THE CLOSER

C. Aimee Hyde

THE CLOSER

1

The Redhead

"**S**on of a bitch!"

Tytus nicks the sharp edge of his jaw and leans in toward the mirror for a closer look. His phone has chirped three times since he got out of the shower and it's making him feel rushed. He's sure it's just Nate texting him the details for dinner. It's his last night in town before heading to Tampa for Spring Training. The start of yet another season.

He loves his career. Baseball is a passion he inherited from his father, and Ty knows that being a pro is a blessing. But it's also a grind. And that grind is just about to get underway. Again.

He'd been drafted by the Yankees out of Harvard when he was 21. Tytus had always been smart, but one of the hard lessons life had taught him was that being smart isn't always enough. You need to be tough and driven. He is both. After three seasons of working his way through the minors, and another five as a middle reliever, he'd finally earned the role of "Closer" for the New York Yankees last season. And this year, his mind is set on being the best damn closer the city has ever seen.

He grabs a towel and dries his face as he walks over to check Nate's text.

Hey Shithead.
Carlyle Hotel.

Beleman's. 9:00

Tytus chuckles at the term of endearment with a shake of his head.

Got it, Douchebag. Don't forget, you're buying.

Cheap Ass. You're a damn millionaire.

And I plan to stay that way.

He throws the phone on the bed and pulls on the shirt he'd laid out over his head.

Nate had been Tytus's roommate at Harvard freshman year. They were best friends within the first month and have remained close ever since. So close, in fact, Nate is also Ty's sports agent.

Going out in public can be a real pain in the ass for any professional athlete, but for a Yankee going out in Manhattan...it's a nightmare. Still, Tytus had promised Nate he would go and he *is* leaving for six weeks in the morning, so he'll just have to deal. They're also planning to celebrate Nate and Chrissie's engagement, and he really likes Chrissie. She's way prettier than Nate.

After deciding on a cream-colored sweater and black chinos, Tytus meets his driver in front of the building and heads out to meet his friend.

Sarah tries to ignore the exhausted look in her eyes as she checks the mirror again. She's been working 60-hour weeks preparing for her current role as Roxie Hart in the upcoming Broadway production of *Chicago*. She has been on Broadway for five years now, but this will be her first lead role and it just may be the death of her.

What she should be doing tonight is sleeping, but instead, she's changed her outfit three times and is running very late.

"I know, Wis. I know." She uses the nickname for her best friend that she'd picked up years ago from Chrissie's little brother. As kids his 'Chrissie' came out as 'Wissie'. *Wis* for short. It stuck. "I'll be down in two minutes. I swear."

Sarah decides the dark red, tight-fitting dress is the winner. Mostly because it's the one she has on, and her time is up.

She'd promised Chrissie a week ago that she would go out with her tonight to celebrate her engagement to Nate. Why is it that every one of her friends is either married or in a serious relationship? She seems to be the only almost 30-year-old who is destined to live her life alone.

Nate is the cutest damn thing Sarah has ever laid eyes on, and she knew the minute she met him that he was the perfect match for her friend. Sarah and Chrissie met back at Yale where they both studied the arts. Sarah theater. Chrissie design. In fact, Wis had made quite a name for herself in the city already despite only being 27.

Chrissie had played hard to get with Nate for almost a year. Sarah knew it was because she'd been leery at first of the *Lifestyles of the Rich and Famous* hotshot sports agent, but Nate turned out to be the most genuine and down-to-earth guy in the world. It's those cocky, idiotic athletes he represents that you have to watch out for.

His long-term driver, Miles, drops Tytus off at the back of the hotel where Nate is waiting by the employee entrance. It's not like he couldn't come in the front, but he'd either spend the next hour signing autographs or looking like an asshole for not signing them.

"Hey." Nate greets his friend with a handshake and a one-armed hug.

"Hey." Tytus pats him on the back. "Where's Chrissie?"

"Running late. She picked up a friend."

Nate keeps walking but Tytus stops. "A friend? C'mon Nate, we've talked about this. No trying to set me up."

Nate turns back toward Tytus and laughs out loud. "Set you up?" Nate shakes his head and puts his finger to his chin. "Let me see if I can put this in terms that a jock like you can understand." He pauses, pretending to consider his words carefully. "She's way out of your league, Ty." Nate chuckles and turns away before the scowl crosses Tytus's face.

They enter the upscale piano bar where the lighting is just dim enough to reduce the chance of a celebrity like Tytus being recognized. Nate reserved a booth in the back corner that provides bottle service and the two men start in on an expensive bottle of scotch and talk baseball while they wait for the women to arrive.

It's been about thirty minutes, when Nate glances at his buzzing phone and looks out over the crowded bar. "They're here."

As Tytus looks out across the sea of people for Chrissie, his breath hitches in his throat as a drop-dead redhead catches his eye first. Looking directly at him, she smiles and then lifts her hand up in a small wave. As if in some kind of trance, and completely out of character, he starts to lift his own hand from the table.

"Nate. Nate," she calls out as her gaze shifts to the man sitting next to him.

Tytus drops his hand to his side and wipes the stupid grin off his face before anyone notices. What the hell had gotten into him? He doesn't wave.

Finally spotting Chrissie on her way to the table, he slides out of the booth to greet her.

"Hello, Gorgeous." He turns on the charm and gets a toothy smile in return.

"Hay-Hay? Is that you? When did you become a gentleman?" She giggles and pecks him on the cheek.

"Sarah," she turns to her girlfriend, "this is—"

"Tytus," he finishes her sentence and takes Sarah's hand. "Tytus Hayes Jr." He flashes her his best smile and fights the urge to kiss her hand and bow like some kind of knight on *Game of Thrones*.

"Sarah Dalton." She smiles, this time actually at him, and his breath catches again. "You don't strike me as a Junior."

"That's what all the girls say." His normal bravado snaps back in place with a Cheshire grin and a cocky wink. "It's an oxymoron."

Sarah simply raises a brow and shifts her attention to the man beside him.

"Nate," she says softly while leaning in for a squeeze and a kiss on the cheek before the four of them sit down.

Tytus picks up Chrissie's glass and pours her some of the sparkling wine Nate had waiting on ice for her, but when he reaches for Sarah's, she stops him.

"I'll have the scotch as well." She picks up the bottle and pours her own. "If you don't mind sharing." She smirks over her glass.

Tytus just clears his throat and looks over at Nate.

Nate sips on his wine with a stifled laugh and mouths, 'Out of your league'.

The conversation is easy between the four of them. Mostly focused on Nate and Chrissie's plans for their upcoming engagement party, and any early wedding plans they have in mind.

Tytus feigns interest for as long as he can but he finds himself eager to learn more about the redhead sitting across from him.

"So, Sarah, what do you do for a living?" The question comes right in the middle of a sentence from Nate about how they chose their venue.

"I'm an actress," she responds, shifting her attention to Tytus.

"Really? Would I have seen you in anything?" he asks, genuinely intrigued.

"That depends. How often do you go to the theater?" Sarah smiles and her entire face lights up. The entire room, actually.

"Ty? The theater? That's hilarious." Nate chuckles as he fills their glasses. "Tytus is more of a sports bars and rock concerts kind of guy, Sarah."

Tytus gives Nate an irritated glare. "I've been to the theater," he scoffs. "In fact, I saw *Ain't Too Proud* on Broadway last year with my dad."

"And from what I remember you went kicking and screaming like an unruly toddler." Nate laughs and Chrissie gives him a disapproving look.

"What?" He shrugs indignantly. "It's true."

Chrissie shakes her head and grabs her fiancé's hand. She pulls him out to the dance floor, leaving Tytus and Sarah to talk without interruption.

Tytus swirls the liquor in his tumbler and wonders why he agreed to this evening when Sarah reaches for his hand on the table. His body responds to her touch like a wick to a flame. A buzzing sensation runs right up his arm and sends blood flow to his groin.

"What do you do, Tytus? Are you a contract lawyer like Nate?"

It takes a moment for Sarah's words to sink in, and when they do, Tytus frowns. It has never occurred to him that this woman might not know who he is. And for some reason, the fact irks him.

"A lawyer? No." He shakes his head. "Although I did go to Harvard," he adds and then immediately regrets. Wincing internally at how pompous it sounds.

"Impressive," she says, pursing her lips, but there is humor in her voice.

"I play baseball," he says flatly. Furrowing his brow at how simple it sounds all of a sudden. "For the Yankees."

"Oh, thank God," Sarah sighs.

When Tytus squints his eyes, she elaborates.

"I don't know about you, but I've been a little concerned all night that this," she gestures between the two of them, "was some kind of blind date the two of them had tricked us into." Her eyes glance in the direction of Nate and Chrissie.

"And now?" Tytus asks, trying not to take her comment personally.

"And now, I know it's not." She shrugs. "Chrissie knows I would never date a professional athlete."

The expression on Sarah's face is one of complete contentment. Like she has no idea that such a comment might be somewhat offensive to an actual professional athlete.

Tytus immediately straightens his spine. But rather than lash out, he plays it cool.

"Seems a little small-minded for a Yale grad?"

He bites back a smirk; he had surprised her. He can see it in her eyes despite the effort she makes to mask it.

"Nate told me you met Chrissie there," he states as he sips on his scotch. "Please. Educate me on the pitfalls of professional athletes." Tytus's tone has a hint of animosity.

"Well, for starters, they make way too much money."

"Big problem." He smirks. "Go on."

"I don't know, they travel all the time, they're obsessed with a game, they sleep around."

Tytus chuckles out loud at that one. "Do they now?" His tone deepens, and he tilts his head just so, his eyes challenging her. Reaching for Sarah's hand he adds, "What about actors?" He leans in closer and whispers, "At least I don't spend my life pretending to be someone else."

"Uh." Sarah gasps and pulls her hand from his. "That was rude."

"Make sure you add that to your list," he responds dryly, sitting back.

Sarah scowls back at him and lifts her drink to her lips. Looking over the rim at him like he might somehow be a danger to her.

Tytus feels...irritated. He shouldn't be concerned in the least about what this redhead thinks of him. He could have any girl he wants, at any time. He glances at her out of the corner of his eye. Well, apparently not *any* girl.

He clenches his jaw as a small inkling sprouts its roots. He's struck with the need to prove her wrong. To change her mind about athletes. About him. It's just to make a point, of course. It doesn't mean anything.

"Let's dance," he says, grabbing her arm and yanking her from the booth.

She doesn't resist. She allows herself to be half guided, half dragged to the dance floor, but Tytus figures it has less to do with him than the fact that she probably just likes to dance.

Tytus holds out his hand and Sarah accepts. She seems a bit surprised at his willingness to dance to this type of music. The smooth jazz flowing from the grand piano is as impressive as the instrument itself.

Placing one hand on her hip, he takes her slender hand in the other. They begin to sway gracefully.

"He's seventy-three," Tytus says.

"Who?" Sarah looks around.

"The pianist. His name is Earl. He's been playing here for twenty-five years."

"You know him?" Her shock is evident.

"My father is a musician. Earl's been around New York forever, so they've crossed paths."

Tytus gives Sarah a little twirl. And she yelps as she bumps into his chest.

"Plus, he's a big Yankee fan." He winks. "Luckily not everyone shares your opinion on athletes," he whispers the snide comment into her ear before spinning her away and back to him.

He's getting to her. He has to give her credit, she's playing it coy, but he feels her body relaxing into their movements. She's enjoying it. Enjoying him.

"I play," Sarah says just above his ear.

Tytus leans back a bit to look at her.

"You do?" His smile is genuine and it has her blushing and looking away. "Well, then you have to meet Earl. Come on," he says as he leads her over toward the musician.

7

Earl smiles at her sweetly when she walks up with Tytus. As soon as he finishes the song, he reaches for Tytus's hand.

"Tytus, my boy. It's about time you bring a pretty young lady in here instead of that old geezer you're always hanging out with."

Tytus lets out a belly laugh as he drops Earl's hand. "I'll tell my dad you said hello." Tytus turns to Sarah.

"This is Sarah. Sarah, Earl Rose."

"What a pleasure to meet you. You play so beautifully." Sarah wraps his fragile hand with both of hers.

"The pleasure is all mine."

"Sarah plays," Tytus interjects with a bit more enthusiasm than he intended.

"Well, is that so?" Earl pats the bench beside him, inviting Sarah to take a seat.

She tries to refuse but neither man will have it so she gives in and sits down.

The two have a quiet conversation before Sarah lays her slender fingers on the keys beside Earl's. They begin to play together as if they'd been doing so for ages, and Tytus can't help but be smitten. He's never been one to impress easily, but something about this woman has him shaking his head in awe.

Sarah starts to sing softly with the melody. Not loud enough for anyone but him and Earl to hear. Maybe more of a hum than actual singing, but enough to be certain she has a beautiful voice. He watches her intently as her fingers move effortlessly across the keys, leaning into her partner and smiling.

In complete contrast to his usual stoic appearance, Tytus's face breaks into a smile right along with hers, and somewhere deep in his gut, he feels what one could only describe as a flutter. It isn't uncomfortable, or painful in any way, but it unsettles Tytus more than any injury or illness ever has. Determined to prove to himself that it is nothing, he wipes the smile from his face and clears his throat.

"I'm just going to grab us another drink," he says to no one in particular as he heads to the bar, scowling to himself as he ponders his behavior. What is it about Sarah that is affecting him this way? She isn't even his type. He scratches at the back of his neck as he waits for their drinks. *Just because you turned thirty last month doesn't mean you have to lose your damn mind, Hayes.*

Sarah can't help but watch him walk away. The view from behind gives that dashing smile of his a run for its money and has her longing for a tall glass of water. Rolling her eyes at herself she attempts to turn her attention back to the music. But focusing on the notes only reminds her of the thrumming she felt just minutes earlier on the dance floor. The way his body felt pressed up against hers made her weak in the knees. She has to admit, Tytus Hayes Jr. may actually be more than meets the eye, and considering he's already a ten out of ten in the looks department, she considers making a bolt for the exit.

Too late. Here he comes.

Sarah gets up from the bench and takes Earl's hand in her own.

"What a pleasure to meet such a fine gentleman," she says as she gives him a kiss on the cheek. "And what an honor to play by your side."

When Sarah turns back toward Tytus, he hands her the drink with his signature grin, right on point.

"You were fabulous."

The sincere look in his eyes nearly melts her on the spot. Yes, more than meets the eye, for sure.

"The sign of a true professional is to make those around you look better. And Earl is a true professional." She turns back for one last smile at Earl and uses her new drink to swallow the lump lodged in her throat.

They make their way back to the table to rejoin Chrissie and Nate. The focus returns to their friends' engagement and upcoming plans. Conversation flows easily between the four of them for the next couple of hours. Every once in a while, Tytus will move his hand so their pinkies touch and she can't seem to move her hand away. In all honesty, she's doing the same with her knee under the table, pressing it ever so lightly into his. It makes her stomach flop.

Nate finally checks his watch and his eyes widen.

"Well, Ty, as your agent I think it's my job to remind you that you do have work tomorrow. I think we better call it a night." Nate raises his hand for the check and their waitress brings it over.

"Let me get this, Nate." Tytus grabs the check. "We came out to celebrate the two of you and seeing as I can't make the engagement party, it's the least I can do."

Something about the way he grabs the check and pulls his card from his wallet causes Sarah's hormones to buzz. It's completely unlike her to be turned on by money or stature. But confidence? Confidence is sexy as hell, and Tytus has it in spades. She focuses on the warm feeling it brings rather than the pang of disappointment from hearing he won't be at the party.

As the group gets up from the table, Tytus feels a foreign tug in his gut at the realization that the evening is drawing to a close.

"Sarah, you want to share a cab with Nate and me?" Chrissie offers as they head outside.

"That's okay, Wis," she gives her friend's hand a quick squeeze. "I'll get my own."

"I could have Miles give you a ride if you'd like." The words are out of his mouth before he can shove them back in. The three others fall silent and look at him, Nate's eyebrows visibly elevated.

What is he thinking? He's not on a goddamn date with this woman. He never offers girls rides with Miles unless he's taking them home. To his place. And he certainly isn't expecting that to happen. Not that he's opposed to the idea...

"Miles?" Sarah cuts through his thoughts.

"His driver," Nate responds with a smirk.

"Driver?" Sarah doesn't hide the amusement in her tone.

"He's a friend." Tytus feels defensive all of a sudden. "Who...drives me around."

The other three laugh out loud and Tytus waves it off.

"You know with friends like you three who needs enemies?" He keeps his tone serious but the humor in his eyes seems to give him away.

Sarah lays her hand on his arm and smiles. The contact causes Tytus's earlier butterflies to return with a vengeance.

The Uber that Nate called pulls up to the curb.

"You're sure, Sarah? You don't want to hop in with us?" Nate double-checks, as Chrissie hugs Tytus and climbs in.

"I'm sure, Nate. Good night."

"Good night." He smiles softly. "Ty, thanks again for tonight. I'll be down in a couple of weeks to check up on you." He reaches for his friend's hand and gives it a firm shake.

As the cab pulls away, a couple of young girls, maybe late teens, approach the two of them excitedly.

"Oh my God, it is you!" one of the girls squeals.

Tytus's spine straightens. He appreciates his fans. He really does. But sometimes he wishes he could just go unrecognized.

"We are so sorry to bother you, but could we get a quick photo? Our friends are going to die," the other girl pleads, looking back and forth between Tytus and Sarah.

"I'm sorry," he leans down and whispers in Sarah's ear. "This happens all the time."

Just as he's about to smile and say yes, one of the girls hands him her phone. "Do you mind?" she asks, as she and her friend flank Sarah while they giggle and jump up and down.

Tytus is literally dumbstruck when the reality sets in. He isn't the celebrity they're after. Sarah is.

He doesn't say a word. He snaps a few photos and returns the camera.

As the girls walk away, he shoves his hands deep into his pockets.

Sarah tries hard to stifle a laugh by coughing into her hand.

"Is Miles nearby?"

"Actually, I texted him earlier to head home. I was planning to walk. It's not too far."

"So, when you offered…"

"I was going to call him back. If you'd said yes, I mean." He offers a sheepish smile and stuffs his hands into his pockets.

"Which way are you headed? Maybe we could walk together for a while." Sarah matches his shy smile with one of her own.

"Towards Upper Manhattan. You?" he replies.

"Same," she replies as she hooks her arm in his.

Tytus's heart hammers as they walk arm and arm down Madison Avenue. All night long, she had him off his game. He doesn't consider himself a player, by any means, but he definitely knows how to get what he wants from a woman, without ever giving much in return. He knows how to remain in control. So, why is it, that all night he's felt like this redhead is in the driver's seat?

"I really am a big deal," Tytus jokes, breaking the silence. "I swear."

Sarah laughs loudly and squeezes his arm with both hands. He tells himself the flex is a natural reaction, but he knows it's not.

They take a left on 80th so they can walk along Central Park.

"So, Nate mentioned work tomorrow. Do you have a game?" She looks up at him curiously.

"A game?" He smiles. It's actually nice to spend time with someone so removed from baseball. "No. I leave for Spring Training in the morning." He looks ahead to the park and wonders why the reality of that makes him sad all of a sudden. He'd been looking forward to it.

"What's Spring Training?" Sarah shivers and tucks her arm a little tighter around his.

"Pre-season workouts and exhibition games," he answers, trying not to let the testosterone she just aroused in him show in his tone. "Six weeks in Tampa."

Sarah's hands go slack on his arm and she stops walking. Tytus takes one more step and turns back. He can't read the expression on her face and even though she starts walking again, she doesn't touch him any longer.

Confused by her reaction, Tytus clenches his jaw as the two walk in silence along the park.

"That's why you won't make the engagement party," Sarah surmises and breaks the tense silence.

"Exactly," Tytus sighs. "I'll be back in mid-March. That's when the real season starts," he answers solemnly. Why does he feel like he'd done something wrong?

Sarah just nods.

"It's getting late," she says as they come up to the north end of the park. "I should really get home."

Tytus's shoulders drop. *I guess that's that.*

A cab pulls up next to them as soon as Sarah hails it. She turns and leans in for a peck on his cheek. Her lips soft and wet on his structured jaw. "It was nice meeting you, Tytus Hayes Jr.," she whispers in his ear, sending chills down his spine.

He wants so badly to ask for her number but his usual confidence has evaporated. Instead, he opens the door for her and simply asks, "Where are you headed?"

"So-Ho," she tells the driver.

Tytus shuts the door and scratches his neck in confusion. Watching as the tail lights disappear in the distance.

Same direction my ass.

2

Breaking the Rules

"*H*ayes. Hayes!" Spencer shouts. "Tytus!" he yells again at the pitcher before throwing him the ball.

Tytus snaps his attention back to his teammate and puts his glove up to show he's ready.

"What is up with you?" Spencer shakes his head. "You've been in complete fucking La La Land since we got here." He tosses him the ball.

Tytus doesn't respond. He just casually receives the baseball and throws it back.

"Good talk," Spencer says sarcastically.

Still nothing from Tytus.

"You know why they call the pitcher and catcher the 'Battery', right, Hayes?" The question is rhetorical so Spencer continues. "Because they're a unit. They work together like two ends of a battery. They *communicate.*"

Tytus communicates with his catcher after that. But not with words. He just starts throwing the ball harder and harder with each toss. He continues to back up as well until he reaches a distance of about 300 feet for what is referred to as 'Long Toss'. Now he can't hear Spencer's whining at all.

Only pitchers and catchers report to Spring Training for the first few days. Workouts are low-intensity and only a few hours long. Things don't really pick up until the following week.

One of Tytus's favorite things about Spring Training is the warm Florida sun in February. Instead of the 40s and 50s he was facing in New York, he's blessed with temperatures in the 70s and 80s, and it is always enough to put him in a good mood. Well, up until this year.

"You wanna go shoot some pool? Grab a beer?" Spencer asks, walking out of the shower, using his towel to dry his hair while leaving the rest of his body exposed.

"Jesus." Tytus, clad only in a towel himself, throws Spencer one. "Cover that shit up, please?"

"My God, you are on your period this week. Forget the fact that I phrased the earlier invite as a question. We are going out for pool and beers. You need to loosen up or I'm going to kill you before the rest of the team arrives."

Sarah has been continuing to burn the candle at both ends. She walks into her apartment, kicks off her shoes, and walks straight to the bedroom. Without even taking off her coat, she falls face-first onto the bed. With only two weeks until opening night, rehearsals have been so demanding, she feels like all she does is work and sleep. Probably because all she does is work and sleep.

Chrissie and Nate's party is this Saturday night and she's looking forward to having some drinks and laughs with her friends. The minute she lets her mind wander there, however, *he* works his way back into her thoughts. That dark hair, those big brown eyes, that damn smile. It has only been a few days, but she feels like he has been haunting her for far longer. When Chrissie had asked her the following day what she thought of Tytus, she had played it off. He was cute, but not her type. *Cute?* Yeah, right.

"You know my rule about dating athletes. Especially professional ones, Wis. Not interested."

Well, she may not be interested, but she can't get him off her mind. Every time she lets her mind relax from a task, he seeps his way in. And it isn't just his image she conjures up. It's the smell of him. An intoxicating combination of whiskey and oak, with a touch of something else. Vanilla?

"Oh, for Christ's sake," Sarah says to the empty room. She catapults herself up off the bed and makes the impromptu decision that a hot bath is just what she needs to wash this man from her existence.

Minutes later she lowers herself into the steaming tub full of bath salts. With candles lit, a glass of wine, and soft jazz on her portable speaker, she is in heaven. Nothing is better to soothe her aching body and mind than this.

As the heat from the water slowly penetrates her skin, she feels the tension in her muscles subside. And with each sip of wine, her mind relaxes as well. With her eyes closed, she starts to drift in and out of consciousness. She's not falling asleep, exactly, but into an almost meditative state.

She feels her body swaying to the soft music, weightless in the water. She's...dancing. Smiling. Laughing. She takes in a deep breath but instead of the aroma of her bath salts, it's an intoxicating blend of sandalwood and scotch. One hand pressed firmly against a taut chest and the other dwarfed by a hard, bulging bicep. Her eyes flutter upward and she meets his gaze; falls deeply into his eyes. The vision of Tytus she's conjured up lowers his head to kiss her. Without overthinking it, Sarah's hand slides between her legs.

It's the second time in three days she's *washed him away* like this.

Tytus has already kicked Spencer's ass twice in billiards and they are both on their third beer.

"So, you gonna tell me what's going on?" Spencer smirks over his bottle. "You may as well just spill it, Hayes. I'm not gonna let up."

Tytus shakes his head and knocks back the remainder of his beer. He knows if he tells Spencer, he will never hear the goddamn end of it. He also knows that if he doesn't, Spencer will incessantly harass him. Furthermore, if he's being honest with himself, he actually wants to say it out loud. He's starting to think that keeping it all in is only making it worse. Like shaking a bottle of soda and watching all the pressure build.

"Sarah. Her name is Sarah," Tytus sighs.

The look on Spencer's face makes Tytus want to crawl into his empty beer bottle. Instead, he raises his hand to the bartender for another. He's going to need it. Good thing he doesn't report until 11:00 a.m. tomorrow.

His teammate's face goes through the entire gamut of expressions as he clearly struggles with a response. Complete and utter shock, to fighting back a laugh, to furrowed brows, and ending on a cleared throat with a head shake. Followed by a big pull on his beer and another shake of the head.

Tytus expects a smart-ass remark. He's braced for it. But when Spencer responds with a sincere and fair question he's impressed.

"What about your rule?"

"I know." Tytus sighs again.

"No distractions."

"I know," Tytus repeats with a little more conviction.

"No dating during the season," his catcher continues as if maybe Tytus forgot his own mantra.

"Fuck, Kline, I know!"

Tytus has a strict rule ever since he has been called up to the majors. No girls during the season. He doesn't go without sex, that would be counterproductive, but he steers completely clear of dating or anyone that might require too much of his attention. He'd been pretty mind-fucked in college by a girl who told him he was basically incapable of making real connections. Now, his world is baseball and pitching. Anything else is just a distraction.

"Okay, okay." Spencer puts his hands up as a shield. "Don't yell at me, man. I'm on your side."

Spencer motions for another beer and scoots his chair closer to Tytus's.

"Tell me about her."

Spencer Kline has always been a pain in Tytus's ass. They were rivals in college and basically hated each other. But in the minor leagues, when things got rough, they had learned to count on each other. They had become teammates and even friends. Generally speaking, though, Spencer is a dick and Tytus would never have dreamed of confiding in him like this. But he can see his friend is being sincere. And Tytus doesn't have many options.

"I met her the night before we flew out." Tytus looks past his friend at nothing in particular but catches the shock that flashes in his eyes.

"Nate and Chrissie invited her to join us for drinks. We were celebrating their engagement because I can't make the party this weekend."

"Were they setting the two of you up? I mean, Nate knows about your rule." Spencer tilts his head.

"No," Tytus answers right away. "No, I don't think so." Only this time it's less convincing and his brows draw together a bit. "Chrissie knew that Sarah had some rule about dating athletes. And Nate knew about my...Son of a bitch!"

Spencer chuckles and takes a drink of his beer.

"I think you've been had, my friend." Spencer grins.

Tytus sits there with his mouth open as the wheels are spinning in his mind. Nate is getting married. He's always harping on Tytus about needing a woman in his life. Now, Tytus has turned 30 and Nate won't shut up about it. Everything about that night reeks of a setup. Right down to Nate's challenge, *she's out of your league.*

Tytus shakes his head in silence. "Well, I'll be damned," he finally says. "I'm going to beat the shit out of him."

"Are you? Sounds like maybe he was right about you and this Sarah? I've known you for a long time, Hayes. And I've never seen you turned inside out over a woman." He takes another swig from his beer. "You didn't really tell me about her. You sure she's not just after your money or your name?"

Tytus chokes on the beer he is just about to swallow. "Now, that, I can assure you, is not the case." He grins as he wipes his mouth with the back of his hand. "She didn't even know who I am." He laughs again and shakes his head at the memory. "Never even heard of me."

Spencer offers a small grin and eggs him on.

"She wasn't swooning and drooling over the great Tytus Hayes Jr.? Yet, you were interested? This I've got to hear."

"She's an actress," Tytus says, enjoying this conversation more than he should. "On Broadway. And she plays piano and has a beautiful voice."

Spencer doesn't comment and Tytus is on a roll now.

"She's witty and smart...not afraid to speak her mind, you know?" He finally looks up from his hands and notices the expression on his teammate's face. Tytus sits up straight and takes a long drink of his beer.

"Anyway." He clears his throat. "She's thrown me off my game a bit."

"No kidding?" Spencer laughs. "You get her number? Why don't you just call her?"

"I didn't ask. Honestly? She probably would have turned me down." Instead of frowning at that revelation, he grins.

"When's that party?"

"Saturday night. Why?"

"Is she going to be there?" Spencer questions.

"I'm pretty sure. Yeah."

"Then, so are you." Spencer downs the last of his beer.

"What?" Tytus croaks. "I can't."

"You can. And you will. Listen, Hayes. You just talked about a woman for ten minutes and didn't say a single word about her looks. You are going to that party."

"Just because I didn't mention her looks doesn't mean—"

"Is she attractive?"

Tytus swallows a sudden lump forming in his throat. He nods once and finishes his beer in one swig. "Very," he croaks.

"Look, Tytus." Spencer rarely uses Tytus's given name. Hayes, Ty, any number of derogatory terms, but rarely Tytus. He clasps his hands together and leans closer to his friend. "I've known you for how long? Ten, eleven years? I've never heard you compliment anything about a woman except her looks. Don't try to tell me that doesn't mean anything."

Tytus feels a wave of something in his stomach. Suddenly he's wishing he just kept his mouth shut like he usually does. It's not that he disagrees with what Spencer is saying, it's the fact that he may be right.

Sarah is blaring her *Favorites'* playlist as she gets ready for the engagement party. She's feeling pretty fabulous today because the tech rehearsal for the show went off without a hitch last night and the town is buzzing with excitement for the revival's opening night on Friday. She had nothing but positive feedback from everyone about her portrayal of Roxie and she is more excited than nervous for the sold-out first week.

Her text notification goes off in the middle of *Miss Independent*. It's Chrissie.

Hey.
Trying not to stress about tonight but sometimes, Nate is such a...MAN! Ugh.
> *ROFL. I wouldn't know, but I can imagine.*

How did your rehearsal go?
I am so excited that you can make it tonight!
> *It was perfect. I can't believe we open in less than a week.*
> *Me too! Getting ready rn.*

YAY! See you soon. XOXO Can't wait!

There is only one thing that's been threatening to put a damper on Sarah's mood. She scrolls back up the text strand and stares at the photo Chrissie sent her from Saturday night. Despite her efforts to not let the picture affect her as it has the hundred other times she'd pulled it up this week, it makes her stomach flip flop. Again.

There is a sparkle in her eye and a smile that spreads from ear to ear. She looks...happy. That, however, is not the problem. The problem is the person taking up the rest of her screen.

Damn that Tytus Hayes. She really needs to move on. She'll probably never even see him again. And even if she does, maybe at the wedding, not that she's been thinking about it, he probably won't even remember her.

Just as before, she lets her finger hover over the trash can icon in the corner. She really shouldn't keep it. It's not doing her any favors. But, she does look damn good...maybe she'll just crop him out. Later.

Tytus is clad in his best Tom Ford as he takes a selfie in front of the private plane he chartered for the night. He shoots it off with a text to Nate.

Too late to RSVP?

The thought of showing up and surprising Sarah makes his palms sweat. He had almost backed out. Used early morning practice as an excuse. But Spencer was all over him like white on rice and if he's honest, he's actually excited.

Luckily, self-confidence has never been his issue. He's always been the cocky type and being a pro player with dashing good looks doesn't hurt. Otherwise, he might let a little doubt creep in about whether she'll even be happy to see him. Or he might fixate on the fact that she's probably coming with a date. Yeah, it's a good thing stuff like that doesn't bother him.

He feels his phone buzz in his pocket as they're about to lift off.

No shit! How'd you manage that?
You didn't get cut, did you? You realize without you, I can't afford this party, Ty.

Very funny, Nathan.
I decided I couldn't miss it. Of all people, Kline convinced me.
In the air now, see you soon.

As Sarah steps out onto the rooftop at Salon de Ning she is literally breathless. The view of downtown is stunning on its own, but the beautiful combination of fairy lights and flames from the fire pits have the entire rooftop glowing.

She's hardly had a chance to take everything in before she spots Chrissie coming toward her.

"Holy Shit, Sarah," Chrissie says, checking out the tight black, floor-length gown. "You look incredible."

Sarah blushes at her friend's overreaction as they exchange kisses on the cheek.

"Look who's talking," Sarah says, spinning Chrissie around. The nude gown shimmers and sparkles with every single light surrounding her.

Chrissie takes Sarah by the arm and quickly grabs two glasses of champagne from the nearest tray.

"A toast," she says, handing Sarah a glass. "To seizing the moment." The joy bursting from Chrissie's giddy face gets Sarah right in the feels.

"Carpe Diem." Sarah echoes and both ladies drink.

On the far side of the patio, Tytus struggles to find air. The moment Sarah stepped out of the elevator his heart rate became erratic. The way her dress clings to every curve of her perfect figure. Her hair frames her face in a way that accentuates her sparkling eyes and sensual lips. Though he is watching her from a distance, he can feel her presence. The heat, the energy, the need. He can't recall a time when a woman impacted him quite like this. He has been with plenty of attractive women, of course, but something about Sarah Dalton grips him from the inside.

A sense of relief washes over him as he witnesses the two girls giggle and drink. No sign of a date. The tension between his shoulder blades loosens slightly, but his nerves are still on hyper-drive. He downs a double shot of Blue Label in one go and makes his way across the patio.

Sarah is standing at the corner of the rooftop looking out at the skyline when the energy around her shifts. She can't put a finger on why exactly, but she senses…sandalwood and scotch. She knows he's there before she can see him, before he even speaks.

"Miss me?" he whispers in her ear.

He doesn't touch her, which only makes her long for it more. He just hovers right behind her. Close enough that she can feel the heat emanating from his body. She closes her eyes. She's pinned. The railing is right in front of her and if she turns, his face will be mere inches from hers. She can't have that. So she responds, without making a move, matching his sultry tone.

"Couldn't stay away?" She tsks. "I get that a lot."

It's a bald-faced lie, of course. She is stunned by his presence. Her legs are wobbly and her heart is racing, but tapping into her acting skills, she does her damnedest to appear unaffected, bored even.

A slow smirk spreads across his face as he reaches up to tuck a few loose strands of hair behind her ear. He leans into her now so his front is pressed lightly against her rear.

Her entire body shudders.

"I'll take that as a yes." His voice is a touch deeper than normal and there's a hoarseness to it that makes Sarah woozy.

"I see you two found each other," Nate says, slapping Tytus on the back and causing him to jump away from Sarah like a kid caught in the cookie jar.

Tytus coughs into his hand and clenches his jaw tightly enough that Sarah worries he might break his molars.

Grinning from ear to ear Nate looks back and forth between the two. Sarah knows it's obvious that she is more than a little flushed and Tytus is hot and bothered.

"Sarah, you remember that corporate lawyer, Charles, I told you about? He's here. C'mon. I'll introduce you." Sarah sees the look that flashes in Tytus's eyes, but he keeps a perfectly straight face. Nate holds his arm out to Sarah and she takes it.

She has no interest in this Charles, but some space between her and Tytus sounds like a fabulous idea.

Tytus can't figure Nate out. He stands, sipping another scotch. He was sure that Nate's intention was to hook him up with Sarah, and now when he's ready to make a move, he introduces her to some corporate douchebag? Tytus can tell the guy's a slimeball without even saying two words to him. The haircut, the annoying Southern accent, the way he keeps laying his hand on Sarah's arm while he laughs. Tytus has the urge to pick him up and throw him over the ledge.

"You know if you wanted to drink alone at the bar, you didn't have to charter a plane and come all the way back to New York." Chrissie smiles as she joins him.

"Just getting tired," Tytus deflects. "I'm glad I came though." He gives Chrissie a half-hearted smile. "It's not too late to ditch the kid and marry a real man." He winks and makes her giggle.

"He's only a year younger than you, Tytus."

"Yeah, but men in their thirties are so much more mature," he teases as he sips his drink and takes a look at his watch.

"I thought maybe you had your eyes set on someone else." Chrissie lifts her eyebrows and motions her head across the patio.

He doesn't need to follow her gaze to know who she means, but he does anyway. Sarah is sitting on the outdoor sofa now practically in Charles's lap. The sight makes his blood run hot.

"Hmph." A sound resembling a grunt comes from Tytus's throat as he looks away.

Chrissie stokes the fire a little more.

"She asked about you," she adds while sipping her champagne.

Tytus's head snaps back in Chrissie's direction. "What was that?" he inquires.

"Sarah. She said she had a nice time last weekend, and she asked me about you."

Tytus wants to ask for details but is well aware this may be a trap. Women are sneaky. So he nods instead and takes another drink of the scotch that he's nearly finished. He has to be in the weight room early tomorrow and he will regret it immensely if this drink isn't his last.

"I had a nice time, too. Will you excuse me?"

He surprises both of them by setting his glass down and walking straight over to Sarah and Charles.

"Sorry to interrupt," he says in his manliest voice, chest slightly puffed out. "I'm Tyt—"

"Tytus Hayes Jr." Charles stands up and shakes the outstretched hand. "Holy shit." Charles just stands there and gawks at Tytus for a moment until it gets awkward for everyone.

"Sorry," Charles snaps out of it. "Sorry. Really. I mean I knew you were a client of Nate's but I didn't expect…I'm a huge fan. Seriously." Charles can't seem to figure out what to do with himself as he moves around nervously. "The strikeout record last year. That perfect inning you threw in the Division Series. I mean, you're the best." He laughs at himself, slightly embarrassed. "Listen to me, I sound like a fucking kid."

Nate is practically pissing himself just a few feet away, and it only irks Tytus more.

"Yeah, well…" Tytus says when Charles just keeps standing there. "As you know, I'm in the middle of training, and I have to catch my flight back soon, so do you mind if I steal Sarah away?"

"Oh no, of course not." Charles is eager to please and drops Sarah like a hot potato. "It was a real pleasure meeting you, Mr. Hayes." Charles reaches his hand out again but when Tytus just nods, he walks away.

Sarah watches the entire scene unfold in front of her eyes. A full-grown man who seemed classy and sophisticated just two minutes prior was reduced to a babbling schoolgirl at the sight of Tytus Hayes.

"Shall we?" He extends a hand down to her. He can see on her face that the whole interchange that just took place has her reeling.

The two walk over and stand near the railing away from the crowd. There's a heat lamp hovering over them and illuminating an orange glow.

"I'm not sure what to say about what I just witnessed back there," Sarah says with a little laugh.

Tytus shrugs his shoulders. "I tried to tell you. I'm a big deal." He flashes her that charming smile, sending tingles from her spine out to all her extremities.

"Tell me about it. I know you're a pitcher. I think I understand that much. But, what else can you tell me?"

"That's what you want to talk about? Baseball?" He raises a brow.

"Not baseball, exactly." She takes her gaze off the city lights and looks into his eyes. "You."

Tytus stares back at her and absently licks his lips.

"Okay," he starts, his voice husky. He clears his throat. "I'm what is called a *Closer*. That means it's my job to get the last three outs of the game."

Sarah nods. "So, baseball is nine innings, right? You always pitch the last one?"

"Well, not always. Only if we're ahead. Or tied, sometimes. And the game has to be close. Within three runs." He clasps his hands together to keep from touching her like he desperately wants to.

"Why is that? It seems like they would need you when the team's losing?" She shrugs, seemingly genuinely curious and awaiting an answer.

"As a pitcher, I can't bring us ahead when we're down. That's on the offense. My job is to hold the lead when we have it. Shut the other team down. It's called a *save*."

"I see." Sarah nods. "Sounds like a lot of pressure."

"It is," he responds honestly. "But I thrive on it. I want to be the best Closer New York has ever had." He's not sure why he just shared that with her. It is a personal goal and he's never said it out loud to anyone.

"Enough about me," he says, eager to change the subject. "What's your next role?"

Sarah's face lights up as she tells him about her lead role as Roxie in the revival of *Chicago*. He can see how proud and excited she is and it fills him with a sense of pride himself. He has no clue what right he has to feel proud, but it's there nonetheless.

"Chicago," he says excitedly. "That's my dad's favorite show. I told you he's a sax player, right?"

"You said he was a musician," Sarah answers. "The sax is my favorite. I love jazz. It's one of the big reasons I'm so excited for this role."

The air between them is palpable. The smiles, the energy, the excitement. Anyone watching them could see it.

"You're a fan of jazz music? That's crazy. Maybe I could take you to see my dad play sometime?" The minute the words are out of his mouth he wants to pull them back from the air.

A silence falls between them for the first time since they started talking.

"When's the show open?" Tytus attempts to redirect the conversation.

Sarah doesn't respond right away and Tytus worries maybe he's pushing too far too fast.

"Friday," she says as she looks back out over the city and away from his gaze.

The mood has shifted. From crackling chemistry to awkward silence. It cuts him deep.

"I have to go." Tytus exhales, finally.

Again their evening is cut way too short.

Sarah turns to face him and gives a strained-looking smile.

"It was great seeing you again, Tytus," she offers.

"You too, Sarah." He smiles softly but there's a sadness in his eyes.

Just as he's about to push away from the railing, Sarah steps closer and places both her hands on his chest. Looking up into his eyes, under heavy lids.

Tytus's gaze shifts down to her lips as he licks his own for the second time. Sarah pushes up onto her tippy toes.

"You were right, Tytus." She whispers before placing a soft, lingering kiss on his cheek. "I did miss you."

3

Break a Leg

*W*hen Tytus arrives at Tampa International, it's almost 2:00 a.m. Miles doesn't come with him to Spring Training so, despite his hatred for them, he has to get an Uber. On the drive, he takes out his phone and pulls up the contact info Sarah gave him before he left the party.

He considers texting her even though it's late. He hasn't been able to stop thinking about her. He'll deny it outright if anyone asks, but in the private walls of his own mind, he knows it's true.

Tytus opens his photo app and takes a long look at the picture Nate had texted him from the night at *Beleman's*. He'd sent it to him with some smart-ass caption about meeting a celebrity. Nate had laughed for hours when he heard the story about the excited fans wanting Tytus to take their photo with Sarah. God knows why he ever shared that story with him.

He has no idea how many times he's gone back to look at this photo. Not just to analyze the two people in it but also the way the picture made him feel. She's beautiful. That's obvious.

Her smile is infectious in a way that you couldn't possibly witness without breaking into one of your own. Her auburn hair. That flawless skin. But what truly haunts him are her eyes. The color an ever-changing swirl of green, brown, and gold. Even more than that, it's the light that shines through them. It's as if someone bottled up all that is good and beautiful in the world and then sprinkled it into her eyes. Like she's a mystical sorceress wielding her magic on all those in her path, and he is simply under her spell.

Tytus chuckles to himself as he looks out the window and tries to remember the last time he'd been this hung up on a girl. To actually have to stop himself from texting a girl too soon? High school, maybe? Doubtful. Sports had been his priority even back then. He guesses the answer is never. Tytus has a sinking suspicion that Sarah Dalton is going to be his first in a whole plethora of ways.

Opening another app on his phone he does a little research. He has an idea. You could even call it a plan. And first thing tomorrow, he is going to set this plan in motion.

When Sarah gets home from the engagement party, the first thing she does is kick off the ridiculous heels she had been wearing. They were fabulous, and did amazing things for her calves, but they hurt like hell, and she was grateful to be rid of them.

As she washes her face and changes into pajamas, she checks her phone at least three times. Telling herself, of course, that it's just a habit and not the expectation of finding a message. Certainly not from *him*. She knows he basically hopped directly onto a flight and probably couldn't use his phone. Not that he would have texted her, even if he wasn't on a plane. They had only said goodbye a couple of hours ago. But, the last thing she is going to do is sit around and obsess about when he might reach out to her. She has never pined after a guy and she certainly isn't going to start now.

As she climbs into bed and turns on *Dateline*, she silently curses herself for doing every single one of those things. There is some relief in the fact that despite giving Tytus her number, she hadn't thought to ask for his. Now, at least, she has no choice but to wait for him to reach out first.

Thank God for that. Because she's pretty certain, she'd be texting him right now.

"Okay, Hayes. Spill it. Was it worth the trip?" Spencer takes a seat on the floor of the weight room next to Tytus and begins to stretch.

Tytus had been the first guy in the gym and more than fifteen minutes ahead of the 6:00 a.m. report time. He was trying to function on about three hours of sleep and he knew he'd need to hit the recumbent bike and break a sweat before lifting.

"Yes." Tytus keeps his face stoic, completely aware that his brief response will annoy his friend.

"Good."

Tytus smirks internally. Two can play at this game. He knows that while Tytus is trying to give the impression that he doesn't want to provide a play-by-play of his evening, he's actually hoping Spencer will press him for details. So, he doesn't.

Over the next several hours, both men keep busy with their training routines and while Tytus tells himself he's relieved that Spencer has seemingly dropped the subject, he can't help but notice a slight disappointment. Later, when the two men head to the locker room, Tytus can't stop himself from bringing her back up.

"So, she's the lead in *Chicago*. It's opening this weekend." He keeps his voice casual.

"I'm sorry?" Spencer scrunches up his face. "Am I supposed to know who you're talking about?" he teases.

"Christ. You really want to make this hard on me, don't you?" Tytus laughs as he gets undressed.

"Honestly? Yes. Yes, I do." Spencer follows Tytus toward the team showers. "But seeing as I'm not a shallow prick like you, I'll ease up. Tell me all about Susie and your night of passion."

Tytus turns on the shower and immediately splashes Spencer with the cold water flowing from the showerhead.

"It's Sarah. And you know it." He blocks the playful punches his catcher throws at him and then turns the handle to the left. Tytus waits for the water to heat up before stepping under the stream.

"And there was no 'night of passion' unless you count a kiss on the cheek and a few suggestive whispers."

The two men carry on a completely normal conversation while showering right next to each other as only a pair of true teammates can do. Tytus tells him all about the evening and his talk with Sarah. He lets Spencer in on his plan before toweling off, getting dressed, and heading back to his apartment to call his dad.

Tytus's family life is complicated. His relationship with his mother is basically non-existent, and according to a girl he dated in college, it's the reason why he will never have *a real relationship with any woman, ever.*

Tytus is the oldest of three. He has a brother, Travis, and a little sister named Tess. His father had been on the road a lot pursuing his dream—turned career—as a musician and a lot of the man-of-the-house responsibilities had fallen on Tytus from an early age. He never resented his father for it, though. In fact, quite the opposite. He basically worships the man. And while having grown up this way serves him well in areas like responsibility and work ethic, it chipped away at his innocence and that natural child-like spirit kids were supposed to have until at least their twenties. It hardened him. Especially in his teen years, when his mother ruined everything, and the entire family fell apart.

Ever since Tytus left home for college, he hasn't spent as much time with his father as he should've. With him being in New York and his dad living in Boston, often too much time passes between their talks or visits. Tytus knows it's usually his fault and he's fairly certain he's owed his dad a return call for over a week.

"TJ? Son. You actually called. Hold on, I think my angina is acting up."

"Very funny, Dad." Tytus grins. Something about just hearing his dad's voice makes his heart swell. "You're not going to believe this, but I'm actually calling to see if you're available this Friday night?"

"To come to Florida? Games don't start until next week, right?" It's easy to hear the confusion in his father's voice.

"Not Florida, Dad. New York." Tytus runs his free hand through his hair, suddenly nervous and second-guessing this idea.

"New York?"

"To see *Chicago*, on Broadway, with me. It's opening night, and...I know you love it." Tytus winces at how unlike him this invitation sounds, and he holds his breath waiting for a response.

"Am I being punked, or whatever it's called?" His dad's voice drifts from the phone like he's looking around the room.

"No, Dad. You're not being punked. I just happened to get a couple of great seats, with backstage access, actually, and I couldn't think of anyone who'd enjoy it more than you." Tytus's statement is one hundred percent true. It's not the whole truth, but it's true nonetheless.

"Well, TJ, of course, I'd love to go. You know how I feel about that show, not to mention just spending a night with my number one son, but I have to believe there is more to this story. Don't you have to be at practice?"

"It's actually our last night off for a while," he answers the outright question but doesn't touch the implied one. "I'm going to book you a flight. Okay, Dad? And Miles will pick us both up at JFK. The show starts at 8:00."

"Tytus, I can book my own flight. Or maybe I'll just take—"

"Dad. Please, I got it, okay?" Tytus stops pacing and sits on the couch. A little relief sets in. "And I don't have to be back in Tampa until Sunday evening so we can stay the night at my condo."

"Ok, TJ. That sounds great." His smile is so big Tytus can hear it in his voice. "I'll see you Friday then."

After disconnecting the call, Tytus exhales deeply. He pulled some serious strings to get these tickets and if the Yankees make the playoffs this year, he is sure he'll be returning the favor with some box seats behind home plate.

He pulls up Sarah's contact info on his phone and starts typing. His thumb hovers over the *send message* for a good minute or two.

Hey.

The second he sends it he regrets it. What a stupid thing—

Hey?

Her quick response brings butterflies to his stomach. The question mark sparks the thought that she may not know it's him.

I figured you were probably missing me again.

He smiles thinking that should do it. Proud of his own flirting.

Who is this?

Tytus's face drops and so does his stomach. He's not sure how to respond to that even though the answer is quite simple.

Lol. I'm joking, Tytus.

Tytus laughs out loud with a mixture of relief and actual humor at her tease.

I knew that. Well, now you have my number so make sure to put it in your phone.

It must be hard to keep all the guys straight.

True. It's Tytus H. Right? Last initials help.

Funny.

How was your practice this morning? Were you exhausted?

It wasn't too bad. It was just weights and arm training stuff. I was fine.

How's the show coming? Ready for the big day?

Just about. I can't believe it's only 5 days away!

Maybe I could come see it? When I'm back in New York?

I'm sure you're going to be just a little busy.

Doesn't your season have you traveling all over the place?

It does get crazy when the season starts, but we have a day off here and there.

And I'd love to see you on stage.

Sarah doesn't respond right away, and Tytus worries maybe he's pushing too hard. He sees the bubbles pop up and clenches his jaw.

I'd love that, Tytus. Really.

And...exhale.

Sarah wakes up on Friday morning with a 'this is the first day of the rest of my life' kind of feeling. To say she's full of nervous energy would be a gross understatement. She is

positively buzzing. Chrissie is coming over and bringing breakfast and Sarah decides that Mimosas are definitely in order. One or two won't kill her. In fact, it's probably exactly what she needs. The girls eat and talk and laugh out loud. Sarah is touched by the excitement and pride in Chrissie's eyes. She hasn't stopped smiling since she walked in the door.

"Sarah, I just can't believe it's really happening." Chrissie's eyes fill up. "I always knew your name would be in lights, but…"

Sarah wraps her best friend in a bear hug as her own eyes begin to well.

"I know, Wis. I know. It's crazy."

Her whole life, Sarah has never been one to take risks, at least since her dad lost everything and she had to live through the consequences. Dave Dalton has a heart of gold, but he had always been more concerned with chasing the next big thing than he was about providing for his family. Sarah's childhood had been full of heartbreaks and disappointments. But when she's on stage, she somehow feels free, yet completely in control. It is the only place she isn't afraid to leap without a net. And now, after all these years, her blind faith is paying off and everything she ever wanted is coming true.

As the morning continues, the girls shift their conversation to a walk down memory lane. Chrissie brings up some of Sarah's college stage performances, sending them both into a tizzy of giggles. The entire time they are talking, Sarah wants to bring up Tytus. They have been texting each other a few times a day all week, and Sarah tries really hard not to get caught up in it. But he's always there, just under the surface. Deciding that not saying something is turning it into a bigger deal than just saying something, she blurts it out.

"So, Tytus and I have been texting each other." Sarah bites the inside of her cheek to keep a nervous grin from spreading.

Chrissie drops the fashion magazine she's looking at on the coffee table and turns to Sarah.

"I'm sorry. What did you just say?" Her mouth agape.

"What?" Sarah tries to play it off. "What's the big deal?"

"You have been texting with Tytus Hayes Jr. and you're just *now* telling me?" Chrissie's voice rises in volume with each word she spits out. "I cannot believe it. Nate is gonna shit."

"Why? Oh my God, Wis, seriously. You're making me regret telling you."

"You were considering not telling me?" Chrissie shrieks as she jumps off the couch and tries to grab Sarah's phone from the counter. "Sarah and Hay-Hay sitting in a tree, k-i-s-s—"

"What are you doing?" Sarah yanks her phone away just in time.

"Hand it over, Red. I have got to see what the two of you have been up to."

"You will do no such thing." Sarah chuckles. "And what is with that nickname, anyway? Hay-Hay? It doesn't seem all that fitting for a guy like Tytus."

Chrissie laughs out loud. "Did I just call him that? I don't even hear myself anymore." Chrissie's grin is from ear to ear. "I stole it from my eight-year-old niece. She's madly in love with him and she writes it all over everything."

Chrissie is still laughing when she tries to grab the phone again. "I need to see those texts."

"Would you just calm down and tell me why you're making such a huge thing out of this?" Sara holds the phone behind her.

"For a number of reasons, Sarah. Don't play dumb with me. How about your rule, for starters?"

Sarah winces. She is well aware of what her best friend is referring to. She has had a strict rule against dating jocks that dated back to just before the girls even met. It is a pact with herself that she never broke. "My rule is about being in a relationship. This isn't a relationship."

"Uh-huh," Chrissie says. "Okay...How about the fact that Tytus doesn't even do...," she waves her hands around in search of the right word, "this." She drops her hands to her sides. "And, I'm willing to bet you that he doesn't text with girls either. Not unless it's for a booty call."

Sarah puts her hand to her chest and opens her mouth in offense. "Well, I can assure you this is not *that*."

"Exactly my point, Sarah. Oh my God," Chrissie says again as she steps closer to her friend. "Tytus *fucking* Hayes is into you."

"Okay, enough champagne for you, missy." Sarah picks up the glass from the coffee table. "You have clearly lost your mind."

When Sarah arrives at the theater on Friday, she is greeted almost immediately by Sebastian.

"Sarah." He smiles with a nod.

Sebastian is the lead stagehand for the theater company and also kind of an *assistant* to Sarah. Even though he is an 'all business — all the time' type of guy, Sarah knows she's his favorite. And she loves to drive him nuts.

"It's the big day, Sebastian. Can you believe it?" She wraps him in a big bear hug and squeals excitedly. The more Sebastian tries to squirm out of her embrace, the tighter she squeezes.

"Okay, okay. I just ironed this shirt," he says as he wiggles himself free. He acts annoyed but Sarah knows that deep, *deep* down he loves the attention and it makes her even more giddy.

"Everything is laid out for you in your dressing room. Make-Up is in…" he glances at his watch, "forty-five and hair right after. You need anything at all, just text me." Despite his efforts, a small smile tugs at the corner of his mouth.

Sarah leans in and kisses him on the cheek.

"Marry me?" she asks in a sweet voice.

Sebastian simply blushes at her pretend proposal and scurries off without another word.

When Sarah walks into her dressing room, her breath catches in her throat. She literally stops in her tracks, bringing both hands to her mouth. Her eyes slowly well up at the sight in front of her. There are at least a dozen bouquets of flowers in all shapes, sizes, and colors filling nearly every surface in her room. The first one is a large arrangement of gerbera daisies and she knows without looking at the card that they are from her dad. As she walks through her dressing room turned greenroom, she picks up and reads each and every card. Her mom, Chrissie and Nate, her director, and one from Sebastian that makes her tear up. Every single one of them wishing her well on her big night.

She is already feeling overwhelmed with emotion when she turns to find the most magnificent display of them all sitting right on her dressing table.

An enormous bouquet of what looks like five dozen roses. A mixture of white and pink that nearly stops her heart. Despite her best efforts, she immediately hopes they are from Tytus. She had been trying all day, unsuccessfully apparently, to stop wishing and hoping he'd be here tonight. She knew he couldn't get away from baseball, and he had called her this afternoon to wish her luck. But as she stands gaping at the most beautiful flowers she has ever laid eyes on, she feels that tug on her heart stronger than ever.

She reaches for the small envelope and slides the card out.

White roses are white
and pink ones are pink.
My first try at romance,
what do you think?

Sarah chokes out a laugh through the emotion building in her throat. It's written in his own handwriting which gets her hopes up even more. How could he have written it by hand and had it delivered from Florida? Sure, it's possible, but maybe he's actually in town.

She sees there is something written on the back, as well.

Break a leg!
— T.H.J.

Sarah looks back up at the arrangement in front of her and plops herself down into the chair, suddenly too shaky to stand. She knows this is the biggest night of her life, but it's not the show that has her heart racing. She has it bad for this guy, and she prays to God, she doesn't live to regret it.

At a young age, Sarah had learned to protect herself. She had been let down more than once by the people she loved the most. It's why she sets rules and plays her cards close to her chest. So why is this baseball player making her want to forget all that and throw caution to the wind?

Tytus had changed his shirt four times before finally deciding on the black long-sleeve button-down he had put on in the first place. Investing this much time and thought into his outfit is another first he can surely blame on Sarah.

Everything with his and his dad's travel arrangements had gone off without a hitch, and Miles is waiting for them at the curb when they exit the airport terminal.

"Mr. Hayes." He nods and takes Tytus's overnight bag. "Mr. Hayes," he says again as he smiles at Tytus Sr. who shakes his head when Miles reaches for it.

"I can handle my own bag, Miles." Tytus Sr. smiles. He still hasn't adjusted to his son's celebrity status, even after all this time.

"When's the last time you saw a show on Broadway, Dad?" Tytus makes conversation once they're on the road. "Was it last summer when we saw *Ain't Too Proud?*"

"Yes. But a few months before we saw that, I saw the *Merchant of Venice* and it was fabulous." His father's eyes perk up as he's talking. "I wasn't really expecting to love it the way I did, but I was blown away by the performance of one of the actresses. In fact, I was so excited when I realized she's actually the lead in this production of *Chicago*."

Tytus's eyes widen as he turns to his father and attempts to swallow the clump of cotton balls that just formed in his mouth.

"Sarah Dalton?" Tytus croaks, completely unable to hide his utter shock.

"You know her?" Tytus Sr. matches his son's surprise.

"Well, yes. I mean, she's a friend of Chrissie's, you know Nate's fiancée?" Tytus bites the inside of his cheek. Now that Sarah has become the topic of conversation, he's afraid he'll get another bad case of diarrhea of the mouth like he had with Spencer.

"Incredible." Tytus Sr. shakes his head in disbelief. "Well, you're in for a real treat, TJ. She lights up the stage like no one I've ever seen."

"I bet," Tytus says before he can stop himself.

"You've met her then, I take it?"

"A couple of times, yes."

Tytus glances at his dad from the corner of his eye as the conversation takes an awkward halt. After all these years he knows his father well enough to see the wheels in his head spinning.

"What?" Tytus finally says, trying not to sound too defensive.

"Nothing." His dad smirks.

"What? You've always had a crappy poker face. I could beat you by the time I was six. Just spit it out."

"You're dating Sarah Dalton, aren't you?" Tytus Sr. cannot contain the humor in his voice. Without even looking at his father, Tytus can hear the smile on his face. His dad is enjoying this way too much.

"No. I am not."

His father's frown is quick and exaggerated.

"But I'd like to be," Tytus exhales as he looks out the window.

And just like that. Tytus Sr. is beaming once again.

The first thing Tytus lays eyes on when he climbs from the back seat of the Lexus is a giant poster of Sarah plastered on the wall outside the theater. She's wearing what looks to him like black lingerie fitted tightly to her body with lace covering her chest and arms. He swallows thickly at the enormous image of her cleavage and the response in his groin is immediate. He clears his throat.

Tytus Sr. looks on with a shit-eating grin he'd passed on to both his sons. He doesn't say a word but he doesn't tamper down the amusement on his face either.

They aren't out of the car for more than a few seconds before the cameras start flashing.

"Mr. Hayes!"

"Mr. Hayes!"

"Tytus. Tytus!"

Tytus wraps his arm around his dad's shoulder and smiles at the cameras flashing in every direction. He gives them a minute or two to do their jobs and then he turns to walk into the lobby, ushering his father to walk in front of him.

As Tytus enters the lobby of the Ambassador Theatre he heads straight for the nearest bar with Tytus Sr. following close behind. His nerves are beginning to hum, and he could really use something strong to calm them down.

He orders a scotch for himself and a beer for his dad and they lean against a nearby wall and enjoy the people watching. You get all kinds in New York City, even at an event like this, and the two men start an old game where they take turns making up names and backstories about the people around them. It's something Tytus Sr. has done with his son since he was young. It helped pass the time at some of his jazz gigs. They have never grown tired of it.

"That's Chuck." Tytus Sr. points in the direction of a short bald man. "He's socially awkward and has a beagle named Snoopy." Tytus shakes his head at his father's humor and can't help laughing at his cheesy joke.

"There's Nathan." Tytus Sr. points.

"Hey, it's my turn," Tytus complains.

"No, I mean, there's Nathan. Richards."

Tytus turns to see Nate and Chrissie approach with the biggest shit-eating grins he has ever seen. He curses himself for not considering that they'd be here. What an idiot.

"What a surprise," Nate practically shouts as he nears the men. "Tytus Hayes Jr. at the theater. What could possibly have brought you here tonight, of all nights?"

"Hilarious." Tytus smirks as Nate comes in for a one-armed man hug.

"You just cost me one hundred dollars you pansy-ass. Chrissie bet me a hundred bucks you would be here tonight. She read you like a damn John Grisham novel," Nate whispers before turning toward Tytus's dad.

"Mr. Hayes," Nate smiles and reaches for his hand. "So good to see my favorite sax player. You remember Chrissie? My fiancée."

"Of course, I do. Chrissie." He smiles and kisses her hand. "I'm still trying to figure out how a gorgeous girl like you ended up with a fully grown twelve-year-old like Nathan here."

"If you figure it out, let me know." Nate laughs.

"It's great to see you again, too, Mr. Hayes." Chrissie smiles. "Nate keeps promising me he's going to take me to see you play but it hasn't happened yet." She shoots her fiancé a sideways glance.

"So Tytus," Nate changes the subject. "I'm guessing you must be here to support Sarah? I heard the two of you have been keeping in touch."

That comment earns Nate an elbow to the ribs from Chrissie.

"Have you now?" Tytus smirks, more pleased than put off by Nate's comment.

The lights in the lobby dim and then brighten to let everyone know that it's time to head to their seats.

"Where are you two sitting?" Chrissie asks. "We're in the Mezzanine."

"We're down here. In the Orchestra section," Tytus answers, purposefully vague.

"Front row," his dad adds with a grin. "You know this is Tytus Hayes Jr., right?" He gestures to his son, wanting to join in on the ribbing Tytus is getting.

"Front row?" Nate's eyes go wide. "Can't wait to hear how you pulled that one off at the last minute."

The action on stage captivates the entire audience from the second the first note plays. Tytus has been to the theater a handful of times, but he's never been this close. He finds Sarah onstage before she speaks her first line and it takes the air from his lungs. He's not sure if it's the blond wig, the sexy makeup, or the get-up she has on, but the combination hits him right in the groin.

There is no denying the way she commands the attention of every person in the theater, and he is immediately impressed. The graceful way she moves across the stage and the uncanny delivery of her character completely transports him. He wholeheartedly believes she is Roxie Hart.

But it's when she opens her mouth to sing, that he finds himself holding his breath. Afraid to exhale for fear it will distract his ears from the flawless sound of her voice.

As he watches her perform on stage in front of a completely mesmerized crowd, he remembers what Nate said that first night at *Beleman's*. *She's out of your league.* For once, he thinks, Nate may actually be right.

The crowd shoots to their feet in thunderous applause. A standing ovation that goes on and on for what feels like an hour. The actors come out one at a time for their curtain calls and the audience continues to roar. When Sarah finally appears for her final bow the entire theater erupts. He can see the tears in her eyes from where he is standing. The smile on her face illuminates the stage more than the thousands of lights had done. As Tytus gazes at her from below, he watches intently as she drops her chin and looks down to the front row. He feels his heart pound as her eyes come to rest on his. The shouting and cheering surrounding him slowly fade away, as do the people on stage beside her and those to his right and left. Their eyes lock in what can only be described as an embrace. Neither moves for several beats until he's snapped back into reality with an abrupt slap on the back from his dad, and all the hoots and hollers fill his ears once more.

The two men make their way to the stage door where security is admitting people with the proper credentials. He finds their names on the list and they get through without incident, making their way up the stairs with all the other VIPs.

They send everyone into a large room filled with wine, champagne, and all kinds of food. A few of the cast members are already there socializing but Tytus isn't able to spot Sarah.

"What did you think?" Nate asks, placing a hand on Tytus's shoulder. "Did I tell you, or did I tell you?"

"Yeah, yeah. I know. Out of my league." He laughs. "She is amazing." Tytus's eyes wander the room.

"She'll be out in a few minutes. Chrissie went to help her get changed."

"That was an unbelievable show." Tytus Sr. turns to Nate. "I think this is the third time I've seen *Chicago* and it is the most impressive cast by far."

The three men grab a drink and a few appetizers and catch up while waiting for Sarah to make her entrance. It's no secret when she finally appears. The whole room breaks into applause. Sarah walks in with her natural red curls hanging loosely over her shoulders. She's wearing a sexy navy dress that shows all her best features including a cut low dip at the chest. Tytus loses his footing and bumps into his dad.

"You alright there, Son?" He chuckles.

Sarah makes her way over to them, accompanied by Chrissie, but is stopped by every person in her path for a hug or a quick selfie.

Nate is the first to step up and wrap her in a hug. "Hot damn. You were something up there, Sarah." He gives her a squeeze. "You nailed it. Simple as that."

"Thank you, Nate." She blushes.

Tytus swallows as she turns to face him, suddenly fearing he's forgotten how to speak.

"Tytus," she bails him out. "What a pleasant surprise." She lifts up on her toes slightly as she places a soft kiss landing just past his cheek and under his ear lobe. "The flowers are beautiful," she whispers quietly before pulling away.

Tytus can still feel the presence of her lips on his neck. Her breath in his ear causes goosebumps to run down his spine.

"Sarah Dalton." She holds out her hand to Tytus Sr. as Nate clears his throat.

"Oh." Tytus snaps his head toward his dad. "Sarah, this is my dad, Tytus Hayes Sr." He gestures between them. "Dad, Sarah Dalton."

Tytus Sr. takes Sarah's hand and kisses the back of it lightly. "I'm a big fan, Ms. Dalton. What an honor to meet you." He looks up to her eyes and smiles softly. "You were breathtaking tonight."

Sarah's face lights up with a little extra glow. "Wow," Sarah gasps. "What a gentleman you are."

"He's right." Tytus finally manages to weigh in. "You were just…spectacular." When Sarah looks back at him from the corner of her eyes, it stirs something primal deep inside of him.

The four of them spend the next thirty minutes or so talking, drinking, and eating. Sarah is pulled away for an interview and some autographs here and there but she seems to find her way back to them every time.

Worrying that they may never get a moment alone, Tytus is relieved when his dad excuses himself to use the restroom, and Nate and Chrissie get caught up with some mutual friends.

"You really were something up there, Sarah. Breathtaking was the perfect word." His eyes gaze into hers to prove he means it.

"You don't look too bad yourself, Hayes." She winks. "And I meant what I said, the flowers, the note, it meant more to me than you know." She looks down at her feet before choosing her next words. "I'm really glad you came, Tytus. I was hoping you would."

"Good," he says softly.

"Good," she repeats.

"So, I don't have to be back until tomorrow. Any chance for a nightcap?" He looks around the crowded room and leans in to whisper. "Just the two of us?"

"I thought you'd never ask." She looks into his eyes with a desire he swears wasn't there before. "Just let me grab my things."

Tytus turns around to find his dad. Apparently, he's going to have to ditch him for a few hours. He finds him talking with the group where Nate and Chrissie are.

"Dad. I'm going to have Miles take you to my condo, okay? I'm going to spend a little time with Sarah. Alone. I hope you don't—"

"TJ, it's fine. I'll be fine. I'm happy for you, Son. She's one hell of a catch. I can tell already."

Tytus gives a quick head nod to Nate and makes his way down the hallway he saw Sarah walk down. After passing a few doors, he finds one with her name on it and knocks lightly three times.

"Come in," he hears faintly through the door.

Tytus opens the door to her dressing room and is met with what looks like a thousand flowers.

"Woah," he chuckles. "Guess my flowers in the dressing room idea was really original, huh?"

45

"Your flowers were perfect, Tytus. I mean it." Sarah steps closer to him and it's as if they both realize at once that they are alone.

He takes a cautious step toward her that brings them basically toe to toe. Their eyes find each other and seem to communicate more than any words could. Sarah's gaze shifts from his, ever so briefly, down to his lips and it's all the invitation he needs. He takes one final stride, his leg slipping just between hers, as he places a hand lightly on her cheek. His thumb grazes her softly as he looks into her eyes with more intensity than either can bear.

As Sarah's eyes flutter closed she moves her face closer, just an inch or two, and he leans in to meet her. Tytus lays his mouth gently over hers, his bottom lip fitting snugly between hers. He holds her there, gradually applying more pressure with his lips as each second ticks by. He slides his hand further around to the back of her neck, as she places her hands on his chest and pushes lightly against him, not to push him away, but to feel his strength. He pulls back momentarily to look at her, and Sarah's eyes blink open to find his before she leans back in for more.

Tytus groans into her mouth this time as he uses his tongue to part her lips and easily slides it inside. He glides his hands slowly down her back and grips her tightly just below the waist, pulling her into him as their bodies press firmly against each other. Sarah's arms wrap around his neck and she runs her hands through his hair.

He had been afraid of this. That she would feel this good. Her lips this soft. Her body this small in his grip. He had been afraid that she would feel even better than she had in every dream he had this week.

But as he deepens the kiss, he lets go of the fear. Let's himself fall freely in a way he has never done with anyone. Ever.

4

Reality Check

*T*here is a saying, 'Time flies when you're having fun'. But to Sarah, it feels more like, 'Time flies when you're busy as hell'.

It's been three weeks since opening night, three weeks since her career launched into hyperdrive, and three weeks since Tytus Hayes Jr. rocked her world with not just one, but two mind-numbing kisses that may have caused permanent nerve damage. She won't know for sure until she kisses him again. And since they haven't seen each other since that night, that task is proving quite difficult.

It's not that they haven't *wanted* to get together, it's just been physically, and logistically, impossible. Tytus started his Spring Training games and hasn't been able to fly back to New York. Sarah is working constantly, performing as many as eight shows over six days and sleeping all day on her one day off.

They have been talking a lot though. Tytus calls her almost every day. Usually in the morning while they are both having coffee or breakfast. Tytus on his way out and Sarah just waking up. She gets in late most nights and he likes to be 'lights out' by eleven. They've been texting too, which she must admit, she is thoroughly enjoying. Their flirting through text messages is steadily picking up heat and she often catches herself blushing or grinning at her phone like a teenager.

But she misses him. It's as simple as that. They've tried Facetime once or twice, but for some reason, they both find it a little awkward, and it just isn't the same as being face to face. She finds herself thinking of him the moment she wakes, and usually, he's the last image that passes through her mind before drifting off to sleep at night.

Some nights when she is lying in bed trying to fall asleep, she worries that she's in too deep already. How can that be? She's only seen the man three times for goodness sake. They've only kissed, and she's done more than that with plenty of other men throughout her adult life. So why the anxiety? Why the fear? She knows why, of course. For starters, she had broken her rule. She'd let herself get involved with an athlete and it had brought back memories that made her stomach turn. Secondly, she thought about him way too often. The kiss they had shared in her dressing room, followed by the drinks and quiet conversation over their nightcap, and another kiss in front of her building that made her want to invite him in, they all swept her up into what felt like a fantasy world that she is dying to find her way back to.

Luckily, she is either too busy or too tired to spend much time overanalyzing, and before she knows it, another week has passed. Tytus will be returning to New York in a couple of days, and she will find out for certain just what she has gotten herself into.

As Tytus is packing up the things he brought with him to Florida, he has one thing on his mind. Seeing Sarah. He's been trying to rationalize this *need* he seems to have for her as something physical more than psychological. Like he's just really attracted to her and really horny because he hasn't had sex for what feels like eons.

The past few weeks have dragged on forever. Part of it is the life of a high-end closer at Spring Training. They barely use him on the mound, saving him for the games that count. But he still has to sit through every inning of every game, knowing he is basically a high-paid spectator. The other part, however, is missing Sarah. The evening they had spent together after her show had really affected him. He continually tells himself it was the undeniable spark between them when his lips touched hers, but he knows it's more than that. He misses her. Her smile. Her laugh. The way her mouth curves just a little when she's impressed with him but doesn't want to show it.

As he zips up his bag and does one last sweep of his temporary apartment, he stops in the bathroom doorway and looks at the shower. His mind drifts to all the fantasies of her he had let himself indulge in while in there. Smiling to himself, he turns out the lights and walks out. He has every intention of making each one of those fantasies a reality. And the sooner the better.

Tytus catches an Uber to the airport and texts Sarah on his way.

Finally on my way.

Yay! Nate is picking you up, right?

Yeah. I told him Miles could do it, but he insisted. He really misses me.

So do I.

Tytus's stomach flutters as his signature smile spreads across his face.

I wish I could see you tonight.

Me too, but we agreed that tomorrow makes a lot more sense.

I know. I'll pick you up at 10:00 for breakfast?

Can't wait.

Tytus tucks his phone back in his jacket and smirks. If she thinks he's really going to wait until tomorrow, she doesn't know him at all.

Tytus exits the United terminal at LaGuardia and spots Nate's new SUV right away. He had described the black Lincoln Navigator to him over the phone.

"It's nice," Tytus says as Nate rounds the vehicle to open the back hatch.

"Thanks." Nate smiles as he wraps his friend in a hug. "It feels like I'm driving a tank, but I needed something new, and Chrissie and I plan to start trying right after the wedding, so—"

"So, SUV it is?" Tytus laughs.

"Exactly."

The two friends shoot the shit all the way into Manhattan, mostly about baseball.

"Let's grab a couple of beers before I take you home," Nate suggests as they get close.

"I can't."

"What do you mean, you can't? You've got plans at 10:30 on Monday night?" Nate looks at Tytus quickly before turning his eyes back to the road.

"Not exactly." Tytus is purposefully vague though he knows Nate won't back down.

"You're going to see Sarah, aren't you? Chrissie told me that the two of you talk almost every day, but good Lord, you've really got it bad, Hay-Hay." Nate clicks his tongue and shakes his head.

"Don't even start." Tytus' voice is flat. "I know this was your plan all along. You basically set the two of us up."

"Doesn't mean I thought it'd actually work." Nate busts out laughing. "I mean, I've known you for what, a decade? Longer, shit. And I have *never* seen you go out of your way to make time for a girl." He glances at Tytus again but he's looking out the window. "First the party, then the show, and now this?"

Nate pauses, seemingly waiting for some kind of response but continues when he gets none.

"Seriously, Ty. You really do like her, right? Because Chrissie protects her like she bore her from her own womb, and if you hurt her—"

"I wouldn't." Tytus's head snaps back to face Nate. His voice more than a little irritated. "I won't."

"Okay..." Nate backpedals a bit. "Good. Just, good."

As they pull up to Tytus's place, Nate tries to smooth things over.

"Look, Ty. I'm happy for you, I am. Sarah is an amazing woman and you are one of the best people I know. I care about both of you, and I just don't want to see anyone get hurt."

"And you think I do?" Tytus huffs.

"No. Of course not. But the season starts the day after tomorrow, and I know how busy you'll be. How focused you get. And with Sarah and *Chicago*. It's just…a lot," Nate explains as he pulls up to the curb.

"I know, Nate. I know. I appreciate it." And he does. "Thanks for the ride. Lunch before Opening Day, right?"

"Wouldn't miss it for the world."

Tytus grabs his bags from the back of the car and waves to Nate as he drives off. He's exhausted. The team played their last exhibition game this afternoon and then he had rushed to pack and catch his flight. Nothing could keep him from kicking off his shoes and falling face-first onto the bed he has missed dearly. Nothing but Sarah, that is.

He pulls on a pair of dark blue jeans and a gray sweater, brushes his teeth and hair, and texts Miles that he's ready.

Sarah is sitting in the chair in her dressing room taking off her makeup and wondering where she will find the energy to even walk outside and catch a cab. Monday nights have proven to be the toughest. With shows every night but Wednesday, and four over the weekend, it catches up with her the most on Monday. At least on Tuesdays, she can fantasize about spending the next day in bed watching Netflix.

She loves it though. She smiles in the mirror. It has been even better than she dreamed it could be. Exhausting? Yes. Physically and emotionally draining? For sure. Stressful and scary as hell? You bet. But it's more rewarding and fulfilling than anything she's ever done. The reviews of her have all been positive. One of New York's toughest critics was even quoted saying, *"Sarah Dalton is the most authentic Roxie Broadway has seen in a decade."* That one made her cry.

Once the makeup is gone, there is relief in seeing her own face in the mirror, and it's the thought of breakfast with Tytus Hayes Jr. that finally gets her to push herself up and out of her chair.

"Time for some much-needed beauty sleep," she says to the empty room as she grabs her bag and heads out.

Sarah says goodbye to Sebastian and the few straggling cast members backstage. She pulls her coat tightly around her body, covering the cozy but not too-flattering jeans and oversized sweatshirt she's wearing home tonight. She is more than grateful that not every night requires her to doll herself up to impress or entertain others. When a woman has finished a long day at work, she should be able to throw on something comfy.

She pushes open the door to the back side of the theater and walks toward the curb with her head down, looking through some messages on her phone. She smiles widely as she presses on one from Tytus that says he's arrived home safely.

Just as she's about to respond to him a voice has her picking her head up.

"Excuse me. Are you Sarah Dalton? I'm a huge fan."

Sarah stops in her tracks and gasps, placing her hand to her heart. She can hardly register the identity of the gorgeous man in front of her as he leans there against the black Lexus, a smirk on his face, and flowers in his hand.

"Tytus?" she chokes.

"Oh good. You remember me." He grins and pushes himself off the car.

He takes two strides toward her but hesitates when Sarah doesn't move.

"Sarah?"

She's not sure why but she's overcome with emotion which seems to have halted all her normal bodily functions. Movement. Speech. Breath. She hadn't fully admitted it to herself, but deep down she had been terrified. Terrified that she had fallen too fast and too hard for this world-famous heartthrob who had waltzed into her life without warning. She had been so nervous that when he returned, the spark between them would prove to be one-sided. That he would have lost interest or simply grown bored. Somehow this small gesture, a ride home and some fresh flowers, means more than a fancy date or a diamond necklace.

She takes the remaining strides and answers his question with action instead of words, wrapping her arms around his neck and laying her head on his shoulder. She can tell her response surprises him as his body initially stiffens but after a beat or two, his arms wrap around her waist and she feels him lay his head on top of hers.

The embrace is interrupted by a voice from behind Tytus.

"Excuse me, Mr. Hayes?" Miles says softly.

When Tytus turns to look at his driver, Miles gestures toward the corner to his right. Tytus turns his attention toward the alleyway.

"Hey!" he yells, drops his arms from Sarah, and turns away from her. "Hey!" Tytus yells again when no one responds or surfaces.

"I think he's gone, Sir," Miles says in a resigned voice.

"Shit." Tytus runs his hand through his hair.

"What?" Sarah finally asks, her pitch higher than usual. "Something dangerous?" She grabs Tytus's arm.

"Not something, someone. And not dangerous, just annoying," Tytus says walking her to the car. "I have a feeling we may be plastered all over social media tomorrow." Tytus sighs as he shuts Sarah's door.

Sarah can't tell if his annoyance is due to a simple violation of privacy or the potential publicity the photos might bring. She gives Miles her address and she and Tytus sit quietly in the back seat for a few minutes. The interruption to their reunion had knocked them both off balance.

"I'm sorry," they say in unison as they turn toward each other at the same time.

"You're sorry?" Tytus asks with his eyebrows raised. "What do you have to be sorry for? I'm sure it was some idiot following me. Do you normally have people snapping your picture back there?"

"No." Sarah shakes her head. "But if you hadn't stopped by to see me..."

"Sarah." He puts his hand on top of hers. "This happens to me everywhere I go. It's basically par for the course, especially during the season." He squeezes her hand lightly so she looks at him. "I feel terrible that your picture might go viral tomorrow because of me."

She smiles at the tenderness in his voice and she knows he means it.

"There are worse things than being pegged as Tytus Hayes's new arm candy." She tries to lighten the mood. "I hear you're a pretty big deal."

That gets a chuckle from Tytus and he instantly relaxes. "Arm candy." He smirks, with a shake of his head.

Conversation flows easily between the two of them the rest of the way to Sarah's apartment.

"Can I walk you up?" Tytus asks as they pull up to the curb. His tone sounds more hesitant than usual. "I know you're exhausted and probably just dying to get to bed."

She's dying to get to bed alright. With him. "I am tired, there's no denying that, but I'd love it if you came in for a bit? Maybe just a quick drink?"

Tytus's finger twitches on his thigh. "I'd love to." His voice suddenly hoarse as he pulls on his pant leg and adjusts himself in the seat.

Twenty minutes later, Tytus is pouring Sarah a glass of wine as she comes out of her bedroom in satin pajama pants and the same oversized sweatshirt.

"You said get comfortable, so I took it to heart. What you see is what you get, Hayes," Sarah says as she strides in and does a mock twirl for him.

Tytus's mouth goes dry at the sight of her. How is it that she gets more and more beautiful every damn time he lays eyes on her? She literally takes his breath away, even in her loungewear. Especially in her loungewear. He clears his throat as he rounds the kitchen island to join her. He hands her the glass and sits down next to her on the couch. Far enough away that he can turn toward her with one knee bent and up on the couch. Close enough that their legs touch lightly as she sits cross-legged in front of him.

"So," she smiles over her wine, "tell me what's in store for you and your team this week. We talked about my shows but not much about baseball."

"That's because you hate baseball." Tytus laughs.

"Uh," she cries and slaps his leg. "I do not hate baseball. I dislike athletes—and only male ones. Female athletes are amazing."

Tytus sips on his wine and smiles over his glass. He loves pushing her buttons. "So, you dislike me then? You realize I'm a male athlete, right? Like, for a living?"

"Well, some exceptions have to be made from time to time. Jury is still out on this one." Sarah winks.

Tytus explains that his season opens on Thursday night. They are hosting the Baltimore Orioles for four games, then the Tampa Bay Rays come into town for three. After that, they head on their first road trip to play in Boston and then Toronto.

As he talks, he notices that Sarah seems to be stretching her feet, even wincing a bit from time to time.

"Do they hurt?"

"What?" she asks, seemingly unaware that she's even messing with them.

"Your feet? Do they hurt?" he clarifies.

"Oh." Sarah blushes a bit sensing his next question. "They get sore. It's really unfair what I ask of them, you know."

"Here." Tytus scoots back and gestures for her to stretch out her legs. "If I'm going to bore you to death with baseball talk, the least I can do is massage your feet while I do it."

Sarah hesitates for a moment, but her feet are killing her, and if he massages half as well as he kisses, she can't afford to miss out. She leans back a bit and places her right leg in Tytus's lap.

He reaches down and takes her slender foot in both hands as he begins to slowly kneed his thumbs into the bottom of her foot. Sarah lays her head back and closes her eyes with a soft moan that brings back Tytus's tight crotch issue from earlier.

"Oh my God, that feels amazing," she says more to herself than to him. "Go on," she prods. "You were telling me about the teams in your division and why that's important."

Tytus can hear what Sarah is saying but he can't really remember the answer. Who were the teams in his division again? What sport was he talking about? All he can think about is the buzzing in his ears and the blood flow to his nether region.

"Ty-tus?" Sarah sing-songs.

"Right." He shakes his head. "Umm. Right." He tries to scoot his body back a little further so Sarah's heel isn't so close to his groin.

"So the four teams we open up against are all in our division which makes the wins twice as important." *Baseball, baseball, baseball,* he repeats internally trying to calm his raging hormones.

Tytus successfully manages to keep his mind off sex for the next few minutes as he gives Sarah a rundown of the projections for this year and their chance at making the playoffs. It's not until he reaches for his wine, several minutes later, that he realizes she's fallen asleep. He laughs quietly but his shaking almost wakes her so he stops and tries to hold his breath. Sarah stirs but turns on her side and falls back into a deep sleep. Tytus considers trying to carry her to bed but the temptation to join her there would be far too strong. So he grabs the throw blanket off the back of the couch and lays it over her as he gently slides up.

"Goodnight, beautiful." He places a light kiss on the top of her head and sees himself out.

Tytus wakes up the following morning to a call from Nate.

"What?" Tytus grumbles into his cell.

"Have you seen them?"

Tytus is still half asleep but the awake half of him knows exactly what his friend is referring to.

"Fuck." He rubs a hand over his face. "No. But I knew they'd be there. Bad?" He swings his legs off the side of the bed. He won't be getting back to sleep now.

"You've had much worse." There is no humor in Nate's tone. "It's dark, you can't really see Sarah that well, but they do correctly identify her in the captions."

"Fuck," Tytus says again. His vocabulary limited without caffeine. He walks into his kitchen to start the coffee. "Anything nasty or damaging?"

"No, not really. Just cheesy budding romance crap."

"Thank Christ," Tytus sighs. "Her career is taking off. I'd hate to…" *get in the way.*

"Hate to—what?" Nate asks when the line goes silent.

"Nothing. It's…nothing."

56

At 10:00 a.m. sharp Tytus pulls up in front of Sarah's building in a metallic gray Aston Martin DB11. He figures if she hates sports, she probably isn't into cars either, but it makes him feel cool, so there's that.

He's just about to text her when she walks out of her building. She's wearing a dark-colored dress, green maybe, that is dancing just above the knee in the March breeze. She hugs her creamed colored coat around her as she scans the street for him.

Tytus rolls down the window and calls out to her.

"Hey, Red. Looking for a ride?"

Sarah spots him and shock registers on her face before a sly smile spreads on her lips.

"Caught her off guard. Point Hayes," Tytus says to his reflection in the rearview mirror.

He jumps out as Sarah comes across the street and he gives her a peck on the cheek.

"Sleep well?" he teases.

Sarah laughs as he opens the passenger door for her. "Yes, actually. Once I moved to the bed, that is."

The two of them head to breakfast in the flashy sports car listening to Tytus Sr.'s jazz on the high-tech sound system. Tytus tells Sarah all about the Car Club he belongs to and explains how cars are another common ground he shares with his dad.

"How about you and your old man? Were you two close when you were growing up?"

Sarah doesn't answer but the way she shifts in her seat screams discomfort.

"Not trying to pry," he continues, "family dynamics can be…complicated. I get it."

Sarah smiles softly, appreciation and relief in her eyes. "You could say that," is all she offers before changing the subject. "Speaking of complicated, I heard about the photos."

"Yeah," Tytus sighs. "I'm really sorry about that, Sarah."

Sarah laughs it off as, "any publicity is good publicity," but Tytus isn't convinced she means it. Even though he's only known her a couple of months, he's starting to pick up on her subtle cues. He's a poker player after all. He may be used to having his photo plastered everywhere and his personal life exposed to the masses, but Sarah deserves better than that.

She rarely even posts on her Instagram account, and when she does it's usually puppy memes. Not that he had been stalking her or anything.

Over breakfast, they get on the subject of college and start trading stories about Nate and Chrissie. Tytus tells Sarah about the time Nate got arrested for underage drinking even though he was twenty-three.

"He had lost his license and the cops said there was no way he was a day over 18." Tytus chuckles at the memory and has Sarah snorting.

Sarah shares a story about Chrissie and how she had joined a bunch of sorority girls at a party who turned out the lights of the pool and then jumped in naked.

"Some frat boys stole all their clothes and then turned the lights back on."

The two of them laugh so hard there are actual tears shed.

They talk more about work and what their schedules will be like over the next month. Sarah mentions that her dad lives in Toronto and is a big fan of the sports teams there.

"I bet he would love to come to a game sometime and see you pitch."

Tytus takes note of the shine in her eyes and deducts that things must not be all bad between them.

Sarah explains that her only night off of work is Wednesday and that she is really looking forward to seeing one of his games as soon as it works out.

After breakfast, they take the car out for a drive to Staten Island. Other than the times when they remain quiet to enjoy the smooth sounds of jazz coming from the speakers, they never run short of conversation. Everything between them feels so natural. Like they are old friends who just found their way back to each other.

When they finally return to Sarah's, they are about thirty minutes behind schedule and she is going to have to rush to get to work.

"So, lunch on Thursday?" Tytus asks before she gets out. They had already agreed that he wouldn't be coming to the show tonight and with Opening Day for him tomorrow, it would be a busy day.

"Already looking forward to it." Sarah smiles. Tytus pulls the car into a metered spot and jumps out. He surprises her by jumping out and jogging around the car to her side.

As she climbs out of the sports car, Tytus closes the door behind her and pins her against it.

"I can't believe we've spent almost six hours together since I got back and I haven't done this yet."

His mouth is on hers in a flash. Hot and hungry, he consumes her in such a possessive way she finds herself trying to grip the car for support. When her hands find nothing there to hold on to, she opts for gripping him instead. Sarah's hands come away from the car and up to the nape of his neck. Tytus's broad hands press firmly along the sides of her body, starting at her ribs and sliding down to her waist. Her fingers glide upward into the short hairs on the back of his head, her thumbs lightly caressing the skin behind his earlobes.

Tytus moans into her open mouth as he pushes his groin into her, his arousal is undeniable and it causes a stir in Sarah's lower abdomen. His tongue works its way skillfully through her mouth with such ease and control, she wonders absently how she ever lived before this. Without this.

With a conscious effort, he drags his mouth from hers. His pupils are full and dark, bordering on dangerous.

"You better go," his tone so husky it makes her skin tingle. He leans his forehead against hers and closes his eyes as if containing himself this way is causing physical pain.

"You sure you can't come over tonight?" She can hear how suggestive her tone sounds, and the way Tytus moans and presses his groin into her, she knows it's not lost on him.

"God, Sarah. Don't tempt me." He huffs and pushes off the car, creating some much-needed space between them. "I have a pre-game routine that I can't break. Not even for…this," he says gesturing between them. "But I can promise you one thing, I've never been more tempted."

He takes Sarah's hand as they wait for traffic to clear, and jog across the street.

"Good luck tomorrow." Sarah smiles sweetly. "Hope you get your first *save*."

Tytus cocks his brow and nods with approval. "Very good. You've been listening after all."

"You must have taught me that one before I fell asleep." She laughs as she walks away and leaves him standing on the curb.

When Tytus steps into the clubhouse it feels more like coming home than his condo had after weeks in Tampa. For the next eight to nine months this will be his home. This is where he will spend countless hours a week. Training. Preparing. Reflecting. He takes in a deep breath and lets it out slowly.

He heads to the corner where his locker has been since he was called up five years ago. His brand-new pinstriped uniform is hanging there, pressed and pristine, with his number 42 glistening on the back. The Yankees have a long-standing tradition that they do not display their last names on the uniform the way most of the MLB teams do. In Tytus's opinion, it makes the number that much more special. He chose his number in honor of Jackie Robinson, of course. He was one of the greatest to ever play the game and coincidentally the uncle of one of his father's band members.

He sits down on the stool in front of his locker and starts unpacking the few things he will keep there for the season. A picture of him with his dad and his little brother and sister. Tytus is only about 14 in the photo and all three of them are wearing Yankee jerseys. Considering he grew up in Boston, it didn't make them very popular with the neighbors. The photo reminds him to keep things in perspective. Some things are more important than baseball. He also puts up a proverb that he found while he was in college. It's become a mantra of sorts over the years.

"I may not be there yet, but I'm closer than I was yesterday."

He hangs it in his locker every season as a reminder that life is a journey. On the field and off. He knows he's not quite the pitcher, or the man, he wants to be. Not yet.

Lastly, he pulls out the game ball from his first save in the major leagues. He's been told he's crazy for not having it locked away somewhere, considering it's worth thousands, and more with each save he collects, but it's not about the monetary value to him. It's another reminder. That with hard work comes success. No one would ever beat him because he hadn't worked hard enough.

As Tytus starts to get undressed, he thinks about the meal he just shared with Nate. They started this tradition of having lunch together on Opening Day their first year at Harvard. They had continued the tradition through the minor leagues and on into the majors. Nate has never missed it. Not even when it meant taking a bus to Connecticut in college or flying out of state when they opened on the road. He is blessed to have a friend like Nate, and the fact that he also serves as his agent is just icing on the cake.

Ironically, the thought of icing has him licking his lips and thinking of Sarah. The temptation to show up at her place last night had been powerful, but he knew if he had, his body would surely have been spent today. And he had a job to do.

As his teammates start to file in, there are lots of high fives, back slaps, and chest bumps all around. The music starts pumping as the guys get their game faces on. It is Opening Day. And other than the playoffs, it is the biggest day of the year.

Sarah can hardly stand the nervous jitters thrumming through her body. She can't believe she's actually making this happen. She had spoken to the director a week in advance about getting tonight's show off. She had gone on and on about having something really important to do, but if he couldn't swing it she would totally understand. After listening to five minutes of her rambling, he told her she was one of the hardest workers he'd ever seen, and that they have understudies for a reason.

Now that she's on her way to the stadium to meet Nate and Chrissie, she is a bundle of nerves. She didn't tell them until yesterday she was coming because she wasn't sure she could trust Nate to keep her secret. In fact, she wouldn't even have told him at all, if she hadn't needed his guidance on where to go and when to be there.

When the cab drops her off, she heads to the marked Will Call area where she finds the two of them dressed to the nines in Yankee gear. She looks down at her jeans and sweater and frowns.

"We got you covered." Chrissie greets her with a smile and puts a navy-colored Yankee hat right on Sarah's head.

Nate is wearing an actual team jersey and Sarah notices the number right away.

"Did Tytus let you borrow that?"

"Borrow what?" Nate wrinkles his nose. "Oh, the jersey?" He cracks up. "No, Sarah. Anyone can buy his jersey. Most of them will even add 'Hayes Jr.' to the back, even though his actual jersey doesn't have his name on it."

"Fascinating." She raises her eyebrows. Sarah has a feeling she's going to learn a lot tonight.

As the trio walks into the stadium, Sarah is amazed by the size of it. "How many people does this place fit? Do this many fans actually come to the games?"

Chrissie smiles sweetly. "The stadium holds about fifty-five thousand, right, Nate?"

He just nods as he shows his credentials to a guard who lets them pass.

"And they sell out most games, Sarah. So, yes, this many people come to watch the Yankees play. Just wait until you see the place when it's full of crazy fans." Chrissie lays her hand on Sarah's shoulder. She knows her friend has a big reality check in store.

Nate leads them down a long hallway covered in championship banners and trophy case after trophy case. Then they finally arrive at a locked door with an engraved placard on it.

'Hayes Jr.'

Nate takes out a key and opens the door for them. Sarah enters the luxury suite and gasps out loud. The vast room is set up with food, wine, and champagne on ice. The entire space is open with an incredible view of the entire stadium. There are flat-screen TVs, leather sofas, a full bar, and a gorgeous balcony where you can watch the action live.

"My God." Sarah spins around to take it all in. "I think my concept of going to a baseball game was just a tad outdated."

"It's not like this for everyone." Nate chuckles. "There are still plenty of cheap seats out there if you want to walk on peanut shells and get drenched in warm beer."

"Oh, no." Sarah plops onto the leather couch and laughs. "This works."

As much as Sarah is genuinely impressed by the suite, there is a different kind of emotion stirring in her gut. She understands, fundamentally, that Tytus is a really good player. And she knows he's famous to some degree and wealthy, of course. But this? This is taking things to a whole new level. And she isn't quite sure how, or if, she fits into it.

The knot in her stomach tightens. A familiar dark cloud of self-doubt and insecurity looms just outside her consciousness. Very few people know the Sarah that lies beneath the witty, self-assured Broadway actress. She spent many years building up that persona, and she protects it carefully. It is the reason for her rule, in fact. How had she forgotten that?

"It's insane, right?" Chrissie comments as she hands Sarah a glass of wine. "Come out on the balcony, I want to show you something."

Sarah gets up and follows Chrissie outside the glass doors. Sipping on the wine and forcing those negative feelings down like she's done so many times before. She never would have thought a baseball field could be described as beautiful, but there it is, stunning in its own right, and once again she is impressed.

"You see that area out there?" Chrissie points out toward Sarah's two o'clock. "It's called the bullpen. It's where the pitchers warm up. Tytus will be out there throwing pitches to the catcher if the coach plans to bring him into the game."

"Okay, yeah. Tytus explained this to me. In order for him to come in, they have to have a lead in the last inning. Right?" Sarah glances at Chrissie for confirmation. "Then he comes in and *closes* the game. They call it a *save*."

"Impressive." Chrissie slaps Sarah's arm playfully. "You've got the basic idea down. Sometimes they seem to change all that, but I don't always get it. Nate says there are exceptions to every rule." Chrissie shrugs.

"Anyway," she continues, "Tytus will run onto the field from the Bullpen over there so we have to make sure we are paying attention."

Over the next hour, the sun sets and casts an orange glow over the field as thousands upon thousands of fans make their way into the stadium. Sarah begins to notice, person after person, wearing Tytus's jersey. Nate was right and many of them say Hayes Jr. across the back. It's just surreal for her to think that all these people are wearing his number. They are die-hard fans of the man who was hanging out in her apartment and rubbing her feet just two nights ago. How is this even real?

The suite begins to fill with strangers, all talking baseball and other sports, making Sarah feel like a fish out of water. Just as she resigns herself to be a complete wallflower, a familiar face walks in. Tytus Sr.

Sarah heads over to him immediately. So relieved to have someone new to talk to.

"Mr. Hayes."

He turns at the sound of her voice and the surprise that flashes there is quickly replaced with a soft smile. If she wasn't so good at reading people, she would have missed it altogether.

"Sarah Dalton. Wow. This night just gets better and better." He ignores her outstretched hand and brings her in for a hug. "And it's Tytus, or Ty Sr., never Mr. Hayes." With an expression of genuine confusion on his face he asks, "Aren't you due on stage in an hour?"

"I...got the night off," Sarah responds with just a hint of awkwardness.

Tytus Sr. tilts his head slightly and nods. "That's great."

A young man next to him clears his throat less than subtly.

"Oh. I'm sorry." Tytus Sr. turns to him. "Sarah, this is Travis, Tytus's younger brother. Travis, Sarah. TJ's..."

"Friend," Sarah finishes for him, seeing he's not sure how to. "Nice to meet you, Travis," she says as she shakes the younger man's hand.

"Friend, is it?" Travis smirks and Sarah immediately sees the resemblance. "I'm pretty sure I can count all of TJ's friends on one hand? And not a single one of them looks anything like you."

"Don't listen to my idiot brother." A gorgeous, young brunette steps in front of Travis and extends her hand. "No one else does. I'm Tess." Her smile is a spitting image of Tytus's and Sarah knows who she is before the words reach her ears. "TJ's much younger sister."

Sarah laughs and returns the handshake. "It's a pleasure to meet you, Tess. Thanks for the advice." Two siblings he'd never mentioned. Interesting. And where might his mom be? "So, TJ? Family nickname?" Sarah couldn't help but notice that none of them seem to use his actual name.

"Oh, yeah," Tess answers once the question registers. "He's always just been TJ to us. Tytus is a strange enough name as it is. We really didn't need two of them." She leans in and lowers her voice, "Especially with egos like those two have." She tilts her head knowingly.

"I heard that," her father chirps.

"You were meant to." Tess laughs and heads toward the balcony dragging Sarah with her.

Sarah is already fond of the three of them and she silently wonders what family holidays must be like.

By the time the game starts, at 7:05 p.m. on the dot, the stadium is roaring and bursting at the seams. The Yankees take an early lead with a two-run home run and the entire place goes ballistic.

Sarah is pleasantly surprised at what a great time she is having. It could be the obvious connection she has with Ty Sr., or the fact that she's on her third glass of wine, or maybe, just maybe, she actually likes baseball after all.

The Yankees are up on the Orioles 4-0 in the seventh inning when Sarah taps on Nate's shoulder.

"So, it's almost the end, right? And we're winning? So Tytus will pitch?"

Nate smiles. He notices she just used the pronoun we. "Not unless Baltimore scores," he explains. "The game has to be within three runs. If they are winning by four or more, it's not a save opportunity and Ty won't pitch."

Sarah pouts a bit as her bottom lip rolls out.

"Then I'm going to cheer for them to get a point."

"A run," Nate corrects, but Sarah just rolls her eyes as she walks back out to the balcony.

Sarah gets her wish when the Orioles hit a three-run shot in the top of the eighth inning, bringing the score within one.

"Sarah! Sarah!" Chrissie shrieks. "There he is! He's up! In the Pen."

Sarah runs over next to Chrissie and looks out toward the area she had pointed out. She can't see him too clearly due to the distance, but she can tell it's his number. Nate walks over and nudges her and then points to the enormous screen in center field.

Sarah sucks in a sharp breath that turns the heads of both her friends. It strikes her as funny that she is caught off guard at the sight of him in a baseball hat, all things considered.

But the hat is just the beginning. The way his uniform snugs his broad shoulders and bulging biceps literally makes her knees go weak.

"You okay, there?" Nate teases. "You need a moment alone?"

"Shut up, Nate!" Chrissie defends her friend. "You're just jealous."

The Yankees hold the lead but don't score in the bottom of the inning. So when the ninth inning starts the score is still 4-3.

Sarah, Nate, and Chrissie, along with Tytus's dad and siblings stand along the balcony watching intently as the small door built into the right-center field wall opens and Tytus emerges.

The intensity of the entire stadium is palpable. The pounding music accompanied by the screams and cheers of the crowd make Sarah's ears ring. The guitar solo that blares through the speakers is one she recognizes immediately as *Thunderstruck* by ACDC. As Tytus breaks into a full sprint the crowd bellows out "Thunder!" along with the piercing whine of the guitar. "THUNDER!"

Sarah is awestruck. She has never witnessed this type of energy coming from so many people at once. Thousands of people, from all walks of life, coming together as one united entity.

All for him. For Tytus.

That stirring in her stomach from earlier returns in full force. The feeling that maybe all of this is more than she can handle. She works in show business, and she understands fame. But this is a completely different world than the one she knows and old voices that she had buried long ago, surface. Whispering in her ear that she could never be enough for him.

The next few minutes pass in a blurry haze. Tytus fires pitch after pitch and the crowd roars louder and louder with each swing and miss. Three players come to the plate, and three players are sent back to the dugout. One by one, Tytus mows them down and the fans can't get enough.

The Yankees win. Tytus gets his first save. Everyone in the suite is cheering, smiling, high-fiving. Sarah should be jumping up and down with excitement, but instead, she feels a little sick.

"Sarah?" Chrissie puts her hand on Sarah's shoulder. "Hey, are you okay? He did it. He was amazing."

Sarah offers a weak smile. He had been amazing. This entire night has been like a dream. Too good to be true, in fact. And it terrifies her.

Over the next fifteen to twenty minutes the suite empties out. It's a Thursday night after all, and people have to work in the morning. Ty Sr., Travis, and Tess say their goodbyes and tell Sarah they hope to see her again soon. Travis makes a crack about her coming to family dinner at the Hayes's and Sarah knows he is trying to tease her. Ty Sr. makes her promise that she will come see one of his gigs, now that they have seen her show and one of Tytus's games.

Sarah isn't really sure what is supposed to happen next. Does Tytus come up here when he's done? Does she go down to the field? Should she just leave and talk to him tomorrow? She hasn't been able to shake the sense of doubt that has been haunting her all night. The reality of Tytus's fame and stature is starting to feel like a heavy load she's not strong enough to carry. The more she learns about him, the more she sees the life he lives, the less she feels like she belongs.

"I think I'm going to head home," Sarah says to both Nate and Chrissie at once. If she claims to not be feeling well, it wouldn't be a lie.

"What?" Nate says incredulously. "Head home? Don't you want to see Ty?"

"Oh, I don't know. I'm sure he's busy with reporters and stuff. I can wait to see him tomorrow."

"Sarah, I'm sure Tytus will be thrilled that you came. Let's just head out to the back tunnel and meet him there," Nate continues with his brow furrowed.

Sarah isn't sure she is ready to see Tytus, but she agrees with a silent nod anyway, doing her best to push through the insecurities she hates so much.

What happened to the girl who told him she was relieved they hadn't been set up? Where was the confident actress that could send an entire theater to their feet in roaring applause? How had she fallen so hard, so fast, that she's doubting herself in ways she had vowed never to do again?

By the time they get down to the player tunnel, it's packed along both sides with avid fans. Sarah notices, as she follows Chrissie, that more than half the jerseys people are wearing are number 42. She swallows thickly as she notices that although there are a few kids, and a handful of middle-aged adults, almost every fan who is wearing his jersey is a young girl between the ages of maybe 18 and 25. The reality of that fact does nothing for her anxiety.

As they stand off to the side and wait, Nate tries to call Tytus. When all he gets is his voicemail, he tells the girls he's going to head around the other way to find him.

A few players exit the stadium after Nate leaves. The fans cheer and call out to them as they stop to sign autographs and even take a selfie or two.

Sarah and Chrissie start talking about this and that's when there is a sudden uproar amongst the fans.

After a minute or two, Sarah picks up on what everyone is yelling.

"Ty-tus!"

"Ty-tus!"

"Mr. Hayes!"

She can't see very well over the hundreds of people so she walks a few steps away from Chrissie and up a small grass berm to get a better view. It only takes a moment for her to regret it.

Tytus is clad in black slacks and a maroon button-down dress shirt as he walks through the screaming fans. They are reaching for him, grabbing his arms, calling his name. His eyes sparkle with pride as he flashes his perfect smile at every single one of them. He looks incredibly happy. So in his element.

Girl after girl run their hands down his chest or along his arms. He stops to sign autographs and take photos with them. A group of four girls, who don't look older than twenty, push their way through the weak barrier and wrap their arms around him.

She can see him laughing as the girls scream declarations of love and snap picture after picture of themselves, and each other, in his arms.

Sarah's mouth has gone completely dry. Her eyes, hazy. This is his reality. Whatever she thought they have, it isn't real. Maybe he'll enjoy her company for a while, but this is the life he is accustomed to. Did she really think he was looking for something…more?

Her heart aches as she watches him from a distance and feels him slipping away. Just then, one of the girls, a gorgeous blonde, grabs Tytus by the neck and pulls him into a sloppy kiss.

"Sarah." Nate jolts her from her trance as he grabs her shoulder. She spins around to look at him, her eyes wide and misty.

"Sarah?" he says again, concern all over his face.

"It's...time for me to go, Nate. Please, let me go."

"Sarah, what happened?" Nate follows Sarah's gaze down the berm and sees security pulling a group of young girls from Tytus. When he turns back, Sarah is walking in the opposite direction.

"Sarah. Sarah," he calls after her. "Sarah, stop, please!"

Sarah turns around to face Nate with tears streaming down her face. She doesn't say anything, she just glares.

"Hey." He reaches for her arm but she crosses them in front of her. "Sarah, they're just fans. You can't let them bother you. It doesn't mean—"

"Don't finish that sentence, Nate Richards. Don't tell me what it does or doesn't mean." Sarah wipes at her face, furious with herself for being so emotional. "I can't do this. That's why I have that damn rule in the first place," she continues.

Nate tries to interject but she holds up her hand to silence him.

"I just...can't."

Sarah stalks away leaving Nate standing there in the dark parking lot, hands stuffed in his pockets, and a sick look on his face.

5

The Past

*T*ytus eventually makes his way through all the fans and finds Nate and Chrissie waiting for him. The smile he's sporting fades slightly when he senses something is off.

"Up high, Mother-Trucker," he says, raising his hand in the air, hoping it's his imagination.

"You didn't get my text?" Nate says, leaving Tytus hanging.

"Text? No. My phone's off."

He starts to unzip his bag to look for it when Nate reaches to stop him.

"Sarah came." Nate sighs.

"Really?" Tytus's face lights up as he scans the area. "Where is she?"

"Gone, Tytus," Chrissie cuts in. "She left."

"Okay, you two are giving me a really bad vibe. What the hell is going on?" He glares at them both.

Nate takes in a deep breath and lets it out with a whoosh.

"I think she was overwhelmed," Chrissie jumps in when Nate fails to explain.

"Overwhelmed? With what?" Tytus starts to push his way past them. "I'm going over to her place."

"Ty." Nate stops him with a hand to his chest. "Maybe you should just give her some space."

"Space? What the fuck does that mean? Did I do something to upset her?" His voice escalates as he throws his hands up in frustration.

"Just...hold on for a minute."

Tytus drops his bag and tilts his head toward his friend. He knows Nate's tone is meant to be reassuring but he finds it ominous.

"What happened?" His voice is thick.

"She wanted to surprise you. She asked her director for the night off over a week ago."

Tytus clenches his jaw and attempts to swallow the lump forming there. A sick feeling rises up in his gut. He is moved by Nate's words, yet he knows there is a *but* coming.

Nate wrings his hands in front of himself. He looks like he's about to tell a ten-year-old kid that his dog died.

"Hey, babe? Can you give us a minute?" he says softly to his fiancée. "I'll meet you at the car?"

Chrissie nods to Nate and gives Tytus's arm a light squeeze, before giving the men their privacy.

"Chrissie and I met her at the gate and took her up to the suite," Nate finally begins. "She was pretty awestruck by everything. Chrissie gave her the rundown on the bullpen and where she could look for you." Nate pauses.

Tytus can see he's struggling with what to say. Or, at least, how to say it. He knows he's not the easiest guy to deliver bad news to.

"She seemed to be having a great time," he finally continues. "She hung out with your dad and Travis. She and Tess really hit it off."

"Travis? Christ." Tytus furrows his brow. He can only imagine what embarrassing things his kid brother may have said.

"Then it was like something just flipped. Like, a switch." Nate twists his mouth in thought. "When the game was over she seemed...off."

"And she just left?" Tytus's voice has a slight crack and Nate winces.

"No." Nate takes another breath. "She came out here with us. We couldn't get to you with all the fans. I tried to go around, to let you know she was here, but it was chaos." Nate looks down at his feet and back up to Tytus.

"She saw that girl kiss you, Ty. I think it really freaked her out."

"She...what? That...I...didn't she see me push her away? Security dragged her off of me for Christ's sake." Tytus runs both his hands through his hair, still damp from the shower. "She can't possibly think..."

Nate reaches for his friend but drops his arm before making contact.

"Fuck!" Tytus spits out as he drops both his hands back down to his sides. Neither of the men speak for the next minute or so. Tytus just drags his hand over his face as his mind searches for a solution.

"I'm going over there." He picks up his bag.

"Ty..."

"No, Nate. I'm going."

Tytus climbs into the back of the Lexus, leaving Nate frowning after him.

"Take me to Sarah's, Miles."

Tytus has just entered the building when the doubt creeps in. What the hell is he going to say? He doesn't do emotions. He's never been good at explaining how he feels. He could show her with his mouth. His hands. His body. He's always been quite good at that. But even without being particularly blessed in the empathy department, he's fairly certain that's not the best approach this time.

He puts one foot in front of the other until he's standing in front of her door, fist raised, staring at the numbered plates reading 221. As he drops his now sweaty hand to wipe it on his pants, a familiar voice in his head urges him to run. He doesn't need her. He doesn't need this. If she doesn't want what he has to offer, then so be it.

But he doesn't move. His feet are glued to the floor. This ache in his chest is suffocating and begging him to make it stop. Knocking briskly three times just to the right of the brass numbers, he waits. In general, Tytus is in incredible shape with a heart rate that sits less than 40 bpm. Currently, however, it's at least three times that.

He's not sure how long he's been standing there. Ten seconds? Ten minutes? He doesn't hear the slightest indication that anyone is coming. She has to be home. He glances at his watch and sees it's after 11:00 p.m.

"Sarah," he calls through the door as he knocks again.

This time he hears movement inside. He holds his breath but the door doesn't open. He feels her presence. She's there.

He lays his hand flat on the door.

"Sarah?" He waits.

"Tytus, what are you doing here?" Her voice is faint but he can still hear the pain in it.

"Sarah." He rests his forehead on the door, unable to resist the need to be closer to her. "Open the door."

She doesn't respond. The door remains shut, but he knows she's still there. Just on the other side.

"Please?"

When he hears the click of the bolt, he pulls his head away from the door and steps back. The door swings open slowly and reveals a puffy-faced Sarah in her pajamas. Her eyes cast down to the floor.

"Hey," he whispers, fighting the urge to reach up and touch her cheek. It kills him that he's not sure he has the right. "Can I come in? Can we just...talk?"

Sarah walks away from the door letting it fall open, indicating her unspoken response.

Tytus follows her in and shuts the door behind him. She plops herself into the chair opposite the couch and he takes it as an indication that she's not interested in being close to him. The pang in his gut is sharp.

Taking a seat across from her, he just watches the flames dance in the fireplace. He has no idea how to do this.

"I didn't want that girl to kiss me. I pushed her off the second I got my bearings." His gaze doesn't leave the fire, but from the corner of his eye, he can see her flinch and cross her arms in front of her chest. Shit. Maybe that wasn't the best way to start.

"Listen, Sarah. I don't really know what to say, because I have no idea what even happened." Tytus just stares at his hands because looking at her hurts too much. "I just know you're mad at me and I—"

"I'm not mad at you."

The sound of her voice snaps his eyes up and their gazes lock on one another. Initially, he is hit with a wave of relief, but the distance in her eyes immediately sobers him.

"Then what is it?" He almost wants to take the question back the moment he verbalizes it, not sure he's prepared to hear her answer.

"It's complicated." She looks away. "It wasn't just that girl kissing you, or the hundreds of girls screaming your name, or the thousands of fans worshiping your every move, it was all of that, it was everything."

"I don't understand." Tytus scoots forward on the couch just to get a few inches closer to her. The need to reach for her hand overwhelms him.

"Of course, you don't. Because you're you." She lets out a huff. "Tytus Hayes Jr., The Best Closer in New York." Her voice is cold and condescending.

Her words are like a slap in the face and the walls he carefully constructed over the years instinctively shoot up.

"Wow. Okay, then." He slaps his hands on his knees and gets up from the couch. He doesn't try to hide the bitterness in his tone.

"I didn't mean to say it like that, Tytus." Her eyes fill with tears but she doesn't get up. "It's just that you don't know what I've been through."

"Because you won't tell me." His voice cracks as he raises his hands and lets them drop. His gut is wrenching. His eyes well up.

"I just can't go through it again. It's the reason I made that damn rule." Her own voice is wavering now as she looks away from him and down to her lap. "I never should have let it get this far."

Another jab to the ribs and Tytus clenches his jaw, biting back the urge to say something hurtful. *Yeah? Well, I wish we'd never met.*

Instead, he stalks toward her door. He's heard enough.

"Tytus, wait."

He stops and turns to face her.

"You know what, Sarah? My past wasn't all sunshine and roses either. You don't have a monopoly on pain."

He looks at her, standing just feet from him, tears staining her cheeks. And as hurtful as her words had been, he just wants to hold her.

"I'm sorry." She lets out a sob. "I don't know how to do this."

He moves toward her but she steps back and puts her hand up to stop him. The rejection hurts more fiercely than any of her words had.

"I need some time," she whispers. "Some space to sort through...everything. Can you give me that?"

Tytus bites down on his back teeth and the tick in his jaw is visible across the room. He balls his fists at his side and then releases them slowly. Afraid that if he speaks, he'll lose control. He gives her a curt nod and shows himself out.

The minute the door clicks shut, Sarah collapses to the floor. She drops her face into her hands and gives in to the tears. She welcomes the pounding headache because it distracts her from the pain in her chest.

As much as she fought it, she wanted him to show up. Needed him to. And when he did, she had shut him out.

Sarah picks herself up from the floor and makes her way to the bedroom. She has worked for years to bury this part of herself. The part that doubts, and worries, and wallows. One thing that has drawn her to acting is the opportunity to put on a mask and become someone else.

She is strong. She has overcome enough disappointment and pain in her life to prove that. She knows she is kind and witty and fun.

She holds a washcloth under the hot water from the tap in her bathroom and wipes her face. With a deep breath, she just holds the towel there to let the heat seep into her skin. As she pulls it away and sees her reflection in the mirror, she regains her balance.

She cares about Tytus. Much more than she intended to, and far more than she's comfortable with. She knows she hurt him tonight. He had done nothing to deserve her rejection, other than to be too much of everything she ever wanted.

Her instinct to run when something feels too good to be true is rooted in relationships from her past and she never should have allowed a man like him to get this close. For either of their sakes. If she can't learn to love herself, she will never be able to let someone else love her. It's as simple as that. She climbs into bed and pulls the comforter up to her chin, and because she's determined to let the pain take over, she lets her mind drift through their brief time together.

The first moment Sarah laid eyes on him, he had his hand in the air in an awkward wave and he flashed that incredible smile. Her staple defense mechanism was activated instantly. Confident indifference. It was her forte. But somehow between the dancing, the piano, and the walk along the park, he found a crack in her walls and, at the time, she'd been grateful for it.

The engagement party was when she really faltered. The feel of his breath on her neck. His husky voice whispering in her ear. He stirred a desire deep in her loins that she couldn't deny.

By the time he sent the roses and the adorable poem, Sarah was too far gone to recover. She was head over heels for him, and the scariest part is that she had let herself believe it could actually be something.

And all of that was before he had even kissed her.

Sarah feels a hum between her legs as she closes her eyes and drifts back to the moment she first felt his lips on hers. His tongue in her mouth. His hands on her body. She squeezes her eyes tightly as new tears threaten to fall.

She's in love with him.

The gravity of it settles on her like a ton of bricks and she clutches the sheets at her side to brace herself. There is something about him that just draws her in. The soft way he looks at her, the way her body responds to his touch, the sound of his voice when he says her name. If only she was brave enough to let go. Let go of the past. Of her fear.

Sarah told him she needed time. Maybe, if he was willing to give it to her, she could find the courage to let him in. To truly open herself up to the love that had planted its roots inside her.

In the safety of her own room, she admits to herself that she wants that more than anything, and within minutes she gives in to sleep.

Tytus's mood couldn't be more of a one-eighty from when he entered the clubhouse yesterday. He went to bed pissed, woke up angry, and now he's walking into the locker room spitting bullets.

He's intimidating enough on a good day. Standing six foot two and a solid two hundred and ten pounds of pure muscle, but when he's in a mood, watch the fuck out.

"Hayes." Spencer nods as Tytus sits on the stool in front of his locker.

"Hmph," Tytus grunts.

"Fastball was crack-a-lackin' last night," Spencer says as he unties his tennis shoes.

Tytus knows his catcher can see the fire coming from his ears. He also knows that he will think it's his job to try and distract him from whatever is up his ass. He doesn't care. Tytus doesn't even bother to grunt this time. He just takes his shirt off and throws it into his locker.

"How's the arm?" Spencer asks after a tense moment of silence.

"Fine." Tytus pulls on his jersey and begins methodically buttoning it up.

"Anything you want to talk—"

"No." Tytus marches into the training room, leaving Spencer with his mouth still open.

The Yankees win again but they don't use Tytus. Thanks to a couple of late-inning home runs they handle the Orioles 8-2 and improve to a 2-0 record.

Nate had texted him before the game that he had some business to discuss with him, and that he plans to drive him home after they have a couple of beers. Tytus wants to say he isn't interested, but the idea of going home and drinking alone two nights in a row is depressing.

They walk into the upscale bar where Nate knows he will always have a corner booth waiting and they won't be disturbed.

"I didn't really get a chance to tell you last night, you looked great out there. Dominant in fact." Nate breaks the ice with a stroke of his friend's ego. It's been known to help in the past.

The waiter drops off two glasses of scotch and hurries away.

"Thanks." Tytus takes a sip of the amber liquid and relishes the familiar burn in his throat.

Nate follows suit as he considers the safest way to broach the subject.

"She doesn't want to see me anymore." Tytus takes another drink of his scotch. He knows Nate took him out to find out what happened and he'd rather just cut the small talk and get it over with.

"Did she say why?" The pained expression on Nate's face indicates he understands his friend is suffering, but he tries to keep the conversation going.

Tytus just stares at his drink. His emotions are all over the place. One minute he wants to pick up the glass and hurl it at the wall and the next he wants to pull out his phone and call her. He purses his lips as her words run through his mind.

You don't know what I've been through.

I just can't go through it again.

I never should have let it get this far.

"Not really," he finally offers. Eyes cast straight ahead. "Sounded like someone hurt her in the past. And for some reason, she thinks I'll do the same."

"Permission to speak freely?" Nate falls into lawyer jargon.

Tytus just shrugs and sips his scotch.

"You've never really been one for long-term relationships." Nate leans back as if he wants to put a little space between them before finishing his thought. "Ever consider she might have a point?"

Tytus huffs dryly and looks Nate in the eyes. "Yes." He takes another drink. "Every time I stop being pissed off for more than two seconds."

Nate nods in a gesture of respect for his honesty but doesn't look satisfied.

"What are you going to do?" He swirls the alcohol around in his glass.

"She asked me to give her some time. Space." Another tilt of his scotch. "To…figure things out."

"And?" Nate raises his eyebrows. "Do you think she's worth it?"

Tytus finishes his scotch in one last gulp.

He tilts his head at Nate. "You know the answer to that."

"Oh, I do. I just wanted to make sure you knew." Nate chuckles.

"What would I do without you?" Tytus deadpans.

Despite being exhausted, Sarah has agreed to meet Chrissie for coffee. She's going to be performing in four shows in the next 36 hours and she has to be at the theater before noon. She's emotionally and physically drained and barely hanging on by a thread. Which is exactly why she's meeting her best friend for coffee.

Chrissie is already sitting at the counter in the coffee shop they deemed theirs when they moved to New York after Yale. The minute she sees Sarah, she hops off the stool and wraps her in a tight embrace. Great. Sarah's eyes are already stinging.

"Hey," Chrissie says softly. "Thanks for saying yes."

"Thanks for not taking no for an answer." Sarah pecks her cheek.

"Let's start with the easy stuff," Chrissie says as the waitress puts down two coffees.

"How are you feeling? Physically, I mean. All these shows must take so much out of you."

"You know," Sarah starts as she sips her coffee, wishing she had some cream, "I'm doing okay with that. All those years of yoga and dance prepared me well." Sarah is about to say 'except for my feet' but that makes her think about Tytus, and she takes another drink instead.

"And emotionally?" Chrissie treads carefully.

Sarah tilts her head at her friend and sighs. "Emotionally, I'm a wreck." Just saying it out loud makes her eyes fill up.

"Oh, Sarah." Chrissie lays her hand on her friend's. "I can't help but feel like this is all my fault."

"Your fault?" Sarah's voice raises in pitch as she sits back in her chair. "Why on earth would it be…Chrissie Elizabeth Grey."

Chrissie puts her hand to her mouth to stifle a laugh.

"You planned this. You knew about my rule and you still set me up?" Sarah is whisper-shouting now, with an incredulous look on her face.

"I set you up because of your rule, Sarah," Chrissie replies. "You never gave me any good reason for it and Nate and I thought you and Tytus were per—"

"You and Nate? He was in on this?" Sarah turns from her friend and shakes her head. One can practically see the wheels spinning in her mind.

"Did Tytus know? That this whole thing was some kind of plan?" Sarah feels like a pawn all of a sudden and her voice starts escalating.

"No, no," Chrissie reassures her. "Tytus was in the dark. Same as you, Sarah. I swear."

Sarah lets out the breath she is holding and gives her friend a curt nod.

"I am sorry, really." Chrissie squeezes Sarah's hand. "But you have to admit…we weren't wrong. The air between the two of you was sizzling from the moment you sat down in that booth."

Sarah closes her eyes at the memory. "Actually, it was from the moment I laid eyes on him."

Sarah spends the next few minutes telling Chrissie about what transpired in her apartment after the game on Thursday night. She doesn't go into detail about what happened in her past, but Chrissie slowly puts the pieces together. Sarah explains how she asked Tytus for time, but that he seemed really upset when he left, so she's afraid she may have ruined things between them. Both women shed their share of tears.

"Listen," Chrissie says quietly when Sarah is finished. "I know this is as cliché as it gets, but if he can't give you time to work through what you're feeling, he doesn't deserve you."

"I'm not sure that's fair, Wis." Sarah wipes her cheek with her napkin. "He has been nothing but wonderful to me, and just because I have old wounds that haven't healed, doesn't mean he's a bad guy for not waiting around."

"Maybe not a bad guy," Chrissie gets up to wrap her friend in a hug, "but a stupid one."

The Yankees suffered their first loss on Saturday night 3-0, which didn't help Tytus's foul mood. He went straight home, drank one too many glasses of scotch, and fell asleep on the couch.

When he wakes on Sunday morning, he has the headache he deserves. With a day game starting at 1 p.m., he has to be at the field in an hour. A hot shower, a cup of coffee, and four scrambled eggs later, his head is still pounding.

He hasn't heard from Sarah since Thursday night and it's driving him mad. He had almost texted her three hundred eighty-seven times and almost called at least twice. Space. He keeps telling himself. She'd asked for space.

Tytus enters the game in the bottom of the ninth inning with a tight 1-0 lead. Their starting pitcher had thrown eight flawless innings and it's up to Tytus to close the door on the game and the series.

He had been a bit wild while warming in the pen, and his focus was all over the place. Things don't improve when he nails the first batter he faces right in the ribs.

"Motherfucker," he grumbles into his glove, as he uses the spike on his cleat to kick at the dirt next to the mound. He needs to get his shit together before he blows this game.

He strikes out the next batter but the runner on first steals second on a pitch in the dirt that gets away from Spencer. So if Tytus gives up a hit, the run will most likely score and tie the game. Spencer calls 'time' and jogs out to the mound to talk to his pitcher. They both cover their mouths with their gloves to hide the conversation from the cameras.

"Hey. You good?" Spencer says as he lays his hand on Tytus's shoulder.

"Good? No. I'm crap. I'm all over the damn place."

"Hayes, look at me." He waits for Tytus to make eye contact. If it hadn't been for their years of history, his glare would have had Spencer cowering. "You own these guys. You hear me? They can't touch you. Just throw strikes, Ty. You got this."

The umpire starts walking toward them which is the universal indicator to wrap things up, so Spencer gives Tytus a slap on the rear and jogs back to the plate.

Digging deep and regaining his focus, Tytus gets the next batter to hit a weak ground ball to first for the second out, but the runner moves to third base.

Ok, Hayes. Keep it together. One more out. Tytus kicks at the dirt some more and spits to the side as he stares down the batter.

His first pitch is high and he curses himself for it. Falling behind in the count can be a dangerous thing. If he throws a wild pitch here, the game will be tied. The next pitch is a ball in the dirt. Spencer makes a great block to keep it in front of him and the runner on third stays put.

Tytus takes in a slow deep breath. *You've got this.* He repeats the catcher's words in his mind.

His next pitch is a fastball that catches way too much of the plate and is driven high and deep to center field. The outfielder goes back, back, back to the wall…and makes the catch.

Game over. Yankees win. Tytus is doubled over with both hands on his knees. He never even turned around to watch the flight of the ball. Off the bat, he was sure it was gone. It's only the cheers of the crowd and Spencer running to him that tell him differently.

He exhales the breath he's holding.

It's in the shower about thirty minutes later he makes a decision. He can't stay in this place he's in with Sarah. It's just not healthy. He needs to either move forward with her or from her. And the answer is obvious.

The minute he gets changed, he heads straight to The Ambassador Theater.

6

Baby Steps

"**S**old out."

The words echo in Tytus's head as he drops his chin to his chest and mutters something about being an idiot. His eyes scan the front of the theater fully expecting to find scalpers holding signs saying, *Need Tickets?* He finds none. Apparently, Broadway isn't Yankee Stadium.

He considers just waiting out back for her to leave after the show, but that's not what he came for. He came to see her. To watch her perform with all that confidence and talent that he found so enthralling the first time he had come.

He walks up to a small group of couples on the sidewalk.

"Excuse me," he interrupts their conversation. "Anyone happen to have an extra ticket?"

"No, sorry," one of the women answers him.

"Hey," the guy next to her practically shouts. "You're Tytus Hayes Jr. Guys. That's Tytus Hayes Jr."

Tytus motions with his hands for the man to quiet down as he scans the area. "Woah, keep it down. I'm just trying to get a ticket to see the show. I'm not looking to get mobbed out here."

"Shit. I'll give you mine if you give me an autograph," one of the other men says, earning him a swift slap on the arm from the girl next to him.

"You will do no such thing," she scoffs.

"Wait, wait, wait," one of the girls says excitedly waving her hands. "I know why you want a ticket. You and that actress have a thing." She claps her hands repeatedly. "I saw the pictures on TMZ."

"Awww," another one swoons. "How romantic."

"So, you'll give me your ticket then?" Tytus flashes his signature smile to hide his irritation.

"We paid $150 for these seats," the autograph guy responds.

"How about this? I'll give you $500 for both your seats." He gestures to him and his date. "Plus an autograph." The man's eyebrows shoot up as he looks at his date.

"I guess." She shrugs her shoulders. "But we're going shopping," she adds.

Tytus takes the cash from his wallet, signs their Playbill, and heads inside. He's especially grateful that at least with two tickets he can put an empty seat between himself and the rest of that group.

When Sarah spots him, she almost misses her line. She's in the middle of the third scene and out of the corner of her eye, she sees him. Tytus. In the audience. His eyes lock on her in an unwavering stare. She loses her breath and almost her footing along with it. The lapse is quick, and the average member of the audience would never notice, but her director did.

"Sarah, are you okay? You looked like you had a miniature stroke out there."

"I'm fine. I'm sorry. I just got distracted for a second," she says, still flustered by Tytus's unexpected presence.

The rest of the night she makes sure not to look in his direction again. The last thing she needs is to stumble or miss a cue. But when the show is over and she takes her final bow, she lets her eyes drift to his seat which is now empty. The disappointment it brings is sobering. Sarah lets the tears come and plays them off as happy ones.

Once she is changed and out of her wig and makeup she pulls her phone from her bag. She sees that she has a text message and hates herself for the tangible response her body has. She wants it to be him so badly, she puts the phone down on the counter without checking. She shakes her hands in front of her as she paces. She's equal parts sure that it is, and also is not, from him.

If it is from him…what will it say? After all, he showed up so that's good, right? But he didn't stay so that's probably bad.

Sarah snatches up the phone and clicks the bubble.

I had to see you. I hope you're not mad. You were amazing.

Her eyes fill with tears so quickly she can hardly read the last couple of words. She plops down in her chair. She reads the message twenty times through her glassy eyes before finally putting it down to grab a tissue.

After a deep breath or two, she picks up her phone and replies.

I'm really glad you came.

She wants to write more. *I miss you.* Delete, delete, delete. *I'm sorry.* Delete, delete, delete. She decides that for tonight, this is enough. If she's going to make this work, it is going to require baby steps. And this is step one. She hits send.

Tytus wakes around 3:00 a.m. sweaty and rock hard. It takes him several moments to get his bearings.

His eyes flutter as he tries to regulate his breathing. Sitting up against his headboard, he takes a long drink from the water bottle on his nightstand. His heart is pounding and the pressure in his lower abdomen is significant. One or two quick strokes would relieve him for sure.

She had been in his bed. In the dream. Naked and beneath him. It had felt so real he was having a difficult time coming down from it.

He closes his eyes and drifts back.

There's a knock on his door. It's so soft, he isn't even sure there is someone there. When he opens it, it's her. Sarah.

She is crying and apologizing and he wraps her in his arms and kisses her. The kiss spirals quickly from tender and loving to passionate and desperate, and before he can comprehend what's happening they are shedding their clothes and moving toward his bed.

She's so beautiful. Perfect. Her skin is soft and flawless. Her hair falls in loose curls around her flushed face. Her breathing is heavy and staggered. Sarah is lying on her back as he just takes in the sight of her. She's gripping the sheets and arching her hips toward him in a wordless plea for contact. But he waits. He wants her need and longing for him to be unbearable.

He holds out as long as he can, but the moment she groans his name and bites on her lower lip he loses his control. He lowers his body closer to hers and runs his hand along the outside of her breast. His thumb barely grazes her nipple as he caresses her reverently. The more she moves and moans under him, the more weight he eases onto her.

It's so real. So intense he can still feel her beneath him.

Tytus opens his eyes and downs the rest of the water on the nightstand as he gazes at the tented sheet covering his body.

He struggles multiple times to swallow the lump in his throat. If ever he had wanted to fall back asleep and resume a dream, this was the time. The tightness in his crotch is quite literally painful. But the torment is not all physical. He feels spent emotionally as well. It's as though he just had everything he ever wanted snatched from his grasp, and it's left him feeling empty and hollow.

He considers just turning the rest of the dream into a fantasy and trying to bring some kind of release. But the dream had been too perfect to turn it into that. So he lays back down, pulls the covers up to his chin, and tries to think of anything but Sarah.

When Tytus wakes in the morning he still feels…pent up. Generally, when he feels tense the best medicine is a good hard run, so he throws on some sweats and a hoodie, grabs his headphones, and hits the pavement.

It's early and the sky is still a pale shade of pink. Tytus loves to run outside, but he only does so occasionally for fear of being noticed. As long as it's early and he keeps his hood on, he's usually safe.

Once he gets his blood pumping along with the beat of his playlist, he falls into a steady rhythm. It's become inevitable, lately, that when he allows his mind to relax, it drifts directly to Sarah. If he's focused on something, like a workout, or a poker game, he can keep himself from thinking of her. But when his mind is clear, and left to its own devices, forget about it. She's always there.

The dream he had last night hadn't been the first one with her cast as the leading lady, but it had been the most vivid. He's guessing because he'd gone to her show and seen her in person.

I'm glad you came.

That's all she had said. He doesn't really know what to make of it. He's glad she was glad, but he'd hoped for more. He had hoped she'd give him some indication of when he could see her again. He'll be leaving on Thursday for a week and he really wants to see her before then.

This whole game is new to him. He had never in his life been the one to pursue a girl. Even at a young age, the girls had flocked to him. He could even remember two girls in middle school getting into a fistfight at lunch over which one of them he liked more. He hadn't really thought much of either of them if he was being honest. His thoughts were more consumed with baseball cards and his next start on the mound. Although the fight was kinda hot, especially at age 14.

All through high school and college, he had been a star athlete and a strong student. When it came to dances or parties, he could have his pick of any girl he wanted. So the idea of putting himself out there for a relationship, of taking a risk and possibly being rejected, is very new. And he isn't a fan.

But there is just something about Sarah that is unlike any woman he has ever met. She's…different. And in his gut, he knows she feels the same way about him. So if he can gamble at cards, or take a chance by throwing a changeup in a three-ball count, why can't he do it now? Sarah is way more important than losing a hand in poker or giving up a base hit.

That's when he makes up his mind. He is going to ask her out for a drink before he leaves town. What's the worst that could happen?

She could say no.

It's Monday, and the blaring sound of a cell phone alarm awakens Sarah from a deep sleep. Fumbling for her phone in an attempt to mute the damn thing for five more minutes of peace, she instead knocks the phone to the floor. God, she hates Mondays. She lays there in denial for another fifteen minutes before finally rolling out of bed and getting in the shower.

It's not until she's sipping her coffee that she starts wondering where she put her phone. As she wanders around aimlessly looking in the usual spots, she remembers it falling on the floor by her bed. When she picks it up and heads to the couch, she notices her text message indicator has the number four next to it. As she lowers herself onto the sofa, she clicks on it and nearly spills coffee on her new white couch. All four messages are from Tytus.

I was thinking maybe we could grab a drink tomorrow night?
I have a day game and I know you said Tuesday is your night off.
I'm heading out of town on Thursday.
Just a drink. If you want?

Each message was about two minutes apart and the last one had been sent an hour ago. Her stomach swarms with butterflies as a warm sensation spreads from her heart out to all her extremities. God, she cannot believe the way this man affects her. She covers her mouth as she thinks about the fact that he's been waiting an hour to hear her response.

She wants to say yes, of course. She misses him terribly, but she knows she's not ready to explain her behavior. Not yet. And Lord knows she is completely terrified that once she does, she'll probably scare him off with her needy insecurities and low self-esteem. No guy out there finds self-pity sexy. Especially not a guy like Tytus. He's attracted to her confidence. Her wit.

Sarah Dalton, the kick-ass actress who doesn't need anyone. But that isn't really her, and she's not sure what will happen when he finds that out.

Sarah stares at her phone for what feels like forever. She thinks back to her talk with Chrissie and about the way Tytus has treated her since day one. The way he keeps showing up even when it's not expected. She reminds herself of her epiphany in the middle of the night.

She deserves to be happy. And if any man is worth the risk. It's this one.

A drink sounds perfect. What time should I be ready?

The Yankees earn their fourth win on Monday night when they beat the Tampa Bay Rays, 5-3. Tytus pitches a perfect inning, striking out two of the three batters that he faces. He feels great on the mound and even agrees to a drink with Spencer after the game.

"To another win and save number three." Spencer raises his beer and clinks it with Tytus's.

"You were great behind the plate tonight, Kline. Really, you called a great game back there."

"You must be in a good mood," he jokes. "I think I can count all the compliments you've ever given me on one hand."

"Come on." Tytus raises his brow. "I'm not that bad, am I?"

"Worse," Spencer says with a smirk before raising his beer to his lips.

The two talk baseball and Spencer's family. He married his high school sweetheart about two years ago and they have a son who's just learning to walk.

"Traci wants to start trying for number two. Can you believe that? Shit, one is hard enough."

Tytus just laughs as he finishes his beer, but something in his gut twists and the beer tastes a bit sour.

When Spencer married Traci, Tytus hadn't been the least bit jealous. Spencer and he had both been called up to the majors around the same time and Tytus had been enjoying the life of a celebrity. He had his share of beautiful women, but there were never any strings attached. And after what had happened with his parents, marriage was not on the table.

But after Spencer had his son, and Tytus had been at their place for a barbecue, he'd felt a twinge of…something. Spencer had always been the immature one. When they were rivals in college, Tytus always looked down on Spencer's 'Playboy' mentality. Tytus was pre-law and took his education seriously when all he ever heard about Spencer Kline was that he loved to party. Now here Tytus is, single and unattached, and Kline is a family man. A dad. It just feels weird. And now with Nate getting married and talking about kids…

"How are things with Red?" Spencer asks, breaking the long silence.

"Her name is Sarah, Kline. And you know it." Tytus picks up his new beer.

"Okayyy," Spencer drags out the word when Tytus stays silent. "How are things with Sarah?"

Tytus knows that Spencer's intentions are good. He's sure that his friend suspects his foul mood the other night had to do with Sarah. He looks at Spencer intently, considering what exactly he should share.

"Not great. But I'm working on it." Honest. Accurate.

Spencer purses his lips and nods his head, eyebrows drifting upward.

"What?" Tytus says frowning.

"Nothing." Spencer looks away and sips his beer. "Just never known you to work at any relationship." He turns back to Tytus and grins. "Good for you, Hayes."

Sarah does something on Tuesday afternoon that she's never done in her life. She tunes into a baseball game on TV. She went to her yoga class first thing that morning, came home, showered, and threw on some comfy clothes.

Chrissie had tried desperately to talk her into coming to the game, but she'd declined. She is actually really looking forward to drinks tonight and she doesn't want to take the risk of screwing it up somehow. Baby steps.

So she makes a plate of veggies, cheese, and humus, pours herself a glass of cold white wine, and turns on the game. If only her dad could see her now, she giggles.

It turns out that baseball on Television is nothing like baseball in the stadium. By the third inning, she finds herself fidgety and a little bored. She keeps herself occupied with folding laundry and Wordle on her phone. She's actually flipping through a magazine when she hears the name *"Tytus Hayes Jr."* echo from her speakers.

When she looks up, she puts her hand to her heart at the sight of him up close and personal in his Yankee cap. He has a headset mic on and is speaking directly into the camera.

"Thanks, Sean. It's a pleasure to be on with you guys," Tytus says with that deadly smile.

Sarah grabs her remote to turn up the volume.

"Tytus," an off-camera voice inquires, "the team is off to a great start and you are leading all closers with three saves. Are you optimistic about the team's chances this season?"

Sarah's stomach does a complete cartwheel as he opens his mouth to speak again.

"I feel great about our chances. We have a group of men in our clubhouse that want to win games. We grind out here every day, and when push comes to shove we support each other. No matter what, we have each other's backs."

"And how about your season, Tytus? There's a lot of buzz about this season possibly being your first All-Star selection."

"I appreciate that, guys, I do. But it's awfully early in the year, and I'm just trying to go out there and pitch. To do my best to help bring home a win for our team and our fans. The rest is out of my control."

"Spoken like a true professional. Tytus, thanks for taking the time."

"Anytime, guys. Thank you for having me."

Sarah listens intently as the two commentators continue talking about Tytus while the game plays in the background. They talk about how he's been getting better every year and that he will be up for a big contract extension at the end of this season.

Sarah hasn't moved a muscle since turning up the volume. She is so flabbergasted by the fact that Tytus was just on her television set. And she finds it pretty hilarious that her main takeaway from all that is, *Lord have mercy, that man is gorgeous.*

Tytus finds himself standing in front of those three brass numbers again with his nerves jumping and his pulse racing. *God, he is pitiful.*

He raises his hand to knock but drops it back to his side instead. Shaking his head, he runs a quick hand through his hair. He really doesn't want to screw this up. Inhale…exhale. Three quick knocks.

Sarah opens the door seconds later and Tytus's mouth goes dry.

He texted her earlier that he had a surprise in store and that she should dress casually. He hadn't seen her the night of the first game she came to until after she'd changed and he wondered absently if she had looked this good that night as well.

Her jeans are tight which accentuates all her curves. Her sweater is baby blue with a V-cut neckline that provides a view that could make a proud man beg.

"You look…Wow." His voice comes out a bit raspy and makes Sarah blush.

Tytus's black sweater is hugging his pecs and biceps in such a way that Sarah needs a minute to find her words.

"So do you, Tytus." She gives him a slow once over before pushing up onto her tippy-toes and pecking his chiseled jaw. It is an innocent enough gesture but it leaves him breathless.

"Ready?" Tytus croaks. His voice, hoarse.

"Just let me grab my purse." Sarah lays her hand on his chest and hesitates to pull it away. She looks up into his eyes but he can't quite read her expression.

Eventually, she turns away to grab her purse and he immediately misses the contact.

In the elevator, Tytus's hand twitches at his side. How is it that she had held on to his arm on the night they met, but now, he's unsure about reaching for her hand? He wants to. He has this feeling that can only be described as a need to touch her. But he's scared to push her too far too fast. He promises himself that for once in his life, he isn't going to take the lead tonight. Just spending time with her is enough. For now.

"I thought about picking up a car for tonight," Tytus says as he opens the door of the Lexus for Sarah. "But there is literally no parking where we are going, so I opted for Miles."

"Well, I'm glad." Sarah lowers herself into the car. "Because I've been missing you, Miles." She reaches up over the front seat and squeezes his shoulder.

"The pleasure is all mine, Ms. Dalton." He looks back over his shoulder at her.

"Oh, no it's not, Miles." Tytus jokes with his driver and makes Sarah smile.

On the drive, they settle into casual conversation and Tytus almost forgets that they had ever had an issue. With his guard temporarily down, he puts his hand on Sarah's knee. She smiles at him, but it doesn't reach her eyes. In fact, her gaze shifts to her knee and then quickly back up to his face. It's subtle, but he picks up on it and removes his hand.

Miles drops them off outside of a small brick building with the name Arthur's Tavern.

"Jazz?" Sarah's eyes light up as they walk through the entrance.

"Not just jazz, real jazz," Tytus says with a smirk.

Tytus sees the group of men he's looking for huddled near the bar and he leads Sarah straight to them.

"I heard this is the best jazz dive in all of New York, so why are you old geezers here?" Tytus slaps the back of a man facing away from him, but the entire group turns around.

"Lord have mercy, will you look at that. Tytus Hayes Jr. in the flesh." The older gentleman gets up to wrap his arms around Tytus, and Sarah spots Tytus Sr. on the stool behind him.

His father gets up when he sees Sarah and steps in for a kiss on the cheek. "Guys, I'd say gentlemen but I'm not a liar, this bombshell is Sarah Dalton, and for some reason I have yet to figure out, she seems to enjoy TJ's company."

That gets a hoot out of everyone, except Tytus that is. Tytus Sr. introduces Sarah to what she realizes are his bandmates and he shows the two of them to a private booth.

"Our set starts in about ten. Hope you enjoy it," he says, as he squeezes Sarah's hand and gives her a wink that is identical to his son's.

Tytus orders drinks for the two of them and they sit and talk while they wait for the band to set up. He explains that his dad is semi-retired and usually only fills in these days when they need someone. The rest of the guys live locally while Tytus Sr. lives in Boston.

"What about your mom?" she asks. "Does she ever come out to see him play?"

Tytus's lips tighten into a thin line as he sits up straighter in the booth. Clenching his jaw, he looks away from Sarah.

"My parents…aren't together anymore."

He sees the concern flash on Sarah's face but she doesn't push. He is graciously saved from a conversation he doesn't care to have when the drummer starts his countdown and music washes over the entire bar.

As the first song turns into the sixth or seventh, and drink number one, becomes number three or four, Tytus notices that Sarah inches closer and closer to him in the booth. He can feel her thigh touching his and it's causing a hum to permeate through his entire lower half. He balls the hand resting on his knee into a fist as he carefully contemplates moving it to hers.

As if she could somehow sense his hesitation, Sarah shifts another inch closer and lays her head on his shoulder. With newfound confidence, Tytus slides his hand from his knee to Sarah's and tightens his grasp, just slightly. This time, he's pretty sure she likes it.

The band finishes their set around 11:30. Sarah and Tytus say their goodbyes and she promises to follow them on Instagram and catch as many gigs as she possibly can.

As Miles drives the two of them home, Tytus notices Sarah's eyes growing heavy. He's guessing it's a combination of the alcohol and being overworked. He lifts his arm up and around her head. She doesn't hesitate or shy away from him. She leans right in and closes her eyes.

When they pull up at Sarah's, Tytus softly jostles her.

"Hey," he says softly. "Come on, I'll walk you up."

When they arrive at Sarah's door, they both stand in awkward silence. Tytus is hoping she will invite him in, but he's met with silence instead.

"I had a great time." Tytus breaks the quiet as he reaches for her hand. He looks into her eyes as he glides his thumb across the back of her hand, trying to get a read on where they stand.

"So did I, Tytus. Really. It was perfect."

Sarah puts her hands on Tytus's shoulders and leans in to kiss his cheek. Without warning, he turns his head so her lips land on his. So much for not taking the lead.

He wraps his hands around Sarah's waist, grasping her left forearm with his right hand, pulling Sarah closer so that every part of her body is pressed firmly to his. Her lips are soft and pliable against his as he tilts his head slightly and slides his tongue past them. The moan he feels coming from her is all the encouragement he needs.

He backs Sarah into the door of her apartment. 221. The numbers are engraved in his memory. His hands run up both of her sides slowly, applying just enough pressure to feel every curve of her body.

He doesn't want to push her too far, but he can't seem to stop himself. The more he tastes her, the more he needs. He keeps his left hand gripping her ribcage so that his thumb brushes ever so lightly on the underside of her breast while his right reaches behind her. His long fingers engulf the back of her neck, pulling her mouth closer as he slides his tongue deeper.

When he finally pulls back slightly to get air into his lungs, she moans his name. "Tytus." The sultry tone is almost more than he can handle, but when he leans back into her, she repeats it. With a different tone, altogether.

"Tytus." It's a request. A plea. She applies the slightest pressure to his chest to signal she's asking for space.

When he looks into her eyes he knows what she's saying. Not tonight.

"Baby steps, Tytus. Baby steps."

7

Broken

*A*s her Friday night show is wrapping up, Sarah can't stop thinking about getting home, getting comfy, and hopefully talking to Tytus. He'd left on his trip yesterday and they had agreed to talk tonight, once they were settled. Tytus picked up his fourth save last night in Toronto and she's excited to see how they did tonight. Sarah Dalton, a baseball fan. Who would've thought?

She knows she needs to greet some fans and sign some autographs, so once she's changed, she heads out to get it done. It had been a packed house tonight, and more people tend to stay for autographs after the weekend shows. Tonight is no exception. As the line moves along and Sarah shares her sweet smile and beautifully crafted signature, she is filled with a warmth of appreciation. Being able to do something she loves this much, and then having people line up to shake her hand for it, can just be so humbling.

But the warmth quickly turns icy at the sound of a voice from her past. She knows it's him before she even turns her head and the bile rises in the back of her throat without warning.

"Sarah Dalton. A sight for sore eyes."

She swallows down the taste of vomit before she plasters on her best fake smile.

"Mason Drake." She keeps her voice steady from years of training, but her knees begin to wobble beneath her. She doesn't make any move to reach for the hand he's extended and he eventually drops it.

"This is my wife Shannon." He breaks the awkward silence and gestures to the big-haired, big-breasted blonde to his right. "Shannon, this is Sarah. We were in a play together at Yale."

And the vomit is back. Gulp.

Sarah is concentrating so hard on just keeping her balance and not darting back inside, that she forgets her basic manners. Eventually, Shannon speaks instead.

"It's an honor to meet you, Ms. Dalton. You were bloody brilliant."

Was that an accent? Is she British?

Sarah's not sure if she ever pictured who Mason would end up with but it certainly wouldn't have been a beautiful and seemingly articulate English woman. She finally manages to find her words.

"That's so kind of you to say." Sarah offers a grimace because under the circumstances it's the best she's got.

She's beginning to feel quite dizzy as sweat begins to bead on her forehead. If she could just lean on something…

"So tell me, are you married, Sarah?" Mason smiles behind his well-trimmed beard and Sarah wonders absently how long he's had it. His voice sounds distant somehow as she turns her focus to the golden flecks in his light brown eyes and wonders if this is what people mean when they refer to an out-of-body experience.

"Sarah?" He reaches for her elbow. "Are you feeling alright?"

She yanks her arm away and steps back. Her reaction is instinctual and must seem overly dramatic to Mason and anyone else who happened to witness it.

"Excuse me," Sarah says between staggered breaths. She turns and bee-lines to her dressing room.

She stumbles her way inside and barely gets the door shut before leaning against it.

The nausea gives way to heartache as her eyes fill with tears. Mason fucking Drake. She never expected to see him again. Had made a distinct effort not to, as a matter of fact. And then bam, just like that, face to face.

Sarah gingerly makes her way across the room to the water bottle on the dressing table. Her balance is still off, so she steadies herself with one hand while lifting the water to her mouth with the other. The majority of the water makes its way down the front of her rather than into her mouth.

Lowering herself into the chair, she concentrates on regulating her breathing. How can pain from over a decade ago still cut this deep?

Save number five. God, he is on a roll and it feels fucking fabulous. As Tytus showers in the visitor's locker room, he can't wipe the grin from his face. The team has won again and he is pitching the best baseball of his life. And on top of that, he had kissed Sarah senseless the other night, and she'd liked it. He could tell.

He knows what she said. Baby steps. He can handle that as long as her steps are toward him and not away.

He is really looking forward to calling when he gets to his hotel.

"Try not to glance my way with that shit-eating grin on your face." Spencer raises an eyebrow below the showerhead next to him. "The guys are going to get the wrong idea."

Tytus lets out a chuckle that makes Spencer laugh along with him. Even Spencer's smart mouth can't put a damper on his good mood.

The team piles into the bus for the ride to their hotel and Tytus puts on his headphones to listen to the new playlist he's been compiling. Mostly jazz, including the song Earl was playing when he and Sarah danced the night they met, as well as a few from Tuesday, and some random ones that just remind him of her.

He watches the Canadian night sky as the bus makes its way along the highway. He knows Sarah is holding back. That she's apprehensive about getting serious with him. He should know what apprehension looks like since he's never truly been able to commit to anyone.

He's never been a guy to think long-term. After what he had witnessed with his mother, he hated even the concept of marriage. And most women didn't want to get serious with a guy unless he wanted that. Marriage. A family. He swallows.

Gradually, Tytus becomes aware of a bad taste in his mouth. It's accompanied by swirling in his gut like he used to get in the backseat of the car when he was a kid. Where exactly did he see this thing with Sarah going? He had been so drawn to her, so caught up in her beauty and the way she made him feel, that he'd let down his usually impenetrable walls. Obviously, she had been hurt in the past, and did he really think he could offer her something more? Something real?

Rubbing a hand down the stubble already shadowing his face, he draws his brows in a tight line. She means something to him. Maybe more than anyone ever has and he's only known her for a short time. The last thing he wants is to hurt her. He wants her to have the happiness she deserves. And he had never really been good at making other people happy.

How quickly one's mood can change. He'd gone from feeling like a million bucks to a piece of shit, just like that.

The buzz of his phone snaps him back to the present. Travis. He declines the call but texts him right away.

On the team bus.

Call me. It's about Mom.

Well, fuck.

That doesn't help Tytus's mood one bit.

"She's sick," Travis says as soon as he answers the phone. "Like, really sick."

Tytus lets the words wash over him, but he says nothing in response.

"Tytus," Travis raises his voice. "Did you hear me? Mom's sick."

"I heard you, Travis."

"You need to come see her, Ty. She's asking about you."

Tytus swallows the lump in his throat. Travis' words hit him hard. Much harder than he'd ever admit.

"How bad?" He clenches his jaw and balls his fist. Angry with himself for caring enough to even ask.

"I'm not a doctor, Tytus. But it doesn't seem too good. They're running a bunch of tests. Danny says—"

"I don't give a shit what Danny says. Don't fucking mention that bastard to me." The mention of his mom's husband brings Tytus's walls right back up. "I'm in Canada, Travis. I can't make it." Tytus's eyes start to fill with tears at the internal push and pull. Even after all these years, the intensity of it feels like it might physically tear him in two.

"I know that, Tytus. But Monday you fly into Boston. I'm not an idiot."

"I have nothing to say to her. A visit from me is the last thing she needs."

How has this night gone to complete shit? Tytus just wants to throw something.

"You're wrong, big brother." Travis exhales into the phone. "And you're going to regret it if you don't come."

"Goodnight, Travis. This conversation is over." Tytus hangs up the phone and stalks toward the wall of his hotel room. He lifts both hands up to his chin as he takes a fighter's front stance. His eyes well up with tears while he battles with the urge to throw a right cross straight into the wall. Knowing he'd only break his hand and potentially ruin his career, he grabs a pillow from the bed.

"Fuck!" he screams into it before chucking it across the room.

He knows he's supposed to call Sarah. He had been so looking forward to it earlier. But now he just feels like a complete asshole who has nothing to offer and won't even visit his own damn mother in the hospital.

Tytus practically rips off the door to the mini-fridge and grabs a beer. He gulps it down like a bottle of water and wipes his mouth with the back of his hand. Despite the fact that it does nothing to calm his mood, it's getting late and he knows he needs to call Sarah.

He gets undressed and lies on the bed. After taking several deep breaths he finally pushes the icon to call her.

"Tytus?"

He can hear it immediately. She's upset. Crying. He immediately sits up and forgets about everything except her.

"Sarah? What's the matter? Are you okay?" His voice is borderline panicked, but he doesn't care.

"Um. Not really." She pauses. "I mean, yes, Tytus."

He can hear sniffling and he knows she's not okay.

"Sarah. Tell me what happened. Where are you?" Tytus stands up and begins to pace around his hotel room. He wants to crawl through the phone and hold her somehow.

"I'm…still at the theater," she answers him in a defeated tone that only breaks his heart more.

"Okay. Okay. So you're safe? You're not hurt or anything?"

"Yes, I mean, no." She stumbles. "Tytus, I want to talk to you about it. I do. But I just need to get home." There is a crack in her voice that nearly kills him. "Can I call you back when I get to my apartment?" she adds.

"Let me call Miles," he practically shouts. "Just sit tight and I'll get Miles to come get you." He needs to help. She has to let him help.

"Tytus, that's not—"

"Sarah, please. Let me help." There is desperation in his voice.

Seemingly too drained to fight him, she agrees.

Miles arrives to pick up Sarah within fifteen minutes, and she wonders if he is some type of superhero. He sure feels like one tonight. So does Tytus.

She showers, slides into her pajamas, and curls up in bed with a blanket.

Oh, and a tall glass of wine. If she's going to tell Tytus about her first boyfriend, she'd better just keep the whole bottle on the nightstand.

Tytus picks up on the first ring.

"Sarah. Thank God. You're home?" The tender tone of his voice makes Sarah well up.

Shit. If she can't get through ten seconds without crying, how can she possibly tell this story?

"Yes. Home, showered, and in bed."

"Good," he says so softly she barely makes it out.

"I ran into someone tonight." She may as well get straight to it. She takes a gulp of her wine. Tytus remains silent, cueing her to continue.

"Someone from my past and it…shook me up a bit."

"A man?" His voice sounds tight. Like he's asking through clenched teeth.

"Yes." Sarah takes another drink from her glass.

Inhale. Exhale.

"His name is Mason Drake. He was my first real boyfriend. I was eighteen."

Sarah walked into the college auditorium for the first day of the summer production of Grease. She found her group of friends giggling and whispering by the corner of the stage.

"What's going on? What are you all whispering about?"

The girls pulled Sarah into their huddle and pointed to the other side of the stage. There, leaning against the wall, was a tall blond with a chiseled jaw and dreamy eyes.

It's Mason Drake. Only the hottest guy on the entire Yale campus," her friend Pam whispers. "He's the quarterback of the football team." Pam shakes her like Sarah's not paying close enough attention.

Sarah knew who he was. He'd been in one of her fall classes and she'd developed an immediate crush.

He was wearing a pair of baggy jeans and his letterman jacket, messing with his cell phone. Confidence was oozing from his pores and you could feel it across the room. She couldn't peel her eyes away.

"Mason Drake? In our play? Why? How?" Sarah was rambling and it caused the girls to giggle even harder.

"I heard he failed his art class," one of her friends whispered.

"Yeah, and if he doesn't make up the credits, he won't be eligible for football," another added, like such a fate would be the end of the world as they knew it.

"We met doing a summer play after my first year at Yale. He was the star quarterback of the football team and I was an awkward theater geek, still growing into my body."

Tytus clenches his jaw. He doesn't like the sound of where this is headed. He remains silent. Afraid an interruption will cause her to change her mind about telling him.

"I know this is as cliché as it gets, but Mason ended up being cast as Danny Zuko and I was Sandy Olsson. The two of us couldn't have been more fitting for those roles. He was popular and…experienced. I was nobody and completely naive."

"Maybe we should grab something to eat after rehearsal. Go over some of our lines?" Mason was standing directly behind her. She could feel his breath on her neck. A strange tingle ran through her body that she had never felt before. It was a little exciting and a whole lot terrifying.

The two of them started spending more and more time together. Mason even suggested they practice some of their kissing scenes.

"So we don't look awkward," he'd explained with a sweet smile and those puppy dog eyes.

Sarah of course agreed. Grabbing a bite to eat here and there and practicing kissing quickly turned into something more. They began spending all their free time together, and instead of kissing as Danny and Sandy, they were kissing as Mason and Sarah.

He was kind and caring and Sarah fell in love for the very first time. He said he loved her too.

"We were inseparable for two months. I know it sounds ridiculous now, considering I was just a kid, but I felt so in love. Like every fairytale I'd read, every romance film I'd seen, it was coming true, for me." She pauses to sniffle and take a sip of her wine.

"It's not ridiculous, Sarah. Don't say that." Tytus's voice is low and pensive.

"Did you have your heart broken by a first love?" Sarah replies.

Tytus huffs into the phone and then remains silent for several beats.

"We aren't talking about me, Sarah. Please, go on."

"As the summer drew to an end, I began to worry about school starting and how things between us might change. He told me he loved me and that we were soulmates. And on the last weekend of that summer, he convinced me to have sex with him." She pauses and swallows another gulp of wine. "It was my first time." Her voice cracks in the phone.

"I'm guessing things changed after that?" he asks. His tone, pained, as if he knows where this is going.

"Not at first." Sarah sighs and adds more wine to her empty glass.

She had done it. She had sex with Mason and she was no longer a virgin. She couldn't decide if she was proud or embarrassed. He had said he loved her, and she had believed him. They were soulmates after all.

Sarah's fears about the start of school changing things were put to rest for a while. Mason was an attentive boyfriend and an amazing lover. Despite his busy schedule, he made time for her and she felt like everything she'd romanticized about relationships as a young girl had come true. She and Mason were meant for one another and they were sure to live happily ever after.

It was a Friday night and the team had just won a big game against Penn. Mason had thrown three touchdown passes and the entire school had been chanting his name. Sarah watched with pride as he and his teammates piled on top of each other out on the field.

The couple had planned to head to a local hang-out after Mason showered and changed, but he texted to say he'd be stopping by his dorm for something and she should just meet him at a restaurant. Sarah agreed, but later decided she would surprise him at his place and they could walk over together.

"Mason." She walked in with a wide smile and a bounce in her step. "I couldn't wait any longer to see—"

Sarah's words got stuck in her throat as the bedroom door swung open and revealed a bare-chested blonde perched on top of the man she thought was her soul mate.

"Sarah." Mason yelled as he pushes the blonde aside. "What the fuck?"

She wanted to yell right back at him but her voice didn't seem to work. Neither did her legs apparently, because her mind was screaming 'run' but her feet wouldn't budge. She just stood there. Blinking. Staring. Her mouth hanging agape. She had given her virginity to him. She loved him. They were soulmates.

"Sarah. Shit." He threw the sheet at the girl sitting beside him looking bored and unaffected. "I told you I'd meet you there."

He sounded angry. Irritated. Like she was in the wrong for showing up unannounced.

Sarah closed her mouth and swallowed. The thickness in her throat made the simple task feel nearly impossible. When she finally brought her eyes up to meet Mason's she was struck by what she found there. Or more accurately, didn't find. Remorse.

As Tytus sits in silence, listening to Sarah's story, he squeezes his eyes shut and clenches his jaw.

She is crying now. Has been for the past several minutes. He can hear the pain oozing from her words and he would give anything to be able to hold her. His stomach is in knots.

"I'm so sorry, Sarah," he says for what feels like the hundredth time, feeling useless to console her.

"That's not even the worst part," she says after a few moments of silence.

Tytus covers his face with his hand. He's not sure he can take any more of this. His empathy for Sarah is painful enough, but his own past and his feelings about infidelity only make it harder to hear.

"The next day, when I confronted him, he wasn't even sorry."

"How could you do this to me?" Sarah raised her voice in the courtyard outside the building.

"Sarah, would you calm down?" Mason looked around at the people walking by.

"Calm down? You said you loved me," she shrieked, throwing her hands in the air.

"Come on, Sarah." Mason just huffed and shook his head.

"Come on what? This isn't how people who love each other behave." Her voice was incredulous. She still hadn't wrapped her mind around the reality of what all this really meant.

Mason looked around again as he shoved his hands into the pockets of his letterman jacket.

"You're making a scene."

His words, accompanied by his clear concern for being embarrassed instead of any actual concern for her, finally helped reality set in.

"You don't love me?"

"Sarah—"

"Say it!" she shouted. Her voice escalated with her heart rate. "Say you don't love me!"

People were actually gathering now. No one could pass up a good show like the one the two of them were putting on. It was ironically like being back on stage.

"Shit, Sarah!" Mason raised his voice to match hers. "I don't love you!" He raised his hands and dropped them back to his sides. "Think about it. I'm Mason fucking Drake!" He gestured around at all the people looking on. "I'm the damn starting quarterback, and you're…you're no one."

And there it is. The final piece. The reason for her rule.

"Sarah—"

"Something broke inside me that day, Tytus." Sarah feels completely emptied out and exhausted. "He took something from me. And I don't just mean my virginity."

"I know, Sarah. I understand."

Sarah can almost hear the wheels turning in his mind through the phone. She knows he wants to help but what can he really say?

"It took me so long to heal," she continues. "It was two years before I even tried to start another relationship." Sarah grabs a tissue from the nearly empty box and blots her eyes with it. "And now…" Sarah stops mid-sentence. Her throat is nearly closed and she has to force the words out. "And now that bastard shows up out of nowhere, and I'm a complete mess." The tears continue to stream down her face.

"Are you still in love with him?" Tytus's voice is thick and strained. Like he's asking a question he doesn't want the answer to.

"With Mason?" Sarah chuckles but there is no humor in it. "God. No, Tytus. I don't even know if I ever was." She sits up and tries to pull herself together enough to make him understand. "It has nothing to do with him, Tytus. Not really." Sarah works up the nerve to share the truth that's eating her up inside. "This is about me. It's about the way I view myself and what I have to give." Biting her lower lip she lays it all out there. "What do I really have to offer someone like…you?" She inhales, holds, and lets the air out slowly. It's a coping mechanism she's learned over time. "I'm broken."

Those words. They break him.

They hit the nail right on the head. Open the valve that had remained secure for so long. All the anger, the hatred, the blame, the pain that he has bottled up inside breaks free. Like a glass bottle dropped on the pavement, he shatters. And the tears rack his body as they pour from his eyes.

"Tytus?" Sarah's tone shifts to one of confusion. Concern. "Tytus? What is it? Talk to me."

The phone sits on the nightstand, speakerphone on, while he pushes the heels of his hands into his eye sockets. He's drowning as the pain of nearly two decades washes over him. Sarah had opened herself up to him and with every word she said, he saw himself. All the pain of feeling betrayed by someone who was supposed to love you. The realization that they took a part of you, and you may never be whole again. The reality that you are indeed, broken.

He knows she's listening and he curses himself for being so weak. So selfish. He's supposed to be the one supporting her, and now…

"Tytus, please. Tell me what's wrong?"

Her voice is so full of concern and worry, that he forces himself to speak.

"I'm sorry, Sarah." He wipes his eyes aggressively and pulls off his shirt to dry them. "I'm supposed to be supporting you and now I'm the one falling apart." He tries to clear the raspiness from his throat. "Nice work, Hayes," he mutters.

"Actually, Tytus. We are supposed to support each other." The soft tone of her voice is even more soothing than her words. "Now, I just spilled my guts over here. I think it's safe to say it's your turn."

Tytus sighs. He's never been much of a talker. But Sarah has a point. And even though he has no idea why, or what it means, he actually wants to tell her.

He gets up to open another beer and sits in the chair at the desk.

After a few deep breaths, he tells Sarah an abbreviated version of the story. His mother had been unfaithful. She had an affair with a friend of his father's that lasted years, and eventually, she left them all behind for him. She'd had her reasons of course. His dad traveled all the time, they grew apart, excuse after excuse. But the whole thing had torn Tytus to shreds. The more he talks about it, the better he feels. It is as though he is unloading a heavy backpack of bricks, one by one.

"With my mom out of the house and my dad's music career, I had to grow up pretty quick. My relationship with Travis suffered the most. He took my mom's side on most things and I took my dad's. It's not something kids should have to deal with, you know?" Tytus sighs and paces around the room. "Not to mention it basically ruined any chance I had at bonding with Tess. And…my mother and I haven't spoken in almost ten years."

"Oh, Tytus." Sarah's voice cracks. "That must be so painful for you."

"Honestly, I pretty much just block it out." He shakes his head and stares at his own reflection in the mirror. "I'm guessing a shrink would say that's not healthy, but it's been working okay for me."

"Tytus, I don't think—"

"She's sick." Tytus cuts her off before taking in a long pull from his beer. He may as well just let Sarah see who he really is. "Travis called earlier and said she's in the hospital. He says I need to go see her." Swallowing the lump forming in his throat he bites down on his fist as his eyes brim with tears again.

"Maybe you should?" Sarah phrases it as a question and he hears no judgment in her tone.

"I can't." Tytus drops his face into the hand he has propped on the desk.

"Listen, Tytus. No one can tell you what you need to do." Sarah's voice is full of understanding and empathy. "That has to come from you. But I can tell you, speaking from experience, the first step to healing is forgiveness."

Tytus nods to himself as Sarah's words sink in and his tears pool on the corner of the desk. He has been told the same by his father and brother over the years, but somehow, coming from Sarah, they finally take hold.

The two of them talk a while longer until they both give in to the exhaustion.

"I can tell you're falling asleep. I should let you go." Tytus is under the covers himself and is physically and emotionally drained.

"I can't wait for you to get home," she whispers.

There is something slightly seductive about her tone and Tytus grins for the first time all night.

"I'll call you when I get to Boston, okay?"

Sarah hasn't asked if he is going to go see his mom or not. He knows in his heart she will support him either way.

"Sarah?" he continues before she responds. "You know I'm nothing like him. I'd never—"

"I know, Tytus," Sarah says softly. "I know."

And he believes her. She thinks he's a good man. Maybe he is.

"Goodnight, Sarah."

"Goodnight, Tytus."

Tytus sets his phone on the nightstand and heads into the bathroom to brush his teeth. As he wipes his mouth with the towel, he takes another long look at his reflection. As if having a silent conversation with himself, he nods. Tytus heads back to the bedroom and picks up his phone to text his brother.

I'll be there, Travis.

8

Forgiveness

*A*s the wheels touch down at Logan International, Tytus's stomach is in knots. He's made the decision to go see his mom and considering Travis, Sarah, and even Tytus Sr. are aware of that plan, he doesn't see a way out of it. Not that he's changed his mind, he's just terrified he's not ready.

Spencer is sitting to his right in the window seat.

"You good?" He nudges Tytus's shoulder. "You look a little pale."

"Yeah." Tytus nods. "All good," he lies.

The team had split the remaining two games against Toronto and neither game had called for Tytus to pitch. They are currently a game ahead of the Red Sox in the division, which makes this next series extremely important. In the past, Tytus had put his career above all else and rarely had to concern himself with being *distracted*. But life has a way of throwing you a curve when you least expect it, and now he has both Sarah and his mom on his mind.

Hey Trav. Just touched down. Pick me up at the hotel in an hour?

Sounds good. See you soon.

For as much as his younger brother can drive him crazy, Travis is a good guy. Tytus knows he left his brother in a really bad spot when he left for college. And even though all the wounds between them haven't healed, they have come a long way.

As promised, Tytus sends Sarah a text, too.

Hey. Just landed in Boston safe and sound.

Can you talk?

About to get off the plane. Can I call you in a few?

Of course.

They had been texting each other all weekend but hadn't spoken since Friday night. Tytus is honestly blown away by how much better he feels after sharing his story with her. He had worked so hard all these years at keeping it buried, that the freeing feeling of letting it out took him completely by surprise. His dad and Nate are the only people in his life he's ever really confided in, but with Sarah, it's different.

The team makes their way through the airport and onto the bus within minutes. Fenway Park and the hotel are only a few miles from the airport so Tytus figures he'll have time to talk to Sarah before Travis shows up.

"Hey," he says through a side smirk when he hears her voice through his phone. "I just got into my room."

"It's good to hear your voice, Tytus."

When she drops her voice down an octave like that, it does things to him. Especially when she says 'Tytus'.

"It's good to hear yours, too." He sits on the end of the bed. "Are you in the car? It sounds like you're driving."

"Yeah, actually. I'm going to see a friend. I just wanted to make sure you were still feeling good with your decision?"

"Well, I haven't changed my mind if that's what you mean." He pauses. "But I wouldn't use the words 'feeling good'."

"I'm not going to tell you it will be easy, Tytus, because it won't be. But, I really believe you're going to be glad you did it."

Tytus feels a twist in his gut as he takes in a shaky breath. He holds his hand in front of his eyes and watches as it literally shakes. He balls it into a fist.

"I hope you're right, Sarah," he says softly.

"Are you sure about this?" Sarah looks over at Nate as she disconnects the call.

"Positive." He takes his eyes off the road long enough to give her a quick glance. "I spoke with Tytus Sr. and he wanted us to come. Both of us."

Sarah wrings her hands in her lap as she watches the landscape zoom by the car window. When Nate told her he was making the trip to Boston, she had wanted to ask about coming along right away, but she never would have. Then he suggested it…and here they are.

"He's going to be so happy to see you, Sarah." Nate reaches across and pats the hand she has resting on her knee. "I spoke with him last night and he couldn't stop saying how glad he was he told you. How you had helped him see that this is what he needs to do."

She smiles at Nate and nods before looking back out the window. To be honest, she's not just worried about Tytus. She's concerned about herself, too. The cat is out of the bag, so to speak. Tytus may know now why their relationship had her guard up, but Sarah isn't sure if that really changes anything about her fear that she's not going to be enough for him. She hasn't been able to keep her mind off of him, and this longing to be close to him is a bit overwhelming. Making a conscious effort, she pushes the doubts away. This is right. Her coming to Boston. Her feelings for Tytus. She's done with all the second-guessing.

"I'm glad you told me to come, Nate." She smiles with more sincerity as she turns to face him again. "I think it was the right thing to do." And she means it.

On the way to the hospital, Travis explains to Tytus what's wrong with their mom. He doesn't really know all the right terminology but he gives him the basics. Her white blood cell count is dangerously low. They think it's Leukemia. It may be terminal if it doesn't improve.

He also explains that Tytus had just missed his little sister, Tess, who came into town for a couple of days but had to get back to school.

Tytus can't remember ever feeling this anxious. Even in his first outing in Major League Baseball, he had remained steely calm. As nervous as he had been standing at Sarah's door, it was a cakewalk in comparison. He is a man who likes to be in control. When he was a kid, he was a boy who liked to be in control. And despite the fact that going to see his mom was his choice, he feels anything but in control.

They pull into the parking lot of the hospital and he sees his dad leaning against his truck. A moment later he notices that he is talking to Nate. Tytus smiles. Nate has always been there for him in the toughest of times, and he is touched to see him here now.

As they drive past them to find an open parking spot, he catches a glimpse of a third person. Goosebumps spread from the nape of his neck all the way down his spine. His breath catches in his throat. Sarah. She's here.

He stares straight out the windshield in front of him as he tries to gather himself. Every time he thinks he's reached the capacity of his feelings for this woman, she surprises him and they grow deeper still.

"You okay?" Travis asks as he puts the car in park. "It was Nate's idea to bring her. He said you'd want her here. I tried to—"

"Nate was right." Tytus gets out of the car, leaving Travis in mid-sentence.

Tytus strides quickly to where the trio is standing. He steps right between his father and his best friend and wraps his arms around Sarah. As he pulls her close his face falls into her hair and he takes her in like a much-needed breath of fresh air.

God, I needed this. I needed you. The words sit on the tip of his tongue but never leave his mouth.

"Thank you for being here." He looks into her eyes as he slowly pulls away. He wants to kiss her, but they have an audience.

Tytus turns to his father and wraps him in a manly bear hug.

"I'm so glad you came, Son. Damn proud." Tytus Sr.'s voice breaks slightly and it's enough to cause his son's eyes to brim with tears. He chokes them back as he turns to his friend.

"Nate." He nods and pulls the extended hand forward so that he can slap his back. "Thank you," he whispers before they separate.

Travis goes in ahead of them to let Judy, and her current husband Danny, know that Tytus has arrived. His mom is expecting him, but no one was really sure if he'd actually go through with it.

As the group of four head into the hospital, Tytus slides his hand into Sarah's. Palm against palm, fingers interlaced. It's just the assurance he needs. When they enter the large waiting room, Travis comes in from the opposite direction. Danny is following right behind.

Tytus knew he would be here. He promised his father and brother that he wouldn't say or do anything stupid. This isn't the time or place for it. He knows that. Danny glances in his direction but neither man makes eye contact.

"She's ready to see you," Travis says as he stands in front of his brother. "You ready?"

Tytus feels the pressure of Sarah squeezing his hand and he turns to see her beautiful face looking up at him. "You're ready." She nods, her eyes glistening. Tytus nods back with a clenched jaw and follows Travis down the hall.

When they get to Judy's room, Travis puts his hand on the knob, but Tytus reaches to stop him. "I'd like to go in alone." He looks his kid brother in the eyes. "I need to do this alone." Travis drops his hand from the door and looks at Tytus hesitantly before stepping to the side.

Tytus enters and notices several flower arrangements and cards spread throughout the room. It causes a sharp pang of guilt in his side. His gaze drifts to his mother, and he is immediately struck by her fragility. Judy had always been a vibrant and lively person. An artist with an infectious personality who never backed down from a fight. This morning, she looks weak, and at least a decade older than she is.

"TJ?" She tries to sit up as he approaches, but her elbow won't support her. Her eyes are full of tears and her voice is hoarse.

"Mom," Tytus closes the distance between them, "don't try to sit up. Just, relax." He can't hide the emotion in his voice. The sight of her in this bed breaks his heart into a million pieces. He hasn't spoken to her in almost ten years, but now that he is standing here in front of her, he knows exactly what to say.

He pulls the nearby chair next to her bed and wraps her tiny hand between his two larger ones. His heart pounds in his chest as he feels heat rising around the collar of his shirt. He knows what he wants to tell her. In fact, he has thought of little else over the past couple of days.

"I'm sorry, Mom," he chokes. "I'm so sorry." Tytus's eyes spill over as he watches his mother's do the same.

"Tytus, sweetie, why—"

"Mom. Just let me say what I came to say and then I'll give you a chance, okay?" He forces a small smile. "If I don't get it out now, I might not be able to."

Judy nods at her son, her eyes full of emotion.

"I've been holding on to all this pain, this anger, for too long, Mom. It's time to let it go." A wave of relief washes over him as the words leave his mouth. He exhales a breath that has been trapped in his lungs for a decade. "We all make mistakes, I'm certainly no exception to that."

"Oh, TJ. My boy," Judy says softly as tears continue to fall.

"I met someone," he continues, "we haven't known each other very long, but she's…incredible." Tytus wipes his cheek with the back of his hand and tries to fight through his instinct to shut down. "I really care about her, and I think we may have a shot at something." He takes in a slow shaky breath trying to steady his nerves.

"I want to be the kind of man she deserves." Tytus surprises both of them with his candor. "And I think that starts with forgiving you."

"I'm so sorry, Son." Judy sobs. "I wish you could understand how sorry I am." She strains to reach across the bed with her other hand so she can hold his between her own. "I love you," she whispers. "I love you so much." Judy's weak body shudders as she cries, and Tytus stands to lean over the bed rail and wrap his mother in his arms.

Neither of them speaks for several minutes. Tytus just holds her and lets his mother cry. Half of his life he has spent angry and bitter, and now it feels like such a waste. He had never stopped loving her, nor she, him. He had let all these years slip away, and now he has no idea how much time she has left.

"Can I meet her? This angel who brought my son home to me." Judy looks at her son with a pleading look in her eyes.

"How did you know she was—"

"Your brother told me. I'd just love the chance to thank her."

Tytus's throat feels thick as he tries to swallow. Somehow telling Sarah about his mom felt good. And telling his mom about her, felt even better. But the idea of bringing them together feels...terrifying.

"Of course." His voice betrays him and his stomach flutters. "I know she'd love to meet you."

When Sarah walks into the room with Tytus's hand in hers, she lays her eyes on Judy for the first time. While her skin is a bit pale, and her eyes tired, Sarah can see the resemblance immediately. The kindness in her eyes and smile calms Sarah's nerves.

"Mom, this is Sarah." Tytus walks her over moving his hand to the small of her back. "Sarah, this is my mom Judy.

"Sarah," Judy repeats with a faint smile on her face. "What a pleasure to meet you."

"Oh, Judy. The pleasure is all mine. I just wish we were meeting under better circumstances," Sarah adds as she takes Judy's fragile hand.

"Sarah, my dear." Judy squeezes her hand gently. "You brought my son back to me. There is no better circumstance than that." Judy's eyes fill with tears again as her hand trembles lightly in Sarah's.

Sarah understands the gravity of her words as Judy mouths to her quietly. "Thank you."

Tytus's phone starts buzzing in his pocket.

"Can you excuse me for one minute? I need to take this," Tytus apologizes and steps out.

Judy looks at Sarah knowingly and pats the mattress next to her. "I meant what I said. There is nothing I needed more in my life than TJ's forgiveness, Sarah." She smiles. "What a blessing you are to both of us."

"I am so glad that he decided to come, Judy." Sarah sighs softly. "But you are giving me way too much credit. Tytus came to this decision on his own."

"No, Sarah. He didn't. He told me as much himself." Judy pauses and Sarah looks up at her. "I know my son. He's always been strong, protective, and stubborn as a mule." She shakes her head with a small laugh. "His father and brother have tried to get him to work through this for years. But here he is. And here you are. It's no coincidence."

Sarah simply smiles and gives her a cautious nod. The weight of her words makes Sarah's mouth go dry.

Tytus comes back into the room and the three of them talk a few minutes longer. As Sarah watches Tytus and his mom interact, she can see just how much both of them needed this.

Sarah is waiting outside while Tytus brings Nate in to see his mom and spend a few quiet minutes with his family. She's grateful for the solitude and fresh air because she desperately needs to regain her balance.

How had she become this intertwined in Tytus's life so quickly? It is more than a little unnerving. Meeting Judy had left her feeling incredibly raw and their private talk had shaken her a bit. She feels emotionally drained but somehow her heart is so full.

Having been broken by Mason resulted in years of trust issues that were only compounded by her father's habit of breaking promises. Sarah was used to protecting herself and constantly trying to prove that she was self-sufficient and independent. So why was it that Tytus seemed to make her want to strip all that away? To just open herself up. To trust. To love.

The reality of that both invigorated and terrified her.

"Hey."

Just the sound of his voice sends warmth through her body. Sarah turns to find Tytus with his hands in his pockets looking more sheepish than his usual cocky.

"Hey," she responds, a little sheepish herself.

"You okay? I hope that wasn't too awkward for you?"

God. When he looks at her that way she feels like she could literally melt into a puddle.

"I'm good," she offers. "I'm so glad I got to meet her. How are you? You're the one who just reunited with his mom after ten years."

Tytus steps closer and takes both of Sarah's hands.

"Thanks to you." His warm smile takes Sarah's breath away. "I've never been better."

They stand there in the cool breeze and something profound surrounds them. Neither one says a word. There is no embrace. No kiss. Yet it may be the most intimate moment they have shared. For a few beautiful seconds, there are no walls between them.

An elderly couple walks by them and the moment passes as quickly as it came.

"How are you getting back to New York for the show?" Tytus brings them back to reality. "Nate said he's staying for the game. I can hire you a private car?"

"I'm not going back tonight." She didn't intend for it to come out the way it had. Her voice, low and sultry as if it had a mind of its own. The sound of it has just as deep an effect on her as it appears to have on Tytus.

Something dark and primal flashes in Tytus's eyes, but he recovers quickly, clearing his throat.

"What do you mean, not going back?" He can't hide the thickness in his tone.

"I mean, I'm staying. I'm coming to the game with Nate." She smiles coyly as she watches Tytus's reaction to her statement.

His eyes light up a bit before his grin catches up.

Jesus, that smile makes her weak.

Tytus says his goodbyes to his family and promises to come back in the morning. He even shakes hands with Danny, though a curt nod replaces any actual conversation between them.

He climbs into the backseat of Nate's Navigator with Sarah and ignores Nate's sarcasm about not being an Uber driver. Everyone is quiet on the drive to Fenway. It had been an emotional morning for them all.

Tytus feels like a brand-new man. He had been full of anger for so long, he isn't sure what to replace it with. At the moment, however, it's fear. Fear for his mom and her health. And maybe just a little bit of fear about Sarah coming to the game.

He's ecstatic that she is staying in town. When she told him earlier, he could have sworn she was suggesting something and it caused a quick and powerful hormonal response. But, he can't shake the memory of what had happened after the last game she attended. He knows it will be completely different on the road. If there is any chanting or screaming, it will be boos and sneers. Shit, maybe she'll even feel bad for him. He snickers to himself. Still, his profession is a hurdle for her, and the last thing he wants right now is something tripping them up.

After dropping Tytus off at the player tunnel, Nate parks in the small private lot across the street and suggests they grab lunch. They have hours to kill before game time.

"Have you been to Eastern Standard?' Nate asks Sarah as he leads her to the sidewalk.

"No." She laughs. "Haven't really spent much time in this area. None actually."

"Wait, what?" Nate stops walking. "You grew up in Connecticut, you live in Manhattan, and you have never seen a game at Fenway Park?"

Sarah wraps her arm around Nate's elbow and pulls him along.

"Nate, Tytus's game last week was only the second baseball game I've ever been to. The first one was a Dodgers game with my dad on a business trip to LA. I was nine."

Nate shakes his head, seemingly unsatisfied with her explanation, and makes Sarah giggle again.

"Here we are," Nate says as they approach the local pregame hotspot. The restaurant is filling up quickly, but they manage to snag a prime spot. The two of them sink into a large red leather booth and Nate orders them each a Whiskey Smash.

"Trust me, it'll change your life."

They spend the next couple of hours talking about Nate's wedding plans and the upcoming rehearsal dinner. Sarah inquires about every little detail, especially the ones that concern her and Tytus's roles as Best Man and Maid of Honor. She knows she sounds a bit like an excited schoolgirl, and the whiskey isn't helping, but at this moment she just feels happy and decides to just make the most of it.

Sarah is a bit tipsy as she and Nate make their way through the crowded streets near the stadium. After two Whiskey Smashes, she was ready to roll, after three, she was leaning on Nate a bit. As they walk by vendor after vendor and her senses are flooded with hotdogs and kettle corn, she finds the whole environment exhilarating. Everyone is so excited. The energy is palpable and you can't help but get caught up in it.

"Hey?" She yanks on Nate. "No Yankee jersey tonight? All these people are wearing their Red Sox ones."

"Yeah, well our seats are in the front row next to the bullpens, and I'm not looking to get beer or worse thrown on me. We are the enemy tonight, Sarah. Trust me on this."

Somehow his comment excites Sarah more than it worries her. Yep. She's drunk.

As they walk into Fenway Park, Sarah is speechless. She had been blown away by the view of Yankee Stadium from the luxury suite but this perspective may be even more impressive. Nate takes her hand as he walks her through the sea of people and she gets her first look at the field. They are mere feet from the outfield grass and she has the urge to run her hand over the pristine blades. The stadium, although small for MLB standards according to Nate, looks enormous and she is again taken aback at the number of fans filling the stadium.

But nothing has ever left her as breathless as the view of Tytus when she spots him entering the bullpen. Okay, well Tytus has left her breathless on multiple occasions, actually, but this time he does it without the use of his tongue.

Sarah's not sure if it's the influence of the alcohol in her system or the way the uniform is gripping his crotch, but she feels a rush of heat between her legs. For a woman who claims to not care for athletes, she feels utterly exposed as he begins to warm up. Somehow Nate had placed another drink in her hand, and despite the inner voice saying she doesn't need more alcohol, she sips on it. And watches.

Tytus has his legs spread wide on the grass as he bends over to reach for the ground. His gray pants hug his massive thighs and toned ass in a way that makes Sarah shift uncomfortably in her seat. Where had that breeze from earlier gone, she wonders, as her body temperature begins a steady ascent.

He is joined along the foul line by several of his teammates and they begin to jog and throw. This close-up view of him throwing the ball is impressive, to say the least. Sarah continues to let the alcohol swirl through her body as her hormones rage in a way she's never quite experienced before.

The ball comes out of his hand so gracefully. It's as though it takes no effort from him whatsoever, yet the ball zooms to his teammate as if shot from a cannon. His biceps bulge from his jersey and…

"Sarah," Nate practically shouts. "Are you alright? I called you three times." He asks in all seriousness when she turns toward him. "You looked flushed."

Sarah blushes and clears her throat, feeling like she was just caught watching porn by her best friend's husband.

"I'm good, Nate. Great actually." She exhales slowly. "I think I just need to switch to water."

The game is exciting from the first pitch. The Red Sox fans clearly love their team and hate the Yankees, but that only adds to the atmosphere. Nate is an excellent teacher and he walks Sarah through all the positions on the field, plus he gives her a breakdown of the general rules.

When the Yankees break the tie and take the lead in the top of the eighth inning, Nate points out that Tytus will be coming in to get the save.

Sarah watches in awe as Tytus stands just a few feet away from them throwing his warm-up pitches. He had waved and smiled at them early in the game, but he is completely focused now.

"That's where the term game-face comes from." Nate laughs pointing at Tytus. "The hitters don't stand a chance." He grins as he shakes his head.

Tytus enters the game as expected and dominates each batter just as Nate had predicted. He strikes out two of them and gets the third to pop up to Spencer. Save number six is in the books.

Wow. That's my boyfriend.

Sarah covers her mouth with both hands and lets out a small squeak. As if someone may have overheard her thoughts. She has no idea where that thought, or that word, came from. But she's just going to go right on thinking it.

Tytus has to ride with the team back to his hotel, so he tells Sarah and Nate to meet him there. Since he had showered in the clubhouse after the game they agreed to meet up at the hotel for a nightcap.

Only when he enters the lobby bar, he sees Sarah sitting alone.

"Where's Nate?" he asks with one eyebrow raised and leaning in to plant a soft kiss on her cheek.

"He said he was calling it a night. Headache or something." Sarah smiles with a shrug of her shoulders.

Tytus makes a mental note to thank his wingman in the morning.

They sit and nurse their drinks while Tytus desperately tries to focus on the words coming from Sarah's mouth instead of just focusing on the curve of her upper lip. He's failing miserably.

He has been inching closer and closer to her and currently, they are nearly nose to nose. Tytus's leg is propped on the crossbar at the bottom of Sarah's stool and his knee has made its way further up between her legs. His breathing is labored as Sarah runs her hand slowly from his knee to his inner thigh. His groin pulsates as his pants grow tighter.

"Do you have a room here?" His voice is husky and full of need.

Sarah shakes her head slightly as she leans in and whispers, "I didn't think I'd need my own."

"Check, please." Tytus nearly knocks the stool to the floor as he stands and raises his hand to the bartender.

9

Naked

Sarah can hardly keep her feet under her as Tytus literally drags her to the elevator. She's been seriously horny since watching him on the field earlier and the heat between her legs has been gradually increasing since he sat down in the bar. But something about the way Tytus is breathing right now, all heavy and uneven, has her panties feeling moist.

Tytus pushes the elevator button with his middle finger. Several times in fact, as if he thinks persistence will bring it down faster. Sarah finds herself in awe of the sheer length of it. His finger. It makes her blush.

No sooner do the doors open than Tytus has her pinned against the back wall. Fortunately, it's late and they don't have any spectators along for the ride to the twenty-seventh floor.

"God, Sarah." It comes from Tytus's throat as more of a moan than actual words. His thigh is pushed firmly between her legs and the way he's grinding into her, lifts her feet nearly off the ground.

Sarah is breathless as Tytus ravishes her neck. She scrapes the back of his head with one hand while trying to find some sort of balance with the other. His name, Tytus, is on constant repeat in her mind but she's temporarily lost the ability to speak. She moans, maybe more of a whimper actually, when he runs his hand under her sweater and slides it around her torso to her lower back.

"You have no idea how much I've thought about this." His breath is hot as he sucks on her earlobe. "I've dreamt about tasting you." He grinds his erection into her abdomen. "Of being inside of you."

Sarah is actually relieved when the elevator reaches his floor and the doors open. She was beginning to think Tytus was going to make her come with just his thigh and some dirty rumblings.

Tytus, however, seems annoyed by the interruption as he spins her around and begins walking her backward toward his room. He now has both hands under her sweater and as they caress her hip bones and lower back, she can't help but revel in the sheer size of them. His palms are warm and just calloused enough to be sexy as hell.

Sarah finds herself up against another wall while Tytus starts fishing through his pockets, looking for his room key.

"Goddammit," He half curses and half chuckles, trying to get the key from his wallet.

"You can use both hands, Tytus." Sarah giggles. "I promise not to run." Her voice is raspy as she does her best to appear coy.

The way his mouth quirks at her comment is a textbook example of a devilish grin.

"Oh. I know you won't."

Sarah's belly flutters under the intensity of his stare. The way he can make her legs go weak simply by lowering his tone that way disarms her. Every damn time. She gulps.

Mercifully, the door finally opens and Tytus yanks her inside. He pulls the sweater over her head before he kicks the door shut with his foot. He backs her up toward the large bed while reaching both arms around the back of her thighs, hoisting her up off the ground. Sarah wraps her legs around his waist as Tytus slides his tongue into her mouth.

When his shins hit the mattress, he lowers Sarah onto the bed and takes a step back. His eyes are almost black as he looks down at her. As he starts to unbutton his shirt, slowly, his eyes rake over her body.

Sarah has never felt sexier in her entire life. The way he's clenching his jaw and watching her, possessively, makes her feel like prey being hunted by a skilled predator. She slides herself further up the bed and unclasps her bra, letting her supple breasts fall free.

Tytus's cheeks dimple as he juts out his chiseled jaw. His eyes move from her face down to her breasts and Sarah watches his Adam's apple bob in his throat. He pulls his dress shirt off and drops it to the floor.

"I've dreamt of this." His tongue slips between his lips as he steps closer to the bed. Sarah hums in response to his admission, wetness pooling at her core.

She knew he was built. She had felt his taut muscles through his clothes more than once. But the sight of his bare chest is even more impressive than she'd imagined. His arms and pecs are perfectly sculpted and the veins protruding his biceps make her mouth water.

"So have I, Tytus," she whispers.

Kneeling on the edge of the bed, he reaches for the clasp of Sarah's pants. Without another word spoken between them, he peels her pants down her slender legs, leaving her naked except for a lacy lavender thong. He groans as he lowers his face to place a light kiss on the inside of each of her thighs before dragging his tongue along her soaked panties on his way up to her chest. She lifts her hips up toward him, but Tytus doesn't give her what she wants. Not yet.

Despite the fact that she's lying down, Sarah feels lightheaded. There is a dream-like fog clouding her vision which she attributes to the lack of oxygen to her brain.

Tytus braces his body over hers with an arm placed just to the left of her ribs causing his bicep to flex inches from her face as he uses the palm of his right hand to make small circles over her hardened nipple. She wants to reach for his chest. To run her hands across those firm mounds of muscle. But the way he's touching her has her paralyzed. Afraid the wrong movement on her part might cause him to stop.

Unconsciously, Sarah arches her back, urging him to touch her. Really touch her, before she dies from the need.

Tytus envelops her entire right breast with his hand as he lowers his mouth to tease the nipple of her left with his tongue. Moving back and forth between them, he elicits a sensual moan from Sarah before lowering his body just enough to press his hardening cock into her center. For the next several minutes he stays right there, sucking, licking, and nibbling until she can't handle another second.

"Tytus." Sarah finally reaches for him. She scrapes the back of his head with her red nails. "Tytus, please." Her hips lift off the mattress and brush lightly against the protruding bulge in his pants sending a searing bolt of electricity up through her core and into her lower abdomen.

With a sharp hiss, he lifts his groin to break the contact, but he answers her plea. Not aloud, but with his actions, as he glides down her stomach slowly, dragging his tongue along her flat stomach.

He slips his middle fingers underneath the thin material on each side of her hips. Twists his fingers around the fabric and begins to slide them down. Stopping almost immediately and causing Sarah to whimper.

"Open your eyes, Sarah." It comes out like a demand. Not forceful, but insistent. "Look at me."

She obeys. Without question. She is putty in his hands and would do anything he asked of her.

As he pulls the last barrier from her body, Tytus keeps his gaze locked on hers. The depth of his stare coupled with the stream of moonlight illuminating his structured frame gives him the appearance of a Greek God. Sarah gasps as her breath lodges in her throat.

"My God, Sarah," he whispers softly, finally letting his eyes wander down her body. Between her legs. "I knew you'd be perfect. But somehow, you're even more beautiful than I imagined."

Through the haze of ecstasy surrounding them, Sarah feels touched in an even deeper way. There is something special about those words, about the way in which he says them, and it shakes her to the core. She has never felt so exposed. Vulnerable. Naked.

Tytus touches the tip of his tongue lightly between her wet folds and Sarah is brought back from her reverie in an instant. Her body shudders and Tytus responds by wrapping his arms around her thighs. His tongue drifts from the bottom of her opening all the way to the top.

Sarah feels the muscles in her hips and legs begin to hum. The stirring in her lower abdomen builds and she grips the sheets and fights against it. Moaning his name and willing the orgasm to hold off just a minute or two longer.

"Tytus," she cries out his name as he continues to lap and probe her center. With every stroke, she calls his name again and again.

"Tytus. Tytus. Tytus."

Far too quickly and not nearly soon enough, she explodes into the pressure of his mouth. Like a firework illuminating the night sky, blinding light flashes behind her eyes, and pulsating vibrations course through every nerve in her body. The pleasure is so intense, so all-consuming, that she gives herself over to it, accepting that it just may be the death of her.

Tytus unknowingly holds his breath as Sarah comes undone in front of his eyes. He is filled with a strange sense of pride for what he's done to her. That he could bring her this level of pleasure. He's always been a skilled lover, but this is more than that. He hadn't just wanted to please her. To turn her on. Tytus had wanted, needed, to make her understand the way he felt about her. To somehow make her feel what he felt. He'd never been good with words. But this. This he could do.

His erection has grown painful. He's eager to unzip his pants, but he waits. Waits and watches as Sarah's body gradually stops convulsing, the moaning subsides, and her breathing returns to normal. Waits until she opens her eyes. He wants her to watch.

Sarah's eyes flutter open as she comes down from her high. She eyes him standing at the end of the bed. His fingers gripping the button of his jeans. She slides her body back slightly and lifts her head onto the pillow, obtaining a better vantage point.

Tytus swallows the lump in his throat. He knows his body is fit and it has always been a source of pride for him. But as confident and cocky as he is, he feels a bit apprehensive. He wants her to like what she sees.

With a deft flick of his thumbs, the button is undone and he pulls the zipper down, revealing a well-manicured V of thick dark hair. The flash of desire in her eyes gives Tytus the assurance he needs. He pulls the jeans down past his firm glutes and over his thick thighs releasing his rock-hard erection. Sarah's pupils dilate at the sight of him and Tytus can see them darken as they take him in. She wants him, and she's going to get what she wants.

Before he has a chance to come back to the bed, Sarah moves to the edge herself. She reaches for his chest and he steps toward her, between the legs she has dangling from the bed. When he feels her soft hands on his pecs, they instantly flex. Tytus lets out a low groan when she grips his chiseled chest and runs her thumbs over his hard nipples. With eyes shut tight, his back arches slightly as her hands venture south over his rib cage, caressing his abs and pausing on his hip bones.

"Tytus." Her tone matches his from earlier. "Look at me."

A hard gulp does nothing to help the tightness in his throat as he opens his eyes and tilts his chin. His brown eyes are met with her hazel ones, almost golden with the yellow flecks more pronounced than he'd seen before. Sarah wraps her hand around the base of his cock, encircling him with her thumb and forefinger while slipping her other fingers under his balls and applying pressure there as she takes just the tip of him between her lips.

Tytus tightens the muscles in his ass and he gasps at the intensity of her touch. His instinct is to pull back, overcome with sensitivity, but as if Sarah could read his mind, she uses her free hand to grip his butt as she pulls him forward and takes the entire length of him into her throat.

A stream of incomprehensible sounds comes from Tytus's throat as he wraps both his hands in Sarah's auburn waves. He loses all sense of reality as she grips and glides her hand along his length. Is he doing that? Is he pumping in and out of her mouth or is she the one moving? Any sense of where he ends and she begins is lost. He can't tear his eyes away from the view of her mouth as he grips her head tighter and watches himself vanish between her lips.

Tytus feels the tightness in his scrotum coil, his balls start to hug closer to his body, and he pulls himself out before he reaches the point of no return.

"Back up," he croaks.

She doesn't question him. She scurries backward onto the mattress as he crawls on top of her. He's not sure if the growling he hears is only in his head or actually coming from his mouth. He wraps his arm around her thigh and lifts her leg so that her knee is nearly at her chin. His eyes are focused between her legs as he gingerly glides his cock along her folds.

So wet, so ready. For him.

Tytus shifts his attention from their intimate contact and searches for her eyes. The moment her gaze finds his, and their eyes lock on one another, he slips the tip inside of her. He holds there, just beyond the entrance, searching her eyes for something. Understanding? He sees her throat bob and a flicker in her eyes and he pushes forward. He buries himself completely into her. And as her walls wrap tightly around him, he moans her name.

"Sarah."

They don't break eye contact as he repeats the motion time and time again. He can see the pleasure on her face. What he's doing to her. What she's doing to him.

"Fuck...Sarah."

Pulling back slowly, pushing in, a little deeper and a little harder with each thrust.

"Tytus. God, Tytus." Sarah's moans only drive him closer.

The intensity becomes overwhelming for him as the pulsing in his groin intensifies and he knows it's coming. There is no holding back this time.

"Sarah. I'm...I'm—" His voice is full of need as he stutters breathlessly. As the orgasm pulses through him, it electrifies every nerve and muscle from his center to the tips of his fingers and toes. And to make the moment even more perfect, Sarah goes over the edge right along with him. His body convulses as he empties into her before collapsing on top of her body. His large and heavy frame dwarfing her slender one beneath him.

Sarah wakes in the middle of the night with pins and needles in her left arm. It's trapped under the massive hunk of muscle next to her. For the next couple minutes, she tugs, pulls, and pushes trying to free herself, but she can't budge Tytus an inch. She doesn't want to wake him, but she's fairly certain the role of Roxie is contingent on having two arms. If she ends up needing an amputation, she's going to be out of a job.

"Tytus?" she whispers, pushing lightly on his chest. She kisses his lips softly when her first attempt fails, but he is still out cold. Sarah giggles at the absurdity of the situation and slips her free hand under the light sheet covering Tytus's lower half. She isn't trying to start anything, just thinking it might be the best way to get his attention. But when she finds him long and hard, her body responds with a humming between her legs.

She uses her palm to rub tiny circles on his tip. A maneuver she had picked up earlier from the way he'd caressed her breasts. Within seconds he moans as that 'Hayes grin' spreads across his face. He thrusts his hips forward and Sarah tightens her grip to stroke him without missing a beat.

"Haven't had enough of me?" His eyes flutter open and his voice is hoarse. He props himself on his elbow and Sarah immediately pulls her trapped arm free.

"Oh, I'm good," she teases him. "You just had my arm pinned and I need you to move." She rolls onto her side, away from him with a grin. "And based on that rod between your legs, you seem to be the one who hasn't had enough."

Her laugh turns into a squeal as Tytus flips his body on top of her pinning her face down on the mattress. He starts to place wet kisses on the back of her neck and down her spine.

"I was dreaming. About you." His tone is deep and husky and it stirs Sarah's insides. "About doing this."

They are both sound asleep when Tytus's phone starts buzzing on the nightstand. He reaches his hand over without opening his eyes and declines the call. When it starts vibrating again immediately, he curses and rubs his face with both hands.

"Hayes," he grumbles into the phone without looking at the caller.

"Tytus, it's Travis."

Tytus shoots up in bed. "Travis?" He's wide awake now. "What is it? Mom?"

"Calm down, Tytus. She's okay."

Tytus exhales a huge breath of air from his lungs and walks to the window.

"Christ, Travis."

"Sorry, Ty. Listen. The doctor said he actually has good news. Can you come to the hospital? The doctor is going to be coming in to talk to us at 9:00."

Good news? Tytus clamps down on the hope that starts to build in his chest. He's never been an optimist and he doesn't plan to change that now.

"Of course, Trav. Thanks for the call."

Sarah wakes up to the sound of water running through the pipes behind the headboard. She feels a little disoriented and she fights to lift her heavy eyelids. There is a dull ache above her left temple that reminds her she had one too many and an ache between her legs that reminds her of something else.

She reaches across the bed and finds it empty. The shower.

Sarah pulls the sheet from the bed and wraps it around her body as she gets up to open the drapes. She has always loved Boston, despite being chastised by Nate for not knowing the bar seen around Fenway. All the red brick, the history, the personality. It is really unlike any other city she's visited. She opens the slider and lets the fresh air cool her flushed skin. Last night had completely rocked her world. He had rocked her world. The sex, of course, was amazing. But it went way beyond that and she knew it.

Tytus had peeled away her carefully constructed layers of armor over the past few weeks. She'd accepted that she was in love with him before she'd made love to him. But now? Now she knows there is no turning back.

"Good morning." He enters the room and is hit with a sense that he's interrupting her thoughts.

Towel tied at the waist, chest damp and hair dripping, he walks over to stand behind her. Wrapping his arms around her, he nuzzles his nose into her hair.

"I love the way you smell."

"Like baseball and booze?" she laughs.

"Among other things." He spins her around and wiggles his brows before kissing her. It's passionate and deep, but not at all about sex.

"Last night was…"

"Perfect," he finishes her sentence with a smile. His forehead against hers as their eyes lock. "Travis called."

He steps away from her to take a long-sleeved shirt from his bag. "He said the doctor is coming to talk to the family at 9:00." He pulls the fitted thermal over his head and turns back to face her. "He said it's good news." There's a slight hitch in his voice, but he recovers quickly.

"Tytus That's amazing." Sarah walks up to take his hand in hers.

He just nods and squeezes her hand. Still afraid to let himself believe it.

Tytus had invited Sarah to join him at the hospital and as much as she'd wanted to, she and Nate had agreed to head back to Manhattan first thing this morning.

He seems disappointed, but he understands.

As they stand on the curb waiting for Nate to bring the car around, Sarah is fighting the tears building in her eyes. The air feels thick and the ache in her chest scares the shit out of her.

God, woman, you'll see him in a couple days.

"I'll be praying for your mom the whole way back," she says to break the silence. "Promise me you'll let me know the minute you find out anything."

Tytus's hands are on her hips as he looks down into her eyes.

"Of course, I will." His grip on her tightens with assurance.

"I'm so glad you went through with it, Tytus."

"Me too," he replies softly. "Someone really special helped me figure my shit out."

The kiss he leans in to place on her lips communicates so much more than she ever thought possible. So soft. So gentle. So deep.

Sarah is hit with a flood of emotion. The words 'I love you' on the tip of her tongue.

"Beep, beep." Nate's horn jolts her from her thoughts. Saves her, perhaps.

Tytus pulls her into him and wraps his muscular arms around her. She squeezes her eyes shut to force the tears away for just a moment longer.

"I'll see you on Thursday." He leans back to kiss her on the forehead and look her in the eyes. She can see his mind working. His eyes search hers. And for a brief moment, she holds her breath, she believes he's going to say it. That he feels the same way.

"Thank you for being here, Sarah. For…everything."

She offers a weak smile and climbs into the front seat of Nate's car, grateful that he doesn't see her tears.

When Tytus arrives at the hospital he is met out front by his father.

"Hey, Dad." Tytus greets him with a nervous smile and a brief hug.

"TJ," Tytus Sr. replies as they separate. "Are Sarah and Nate coming?"

He shakes his head in response and explains that they had to head back to the city. The two men enter the hospital and Tytus follows his father down the hall to Judy's room. Tytus Sr. smiles with a subtle twinkle in his eye as he looks back at Tytus and swings the door open.

The first thing that catches Tytus's attention is that the room feels brighter. Whether the change is literal or figurative, he's not certain, but it feels much better either way.

Mom?" His voice swings upward in a questioning tone as he sees his mother across the room. She is sitting up in bed. Her coloring has improved and her eyes are far clearer than yesterday. Everyone's eyes are, as a matter of fact, as they all shift their gazes in his direction.

"TJ." Judy's voice is full of joy as she raises her arms from her side, gesturing for him to come and give her a hug. "Two days in a row," she says as he leans down to hug her as best he can. "How lucky am I?"

"Mom, you look good." His brow is furrowed in confusion even though his voice is well disguised.

She laughs quietly. "Try not to look so shocked."

Travis steps up and places a hand on his brother's back, bailing him out.

"Her counts are up, Ty. The medication seems to be working."

Tytus looks across at Danny, sitting next to Judy on the opposite side of the bed. He offers him a sheepish smile which Danny immediately returns. He nods at Tytus with glistening eyes. Tytus may not care for the man, but he can see the love he has for his mother all over his face.

"That's amazing." Tytus takes his mom's hand and gives it a light squeeze.

There is a quick knock on the door followed by the entrance of a small, round doctor.

"Good morning," he exclaims with a cheery tone. "How is my beautiful patient feeling today?" The doctor smiles at everyone in the room but makes his way straight to Judy.

He spends the next ten minutes walking the family through Judy's most recent test results and explains that her cells have responded well to the treatment.

"It appears that her drastic drop in white blood cells was caused by a viral infection, and although she is not out of the woods, yet, we do believe she can make a full recovery."

"So, it's not cancer?" Tytus clarifies. Sometimes doctors have a way of talking in circles and he just wants it to be crystal clear.

"That's right." The doctor turns toward him. "It's not cancer. However, her immune system is compromised and that is a very real concern. So we will keep her here and monitor her counts very carefully."

"For how long?" Danny is the first to verbalize the question everyone has.

"That is hard to say at this point." The doctor tilts his head. "But I can promise you she is in great hands, and we are doing everything in our power to work toward sending her home." He looks around the room and smiles. "Just as soon as it's safe to do so."

Just outside Worcester, the phone in Sarah's hand rings.

"Hello. Tytus?"

"Hey, Sarah. Can you put me on speakerphone so I can talk to you and Nate together?"

"Sure." She smiles. She can hear in his voice that the news is indeed good. "Go ahead, Tytus."

"Hey, Nate."

"Don't keep us waiting. What did the doctor say?"

There is a brief pause on the line. Sarah looks at Nate as she anxiously awaits Tytus's reply.

"It's not cancer." His voice cracks as his chest swells. "She's going to be okay, you guys. My mom is going to be okay."

10

The Thorn and the Rose

Sarah has just set the Thai food on the counter when she hears another knock on the door. Had she tipped the delivery guy too much? Too little? But the second she opens it, Tytus flies through the doorway and sweeps her up into a twirl before setting her back on her feet with a thud and kissing her silly.

"I missed you, too." She giggles against his mouth.

Tytus's flight from Boston had arrived after midnight last night so they'd agreed on lunch. Originally, they were going out, but Tytus had texted this morning with a different idea in mind.

How about we just order in? You pick out lunch and I'll bring dessert.

"Is that dessert?" Sarah points to the brown paper bag Tytus is clutching. She hadn't thought he meant *actual* dessert on the phone. "Strawberries?" She reaches to take the bag from him, but he pulls it away and walks to her refrigerator.

"Strawberry shortcake." He looks back over his shoulder at her and wiggles his eyebrows. "What's for lunch?" He opens the box sitting on the counter. "Chinese?" He takes a sniff.

"It's Thai, Tytus. From this little place around the corner." She reaches for two plates from the cupboard above the counter. "It's my favorite."

"Is it?" He pins Sarah against the counter and kisses her again. Although this kiss isn't, *Hi, I'm so excited to see you.* This kiss is, *Remember me? The one you've been longing for.*

He slides both his hands around her waist and into the back of her loose-fitting linen pants. When his hands find her bare skin he moans. Heat spreads through Sarah's body, starting at the point of contact and making its way up to her cheeks.

She hadn't forgotten the way he'd made her feel. In fact, the past two nights without him she'd brought herself to climax replaying every vivid memory of exactly that.

Just as she's forgotten all about lunch, or even the concept of eating, Tytus pulls away and walks into the living room. Leaving her panting and flushed.

"Quit trying to seduce me, Sarah." He tsks with a shake of his head. "No sex until after dessert."

Once Sarah catches her breath, she laughs out loud and a snort comes from deep in her throat.

"What was that?" Tytus laughs as he plops onto her couch.

God, she cannot get over the way this man makes her feel. He can bring her to an orgasmic state in about three seconds and have her laughing like a hyena with just a smirk or a witty jab. *Where have you been all my life, Tytus Hayes Jr.?*

They had agreed over the phone that they were going to start a new tradition of watching their favorite movies together, alternating picks. Tytus had won the privilege of going first after stumping Sarah in the movie trivia game they'd made up over the phone Tuesday night. They had talked until nearly 2:00 a.m.

"The Princess Bride," he'd announced over the phone. "Tell me you've seen it."

"I think," Sarah replied laughing, "when I was like 6."

Despite Tytus's excitement about the cinematic genius of the 1980s comedy, neither of them paid much attention to it. Instead, they were chatting nonstop.

"Sarah, can I tell you something?" Tytus mumbles, his mouth full of pan-fried noodles. "This Thai food is crap."

Sarah gasps in mock offense as she puts one hand to her mouth and smacks his shoulder with the other. They talk about *Chicago*, about baseball, about Judy, and how she is continuing to improve.

Sarah takes the plates over to the sink and grabs Tytus's paper bag from the fridge. "Time for dessert?" she asks casually, opening the bag. She pulls out a small container of strawberries and a canister of whipped cream.

"Tytus, oh." She turns back toward the living room and he's right in front of her. "You forgot the shortcake."

"I'm on a low-carb diet." He nibbles on her neck.

"You just ate a pound of noodles."

"Okay. I'm not on a low-carb diet." He licks Sarah just below her ear lobe bringing back the blood flow from earlier. "But I didn't forget anything."

He picks Sarah up in a fireman's carry, grabs the items off the counter, and takes her straight to the bedroom.

Over the next couple of weeks, life is good. Better than good, actually. Judy is released from the hospital. *Chicago* continues to receive rave reviews, and the Yankees lead the division by three games. Tytus is the talk of the MLB and a perfect 12-0 in save opportunities.

Despite both of their demanding schedules, they make time for each other. They spend most of their nights together at either her place or his, and they meet for breakfast on the days they don't wake up together. She goes to his games when she can, he sees another one of her shows, they make love. They make lots and lots of love.

It seems that all of Sarah's fears and insecurities have been put to rest. Tytus is perfect. They are perfect.

Until they aren't.

It's her night off and Sarah is watching the game. Not live, but on television. The team is on the road in Houston.

She ordered in, poured some wine, and tuned in from her couch.

She isn't worried when he comes in to pitch with a one-run lead in the bottom of the ninth inning. She's seen him close out several tight games. In fact, she just expects him to win at this point. So, when he walks the first batter and puts him on base, she thinks nothing of it. She even gets up to get a glass of water. When the voices on the TV escalate, she assumes the game is over. And she is right. It's over. But not in the way she'd imagined.

She stands in the middle of her living room, glass halfway to her mouth, and watches as Tytus stalks off the field, while the Houston Astros pile on top of each other. The screen switches quickly to a replay of Tytus throwing a pitch and the batter hitting the ball deep over the fence.

"And that's a walk-off homerun for the Astros, folks. Previously untouchable closer, Tytus Hayes Jr., takes his first loss and proves he is in fact human."

Sarah is still no baseball expert, but she knows a "loss" is not good. And if she hadn't been sure, the look on Tytus's face confirms it. The hairs on the back of her neck slowly rise and an uneasy feeling passes over her.

She waits up until 12:30 a.m. but she still hasn't heard from Tytus. The game ended around 11:00, 10:00 in Houston, and normally it only takes him about an hour to call or text her. Sarah has been telling herself since she shut off the TV, that the team had lost several games already and she was sure Tytus would be fine. She understands that this is different, because he had "blown the save" as she heard the commentator say, but losing was part of sports. Everyone knows that.

At 1:00 a.m., when she still hasn't heard from him, she finally texts him.

Hey.
It's getting late and I'm having a hard time keeping my eyes open.
Can we talk for a bit?

...

She sees the bubbles pop up and disappear several times. He obviously has his phone out. When no message comes through, she takes a chance and texts him again.

I saw the game, Tytus. I'm sorry about the loss.

Sarah bites down on her lip waiting for his reply. Her stomach is swirling and that bad feeling from earlier is still looming. Finally, a response.

I'm exhausted. I'll call you in the morning. Okay?

Sarah's face falls along with her shoulders. He's been gone since Thursday and she suddenly misses him terribly. There have been several times when she wanted to say those three big words to him, and she is tempted to say them now. She can't stand feeling this distant. But she certainly isn't going to do it in a text.

Okay. I miss you.

She settles for those three words instead and falls asleep with no reply from Tytus. The fears and insecurities of the past she had been ready to let go begin creeping their way right back in.

Tytus lies awake in his hotel bed staring at the ceiling.

He knows it was unfair to push her away, but if he had called her, he would have told her. She had a way of getting him to talk. Like she emits some kind of truth serum and he has no choice but to open up to her.

It wasn't the fact that he'd given up the game. Well, it was partly that. He hates to lose. But it was something else. Something far worse than blowing a save. He rubs absently at the aching pain in his shoulder.

Tytus is surprised to find Sarah waiting at the airport a few days later when the team arrives from Houston. They had barely spoken since he blew the game on Monday night. And when they had, he'd been dismissive and distant. He was angry and bitter. And even though it had nothing to do with her, he directed it her way. Yet, here she is.

145

Before he knows it, she has her arms around him. The warmth of her embrace immediately permeates through his body. The smell of her hair fills his nostrils. For a brief moment, he almost gives in. Almost drops his guard and lets go of all the fear and doubt he is harboring inside. Almost trusts her to hold it. To help him.

"Hey," he says, setting down his bags and returning the hug.

"Hey." Sarah smiles up at him, but he can see the worry and concern in her eyes.

So instead of letting her in, and shedding his armor, he clenches his jaw, lifts his chin, and listens to the too-familiar voice in the back of his mind telling him to *man up*. Telling him that he shouldn't burden her with his weakness.

They head to his place straight from the airport. She tries several times to get him talking on the drive, but he finds a way to quiet her questions. By kissing her senseless or changing the subject. And when they arrive at his place and she straight up asks him if they can talk, he flirts and charms his way into having sex first, and then pretends to fall asleep.

In the morning, when she tries again, he raises his voice at her for the very first time.

"Sarah. I said I'm fine!"

He hates himself for it. For raising his voice...and for lying.

The next ten days that he's home in New York are strained between them. They only spend the night together twice and Sarah feels like the more she tries to pull him in, the more he pushes her away.

He blows another save. Giving up three runs in the top of the ninth inning against Seattle, and despite being at the game, she goes home alone. He had texted her that it would be a late night with interviews and that she should just go. She watches the interviews on TV when she gets home and they're brutal. She cries, listening to him say how he let the team and the fans down. Seeing the pain in his eyes through the cameras is torturous.

When they meet for lunch the next day. She makes the mistake of bringing it up and asking if he's okay.

"I know theater and baseball don't have a ton in common," she reaches for his hand across the table, "but I do understand what it feels like when my performance doesn't meet the high expectations I have for myself."

"Listen, Sarah. I know you are trying to help," Tytus pulls his hand out from under hers, "but I like to keep my professional and personal lives separate as much as possible." He sits up straighter in the booth. "I'd appreciate it if you'd just stop bringing it up."

It feels like a slap in the face.

The following Monday, Tytus is on the road again. Tampa.

Sarah's hand trembles as she stares down at her phone. She'd put him on speaker so she could talk to him without trying to hold it steady.

"I just want you to talk to me." She doesn't even realize she's crying until the tears start forming a pool on her dressing table.

"I am talking, Sarah." His voice continues to escalate. "Every fucking day. Every time you call. That's what we do. Talk, talk, talk."

Her entire body feels numb. She doesn't even flinch at the bite in his tone.

"This isn't talking, Tytus." She fights to keep the tears from affecting her voice. "You're not letting me in. There's something going on here and you're not—"

The line disconnects. Mid-sentence. Just like that. He hung up.

Sarah bites her bottom lip and grabs a tissue, wiping the moisture from her desk, but too dazed to think of using one to stop the actual flow from her eyes. All the old wounds are opening. All her fears rising to the surface.

Despite being seated, she's dizzy. Teetering at the edge of a dark rabbit hole. One small step forward and she'll fall.

Sarah lifts her head and stares at her hollow reflection. There is no denying there had been warning signs. It's not as if things had been going swimmingly between them lately.

147

🔘

"Son of a bitch!"

Tytus hurls his phone against the taupe wall of his dimly lit hotel room. He had just said several things to Sarah he didn't mean and then hung up on her before she had a chance to respond.

Dropping his face into his hands, he presses his fingertips into his eyes before dragging his hands through his hair. When had everything become such a cluster fuck? He hadn't meant to hang up on her but he'd lost his temper. Again.

Every damn time they talk lately it's, *I'm worried about you, Tytus. Talk to me, Tytus.* It never stops. And it isn't just Sarah. It's his dad, Spencer, even Nate has been riding his ass. Although he can't really blame Nate. If he continues on this downward spiral, it'll be Nate's paycheck as well as his own.

On that note, he picks up the glass decanter and refills his scotch. Again.

Tytus rubs his shoulder. The ache is dull and unrelenting. He's so careful not to let on when he's around the guys, but when he's alone, he can't help it. So far, he's been able to keep the discomfort in his shoulder at bay with a few extra painkillers here and there. Spencer is really the only one he's concerned might be on to him. If anyone can tell his pitches aren't doing what they should be, it's his catcher. But since Tytus had torn his head off after blowing his third save in two weeks, Spencer had dropped it. For now.

Staring at the amber liquid in his glass, he swirls it around, before draining it with a thick swallow. He had never been good at communicating. Especially when it came to talking about feelings. He had a good relationship with his dad, and he could count on him for sound advice from time to time, but they never really talked like that. Nate was a great wingman, and as loyal a friend as you could ask for, but anytime he tried to get into Tytus's mind, he'd shut him out.

Sarah was the only one who seemed to hold the key to his emotions. Even on the night they met, she had him babbling. Thinking back to the way he actually asked her to dance has him shaking his head. It had just been natural to talk to her. Easy. And then within a few months, she had helped him reconcile with his mom, something he'd believed impossible for his entire adult life.

But the past couple of weeks he had been pushing her away. She had tried time and time again to get him to open up and he'd shut her out. That pull to open up to her, to let her in and share his secrets was constantly met with an even stronger push to keep her a safe distance and lock himself away behind the armor he'd worn for so long. Tytus' eyes sting as he digs the heels of his hands into them. His stomach is in knots. It's not that he doesn't want to tell her. It's that he can't.

How much longer does he really expect her to keep putting up with his bullshit?

Sarah is dreading Nate and Chrissie's rehearsal tonight. The wedding isn't for another week, but Nate had to work around Tytus's schedule and since the Yankees are off until tomorrow, they are having it tonight. *Fucking fabulous.*

Tytus sent her flowers to apologize for his behavior Monday night on the phone, but even after two days of cooling off, she is still pissed. She hasn't spoken to him since, sending him to voicemail every time he had called. And now she is going to walk down the aisle with him? The thought makes her feel ill.

She hadn't gone to meet him at the airport this morning. She's so exhausted from trying to get him to open up about whatever he's going through. And if she is being honest with herself, she's not sure she wants to keep trying. He has made it pretty clear that baseball comes first.

For the first couple of months in their relationship, when baseball had been going well, he was attentive, caring, perfect...really. Then he gave up that homerun to the Astros, and it was like something just snapped.

Tytus was moody all the time. When they were together, he always seemed distant. Like his mind was on something else. She even noticed it in the way they made love. Their first night together, he had been so open. She felt like she could look into his eyes and see inside of him. See *all of him*. Lately, it was as if he was avoiding really looking at her at all, and when he did, he was guarded. The moment something real would flash into his eyes, he would immediately look away.

Sarah had tried. She really tried to find the Tytus that she knew was in there. But every time she asked about it, he'd get defensive. Angry even. *I'm fine!* was his token response. And when he hung up on her the other night, she started to think this may all have been a huge mistake. And it tore her into tiny little pieces.

Looking at her reflection in the mirror, she dabs at the tears forming in her eyes. She has been trying to finish her makeup for the past thirty minutes.

Her phone starts buzzing on her nightstand and her throat closes. Frozen in place, she just stares into the mirror. She knows it's him. With a huff of air, she forces herself to answer it. She's going to see him soon enough, and avoiding his call again, will only make it more awkward.

"You're home," she says instead of a greeting as she pushes herself up from the chair.

"Sarah," he breathes into the phone. His voice, full of relief and something else. Regret?

A heavy silence fills the space between them. She really has nothing to say to him.

"I'm sorry."

Her shoulders drop as she sits on the edge of her bed. She knows he is sorry, but she fights her instinctual need to comfort him. To say it's okay when she knows it's not.

"I know." She squeezes her eyes shut and wills herself to keep it together. "Listen, Tytus. Tonight is really important to Nate and Chrissie. They are our best friends, and I don't want whatever is happening between us to ruin their night. So, let's just be there for them and deal with *this* later. Okay?"

It comes out a bit harsh. And it hurts far more than her tone lets on.

"Okay, Sarah. I'll see you tonight."

The call disconnects and her eyes well up. She is certain she heard a crack in his voice. Maybe he is hurting just as much as she is, after all.

She gives up on her makeup and calls Chrissie.

When Tytus climbs into the back of the Lexus, Miles greets him with a smile.

"Lookin' sharp, Mr. Hayes." He nods into the rearview mirror looking back at his boss. "Big night for Mr. Richards, right?"

Tytus's stomach has been in knots since talking to Sarah this afternoon. Well, actually, a lot longer than that.

"Sure is, Miles." He offers him a half-hearted smile before looking out the window.

"Picking up Ms. Dalton, Sir?"

Tytus clenches his jaw, as well as the fist sitting on his thigh, and exhales slowly and through his nose. Even Miles is reminding him what an asshole he is.

"No."

Neither man speaks another word the rest of the way to The Church of St. Francis Xavier.

When Tytus enters the church, the first thing that strikes him is the architecture. Oddly, the ornate Roman-like pillars remind him of Caesar's Palace in Las Vegas. He snickers to himself at the irony. But the laugh is quickly replaced with a frown when he brings his eyes down from the decorative ceiling and casts his gaze on Sarah.

Tytus has never really been a fan of rollercoasters. All his life he'd been seen as a thrill seeker, an adrenaline junky, and he is. He enjoys taking risks and living life... fast. It's why he loves cars so much. But driving fast and playing poker doesn't make your stomach lift up to your throat and then drop to your ankles. Roller Coasters do that. And so, apparently, does Sarah Jeanne Dalton.

Tytus takes in a steadying breath and walks up toward the altar where Sarah, Nate, and Chrissie are talking with a priest. He turns on the Hayes charm and offers them all his best smile.

"I can't believe a beautiful church like this is letting a sleazeball like Nate Richards get married here." He gives Nate a man hug and a slap on the back. He has yet to make eye contact with Sarah and chooses to ignore the way Nate's eyes shift quickly from him to her. "It must be a connection of the classy bride-to-be," he winks at Chrissie as he plants a kiss on her cheek.

"Actually," Nate scoffs, "Father Kerry is an old friend of mine. I'm the classy connection." He lifts his chin in mock pride.

"The lies we tell ourselves," Tytus teases before facing the inevitable.

He swallows thickly before turning to face Sarah.

"Sarah. God, I've missed you." The words out of his mouth before he can stop them. It's as if his heart just forced them out without consulting his brain. Their eyes meet briefly before he steps in and wraps his arms around her waist. He feels her body stiffen, just barely, before she wraps her arms around his neck.

"Tytus," is all she offers.

He's reluctant to let go. He turns his head to kiss her below the ear, but with a subtle push, unnoticeable to the group, she separates from him before his lips reach her skin.

It is a sharp punch to the gut.

The moment is interrupted by a loud clap and squeal as a small, round, balding man approaches the group.

"Oh my God. Would you look at the four of you. I don't think I've seen so much beauty in one spot since before the idiots on Broadway canceled *Cats*."

Tytus moves half a step back, feeling crowded all of a sudden just by the man's presence.

"Bruno." Chrissie steps up to him and the two lock hands and exchange kisses on each cheek like they've all been transported to France all of a sudden.

"Guys, this is Bruno St. Croix. He's the best wedding planner in all of Manhattan and also a dear friend of mine." Chrissie turns to Sarah and Tytus.

"You are stun-ning." He exaggerates the syllables as he holds Sarah's hand and spins her in a circle. "Blue is absolutely your color, although I imagine you'd look ravenous in anything...or nothing." He wiggles his eyebrows as Tytus loudly clears his throat.

"And you." He turns to Tytus. "My God, my God, why have you forsaken me?" He gives Tytus a slow once-over that makes Sarah snort with a laugh, before covering her mouth. "Let me guess, a dancer? No, tennis."

"Baseball," Tytus says, feeling extremely awkward.

"Hmph. What a waste, what a waste." Bruno waves his hand and gestures for them to follow as he walks to the front of the church.

The next twenty minutes, he walks them around to the different parts of the church and explains the flow of the ceremony and what Nate and Chrissie will need to do as well as the jobs that Tytus and Sarah will have. They are joined by Chrissie's parents and a young boy and girl who would be serving as the ring bearer and flower girl, apparently cousins of Chrissie's. Tytus is really the only family Nate has, so it's up to Chrissie to fill all the key roles.

Tytus doesn't fail to notice the lack of physical contact between him and Sarah throughout the evening. Standing this close to her and not being able to touch her is causing him literal pain.

At one point, when Bruno and Father Kerry are talking, he brushes his finger across the back of her hand. Testing the waters, so to speak. She quickly brings her hand up to twirl her hair and he has his answer. His chest tightens right along with his throat.

Bruno steps up behind Tytus and Sarah and walks them to the back of the church.

"Okay, lovebirds." He positions them next to each other. "The two of you will walk arm in arm right before Chrissie and her father. And try not to look too perfect together, okay? This is Chrissie's big day. Yours will come soon enough."

"Oh, no...we aren't...we won't."

Sarah's stuttering and horrified expression feels like a slap to the face, and Tytus furrows his brow in irritation.

"Pa-lease. As if." Bruno chuckles. "Listen, sweetheart. I read people. It's what I do. And the two of you," he waves his hand between them, "the two of you are meant to be." He lays his hand on Sarah's cheek. "With you being the luscious red rose, and him being the," Bruno drags his eyes up and down Tytus's rigid frame, "hard and sharp thorn always by your side to prick anyone who gets too close." He waves his hand through the air again and walks away adding, "Anyone can see that."

Tytus isn't sure if that strange little man just called him a prick, but he likes the sound of *meant to be*. Maybe Bruno isn't so bad after all.

He wraps his arm around Sarah's elbow and grips her just tight enough to let her know he's not letting go. When the organ music starts to play, he tilts his chin just slightly to his right to peek at Sarah from the corner of his eye. She must feel his gaze, for her eyes drift to the left and find his. A warmth spreads through him as their eyes connect. Tytus sees something there, in her eyes, he feels it in his bones. *Yeah, maybe Bruno has a point.*

Sarah reaches up and lays her right hand on his forearm, just below their interlocked elbows. A simple gesture, that may be just for show, but for Tytus, it's like a cold compress on a fresh wound. He reaches over and places his left hand on top of hers and as they direct their eyes forward and start their march down the aisle, he brushes his thumb over the back of her hand, praying that she feels what he does.

The rest of the rehearsal Tytus feels as though the elephant that had been sitting on his chest has lumbered off to a watering hole somewhere. He knows that he and Sarah aren't exactly good, but at least they have made a small connection. When he had touched her, she hadn't recoiled. Seems like progress.

He continues to cast his eyes in her direction as Nate and Chrissie walk through the rest of the ceremony. She looks at him too, but never holds his eyes for as long as he wants. It seems like she is longing for a connection as much as he is, but now it is Sarah who is holding back.

Once they finish up with the rehearsal, the entire group makes the short walk around the block to Yakiniku Futago for some upscale Japanese Barbeque.

The minute they walk into the dimly lit, upscale bar, Sarah excuses herself to use the restroom. She pushes past the swinging door and braces herself with both hands on the sink. She knew this wasn't going to be easy, but it is far worse than she thought. Not because he's distant and unavailable, but because he isn't those things. She just doesn't know if she can handle this back and forth.

"Hey."

Sarah looks into the mirror and sees her best friend behind her.

"Hey," Sarah whispers, looking back down at the sink.

"You okay?" Chrissie steps closer to her friend.

"I don't know, Wis." She sighs and turns to face her. "I was so scared at the beginning. I was terrified to let him in, but it was like, I couldn't stop it. You know?" Sarah dabs at her eyes to try and salvage her makeup. "The pull between us was so strong. He was open and sensitive, and...after Boston, I just thought..."

"Hey, hey." Chrissie takes her hand and squeezes it lightly. "Love is hard, Sarah."

She knows the statement is really meant as a question when she looks up at her friend and Chrissie tilts her head with her eyebrows raised. Sarah sniffles and nods in confirmation.

"That's what I thought." She smiles softly at Sarah. "Things were all over the place with Nate and I at the beginning, too. You and Tytus both have issues in your past that make it hard to commit. To take risks with your heart. And there is no bigger risk than falling in love, my friend."

"I know, Chrissie. Trust me, I know." Sarah turns to the trashcan and drops in the paper towel she is holding. "It's because of my past that I can't play second fiddle to a game."

"Sarah." Chrissie stops her walking out with a hand on her shoulder. "That's not fair and you know it. It's not a game to Tytus, it's his livelihood. And it's all he's had for a very long time."

Sarah keeps her eyes forward, staring at the door. "I just can't be with a man who won't let me in when things get tough. I can see that he's hurting but he won't share the burden with me. That's not love, Chrissie."

Sarah walks out of the restroom to find the group seated around a long rectangular table for eight. Father Kerry, Bruno, and Chrissie's parents on one side. Nate, Tytus, and two empty seats for her and Chrissie on the other. She sits next to Tytus with her *pleasant girlfriend mask* firmly in place.

The rest of the evening is manageable enough. Tytus keeps his hands to himself for which Sarah is both grateful and disappointed. She knows that it's completely irrational, but it's the truth. She feels what she feels.

As the dessert is placed in front of them, the mood shifts completely when Chrissie's father, Curtis, asks Tytus about baseball.

Curtis explains that he is more of a football and golf fan, but that he follows baseball to a degree. He mentions that he's heard Tytus's name in the media and that it sounds like he's on pace for a record year.

Apparently, Curtis hasn't been watching *SportsCenter* for the past two weeks. Sarah takes a gulp of her wine.

Tytus clears his throat and straightens his spine.

"Yes, Curtis." Nate jumps in when Tytus seems tongue-tied. "The team is doing very well. Leading the division, actually."

"Thanks to your friend, Tytus, here." Curtis smiles and nods to Tytus.

"No. More like in spite of me." Tytus pushes his chair back and stands up. "Excuse me."

Sarah closes her eyes as Tytus stalks off toward the restroom. Any mention of baseball is an immediate trigger for him and she fights off the need to follow him. Whatever she might say to Tytus right now won't help the situation. Instead, she does what's natural for her and attempts to smooth things over at the table instead.

"You'll have to excuse Tytus. He is just a tad competitive." She offers her warmest smile. "He's had a few tough games in the past couple weeks, and well, he isn't happy with anything but perfection." Her smile fades as she lifts her glass to her lips.

Chrissie successfully changes the topic and the awkward tension slowly lifts. By the time Tytus returns to the table, everyone is getting up to leave.

Tytus tries to reach for the check before Curtis snatches it up. "It's tradition, Mr. Hayes, for the father of the bride to take care of this." He nods curtly at Tytus, and the switch from 'Tytus' to 'Mr. Hayes' doesn't go unnoticed by anyone.

Nate and Chrissie are staying a bit longer with Bruno to discuss some details about the reception. They stand and say their goodbyes to their guests. Chrissie holds on to Sarah a little longer than the rest.

Tytus finds himself alone with Sarah outside. Chrissie's parents had caught a cab, and Father Kerry was headed back to his parish.

The two of them are both aware they need to talk but neither seems to want to speak first.

"How about a walk?" he finally offers.

Sarah nods and falls in step beside him. More than anything, Tytus wants to reach for her hand. To just place his lips to hers and kiss all the pain away. His and hers. But he knows that's not what Sarah needs or wants from him right now.

"You know how sorry I am, right? For the way I've been acting." His hands are shoved deeply in his pockets and his eyes are straight ahead.

"It's not about being sorry, Tytus."

He nods. He'd expected her to say as much. But he's not really sure what else he has to offer her so he stays silent.

Sarah stops walking and Tytus turns back to face her.

"Well?" Her voice cracks as she lifts and drops her arms in frustration.

"Well, what, Sarah? I don't know what else you want me to say." As the words leave his lips, his stomach tightens and the elephant from earlier is back on his chest. He knows he is fucking this up, but he can't seem to stop it.

"I want an explanation, Tytus." The tears building in Sarah's eyes sparkle with the lighting from the overhead street lamp. Her voice escalates. "I know your career is important to you. I know that you are struggling and I want to be there for you. But you won't let me in." Sarah shakes her head and sighs as Tytus just blinks at her in response. "I need you to tell me why?"

He tightens his jaw as he feels beads of sweat form on his forehead. *I'm hurt, Sarah. Something is wrong with my shoulder. I'm scared.* The words are there, the explanation she needs, but he can't force them out. He can't speak them into the universe and make them real.

"It's...complicated." He closes his eyes and shakes his head.

"Well, you know what isn't complicated, Tytus?" Her tone is harsh and bitter.

He opens his eyes, tears of his own forming, and looks into hers.

"I'm done. We are done."

She turns to walk away from him when he calls out to her.

"Sarah. Sarah, please." Tytus feels his heart crack along with his voice. He has never felt this kind of pain.

She turns around and looks at him. Her eyes pleading with him to give her what she needs.

He tries. He really tries. To open his mouth and tell her what he knows is true. But he can't. He doesn't.

Sarah exhales the breath she was holding. She shakes her head, tears streaming down her face.

"I love you, Tytus."

He feels dizzy. His vision fades in and out of focus as he watches her walk away. He reaches out for her, at least he thinks he does. Tries to call after her, but he can't form any words. He can't seem to breathe at all. The pressure on his chest increases as he stumbles back to lean against the brick wall. Sweat drips from his forehead as he clutches at his collar and tries to loosen what suddenly feels like a noose around his neck. Tytus fumbles in his pocket for his cell phone and manages to push the call button for Nate before sliding his back down the wall and dropping the phone next to him.

11

Drowning

"*H*ey, Ty. Miss me already?" Nate's voice is cheery and crisp coming through the phone lying a couple feet from where Tytus is hunched over.

Tytus uses all the air he can muster to try and answer his best friend. No words come. Only a muffled grunt and a few staggered gasps.

"Ty? Tytus?" Nate's tone shifts from upbeat to concerned. "Where are you? I'm on my way."

He doesn't respond. He can't. His vision is fading in and out as he faintly hears his friend's now distant voice through the small speaker.

"Call 9-1-1. Right now." He hears Nate saying. "I think Tytus is having a heart attack."

Nate keeps the line open even though Tytus isn't responding to him. He can hear his friend's soothing voice as he keeps speaking calmly into the phone.

"I'm coming, Tytus. Help is on the way. I need you to try to slow your breathing." Nate keeps the advice coming and Tytus is grateful for it. Anything to distract from the caving in of his chest cavity. "Deep breaths, Ty. Come on, don't be a pussy. Breathe."

Tytus can only hear Nate faintly through the cracked phone. He can't quite make out all of the words over the pounding in his temples. But he's coming. That much he knows.

Despite the trembling in his hands, he manages to unbutton the dress shirt that has a choke hold on his neck. The navy sweater he's wearing becomes suffocatingly warm as sweat beads build on his forehead. Tytus works desperately to focus his eyes. To establish a reference point around him that can provide a semblance of balance. Something to ground him. Instead, his vision continues to blur as his heart pounds erratically in his chest. The pressure building there makes it feel as if his heart is swelling and about to burst. Any moment now, his chest is going to crack open.

He hears a voice. It's muffled. Distant. The combination of cloudy vision and echoing voices reminds Tytus of being underwater and he wonders if this is what drowning feels like. Are those sirens? Why is he so nauseous? A viscous wave rolls through his abdomen and he heaves aggressively, releasing all the contents of his stomach right there on the sidewalk.

"Tytus?"

He hears it more clearly now. The pounding in his head mercifully quiets a bit.

"Ty, it's Nate." The cooling touch of Nate's hand on his forehead brings instant relief as his eyes settle on the worried face of his best friend. "I used that app you installed on my phone to keep track of me." Nate smiles down at him, but his eyes are full of concern. "I bet you didn't know I could use it to track you right back." The moment is short-lived when the paramedics move Nate away from him and start explaining that they are there to help as they encourage him to take slow, deep breaths. With a man on each side of him, they hoist him up onto the gurney and load him into the ambulance within seconds.

"Nate?" Tytus croaks out. His voice is dry and hoarse and the taste of bile in his mouth unbearable.

"I'm right here." Nate takes Tytus's hand as he sits next to him in the ambulance. "I'm not leaving you, Ty."

Tytus clenches his jaw and nods. He had never liked the feeling of needing someone, but he can't ever remember feeling this helpless, and his eyes well up in gratitude. Nate talks to him the entire ride to the hospital.

Sarah hasn't even set her purse down on the table when her cell phone starts ringing. Her mind immediately goes to Tytus. Actually, her mind hadn't been on anything but Tytus. She'd been wondering if he'd call. In fact, the entire drive she'd been mentally rehearsing just what she would say if he did.

When she finally wrestles the phone out, she's deflated to see it's not him, but Chrissie.

"Wis, I just walked in the door and—"

"Sarah, it's Tytus."

The blood drains from Sarah's face. The chilling tone in Chrissie's voice is unmistakable. Something had happened. Something terrible.

"What happened?"

Sarah places her hand on the wall. Palm flat along the course surface as she leans her weight against it. Fear is a strange phenomenon. A person can go from any emotion, happiness, anger, indifference, to sheer terror in a matter of a split second. Most emotions have to build their way up, bit by bit. But fear? Fear can grip you from the inside in a flash and erase the ability to think of anything else.

"Sarah…" Chrissie whispers.

"Jesus, Chrissie. Just spit it out." Sarah's voice shakes as it cracks, making her tone sound more desperate than angry.

"I don't know, Sarah. But Nate is with him and they are on their way to the emergency room."

Despite the loud ringing in her ears, Sarah can hear Chrissie crying through the phone.

"But, I was just there. I was with him. I left him on the street. He was…fine," Sarah rambles, talking more to herself than Chrissie. "What…"

"He called Nate." Chrissie takes a deep breath, seemingly trying to remain calm. "I couldn't hear what he was saying, but Nate took off to find him." She pauses. "He told me to call 9-1-1." Another pause. "He said he thought Tytus was having a heart attack."

Sarah hears the words come from the speaker on her phone but a strange sense of disconnect washes over her. This is just a bad dream. Tytus? A heart attack? She almost laughs at the absurdity of it. None of this is real. It can't be. She stumbles into her living room to sit down, but the room just keeps spinning.

"Sarah. Did you hear me?"

Chrissie's voice snaps Sarah from her downward spiral and brings her back to the present.

"I said Nate is sending Miles. To pick you up." Chrissie pauses. "You want to go, right? To the hospital?"

Sarah sits down on her couch and tries to put the pieces together. Why can't she speak? Why is this all so hard to understand? It's as if her mind has turned to mush.

"Sarah? Answer me. You're scaring me." Chrissie pleads with her friend.

"Yes. Yes, I want to go." Getting the words out seems like a monumental task. But once she's accomplished it, her instincts kick in. "I'll be downstairs in two minutes."

Sarah disconnects the call without another thought. She grabs her coat off the hook where she'd just hung it and flies out the door to meet Miles.

On the way to the hospital, in the back of the Lexus, Sarah replays the entire scene of Tytus and her on the street. It unfolds in her mind like a silent movie running on a projector. She closes her eyes and focuses on the memory. The expression in his eyes had been so loud, even though he couldn't seem to find the words. There was something there. Something heavy and daunting. Fear? Pain?

A cool feeling runs through her body and causes her to shiver. Regret, maybe? Had she been too harsh? Had she pushed him away when what he really needed was her trust and compassion? Had she done this to him?

By the time Sarah arrives at the hospital, she has put on her familiar mask of calm and collected. When she walks through the automatic doors to Bellevue ER, she looks like a woman in complete control. Until she sees Nate.

He's standing on the far side of the waiting room, sleeves rolled to his elbows, hair disheveled, and pacing back and forth.

"Nate?" She bursts into tears.

Nate reaches her in two seconds flat and wraps her in a tight embrace.

"Sarah. Shhh. Shhh." He strokes her hair and wipes it from her tear-drenched cheeks. "He's going to be fine, Sarah."

Her body convulses against Nate as she really lets herself cry for the first time since Chrissie broke the news.

"Sarah," Nate says again softly, pulling her from the hole she's burrowing in his chest. "Sarah." He waits for her to look at him. "He's going to be fine. They're just running some tests."

Sarah welcomes the relief as it washes over her. She can see that Nate is telling her the truth. Tytus will be okay. She sniffles and nods before letting Nate go.

"The paramedics said they don't think it was a heart attack," Nate says, running his hand through his hair and exhaling a heavy breath. "They think it was a panic attack."

"A panic attack?" Sarah brings her hand to her mouth. Tytus? A panic attack? The man has ice in his veins.

"I think it's my fault," Nate croaks. "He's been under so much pressure and I...I haven't been there for him. I was so distracted with the wedding. And he's always just been so damn strong. I mean," Nate wipes at his eyes, "he wins, Sarah. He always wins."

Nate shakes his head and starts pacing in front of her. "I tried to get him to talk to me. I did. But he just shuts me out. He kept saying he was fine. I should have pushed harder."

Sarah reaches for his forearm.

"Nate. It wasn't your fault. If it was anyone's fault, it was mine." Sarah's throat closes up on her as she remembers what she said to him before walking away. The look in his eyes.

"I told him we were done."

Nate visibly flinches at her confession.

Tears start to flow from Sarah's eyes as Nate steps forward to embrace her. Both are ridden with guilt and concern while they wait another two hours for any news.

Finally, a young doctor walks up to the area where they are sitting.

"Nate Richards?"

Nate shoots to his feet. "Yes, yes, that's me."

"My name is Dr. Hansen. Dr. Adam Hansen."

163

The doctor smiles and gestures for Nate to sit back down as he pulls up a chair in front of the two of them.

"Mr. Hayes is awake and his vitals have returned to normal. His heart is in excellent condition and he shouldn't suffer any lasting effects from tonight." He looks back and forth between the two letting the good news sink in.

"The episode Mr. Hayes experienced was a panic attack. Anxiety and depression are extremely common in people with high-pressure jobs. Professional athletes are no exception. I have prescribed him an anti-anxiety medication that is approved by Major League Baseball and should help to reduce the risk of future attacks."

"Thank you, Doctor." Sarah's words hardly a whisper. "Can we see him?" she asks anxiously.

"Medication is not the only answer." The doctor offers a small smile toward Sarah. Letting her know he isn't finished. "I'm recommending Mr. Hayes start regular therapy sessions to help relieve some of the stress a job like his brings on."

Nate raises an eyebrow at that. Tytus is gonna lose his shit.

"And I know you are his agent, Mr. Richards, so listen carefully. He needs rest. He shouldn't pitch for at least a few days. He will make a full recovery, this time. But these attacks should not be ignored, and I promise you, they will continue if he doesn't find a way to deal with his stress."

"I understand. Thank you, Dr. Hansen." Nate reaches to shake the doctor's hand as they both stand up.

"You may go in and see him. One at a time. You first, Mr. Richards, as he asked for you, specifically."

Nate looks at Sarah awkwardly.

"He doesn't even know you're here." He shrugs one shoulder. "I'll just be a minute, and then I'll come back for you."

Sarah nods at Nate and watches him follow the doctor down the corridor. She sits back in the hard chair and buries her face in her hands.

Tytus has his eyes closed and his head laid back. The humming of the machines and the occasional drip from his IV provide him with a soothing kind of white noise. When the door quietly opens, he's relieved to see who walks through it.

"Nate." He's had plenty of alone time to think about how he would handle this conversation. And he'd decided not to hold anything back. After all, holding things in is what put him in the ER to begin with.

"You scared the shit out of me, man." Nate chuckles but Tytus knows it's not really meant to be funny. The heaviness in his friend's eyes tells a different story.

"I scared the shit out of me, too. Trust me." He smirks at Nate as he takes a seat next to the bed. Both men, seemingly trying to lighten the mood.

"Look, Ty, I'm sorry I didn't see this coming. I'm sorry—"

"Nate," Tytus cuts him off and waits for him to make eye contact. "Nate," he says again. "This is not on you." Tytus continues when Nate looks up from his lap. "This is on me. It's not like you didn't try to get me to talk." He raises his eyebrow and nods at his friend.

Nate's eyes fill as an understanding seems to pass between the two men. They have never needed many words to know their love for one another runs deep.

"She's here, Ty."

Tytus's back stiffens as his eyes grow wide. His stomach shoots right up into his throat.

"Chrissie called her."

Tytus runs his hand over his face and just blinks at Nate. His throat thickens.

"Sarah told me," Nate continues and looks down at his hands, "about the fight." He rubs his palms on his knees and lets his eyes drift around the room before bringing them back to his friend. "We didn't know, Ty. I'm sorry."

Tytus swallows hard and forces the lump in his throat down. He knows what happened to him tonight was not the direct result of any one thing, but the sum of several parts. The final snap, however, was definitely brought on by what happened on that street. What happened with Sarah.

"She wants to see you, Tytus. She's worried sick."

Tytus just nods at Nate as his eyes threaten to spill over.

"I'll, um…I'll get her."

"Nate?" Tytus croaks, stopping him in his tracks. "Thank you," he says softly as his friend looks back at him over his shoulder.

Not two minutes later there is a soft knock on the door.

"Come in," Tytus says. Keeping his voice as steady as he can.

The moment Sarah surfaces in front of him the scene from earlier floods his senses. His heart clenches in his chest when he sees the tears staining her cheeks.

"Hey," Tytus says, the timbre of his voice warm.

"Hey." Her smile is uncertain and so is her stance.

Considering they had essentially broken up just hours before, neither seems to know what to say.

"I'm sorry," they say in unison.

Tytus furrows his brow in confusion. "You're sorry. For what?"

"For what?" Sarah gasps. "For not being there for you. For not seeing how much you were struggling. For leaving you there on the street after saying…everything I said." The words flow from her mouth in a rushed stream accompanied by a fresh wave of tears.

"Sarah, Sarah, Sarah." Tytus tries continually to stop her. "Come here." He reaches his hand out to the side of the bed where Nate had been sitting moments ago.

"This was not your fault," he says, squeezing her hand the moment it makes contact with his. "Do you hear me? None of it."

Sarah doesn't reply; she just takes her other hand and lays it on top of the one she's holding.

"Don't you see? You were there for me. You did see I was struggling. And I deserved to be left on the street after letting you down the way I had."

"No, Tytus." She shakes her head adamantly.

"Yes, Sarah." He reaches for her face and wipes her cheek with his thumb. "This was not your fault. All my life I've struggled with asking people for help."

Sarah looks into his eyes like she's searching for something.

Tytus inhales a deep breath and lets it out slowly.

"I think it started when I found out my mom was cheating. For some reason, I felt like I was the one she was unfaithful to. I felt so abandoned. Then, when she left, I trained myself not to need anyone anymore. I told myself that if I didn't let anyone else in, I could never be hurt that way again." He stops and looks out the window at the street lights. "But tonight." He swallows. "When I watched you walk away— Something inside me just broke. Like a dam, I had been carefully constructing for years, just burst and all the pain and fear that I had tucked away just washed over me like a wave. I thought it was going to drown me." His eyes are so full that a single tear escapes before he can blink it away. And it's Sarah's turn to wipe it with her thumb.

"I meant what I said on the street, Tytus." She dabs at the tears in her own eyes and then chuckles softly. "No, not the part about being done, silly." She leans in and kisses him softly on the cheek. Then the lips. "The part about being in love with you." She whispers it in his ear and lays her head on his chest.

With her eyes closed, they lay there in silence. Tytus, taking in the scent of her hair. Tomorrow he'll have to figure out how to deal with this mess he is in. The road ahead is not going to be easy, and maybe for the first time in his life, he isn't going to try to handle it alone.

At some point, after Tytus had forced Nate and Sarah to go home, they moved him into a private room. They assured him he'll be able to leave in the morning but some of his test results still weren't in and they wanted to be extra cautious.

He lies awake staring at the ceiling thinking about the choices he made that put him here. Tytus never really spent a lot of time second-guessing himself, personally or professionally. He'd never bought into things like meditation, visualization, or reflection. He'd never seen a therapist, even though many of his teammates swore by it, but he has a feeling that is all about to change.

Sarah had come back. She stood by his side, held his hand, and let him explain. Not only had she forgiven him, she had said she loved him. Twice.

Pride isn't foreign to Tytus, but the kind of pride filling his heart right now is new. Different. He let Sarah in. Maybe not as soon as he should have. Okay, definitely not as soon as he should have. And it may have taken a near-death experience to get him there, but he told her the truth. At least, part of it. He had opened up to her just the way he had with his mother and she had hung on every word. Compassionate and forgiving. It felt good. Right.

Tytus closes his eyes as the realization of what has to be done next sinks in. He has to tell Nate about his shoulder. And Sarah. And Spencer. Everyone. He reaches over to massage the arm that had been the key to his success and what he had once believed was his only ticket to happiness. What an idiot he had been.

The injury to his shoulder had already cost his team three games and he couldn't keep pretending it would just get better. He'd been selfish and stupid to let it go on this long and he has a duty as a professional to take the proper steps toward healing. It could mean the end of his best season, but that is far better than the end of his career.

He knows what has to be done and figures he should probably get some sleep.

Sarah has been tossing and turning all night, never really able to sleep. She is relieved Tytus opened up to her the way he had tonight, but she also knows his issues run deep, and considering she has her own baggage, they will have to learn to trust each other even more.

He had taken all the blame for what happened, but Sarah can't shake the guilt she still feels. She should have found a better way to get through to him than just walking away. To say she was done, and throw out, "I love you" was petty. She had just been so scared. The reality that maybe he didn't love her the way she loved him had cut deep, and she had wanted to hurt him back.

Sarah rolled over and flipped her pillow to the cool side.

She told Tytus she loved him, twice, and she meant it. And when you love someone, you don't just quit when things get tough. She is in this for the long haul and she will make sure he knows it.

When Sarah arrives back at Bellevue the following morning, Nate and Chrissie are already there.

"Sarah," Chrissie says as she wraps Sarah in a hug. "Nate told me you and Tytus worked things out last night?" Chrissie's face is hopeful but her smile is tentative.

"It was a big step in the right direction," Sarah says with a smile of her own.

"Morning, Sarah." Nate steps in for a hug of his own. "The nurse said Tytus will be discharged in an hour or two. He said he has something he wants to talk to us about. All three of us."

Sarah nods as her stomach turns a bit. Here she had been begging Tytus to open up to her and now that he's ready, the possibilities make her nervous.

When the three of them enter Tytus's room the first thing that strikes her is his eyes. They are bloodshot and puffy. Looks like she's not the only one who didn't get much sleep.

"Hey, guys," Tytus says softly as he sits up higher in the bed. "Thanks for coming."

Chrissie steps up and gives Tytus a kiss on the cheek, followed by a handshake from Nate. They both sit down to make room for Sarah to get to Tytus.

"You okay?" She touches her hand lightly on his cheek. He closes his eyes and leans, just slightly, into her palm. The gesture makes her heart skip.

"I am now," he says, opening his eyes and making contact with hers. Sarah swallows at his sincere gaze and she leans over to kiss him softly on the lips.

Rather than pulling up a chair, Sarah sits on the edge of his bed and takes his hand. Intertwining their fingers and preparing herself for whatever Tytus is about to share.

Tytus clears his throat and sticks the tip of his tongue out between his lips as he works up the nerve for what he's about to say. Looking between the three of them, he takes a deep breath in and holds it for several beats.

"First of all, I owe all of you an apology." He holds up his hand when Nate tries to interject. "I have been a complete dick the past couple of weeks. Well, I've always been a dick, but this isn't about that." He smirks trying to keep things light.

"I haven't been honest and it's driven a wedge between Sarah and me, and it's put both of our careers at risk." He looks to Sarah first and then to Nate as his tone becomes more serious.

"I hate to lose. There is no mystery there. I've always been a winner. I work hard for it. And I expect it. I do whatever it takes to put myself in a position of power. I outwork my opponents. I outsmart my opponents."

He stops briefly and glances toward the window as he feels his throat growing thick and his eyes getting moist.

"But not everything is within our control," he sighs.

"You're hurt."

It comes from Nate. And once the words are out, an ominous hush spreads through the room like dense fog rolling in over a lake.

Tytus keeps his eyes focused outside but he clenches his jaw and nods. He knows if he turns to look at him, the tears will come.

No one says a word for several minutes.

"How bad?" Nate finally asks.

Tytus knows that Nate is upset. He can hear it in his voice and when he finally turns to his best friend, he sees it in his eyes as well. Not upset that he's hurt, exactly, but upset that he kept it from him. It wasn't just hurtful as his friend, it was selfish and irresponsible as his client.

"I don't know." Tytus chokes on the response and shakes his head. "I'm sorry, Nate."

Sarah squeezes his hand. "Maybe Chrissie and I should give you guys—"

"No." Tytus holds onto her hand when she starts to let go. "I didn't just keep this from Nate. I kept it from all of you. And...I need to explain."

"Not to me, you don't." Nate pushes up from his chair and walks to the side of the bed opposite Sarah.

"It doesn't matter, Ty." He places his hand on his friend's shoulder. "All that matters is getting you healthy. And I don't just mean your arm." Nate takes a deep breath and walks to the end of the bed. "Here's what's going to happen, I'm setting up two appointments for you this afternoon. One for an MRI, so we can find out just what we are dealing with. And two, an appointment with the team psychiatrist so you can figure out what you're dealing with." He leans down towards Tytus's ear and mock-whispers loud enough for everyone to hear, "Cause I'm your best friend and your agent, but what I'm not, is your therapist."

Nate pats Tytus on the shoulder and gestures for Chrissie to get up. Tytus fights back the tears building in his eyes as he chuckles softly at Nate's words. He has always felt blessed to have Nate in his life, but never more than at this very moment.

"I'm so sorry, Tytus," Chrissie says before she follows Nate out. "I'm here if you need anything. Anything at all."

"Thanks, Chrissie." He nods and watches them both walk out.

Sarah pulls up a chair next to the bed and sits beside him. He looks at her and sees the same compassion and concern he'd seen at the airport over a week ago. Only this time, instead of scaring him off, instead of flipping some internal switch that sends up his self-isolating barriers, it makes him feel safe. Loved.

He begins with the moment in Houston, when he felt the pop in his shoulder, and tells Sarah the whole story.

Tytus was warming up in the bullpen in the eighth inning. They were up by one, but the Astros were the reigning World Champs and the game was far from over. He wasn't nervous. He didn't really get nervous anymore. People called him cocky and arrogant, but he saw it as confidence. To-mate-to, To-mat-to.

The closer he gets to entering the game, the more he lets loose on his fastball in the pen. Starting with easy tosses and building up as he goes. Only his last few pitches before taking the field are thrown at one hundred percent.

It was the second to last pitch when he felt it. A pop. In his shoulder. It had happened before. In high school. He was out for 6 weeks and nearly missed the State Championships.

The pain was sharp and undeniable, and the pitch sailed over the catcher's head while Tytus winced in pain.

His bullpen catcher jogged over. "Tytus? Tytus, you okay? You good?"

He can't be hurt. He'd worked his whole life to get to this point in his career. He's on pace to set an MLB record and make his first appearance as an All-Star.

"I'm good," he lied, nodding at his teammate. "That one just got away from me."

As Tytus ran out to take the field, he told himself he would be fine. It was just a pinched nerve or something. A little soreness he could push through. He was no pussy.

Less than ten minutes later he was walking off the field to the deafening screams of what sounded like the entire population of Houston, Texas. Astros players were dogpiling and cameras were flashing in every direction. Not only had he blown his first save, he'd given up the first walk-off home run of his career. And instead of admitting he was injured, he buried it. Just the way he had trained himself to do for years. And he stood in front of the cameras and took all the blame for letting his team down.

When he felt the pain again a few days later, he had seriously considered telling Spencer. But instead, he convinced himself he could push through it. And he gave up another save. Costing his team a second loss in as many appearances.

Spencer had confronted him in the locker room after that game. Not accusing him of anything, per se, but concerned that something was wrong. Tytus lashed out. Pointed out past failures of his catcher and threw out the old, Nobody's Perfect *cliché while the entire team looked on.*

It was after the third loss, when he hung up on Sarah and threw his phone against the wall, that he knew he had lost control. But he had just shut out the one person who seemed to know how to help him the most.

And he let the loneliness swallow him whole.

Tytus gets discharged around noon and the four friends load into the Navigator. Sarah needs to be at the theater by two and Tytus has to get to the stadium to meet with his coaches, the team doctor, and apparently the team psychiatrist.

They stop at her place first, and Tytus jumps out to walk her up. He taps on Nate's window.

"I'll get Miles to come get me. I need to go by my place and change. Why don't you meet me at the stadium in an hour?"

Nate makes a crack about Tytus being scared to go alone which earns him a rabbit punch in the bicep before closing his window.

He rounds the car and flashes Sarah his signature smile and raised eyebrow. She gives him an exaggerated eye roll, but on the inside her stomach flutters.

Sarah stops at her door to get out her keys and suddenly feels a bit nervous. They had been fighting for the past several days and at the hospital there had been a kind of bubble surrounding them. In fact, they hadn't kissed, really kissed, in 10 days. Not that she's counting.

"Thanks for walking me up, Tytus, but I know you have to get going and I need to—"

Before she can finish her sentence or get the key from the lock, his hand is on her cheek and her breath catches in a gasp.

"I'm so sorry, Sarah." His eyes move down to her lips and his tongue darts out to lick his own. "God, I've missed your mouth."

The kiss is slow and deep. It's not aggressive, but it's full of passion. His tongue finds its way around her mouth like it has finally come home after a long absence. Sarah's knees buckle as she gives herself over to everything he is giving. All the intimacy she has missed so dearly.

His hand snakes up her back and into her hair as she wraps her arms around his neck and tilts her head wishing for a way to dive even deeper into his mouth.

Moments later, Tytus finally pulls back and looks at her, his breathing choppy. Sarah has never seen eyes as expressive as his, and what she sees there now makes her hold on for dear life. His eyes are glistening with unshed tears and the words may not leave his lips, but they are spoken all the same.

I love you, Sarah.

Tytus's eyes are locked on hers and he feels something stir in his chest. It knocks him off balance. He fights the urge to break eye contact. To pull away. But the feeling also comforts him. Warmth spreads through his body starting in his chest and working its way out through his limbs. He wants to give in to it. To embrace it.

He gulps down the lump in his throat, causing his Adam's apple to bob dramatically. His words cut through the tension of the moment like a knife through butter.

"I should go."

Sarah just blinks back at him. His calloused hand wrapped around her jawline with his long fingers in the back of her hair. Despite his words, neither of them moves.

"Why?"

"You know why." He drops his hand and turns from her. "I have to get to the stadium, and you have to get to work," he continues as his heart rate slowly returns to normal.

Sarah doesn't respond for several beats.

"You're right. You have a big afternoon," she finally says as she lays her hand on his shoulder. "You gonna be okay?"

He turns back to her and sighs, "I'm not looking forward to it. But yeah, I'm gonna be okay."

He leans in and places a gentle kiss on her cheek.

"Call me after your show?"

"The second I'm done." She squeezes his hand. "Good luck. If you get results from the MRI, don't make me wait. Text me and I'll check my phone between scenes, okay?"

He nods in response, eyes cast down at his feet, but when she squeezes his hand again he looks up at her.

"Promise me." Her eyes plead with him.

"I promise."

Tytus steps out of her apartment building and is grateful for the fresh air. He takes in a long, deep breath as he stands there to center himself.

He has no idea what just happened to him in there. The feeling that flowed through him like morphine in an IV...had taken his breath away.

Well, he admits as he runs a hand through his hair, he may have *some* idea.

12

The Injured List

First on Tytus's agenda at Yankee Stadium is a meeting with Nate and the coaching staff. When he walks into the clubhouse, he's surprised to see Spencer there.

"Who told you?" Tytus asks, jutting his chin in Spencer's direction.

"No one had to tell me, Hayes. I knew." Spencer shoots him a knowing glare.

"Well unless you're a damn psychic, you didn't know about his meeting." Tytus sits on the couch across from his catcher. "And I know you're no psychic because you can't hit for shit." Tytus throws a towel from the nearby hamper at him.

"So, who told you?" he repeats his earlier question.

"Nate. He called me."

"Shit." Tytus shakes his head.

"Look, Tytus, I thought we were friends, not to mention teammates," Spencer says in a more serious tone.

"Alright, alright don't get your panties in a wad, right after this we can start couples counseling." Tytus quirks his eyebrow and smirks like a smart ass. "Will that make you feel better?"

Spencer doesn't get a chance to respond because the team manager and his two assistants walk in and both men get up to shake their hands.

"Tytus," his manager frowns, "this sure is some shit news."

"I know, Skip." Tytus shakes his head. "I know."

Before they finish greeting each other, Nate walks in and says his own hellos.

"Really?" Tytus says quietly to Nate gesturing toward Spencer.

"He should be here, Ty." Nate's tone leaves no room for argument.

"I know." Tytus sighs and sits between his two closest friends on the couch.

The meeting lasts about an hour. It's basically Tytus doing all the talking and answering a few questions from the rest of the group. He walks them through the entire story the way he had with Sarah. At one point, about halfway through, it hits him how much easier this is because he'd already been through it all with her. The gratitude consumes him and he loses his train of thought.

"Tytus?" Nate nudges him with his elbow to bring him back to the present.

He continues his retelling of events and answers the rest of their questions without incident.

"Okay, guys. Tytus and I appreciate all your support. I'm going to take him for his MRI and to meet Ruzzoli." Nate is the first to push himself up from the leather sofa.

"Ruzzoli?" Spencer chuckles. "Watch yourself, Hayes, that man does some serious Jedi mind trick shit," he whispers behind the back of his hand.

Tytus smiles but it doesn't reach his eyes. Spencer may have laughed but there is honesty in his eyes that unsettles him.

When Sarah arrives at work, she is greeted with a hug and then a slight push in the back from Sebastian. If ever there was a man who is all business all the time, it is him. And she loves him for it.

"How was your night off?" he asks, ushering her into the dressing room.

"You wouldn't believe me if I told you. Tytus—"

"Actually, no time for that," he cuts her off and hands her an article from the *New York Times*.

Sarah literally flinches at his abrupt interruption. She has noticed a less-than-subtle irritation every time she mentions Tytus's name around him.

When she glances down at the article she freezes in place.

World-renowned theater critic Cam Stewart to see Chicago *and the up-and-coming Sarah Dalton.*

"Cam Stewart? Holy Shit." Sarah sits down in her chair. Wait until her mother hears about this. She's loved Cam Stewart since Sarah was a girl.

"Holy shit is right. And he will be here tomorrow night, so let's think of this as a dress rehearsal for the biggest night of your life."

Sarah smiles as she watches him busily bustle around her dressing room. He seems pissed off somehow at the idea of her opportunity, but she knows it's really his way of dealing with a different emotion. Pride.

"Okay, Sebastian." She smiles at his back. "I'm all yours."

The MRI is done and Tytus and Nate are waiting patiently for the team orthopedic to come in and give them the results.

"Nervous?" Nate asks. "Because I am." He gets up and paces the room.

"Of course I'm nervous. But I keep telling myself it's out of my control." Tytus sighs and lays his head back against the wall. "Whatever it is, we will deal with it."

"At least it's not your elbow, right? He won't be coming back in saying you need Tommy-John."

Tytus nods at Nate. Tommy-John surgery isn't his fear. The ligaments in his elbow are stronger than ever. It's his rotator cuff. Another tear and his pitching career may be over. He had successfully managed to block that thought out since he'd first heard the pop. But now, as he knows he's minutes away from the news, it's got a vice grip on his insides.

The two men sit in silence for another ten minutes before the doctor finally pushes open the door.

Tytus stands up immediately, his nerves firing like a Fourth of July firework finale.

"Thank you for your patience, gentleman. I'm Will." He stretches out his hand. "Will Workman," he adds with a firm shake. "Mr. Hayes, please," he gestures to the chair in front of him, "take a seat."

The blood drains from Tytus's face. He can't even bear to look at Nate. Everyone knows, *maybe you should sit down*, really means, this news is going to suck.

"I have good news and bad news." The doctor sits down right in front of Tytus. Their knees, almost touching. It has the distinct feeling of a heart-to-heart lecture and he suddenly feels like a ten-year-old kid.

"If you had continued to throw, your career would most likely have been over within a month. You're a grown man, Mr. Hayes, and a professional, so I am only going to say this once. You need to listen to your body. And when it tells you something's wrong. Something's wrong."

Tytus has never been a big fan of authority figures and the way he's being spoken to at the moment would normally have him puffing out his chest and hurling derogatory names, but the Yankee Orthopedic Surgeon is the best in his field and Tytus knows every word he's said is true. So instead, he clenches his jaw and nods curtly.

"It's not a tear. It's a severe case of tendonitis."

Nate exhales loud enough that both men turn and face him.

"Sorry." Nate holds up his hands and grimaces.

"The popping you heard was the result of your rotator cuff tendon getting trapped under your acromion, or the highest point, of your shoulder."

Tytus leans back in his chair, cautious not to take the news too lightly. "And…"

"I'm going to give you a Corticosteroid injection. The relief should be immediate, but you will need physical therapy and rest."

"How long?" Nate interjects the question on the tip of Tytus's tongue.

"I'm going to recommend they start with the 15-day injured list and we will see how you respond to therapy. I think it's reasonable to say you could begin throwing again in two weeks and pitching in three to four." The doctor stands up and turns to Nate. "But there is no rushing this, and there are no guarantees. If his shoulder doesn't respond to the treatment we will move him to the 60-day DL in a heartbeat."

"Of course." Nate heeds the warning the doctor is giving. "Understood."

"Mr. Hayes." The doctor turns toward him.

"Tytus, please, Doc. Mr. Hayes has shaggy hair and plays the saxophone, not baseball."

"Tytus." The doctor smiles and extends his hand. "I'm a huge fan, and I know you have big goals for yourself and the team this season. But trust me when I say, rushing back isn't going to be good for anyone. Especially you."

"I get it. I do." Tytus gives the doctor's hand a firm shake before he heads out leaving the two friends alone.

Tytus turns to Nate and is caught off guard by the tears in his friend's eyes. The men nod at each other and step into a back-slapping embrace.

Sarah has just finished her final makeup when she gets Tytus's text.

Hey. Doc says it's just tendonitis. 3-4 weeks with PT and rest.
Best I could have hoped for. Break a leg, tonight.

Oh, Tytus! That's such great news.
I have good news too but I'd rather tell you in person.
Talk to you after the show?

Looking forward to it. Off to "therapy". Wish me luck.

Just be you, Tytus. The real you. XOXO

Sarah sets her phone down and glances at her reflection. The smile on her face shows every one of her 32 teeth.

⚾

After Tytus gets his Cortisone shot, Nate drops him at the therapy appointment and they agree to meet back at the game.

When Tytus enters the office there's a definite sense of warmth. The decor is masculine with walls painted in both light and dark shades of taupe separated by a white chair rail. There are two leather chairs across from a sofa with a wood slab coffee table that reminds Tytus of a cabin in the woods.

"Tytus, what a pleasure to meet you. Levi Ruzzoli." The therapist extends his hand as well as a warm smile.

Tytus returns the sentiment as he takes in the seemingly harmless, slightly taller, bald man and immediately remembers his teammate's warning.

"Nice to meet you too, Doctor Ruzzoli," he responds with a bit of hesitancy in his voice.

"Is it?" Ruzzoli laughs. "Please, call me Levi. Have a seat." He nods toward the couch while he sits in one of the chairs.

Tytus takes a seat and rubs his sweaty palms across his thighs. A quick glance at the notebook on the therapist's lap doesn't go unnoticed.

"It's for notes. Does it make you uncomfortable?"

"No." Tytus purses his lips and shakes his head. "No, it's fine."

They spend the next twenty minutes or so just getting comfortable with each other. Tytus likes the man right away. He knows he's probably using the *force* to brainwash him, but he doesn't mind. He feels relaxed and at ease. The only other person who ever makes him feel that way is Sarah.

Once Levi decides it's time to get into the meaty stuff, he focuses on baseball first. They talk about how he started playing, what the game means to him, his goals for the future. Then, just like that, it's like he flips a switch.

"Did you know you were hurt, Tytus?"

Caught off guard, Tytus sits up a little straighter and coughs into his hand.

"Yes." Surprising himself, both of them maybe, his answer is honest and his eyes are straight on Ruzzoli's.

"So, why did you try to hide it?"

Tytus inhales a breath and holds it while wringing his hands in his lap. He looks at the books on the built-in shelves on the wall. Then he lets the air out slowly before looking back to the therapist.

"It makes me feel weak."

"What does? Being injured?"

Tytus doesn't respond right away. They sit in silence.

"Needing people." Tytus looks at his hands before adding softly, "Needing help."

Ruzzoli nods thoughtfully. "That is a big step, Tytus. Not just the fact that you admitted that to me, but the fact that you even know it at all." He smiles softly as he takes a few notes on his pad.

"It seems like you've been making some progress on getting to the root of your issues on your own?" he asks when he looks back up.

"On my own?" Tytus scoffs. "No, not on my own."

Levi simply raises his brow and waits for him to elaborate.

What comes out of Tytus's mouth next catches both men completely off guard.

"How do you know if you're in love?"

Chrissie is waiting for Sarah backstage when she comes out of the dressing room.

"Heeeey," Chrissie squeals and wraps her arms around her. "I never get tired of watching you up there, Sarah."

"Thanks, Wis."

Sarah is happy to see her friend, of course. But for some reason, tonight's show took a little something extra out of her. She's always tired after a show but tonight she's just plain exhausted.

"Drinks?" Chrissie asks, not picking up on Sarah's current state.

"I'd love to. I would. But I didn't sleep well last night, and with all the craziness, I think I'm just worn out."

Chrissie reaches up to place her cool hand on Sarah's forehead.

"Yeah, you look a little flushed, actually." Chrissie tilts her head. "Are you coming down with something?"

Sarah shakes her head. "I don't think so. Unless *fatigue* counts as something.*"*

"Let's get you home, then. We can share a cab."

Sarah sends Tytus a quick message while they wait for the cab, letting him know that Chrissie is with her and she'll call once she gets home.

When they arrive outside Sarah's place, Chrissie offers to walk her up but Sarah declines.

"Take this cab and head home, Wis. I'm fine. I promise."

When Sarah steps on the elevator she checks her phone again but there is no response from Tytus. She knows the team won tonight because she gets ESPN alerts on her phone, which is hilarious when she thinks about it. And they had won big, so even if Tytus had been available to pitch, he wouldn't have needed to.

She's still scrolling through her phone when she steps off the elevator.

"You should really watch where you're going."

Sarah yelps and drops her phone. She puts both hands to her chest and looks up to find Tytus sitting with his back against her door. He's wearing dark blue jeans and a black fitted T-shirt that screams *sexy*.

"You scared me half to death, Tytus."

"As I said, you should really watch where you're going." He stands up and slides one arm around her, pulling her in for a soft kiss.

"I missed you." He purses his lips and gives her his puppy dog eyes. "Plus. I had good news today, you said you had good news today, so…" He holds up the bottle of wine in his other hand.

Sarah had been so looking forward to climbing straight into bed, but she couldn't be more touched by his gesture. And she's really glad he's here.

They head into her apartment and Tytus pours them both a glass of wine while Sarah changes into her pajamas. When she walks out and finds him waiting there, she is reminded of the first night he came over and it brings a smile to her face.

"What?" He laughs, squirming under her stare.

"Nothing," she answers him. "I'm just glad you're here." She takes the glass he's offering and sits on the couch beside him. "Tell me about therapy."

"No way. You first. What's your good news?"

Sarah tells Tytus about the article in the *Times* and about Cam Stewart. She explains that he is a really big deal and a well-respected critic.

"And he's coming tomorrow night to see me, so..."

"So, that's amazing. But also scary as hell."

"Exactly." Sarah exhales.

Tytus leans in and kisses her on the cheek. Then the lips. His thumb caresses her cheek softly. "You'll knock his socks off." He pecks her on the lips. "You'll take his breath away." Another kiss, this one with just a little tongue. "I may have to beat the shit out of him when he comes after you." His words are mumbled against her lips.

"He's gay, Tytus," Sarah says between moans. His tongue is causing a rush of heat between her legs.

"Perfect."

Sarah giggles and pushes on his chest. "Nice try, Mister. Your turn. How was your appointment?"

Tytus huffs with an exaggerated pout and sits back.

"Really good, actually."

As Tytus is summarizing his visit with Ruzzoli, Sarah is struggling to keep her eyes open. It's not that she isn't interested, she's just completely wiped out.

"And, I'm putting you to sleep."

She hears Tytus's words and opens the eyes she hadn't realized she'd closed.

"I'm sorry, Tytus. I'm not sure what's wrong with me tonight."

"You're exhausted. That's what's wrong. Off to bed," he says, pulling her up from the couch.

Sarah wants to object. To apologize for falling asleep on him. She really did want to know about his session. But she has no energy to do or say any of those things. In fact, she barely makes it to the bed before collapsing onto it.

Tytus pulls the covers up over her as she closes her eyes and nuzzles her head into the pillow.

The last thing she remembers is forcing out one word as Tytus walks out of the room and shuts off the lights.

"Stay."

And stay he did.

When Sarah wakes in the morning, she reaches across the bed not sure what she expects to find there. As her eyes blink open she stares at the window on her wall and the light casting a stream on the floor. Her heart sinks a bit in her chest. She must have been dreaming, because she could have sworn Tytus had been cuddling her during the night.

When she hears a cupboard in the kitchen close, she smiles to herself. It hadn't been a dream, after all. She tiptoes into the restroom before heading to meet him in the kitchen.

"Did you take advantage of me last night when I fell asleep on you?" she asks with a seductive smile as she walks into the kitchen.

"Take advantage of you? Please," he says when she steps into his arms. "More like took care of you. And then you practically begged me to stay." He kisses her on top of the head.

Sarah looks up at him with her chin on his chest. "You're a good man, Tytus Hayes."

Something tender flashes in his eyes, but he recovers quickly. He spins her around and she braces herself putting both hands on the counter in front of her.

Tytus slides his hands from her hips up the front of her body and grasps her breasts tightly.

"Oh, I'm a bad man, Sarah Dalton," he whispers in her ear as he pushes his groin into her from behind. "A very bad man." He grinds into her as he kisses her right below the ear. "And I'm going to show you just how bad I can be." He sucks lightly on her earlobe. "Right after I feed you some breakfast."

He lets her go and walks away, leaving her breathless and panting. The smirk on his face is so big she can see it from behind him. *Asshole.* She smiles.

While she is definitely feeling better than last night, she is starving. And with two shows today and Cam Stewart coming tonight, she needs the fuel. So she doesn't argue when he sets the table with what appears to be a spinach and mushroom omelet and a glass of orange juice.

Tytus raises his eyebrows as he sits at the table placing his plate in front of him. "What, too turned on to eat?" He takes a bite of his eggs and then almost chokes at his own joke.

She rolls her eyes and sits down doing her best to look irritated.

The truth? She adores him. That damn smile, those eyes, the way he flips back and forth between cocky and closed off to soft and vulnerable, not to mention he has the body of a god and a cock that would make any woman weak.

"What?" Tytus says, grinning over his glass. "You mad at me?"

"Just eat, Hayes. You're going to need your strength." She lets her tongue linger on her upper lip after licking a drop of juice from it.

Even though he plays it off, Sarah sees the heat in his eyes and the way he shifts in the chair. He isn't the only one who can play this game.

The two of them finish their breakfast like they'd been starved for days and the sexual tension in the room builds with every bite. Sarah finishes first and gets up to rinse her plate in the sink. She can feel him watching her every move, eyes growing darker with each sway of her hips.

"I'll be in the shower." The sultry tone of her voice is intentional and she can sense that it hits Tytus right where it counts. Then with her eyes locked on his, she takes her index finger and wipes a bit of salsa from the side of Tytus's mouth. She slides her finger through her own lips and pulls it out slowly with a pop.

"You missed a spot."

She runs the wet finger across the back of his neck as she walks past him.

Sarah saunters out of the room but before she even makes it to the bathroom, Tytus grabs her from behind and pushes her up against the wall. Both her arms pinned above her head, he grinds his erection into her ass. It takes the wind from her lungs.

"Careful who you tease." His breath is hot. "Maybe you don't know who I am?" He licks her neck and whispers, "I'm Tytus fucking Hayes."

She turns her head, prepared with a witty comeback, and is immediately shut up with his mouth on hers. His specific choice of words causes her mind to flash to a painful moment from the past, but this time, with Tytus, they elicit a completely different response. He presses her firmly against the wall and flattens her with the pressure of his body. His tongue forces her mouth wider as his hands grip her wrists possessively. She can feel exactly how turned on he is and...it does things to her.

"Tytus?" she pleads. She doesn't even know what she's asking for? Stop? Never stop?

"You know what happens when you mess with the bull, Sarah?"

He lets go of her wrists and yanks her silk bottoms to her ankles. Her hands are free but she keeps them on the wall, unable to move or speak. Now on one knee behind her, Tytus spins her around so her back is against the wall and her wet throbbing center is an inch from his face.

Sarah keeps her hands above her head wanting to expose every possible inch of her body to him. Tytus looks up at her to make sure she's watching as he slides his tongue between his lips and into hers.

The ecstasy rips through her like an electric shock and her legs give out, causing her to lean more weight on his mouth. Tytus groans loudly as he supports her leg by lifting it onto his good shoulder. Sarah gasps for air as she finally drops her arms and grips his head with both hands. Moaning loudly, she rakes her nails through his hair and glides her hips forward and back against his hungry mouth.

Since they are playing a ruthless game of who can tease who more, he stops just short of making her come.

"Tytus, please..."

The evil grin he flashes up at her is the sexiest thing she's ever seen. He's on his feet without another word. He grabs her by the hips and hoists her up. She wraps her legs around him and dives back into his mouth. The taste of her all over his tongue.

He carries her straight to the shower and shows her exactly what happens when you mess with the bull.

Tytus stands on the balcony clad only in the jeans he wore over last night and with his hair still wet from the shower. His chest is feeling a little extra buff as he had just shown Sarah that his skills extended far beyond the pitcher's mound.

He's rehydrating with a glass of water while Sarah finishes getting ready. They had agreed that Miles would drop her off at the theater before Tytus heads to physical therapy.

The view from here doesn't hold a candle to his, but it still provides a perspective of the city that makes you stop and take notice. Makes you think.

Last night, when he had been telling Sarah about his talk with Dr. Ruzzoli, Levi, he had thought about telling her what he'd uncovered. But then she started falling asleep and the moment slipped away.

While he had watched her sleeping, he had let the feelings come right up to the surface. Almost whispered it to her a hundred times. But he kept the words locked inside. He wants to make sure when he finally says them, they come through loud and clear. *Soon*, he thinks, as he walks back inside to find his shirt.

When the Lexus pulls up to the Ambassador Theatre, Tytus gets out to open the door for Sarah.

"You are going to be amazing." He smiles and places both his hands on her hips. "Might even turn the man straight."

"Thanks, Tytus." He can still make her blush.

He reaches up to touch her face and leans in for one last open-mouthed kiss.

"Hey, Tytus!" A voice calls and they both turn to find a large telephoto lens pointed in their direction. "I guess we know how you are going to fill your time on the injured list," the reporter next to the cameraman yells out. Before Tytus can respond the two men disappear around the corner.

Tytus drops his hand, as well as his head.

"Fuck."

"Tytus. I'm sorry." Sarah lays her hands on his chest, concern in her eyes.

He looks back up and offers a half-hearted smile.

"It's fine, Sarah." He kisses her on the forehead lightly and pulls her in for a hug. He lifts her chin as he pulls back. Eyes locked on hers. "It's fine," he repeats with more conviction. Sarah nods back.

"Knock 'em dead." He winks and waits until she's safely inside, before climbing back into the car.

As they head to the stadium, he pulls out his phone to text Nate.

Nate, something came up. Call me.

13

I Do

$\mathcal{T}$he show was perfect. She was perfect.

As she steps out for her final bow the crowd lets her know it. The audience is on their feet, cheering, clapping, whistling. She has never felt prouder. She sees Cam Stewart, front and center, with his playbill tucked under his elbow as he applauds along with everyone else in the theater.

She hadn't thought the moment could possibly get any better.

Then off to her right a sharply dressed man comes up on stage with a beautiful bouquet of flowers. The bright lights shield her view as her breath lodges in her throat. She's certain her heart stops for a solid three beats before he emerges from the glow. Like a scene from a big-screen romance, there is Tytus, flowers in hand, eyes sparkling, and that million-dollar smile.

"Brava." He extends the flowers in her direction as he steps up closer.

Sarah blinks repeatedly as her eyes fill with tears. The crowd erupts yet again, taking the volume to a whole new level.

The two of them stand inches apart, eyes locked. She has been completely caught off guard and her heart is beating out of her chest. But he's got her. Just the look in his eyes begins to slow her pulse and grounds her.

He leans in, ever so slowly, and kisses her softly on the lips as his arm slides around her waist. He holds it long enough for several cell phone cameras to flash and then turns her back toward the audience, grinning proudly by her side. Just in front of them the photographer who had accompanied Stewart focuses his lens and snaps a few photos of his own.

The moment is surreal on many levels and Sarah can't quite process what is happening. But Tytus's strong hand on the small of her back eventually guides her backstage.

"What...how did...where...?" Sarah stutters once they are backstage.

"You're speechless," he laughs. "Let's get to your dressing room and I'll explain."

Tytus ushers a mesmerized Sarah through the business backstage and into her dressing room.

"First of all," Tytus says with a devilish grin, "I have to confess, I didn't actually see the show, but based on the reaction of the audience, you were amazing."

That gets a giggle out of Sarah as Tytus steps in to kiss her again.

"How did you make it here at all?" She's finally settled enough to ask.

"Well, considering I didn't have to shower or do interviews, I bolted the minute the game finished."

"But...why?"

"I had a heart-to-heart with Nate and he helped me see things clearly. Boy genius that he is, suggested we go on the offensive," Tytus explains to Sarah as she takes off her wig and makeup.

"The offensive?"

"Yeah. If our picture is going to be all over the internet tonight, or the paper tomorrow, then let's give them the photos we want them to have. Not blurry, back alley photos that make it look like we have something to hide." Tytus walks behind her chair and rubs her shoulders with his strong hands. "But vivid, clear photos that show everyone just how proud I am to stand by your side."

He lowers his face to her neck and then kisses her softly between words.

"Tytus Hayes and Sarah Dalton." Kiss. "New York City's." Kiss. "Newest." Kiss. "Hottest." Kiss. "Power couple."

Sarah lays her hands on top of his and tilts her head up to look at him.

"I think you mean, Sarah Dalton and Tytus Hayes. Didn't you hear that crowd?" Her laugh is smothered by Tytus's mouth on hers.

Tytus has been waiting for Sarah for a little more than forty-five minutes. She had autographs to sign and a private talk with the big wig critic who had come tonight. By the time she meets him at the back door, she looks completely worn out.

"Hey," he half laughs at the sight of her.

"I know." She scoffs at him. "You don't have to laugh at me. I think I may have blacked out during that interview for a couple of seconds." She shakes her head tiredly.

"So going back to my place for a full body massage is out of the question?" The corner of his mouth turns upward. "And by full body massage, I mean you giving me one."

Sarah laughs at his joke but it quickly turns into a whimpering pout as she drops her head straight into Tytus's chest.

He caresses her hair with his hand and kisses her on top of the head.

"Come on, let's get you home."

As he opens the back door to the Lexus for her, Tytus fights off the pang of disappointment. He had planned to ask Sarah to spend the night with him at his place tonight. He had pictured the two of them having a drink on the balcony and finishing the conversation about his session with Ruzzoli. Not that he wants to talk about therapy, but he wants to talk about them. About the way he feels.

But Sarah doesn't just look worn out, she looks like she's coming down with something and he's actually a little worried.

When he climbs in next to her, Tytus reaches over and lays his hand on Sarah's forehead.

"Do you think you might be fighting a bug or something?" he asks as he moves his hand from her forehead to her cheek and then her neck. She's not warm but she's awfully pale.

"No, no. I'm fine, Tytus, really." She takes his hand from her face and slides her slender fingers through his masculine ones. "Saturdays are always tough and after the ordeal you put me through this week, I think I have a right to be exhausted." She smirks and gives his hand a squeeze.

"Oh, you mean all the life-altering sex? That's fair. Not everyone has the stamina of a professional athlete." He tilts his head.

"Stamina? You use that term pretty loosely. I've been to your games, Tytus." She lays her head on his shoulder. "You sit around for two and half hours and then throw the ball a few times. I'm not sure that requires all that much endurance."

He smiles to himself as Sarah closes her eyes. He's never known a woman with as much sass as Sarah. At least not one who was confident enough to use it on him. It's one of the many things he loves about her.

When they arrive at her place, Tytus walks her up. She doesn't ask him to stay and he doesn't bring it up either. She needs rest and they both have early starts tomorrow. He almost suggests that she take the early show off tomorrow and stay home in bed, but he just doesn't feel it's his place. Not yet, anyway.

"Right to bed, okay?" He kisses her lightly on the cheek and looks into her tired eyes. "Tomorrow night Spencer and Traci are joining Nate, Chrissie, and me for the show. I can't wait."

Sarah offers a soft smile but the normal sparkle is absent from her eyes. "That's great, Tytus. I can't wait either."

Another soft kiss and they both say goodnight.

Sarah sleeps like a rock all night and wakes up Sunday feeling rested and excited about what today may bring. Especially once she sees messages from Tytus, Chrissie, Sebastian, her mother, and her director. All with links to the *New York Times* article featuring a rave review from Cam Stewart and several amazing photos. The largest of which is one of her and Tytus looking like star-crossed lovers at center stage.

The text from Tytus reads, *Sorry I look so dashing. Didn't mean to steal your spotlight.* It makes her laugh right out loud. He had sent it nearly two hours earlier and is probably already at the field doing treatment.

He does look amazing. But so does she. There are a few photos from throughout the performance as well and no sign of the surprise one taken earlier in the day. Apparently, Nate had been right.

Sarah texts Tytus back saying she is sure he can make it up to her, then pours herself a cup of coffee, sits out on her balcony, and reads the article over a few times. She answers the messages from all her friends and even calls and talks with her mom for a good thirty minutes.

By the time she eats breakfast and heads off to work, she feels almost like her old self. The exhaustion and headaches of the past few days are hopefully behind her.

The Yankees lose a tough one to Boston that afternoon. They had a lead in the top of the ninth and the bullpen gave it up. It leaves a bitter taste in Tytus's mouth but he really doesn't want it to ruin the evening. They still have a two-game lead in the division and a long home stand in front of them.

The plan he and Nate had put together to get ahead of the whole media thing had worked. The photo from that afternoon did turn up on social media and there are some smart-ass comments about the type of 'rehab' Tytus Hayes was getting in his off time, but the article about Sarah and the photos along with it are perfect. Just thinking about it makes him smile.

"My God, you are whipped." Spencer peers over his shoulder as Tytus stands in front of his locker looking at the article. "All these years I admired your gameplay with the ladies, just for you to turn out like the rest of us." He mocks disappointment, shaking his head.

"Kline, if I ever turn out just like you, do me a favor and shoot me."

The two friends laugh it off and head out for Sarah's show.

Traci is waiting for them by Spencer's car. Of course, a guy like Spencer Kline drives a souped-up Hummer. It's one of the big differences between the two men and their tastes.

Spencer does have excellent taste in women though. Tytus smiles as he brings Traci in for a hug.

"When are you going to leave this loser for a real man?"

"From what I've heard this actress we are going to see tonight took your manhood?" Traci teases back. "The great bachelor, Tytus Hayes Jr., is as smitten as a teenage groupie."

"When you see her, you'll understand." He's not even going to deny it. Traci will read it all over his face soon enough.

The trio climb into the SUV and head to meet up with Chrissie and Nate.

Sarah feels fabulous. No headaches. Great energy. Ready to take on the world. For about three hours.

She'd powered through the first performance earlier and seeing Tytus in the audience with the group of friends he'd brought for the evening show, did provide a second wind. But by the time she takes her final bow, her temples are pounding.

The group had planned to go out for drinks and she isn't going to spoil it by saying she's tired. Again. Sarah has always had energy in spades and she is really starting to wonder if something is wrong. But, she is looking forward to getting to know Spencer and Traci, so she throws back several Advil, puts on her best smile, and heads out to greet them.

About an hour later, the three couples slide into a large booth at *Beleman's*. Sarah can tell that Tytus is pretty excited about his idea of returning to the bar where they'd first met. She finds it incredibly sweet, and after a few sips of wine and a visit to Earl at the piano, she's feeling better again.

The conversation and laughter are non-stop for the next hour and a half. They take turns telling stories about each other from the past, Tytus about Nate and vice-versa, Sarah and Chrissie about rushing sororities in college, and Traci even tells the group about her and Spencer's first time, which makes all the guys want to cringe and all the girls to order another round. Traci is the life of the party even though she is the only one not drinking. She and Spencer share with the group that they are trying for baby number two.

"Would you guys believe that Spencer had a picture of Tytus on his dartboard in college?" Traci laughs. "God he hated you, Tytus."

"They say hatred is the highest form of flattery." Tytus tilts his scotch toward Spencer.

"No, Hayes. They don't." Spencer clinks his glass against Tytus's.

When Sarah checks the time and sees it's after 1:00, she's shocked. She'd been having such a great time, she hadn't even noticed.

"It's late," Tytus says, seemingly reading her thoughts. "And Sarah has had a long week, no thanks to me. We'd better head out."

All the couples agree it's time to get home, and they slide out of the booth and say their goodbyes.

"Traci, it feels like we've been friends forever. It was so great to meet you."

"I must say, Sarah, when Spencer told me that a woman had stolen Tytus Hayes's heart, I couldn't wrap my mind around it. But now that I've met you, and I've seen the two of you together, it's like you were meant to be."

Sarah is so touched by Traci's words that her eyes well up. She's embarrassed by her emotional reaction and quickly plays it off with a witty remark about Tytus's heart belonging to the Yankees, but she'd gladly settle for his body belonging to her.

Tytus hails a cab when they walk out of the bar and the two climb in together. When Tytus gives the driver his address instead of hers, she doesn't even question him. She just wraps her arm around his and snuggles in.

They make love in Tytus's bed for the first time, and Sarah sleeps soundly with her head on his chest and his strong arms wrapped securely around her.

The week drags on and Sarah feels less and less like herself. With the wedding coming up on Saturday, she is determined to get as much rest as possible and get over whatever has been slowing her down.

She had originally planned to go to the baseball game on Wednesday night and hang out in the suite with Chrissie, but she ended up going to bed early and slept for fourteen hours straight. She and Chrissie had met up several times to run various wedding-related errands and work on centerpieces.

Tytus had been on her all week about going to the doctor and when she doesn't feel any better on Thursday morning, she finally calls and makes an appointment for the following day.

She gets through the Thursday night performance and Tytus is waiting to take her home when she finishes up for the night.

"I made an appointment," she says as she steps into his outstretched arms. She knew it was going to be his first question so she answered it before he even asked.

"Tomorrow?"

Sarah nods into his chest.

"What time?" Tytus asks, opening the car door for her.

"10:00."

"Do you want me to come along? I don't start treatment until 1:00."

"No, that's okay." She smiles and then looks at him with her sleepy bedroom eyes. "But if you want to take me to my place, make me some dinner, and caress my entire body with those incredible hands of yours...I could be persuaded to agree to that."

Friday morning, Tytus gets Sarah to agree to at least let Miles take her to and from the doctor. He realized after offering to go with her that he and Nate were picking up tuxedos this morning and he wouldn't have been able to come even if she'd said yes.

His kiss goodbye is a little extra soft and his hug a little extra tight.

"Call me and let me know if they give you any answers, okay?"

"I will." She smiles softly. "Good luck tonight. Light a fire under those guys. We can't have you losing to the Mets." She tilts her head in mock disapproval causing Tytus to laugh.

"I can't believe I'm not going to see you until after the game tomorrow." His tone switches to a childish whine.

"You're a big boy Tytus. You'll be okay without me for twenty-four hours." She combats his childlike tone with a motherly one.

"Hmph," he grunts for emphasis. "I just don't see why we can't see each other tonight? It's not like we're the ones getting married tomorrow."

"Because I'm spending the night with Chrissie and you...you are doing whatever guys do with their best friend the night before he gets married."

Sarah pats his cheek and walks out, leaving a pouty Tytus behind.

Nate pulls up in front of Tytus's place around 10:30. They talk for a bit about Tytus's rehab schedule but switch to wedding talk and the plan for Saturday. Nate chose this date because the Yankees have a rare noon Saturday start time. The wedding ceremony will be at 5:00 with the reception following at 7:00.

"How's Sarah feeling?" Nate asks as they park in the back of the tux place. "Has she finally kicked whatever's been bothering her?"

Tytus sighs and shakes his head. "Not really, she's actually at the doctor right now. She's been so exhausted lately, it's not like her. And she seems...emotional." Tytus looks over at Nate with a pained expression on his face.

"Tytus? You don't think..."

"Don't think, what? I'm sure it's nothing serious, Nate." He completely misses his friend's meaning.

Nate turns in the driver's seat to look at Tytus head-on.

"You don't think she could be...pregnant?"

The word just hangs in the air between them. Tytus hears it. He most definitely hears it, but his mind seems to go completely blank before the meaning of it can actually take hold.

Ba—bump. Tytus's heart thumps. Ba—bump.

The air grows thick and his next breath lodges in his throat.

Preg…preg…pregnant*?*

He turns from Nate and looks out the windshield. Eyes cast directly forward but not focused on anything at all. Sarah? Pregnant? He feels foolish now, that the thought hadn't once crossed his mind. But what did he know about pregnancy? Nothing. Not a single damn thing.

"Tytus? Did you hear me?" Nate reaches over to shake his knee. "I said, I'm sure it's not that. I'm sure it's nothing." His eyes betray him, however, and Tytus can clearly see the concern his friend is trying to mask.

"Yeah," Tytus exhales. "I'm sure it's nothing."

And both friends seem to prefer to leave it at that rather than explore the subject any further.

By the time Sarah finishes up at the doctor, she can't wait to get the hell out of there. As she hails a cab, she thinks absently that she feels worse leaving the appointment than she had when she arrived.

Any chance you could be pregnant?

The doctor had caught her so off guard with the question she had choked on her response. It had been so matter-of-fact, like do you smoke? Or are you getting enough rest?

The blood had drained from her face while she sat there gawking and staring at the calendar on the wall. How had she not even considered the possibility? Because she takes the damn pill, that's why. And when the doctor offered the urine test, she declined right away, still not letting the reality of the idea take hold.

She does the math in her head while she squirms in the backseat of the cab. While it's not plausible, it's certainly possible that she could be. Her cycle has never been all that predictable and she'd heard of people getting pregnant on the pill. But she doesn't feel pregnant. Whatever that means.

It's not until she's nearly back to her apartment that she lets her mind wander to the thought of how Tytus might react. The image she conjures up in her mind scares her half to death.

⚾

Tytus knocks on his therapist's door later that afternoon. He's relieved that they had his second session scheduled for today because he can't stop thinking about his conversation with Nate.

As usual, Ruzzoli warms him up with a few minutes of small talk and a discussion about the rehab on his shoulder. Technically the Yankees are footing the bill, so Tytus figures they should spend some time on baseball.

He tells Levi that his physical therapy is going well and that he's anxious to start throwing again, but he knows he can't rush it. Ruzzoli asks some questions about how the break is affecting him mentally, and the atmosphere in the clubhouse and around the guys. Which Tytus eventually figures out is the man's way of leading into the pictures in the paper and his relationship with Sarah, which is where he wanted it to go anyway.

Before Tytus knows it, he tells him the whole story about the surprise photo, his and Nate's plan, and the amazing article that was written about Sarah. Ruzzoli knew about the article of course, but what he didn't know was how Tytus felt about it. Until now.

"So, you were happy about the picture in the paper? You have no issue with your relationship being public?"

"Why would I have an issue with it? I care about Sarah, and I don't care who knows it."

"You care about her?" Levi repeats, wiggling his pen between his fingers.

"Yes. Of course."

He looks at Tytus pointedly. "You haven't told her you're in love with her then?"

"I—" Tytus opens and shuts his mouth like a cod fish. He shifts his weight back on the couch and lets out a puff of air that had been filling his cheeks. "I never said I was in love with her." His eyes are cast toward the floor.

"True, you didn't *say* it. But you are." He waits for Tytus to look up at him.

"I am." His eyes rest on his therapist's and his voice does not waver.

"So, the question is, why haven't you told her how you feel?"

"I know what you're implying here, Levi, but you're actually barking up the wrong tree."

"Is that so?" Ruzzoli can't hide the amusement in his eyes. "Please, do tell me."

"I want to tell her. In fact, I have almost told her at least a hundred times this week."

Ruzzoli simply raises his eyebrows to signal Tytus to continue.

"But, it's never been the right time. Sarah...hasn't been herself." He feels a lump forming in his throat. He's set the ball rolling and there's no stopping it now.

"I...I think she might be pregnant."

Tytus clenches his jaw and braces himself for God knows what. But Levi doesn't bat an eye and Tytus has to give him credit. Man's got balls of steel to just sit there and give no reaction whatsoever.

"And how does the possibility of that make you feel, Tytus?"

He doesn't answer. How can he find words to explain the range of emotions he's gone through today?

Tytus looks at the floor and wipes his hands on his thighs. Ruzzoli starts jotting down notes in his notebook.

"What are you writing?" Tytus can't hide the fact that he's uncomfortable, and he doesn't get an answer to his question.

"Tytus. You're in love with Sarah and she may be carrying your child. I understand how overwhelming that must be."

Tytus lets out a slow stream of air that had been inflating his chest. But since there is no real question there, he remains silent.

"Have you ever thought about having a family of your own?" His voice is soft and comforting.

Tytus looks up at him for the first time in several minutes, and with eyes full of emotion, he swallows and nods.

Sarah hears the knock on the door, and she squeals as she yanks it open. It's her last night with her best friend before the wedding and she's not falling asleep early. She had requested today and tomorrow off before the show even opened and she's grateful for the break and the time with Chrissie.

"There's the beautiful bride-to-be."

"Sarah." Chrissie brings both her hands up to her mouth. "This is really happening. I'm getting married tomorrow." Chrissie jumps up and down in place like a teenager at her first concert.

"You sure are, Wis. And you're going to be the most beautiful bride New York has ever seen." Sarah pulls her inside and hands her the glass of wine she has waiting for her.

Chrissie heads to the couch while Sarah grabs the tray of appetizers from the counter.

"How was your appointment?" Chrissie asks as Sarah walks toward her. "Get any answers?"

Sarah sits next to her and shrugs. "Not really, they did some tests, but I won't have the results until next week." She plops a carrot covered in dip into her mouth.

Chrissie sips her wine and raises her eyebrows.

"What?" Sarah says with her mouth full.

Chrissie shifts her eyes from Sarah to the glass of water on the table and back to Sarah.

Sarah's stomach flips over as she catches exactly what Chrissie is asking.

"Oh, c'mon, Wis. The doctor said to lay off the alcohol for now until I get the results back. They may need to do follow-up bloodwork on Monday." Sarah keeps her expression neutral but her arms are covered in goosebumps.

"Uh-huh." Chrissie's face breaks into a mischievous grin. "C'mon yourself, Sarah." She sets her wine glass down and looks at her friend intently. "The thought has to have crossed your mind. I mean, could you be?"

"Chrissie." Sarah gets up from the couch and starts pacing. "Don't look at me like that. You say it like it would be a good thing." The emotions Sarah has been pushing down all afternoon, rise to the surface and it's evident in her voice.

"Hey, hey." Chrissie gets up and walks to Sarah's side. "I'm sorry. I'm not making light of it, Sarah."

"I know you're not." Sarah dabs at her eyes as tears threaten to spill over. "And to answer your question, I've done the math. It's possible, yes."

Chrissie takes her hand and tugs lightly. "Want to find out?"

When Sarah turns to face her, brows furrowed, Chrissie tilts her head.

"We could go buy a test?"

Sarah's eyes widen and she shakes her head.

"Sarah, it's better to know for sure, isn't it?" She lays her hand on Sarah's arm. "You're in love with him. Isn't that what's most important?"

Sarah just blinks at her friend. Eventually turning away from her and walking toward the window.

"No, Chrissie. That's not what's most important."

When Miles drops Tytus at the church Saturday afternoon, he's a bundle of nervous energy. He's actually pretty damn excited for Nate and Chrissie. And he hasn't stopped thinking about Sarah and the…situation.

He meets Nate in the small room on the side of the church. They down a couple measures of the Blue Label Tytus brought and take several photos in the courtyard. Tytus feels a bit awkward around Curtis after the way he'd behaved at the rehearsal dinner, but Curtis shows no signs of harboring a grudge. In fact, he's downright beaming.

Once Nate gets started taking photos with his soon-to-be father-in-law, Tytus sneaks off to find Sarah.

It turns out to be an easy mission considering the church grounds aren't that large and the room is clearly marked 'Bride's Chambers'.

Three light knocks on the door and he's hit with a fresh wave of nerves. Chrissie's mom, Kathy, opens the door slowly, careful not to let anyone see too far inside.

"Tytus?" She steps back and gives him a full once-over. "You look dashing."

"As do you, Kathy." He flashes the Hayes grin.

"What can I help you with, Sweetie?" She smiles in return. But her stance is that of a gatekeeper.

"I was hoping to see Sarah." He shrugs his shoulders and gives his best sheepish look. "Just for a minute?" Suddenly he feels like he's in high school, trying to get Sarah's mother to let him in.

"One second," she says as she closes the door.

Tytus leans against the wall, drumming his fingers on his thigh. When the door opens he props himself on the wall with his elbow and his hand behind his head. *Smooth as silk.*

When Sarah steps across the threshold his mouth goes dry. He drops his arm from the wall and stands up straight. The dress is a dark shade of burgundy, with a deep cut at the breast and a long slit up past her knee. Her hair is tied up leaving her neck and shoulders bare. He can't decide where to focus his gaze.

Sarah clears her throat and puts her hand on her hip. "My eyes are up here, Hayes."

"Absolutely beautiful." He slowly rakes his eyes upward from her killer heels to her skeptical eyes.

She tilts her head and raises a brow.

"Undeniably breathtaking."

Sarah's cheeks blush lightly and she adjusts her stance under his stare.

"So damn hot."

"You're an idiot." She laughs playfully and steps right up to him. Her face, not even an inch from his. All his previous musings about weddings, and babies, and unsaid declarations of love slip from his mind. His consciousness, overwhelmed by the heat rising between them, threatening to burn him to ash on the spot.

"Just, wow." His breath catches as he watches her eyes flash to his lips.

"Sarah?" Kathy's voice cuts through the air as the door reopens.

Tytus concentrates on regulating his heart rate as Sarah steps away from him.

"Yes, Kathy?" Her voice, hoarse.

"Chrissie's hair. One of the pins came loose. I need your help." She glances at Tytus and then back to Sarah. "If you don't mind?"

"Of course." Sarah smiles. "I'll be right there."

The door closes again and Sarah looks back to Tytus. He can't quite get a read on her now. Whatever had just transpired between them has passed.

"I better get in there."

She turns to walk inside but looks back at him over her shoulder. "And for the record," her eyes skim up and down his body, "not bad."

The wink is slow and sultry.

Sarah inhales a long and steady breath. It's time. She walks out into the foyer. He's there, waiting for her. He looks nervous and it makes her lip twitch.

As she walks toward him, her stomach swirls with butterflies. Sometimes she can't help but be in awe of how gorgeous he is. He lifts his elbow from his side and she wraps her arm around it, struck by how far they've come since they'd rehearsed this moment. It feels like a lifetime ago.

When it's their turn, Tytus guides her toward the aisle.

"You ready?" His eyes are warm and reassuring and he tightens her arm against his body.

As they walk down the aisle adorned in white ribbon and flowers, arm in arm, organ music playing, it feels like a dream. She knows, of course, that if they were the ones getting married, he wouldn't be walking her down the aisle this way, but it doesn't stop her mind from going there.

Her thoughts wander then, to the elephant in the room. She hadn't taken Chrissie up on her offer. She explained that this weekend was about Chrissie and Nate, not her and Tytus. That the test could wait. And she meant it. But she is also stalling. The reality of what this could mean, of the impact it would have on her life, her career, not to mention what it might do to Tytus, to them. She just couldn't bear it. Not yet.

Tonight, she would enjoy this beautiful occasion with the man at her side. The man with whom she'd fallen so deeply in love.

They reach the end of the aisle and Sarah reluctantly releases his arm before they head their separate ways.

The ceremony is beautiful. Tytus doesn't really consider himself romantic or sentimental, but he'd be lying if he didn't admit to getting misty-eyed more than once. The first time is when the wedding march starts and Chrissie appears at the end of the aisle. He glances in Nate's direction and he can see him practically glowing. Keeping his head pointed in the direction of the bride, he lets his eyes drift to the side to peek at Sarah. Her eyes are full of joyous tears and her smile takes the breath from his lungs.

God, he loves her. There is no doubt about it now. And as the ceremony continues, the feeling inside him seems to take root and fill him up in a way that is both terrifying and exhilarating.

While Nate and Chrissie exchange their vows, he is struck with another wave of emotion. Sarah's eyes find his as Chrissie repeats the words after Father Kerry. He envisions her to be the one dressed in white, across from him, as he slides a ring on her finger. His eyes drift down to her belly as he feels a surge of love for a child that may not even exist.

He needs her to know that whatever life throws their way, he can handle it, they can handle it. *Together.*

After the ceremony, they all head to The Plaza Hotel for the reception. Sarah and Tytus are expected to take photos along with the bride and groom and some of Chrissie's family.

Sarah has been noticing all evening that Tytus seems to be giving her a lot of lingering looks. Not that she minds them, she doesn't, but it's beginning to make her wonder what's going on in that head of his. Is the wedding getting to him, or could he possibly know about…?

"You seem a little extra doe-eyed tonight, Hayes," she whispers between photos. One hand on his lapel and the other on his back. "All this wedding stuff making you soft?"

"Trust me, Sarah, with you pressed up against me like this, I'm anything but soft." He kisses her under the ear lobe as the photographer's flash goes off.

When they finally take their seats at the large round table, they find themselves seated with Spencer and Traci. When Spencer suggests they head to the bar, Tytus turns to Sarah and asks what she would like.

"Just soda water with lime. Thanks." She watches something flash in his eyes and she knows this time she doesn't imagine it. He just nods before walking away, but there is a question left hanging in the air behind him.

Sarah and Traci get right into catching up as if they are old friends until the two men return to the table. When they both set non-alcoholic beverages in front of their dates, there is awkward silence all around. Sarah looks down at her drink and then at Traci's and attempts a smile.

"Okay, okay, twist my arm." Traci beams. "We're pregnant." She wraps her arm around Spencer's waist and leans into him. His smile is just as bright as he grins with pride.

Tytus glances at Sarah but quickly shifts his attention to the happy couple.

"Congratulations, Spencer. Traci." He gives a firm handshake to his friend and a smiling nod to his ecstatic wife.

Sarah is truly happy for them both but there is something else stirring in her gut as she smiles and congratulates them. Just as she's about to give what she feels is a needed explanation for her drink, she is saved by the booming voice of Bruno, the wedding planner, on the microphone. It's time for the new bride and groom's entrance.

Everyone seems to be having a great time. Tytus had given his speech and all the traditional 'first this' and 'first that' had gone off without a hitch. Chrissie and Nate seem to be having a wonderful time, and on the surface, everything is perfect.

Under the surface, Tytus can tell that something is off with Sarah. She is the quintessential Maid of Honor, and her face is constantly lit up with a smile. He knows she's been struggling with fatigue but this is more than that. There is something in her eyes. Ever since Traci had made her announcement, Sarah had been skittish. He's starting to wonder if maybe she already knows...one way or the other.

"Hey, can we talk?" He takes her hand and gestures toward the balcony with his head. "Some fresh air?"

"Fresh air sounds wonderful."

The couple walk out onto the small balcony adjacent to the banquet room.

Tytus feels his nerves start firing as he turns to Sarah and takes both her hands. His stomach is in knots and he just hopes his palms aren't sweaty.

"How are you feeling? It's been a long day for you and I'm sure you're exhausted."

"I'm running a little low on fuel, I won't deny that. But this night is so spectacular, I just keep finding another gear. I don't want it to end."

The way her eyes sparkle when she looks at him gives him just the boost of confidence he needs. He considers for a brief moment asking her, right there. *Are you pregnant, Sarah?*

"Really? To me, you seem like you're not here at all. Like you're...off somewhere else." He pauses when he feels her stiffen, just slightly. "You know you can talk to me, right? Tell me anything, anything at all."

"Tytus." She looks away. "I don't know what you're talking about." She tries to gently pull her hand from his but he only tightens his grip.

"Sarah." He waits for her to look at him, stroking the back of her hand with his thumb. She lifts her chin slowly and brings her eyes up to meet his. With his heart thumping, he takes the leap and lets the words he's guarded so carefully fall from his lips.

"I love you." Saying it out loud feels so good he does it again.

"I love you, Sarah."

He brings her into his arms and holds her tightly. She lays her head on his chest and neither says a word for several minutes.

Finally, Sarah pulls away from him enough to look him in the eyes. She wipes a stray tear from her face and takes in a shaky breath.

"Tytus." She swallows, trembling. "There's a chance I might be pregnant."

"I know." He smiles softly, placing his hand on her cheek.

"You do?" She gasps.

"I do."

14

I Need You to Know

"You want to get out of here?"

Sarah barely hears Tytus's question. She's completely lost in the moment. He loves her. He *knows*. With her cheek pressed firmly against his chest, she is focused on the beating of his heart and the warmth permeating through his dress shirt and into her face. She feels…*safe*.

"Sarah?" Tytus tries to gently pull back, but she wraps her arms tighter around him.

"Not yet," she replies softly.

She doesn't want this moment to end. This feeling. Since the night Sarah met Tytus Hayes, the balance she worked so hard to maintain had shifted. Her heart was exposed and she was constantly struggling with the fear of what-ifs. What if this was all a big mistake? What if he doesn't love me? What if he leaves? And most recently, what if I'm pregnant?

But he does love her and this is no mistake. He isn't leaving, whether she's pregnant or not.

She just wants, needs, to revel in it a bit longer. Reluctantly, she pulls back, creating just enough space between them to look into his deep gaze.

"I love you, too, Tytus." She reaches up and places her hand on his cheek. "So much."

Her voice cracks and Tytus's throat bobs before he leans in to place his lips on hers. Incredibly gentle and soft but with a hint of something else just below the surface. Desire.

"You want to get out of here?" he repeats his unanswered question from earlier.

"What about—"

"They'll understand."

Tytus takes her hand and leads her right back through the wedding reception and to the elevators.

"Where are we going?" Sarah questions him, genuinely confused.

"To our room."

"You got us a room at the Plaza?"

"How else could I make love to you all night and then treat you to breakfast in bed?"

The combination of humor and heat in his eyes makes Sarah swoon. How had she gotten so lucky?

Tytus swipes the key card and opens the door to the suite. He stops in the small entry hallway to hang his jacket while Sarah continues into the living room.

"Planning on a celebration?" she asks, eyeing the fancy bottle on ice and the tiered tray of chocolate-covered strawberries.

Tytus smirks to himself and turns. "I was." He walks into the room to join her. "I am." He notices the weary expression in her eyes.

"Take a closer look." He gestures with his chin toward the table.

Sarah reaches and pulls the bottle from the ice. Her eyes blur with moisture when she reads the label.

"Sparkling Cider," she says softly, bringing her eyes up to his smiling face.

Tytus takes it from her hand, opens it, and pours them both a glass. They sit down on the elegant sofa and face each other. He hands her a flute and raises his while his heart pounds so loudly in his chest he's convinced she can hear it. He's not nervous, not really. He's anxious. In the best possible way.

"A toast." His voice is deep and full of emotion.

The vulnerability in her eyes forces him to swallow. Her gaze locked on his, so full of trust, he feels moved in a way that is brand new. She extends her glass toward him, her hand trembling slightly.

"To love," he begins but doesn't move. "To our future. Together."

Tytus clinks his glass to Sarah's and they each take a sip, their eyes never wavering from one another. He reaches for her cider and places it gently on the table next to his own. He extends his hand and she reaches for it without another word between them.

This time, she is the one who leads, walking Tytus from the living room to the bedroom with a seductive look back over her shoulder.

By the time they stand at the foot of the bed, his breathing is short and choppy. He places his hands on Sarah's hips and begins kissing her shoulders and neck. With each touch of his lips and tongue to her flawless skin, his groin pulsates and his pants grow tighter. But it's when she moans his name and her legs buckle, requiring him to hold her weight and steady her, that his self-control nearly snaps.

Tytus turns her away from him and runs his hands slowly from her hips up her ribcage and then slides them around to grip her breasts. Sarah pushes back into him, her ass pressing against his straining cock, and she lays her head back against his shoulder.

"Do you know what you do to me?" he groans into her throat. "When you stepped out of that bridal room today, you took my breath away." He reaches a hand between their bodies and lowers the zipper of her dress, one torturous inch at a time.

He feels her body shudder from the cool air, and he slips his warm hands inside the opening of her dress. Gliding them across the small of her back and then around to her abdomen, he transfers his body heat to her, his warm breath on her neck, his center pressed against her backside.

Tytus glides his fingers up to her shoulders and slips the straps of her dress over them. The gown falls to the floor gracefully, revealing her gorgeous figure and drawing all the air from his lungs.

Sarah turns to face him, eyes dark with desire and need. Her body covered only in the most intimate place by a thin layer of dark red lace. It's her turn to undress him now. And she does so with painstaking care and patience.

"What I do to *you*?" She finally responds to his long-forgotten question with one of her own.

The tone and timbre of her voice is so sexy, Tytus struggles to swallow the thickness in his throat.

"What about what you do to me?" She takes his hand and drags it lightly against the thin strip of lace between her legs. The heat and moisture there threaten his resolve as he clenches the muscles in his groin to clamp down the desire. A moan rumbles from the back of Tytus's throat as a seductive smirk spreads on Sarah's face.

His eyes remain locked on hers while she unbuttons his shirt and peels it from his muscular body. He leans in for a deep and passionate kiss as her hands finally meet the bare skin of his chest. Gripping his bulging pecs, Sarah tilts her head slightly allowing him access to slide his tongue deeper into her mouth. Backing her up slowly toward the bed, his kiss is unceasing and relentless. His hands completely envelop her tight ass, eliciting a whimper from her that makes him weak.

Seemingly determined to finish the job she'd started, Sarah tears her mouth from his and pushes her hands lightly against his sculpted chest. He grunts in disapproval as he lowers his eyebrows into a scowl of sorts, but she pays him no mind. Her slender fingers unclasp his pants swiftly and she lets them fall to the floor, quickly gripping the protruding bulge trapped in his tight black underwear.

He strains against her hand, arching his back slightly and flexing his core. She does things to him no other woman has ever done. She makes him feel things in ways he's never felt, in places he didn't even know existed. He grabs her wrist in a quick and possessive move. The look in his eyes shifts from dark to tender.

"I need you to know."

His words cut through the fog of need and hunger they are so caught up in. Sarah tilts her head as her eyes meet his.

"I need you to know," he repeats. "What I feel for you..." Tytus hesitates, words have never been his strong suit. "It's more than just this." He looks down at their nearly naked bodies. Then he lays her hand on his chest to feel his pounding heart. "It's this."

Sarah's eyes fill but she doesn't respond.

"You mean everything to me, Sarah. I never thought I was capable of this kind of love."

Before she has a chance to reply, to breathe even, he's lifting her off the ground and placing her under him on the bed. Literally, sweeping her off her feet.

Tytus hovers over her and takes her in. His eyes rake over her body like they had this afternoon. He runs his hand from her hip bone up along her side, his fingers slide around to the outside of her breast and his thumb sits just underneath the front of the perfect mound. He pushes upward, squeezing her gently as she moans and arches her back.

Heat courses through him, blood surging through every vein in his body. An unbearable struggle between giving in and holding back threatens to break him. He grapples for the last ounce of his control as he opens his mouth and sucks softly on her supple breast.

"Tytus..." Sarah moans as she drags her nails from his shoulders to his lower back.

He needs her just as desperately as she needs him, so he pulls his mouth from her chest and sits up on his knees between her legs. Tytus slides his fingers under the thin straps of her thong and pulls them down, revealing a view of her that has quickly become his favorite. His tongue darts out to lick his lips as even from this vantage point he can see how wet she is for him.

He starts to lower his face toward her when Sarah reaches for his shoulder and stops him. When he looks up along her naked body to her eyes, she simply shakes her head once and curls her finger, signaling him to what she really wants.

Tytus doesn't hesitate. His boxer briefs are discarded in a heartbeat and he climbs over her with every muscle in his body flexed, every nerve on edge.

Their eyes are locked, and they are both completely exposed, open, and vulnerable in ways neither thought was possible. And as Tytus enters her, deep and full, their love for each other becomes complete. With every thrust and every moan, they fall deeper and deeper into one another and into a life that will never be the same.

Sarah slips from the bed around 3:00 a.m. and wraps the loose sheet around her. She's surprised her legs still function after the way she, well more like Tytus, pushed them far beyond their expected limits. Repeatedly. They're sore but they do function.

She walks to the vast window and carefully pulls the drapes apart, not wanting to allow too much additional light into the room but enough to see the view of the city.

Tytus had surprised her last night. Shocked is more accurate, really. She had been fairly confident that he loved her. She had seen it in his eyes, felt it in his kiss. But just because a man is in love, doesn't mean he understands how to share that love, to cultivate it into something real and lasting. She knows now that that is what she had been most afraid of. That despite loving him, and regardless of whether he loved her, they wouldn't be able to make it work. With his career, and hers. His baggage. Her past. She had been afraid to really let go, for fear that life would somehow get in the way. And then this whole fatigue thing started…and when the doctor said the word "pregnant" her heart stopped. *There it is,* she'd thought. The reason they wouldn't last. It had terrified her.

She looks out at the brilliantly lit cityscape and lets her mind venture to those dark corners she usually avoids. She isn't opposed to having children. In fact, as a young girl, she often daydreamed about a future when she'd have a home with a yard, a dog, and a couple of rugrats running around with dirt on their faces. Although her childhood had been far from perfect, her relationship with her mom had been special, and she thought she'd be pretty good at it.

But it was just that. A dream. A someday.

The reality of having a baby now is overwhelming. Although the look in Tytus's eyes last night when he told her knew, had eased her mind and heart exponentially. Knowing that he'll be there for her, for them, sheds a different light on the concept.

She makes her way back to the bed and carefully lies down next to Tytus, the dim light from the window casting a glow over his face. She smiles to herself as her mind slips to the image of a little boy running around with his gorgeous smile, or a little girl looking up at her with his deep brown eyes.

She settles her head onto the pillow but keeps her gaze on Tytus's face.

A baby was not part of her immediate plan. She's not sure she's ready to be a mom, and she has no clue how a change like that would impact her career just as it's really taking off. But one thing she does know is that someday she wants a family with this man who has stolen her heart. As her eyes grow heavy, she drifts off to sleep and dreams of Tytus playing catch with their child in that yard she had pictured all those years ago.

Tytus wakes in the morning to the sound of running water. It takes him a minute or two to get his bearings and put together that Sarah is in the shower. He wastes no time throwing the covers off and joining her. He has the most innocent of intentions. Just to be close to her, to wash each other's bodies, because as he told her, it's not all about the sex. But you know what they say about a road paved with good intentions.

By the time they are both *finished* and wrapped snugly in their plush robes, room service knocks lightly on the door. Tytus rolls the table into the bedroom and the two sit in bed and devour the eggs, French toast, and fresh berries. The bubble they find themselves in feels incredible and neither one of them wants to say or do anything to burst it. But as the minutes tick by, Tytus knows the upcoming conversation is inevitable.

It had occurred to him at some point during the night that he would be leaving Monday morning for one of the longest and farthest road trips of the season. Thousands of miles and a three-hour time difference would soon be separating the two of them and for the first time he could remember, he wished he could skip the trip.

"So," he finally starts, "I know we both have jam-packed schedules today, and tomorrow the team heads to California so—"

"California." Sarah doesn't hide the shock, or disappointment, in her tone.

Tytus flinches slightly at her outburst. She has his schedule, he had assumed she knew.

"I know." His tone is soft and his eyes are full of regret. "The timing couldn't be worse."

Sarah gets up from the bed and starts picking things up and putting them down again, clearly trying to get her emotions in check. Neither one of them had spoken a word about the potential pregnancy since the balcony last night but it's clearly the elephant in the room right now.

"I hate that I can't come with you to the doctor tomorrow, Sarah. Our flight is at 10:00."

She just nods at him and he can see the tears filling her eyes from across the room.

Tytus scrambles off the bed and goes right to her, taking her hands in his.

"Hey, you okay?" He bends his knees to bring his eyes down to where she's casting her gaze at nothing in particular. When she just nods again, he wraps her into a tight embrace.

Fuck! He just isn't good at this kind of thing. He wants more than anything to say all the right things and do all the right things, but he doesn't know how to fix this.

"I'm so sorry." He guides Sarah over to the bench at the end of the oversized bed and they sit down next to each other.

"We could take a test tonight?" He lifts her chin. "After work? Like one of those home tests?"

When she just shakes her head and closes her eyes, Tytus shuts his eyes tightly as well. His heart is breaking at the deflated look on her face.

"Sarah, talk to me."

Sarah inhales a long and shaky breath before finally responding.

"You don't need to be sorry, Tytus." She looks back up at him. "This is your job and I knew that when we started this relationship. It's just that I've been reeling the past couple days and last night, when you said you knew and that we'd go through this together, one way or the other," she stops to wipe a tear just as it leaves her eye, "it just meant so much to me." Her voice betrays her as it cracks with emotion.

"But we are going to get through this together. I'm right here. I may be leaving tomorrow, Sarah. And I may not be at that appointment, but I'm still here." Tytus takes their intertwined hands and places them on Sarah's chest. "And whatever the result, I'm ready." He pauses and takes a deep breath of his own. "I love you, Sarah."

She smiles and her eyes soften.

"I know, Tytus. I know you do." She lays her head on his chest and he pulls her closer. "I don't want to take a home test." She pulls back slightly to look at him. "My mom had a false positive test when I was about 6, and I've never forgotten it. She was so excited, and it just crushed her when she found out."

Tytus nods. *Is that what you want? The test to be positive?* He's so close to letting the words tumble out. He had almost asked her last night. After they had made love and she was nestled into the crook of his arm. He had almost asked.

The couple just sits quietly for several minutes. Starting tomorrow they won't be able to hold each other like this for almost two full weeks.

"I'll be fine going to the doctor on my own." Sarah sighs. "It's what I had planned on since Friday."

Tytus clenches his jaw and fights the stinging in his eyes by biting the inside of his cheek.

"I'll call you the minute we land."

After a few more minutes in each other's arms, they both get up and prepare for the busy day ahead.

Sarah powers through the day with a decent amount of energy and manages to successfully keep her mind on being Roxie Hart. But around 8:00 p.m., an hour into the second show, she hits a wall. Physical exhaustion leads to emotional exhaustion in about ten seconds flat and Sarah finds herself blotting her eyes between scenes. Suddenly the idea that her entire life may change tomorrow feels just a tad overwhelming.

"Sarah, are you okay?" Sebastian asks from the doorway of her dressing room. When she turns to face him he sees the tears. "Oh my God." He rushes straight to her side. "What is it? Is it that asshole Tytus Hayes?"

Sarah literally chokes at Sebastian's description of Tytus.

"Sebastian. Tytus is not an asshole." She shakes her head with a small laugh. Already feeling a little better. "And no, it's not him." She lays a hand on her concerned friend's shoulder. "I'm just not feeling too great is all."

"Do you need a doctor or something?"

"I'm fine, Sebastian. Really."

Sarah manages to get through the night without any more nervous breakdowns and by the time she gets out of the theater, she's made up her mind to head straight to Tytus's. He had been so amazing last night, and again this morning, and knowing that he is leaving tomorrow, she wants to cherish every minute she can with him. He had given her a key and she planned to use it. According to the app on her phone, the game was in the 8th inning so she would surely beat him there.

It's a little over an hour later when she hears his keys in the door. She had put on a t-shirt and a pair of his boxers, rolled them up a few times, and planted herself under a blanket on his sofa. A fire burning warmly in the fireplace.

He walks in looking at his phone, probably wondering why she isn't taking his calls when he looks up and spots her.

As the grin spreads slowly across his face, wrinkles gather at his eyes.

"Hey."

"Hey," she whispers.

"I guess that answers the question of why you're not picking up my calls."

Tytus walks over and holds out his hand. When she takes it, he pulls her up into a deep kiss. Like there is nothing he wants more in the entire world than her. It makes her weak.

"I guess it does," she answers hoarsely when he finally removes his tongue from her mouth.

Tytus walks over to pour himself a drink but stops before reaching for the decanter.

"You can have a drink, Tytus. It's okay, you know." She smiles at his back but he doesn't turn right away.

"Don't need one," he says with his back to her. He turns around then with a smirk and a mischievous glint in his eye. "I have good news." He walks back over to her and places his hands on her hips.

"You won?" She smiles, knowing full well that they did. She lets her hand squeeze lightly on his chiseled chest, causing a coiling in her abdomen.

"I got a later flight."

She doesn't speak. She can't. She just lets her heart fill, overcome yet again, with the intensity of her love for this man. Every hurdle, every heartache, every hard lesson she has learned has brought her to this place. To this moment in time. To this man who is everything she never thought possible.

She presses her face into the muscles she was admiring just moments ago and sobs. He doesn't question her or ask if she's okay. He just lets her get it all out as he caresses her back and kisses the top of her head.

They don't talk much the following morning before the appointment. Tytus considers starting a conversation about the potential results of her tests multiple times, but he never gets the words out. Probably because he's not even sure how he feels about it.

He had thought about being a father, of course. He admitted as much in therapy. As a kid, and a young man, he had pictured himself with a family someday. Coaching Little League or Girl's Fastpitch. But when he caught Judy cheating and his parent's marriage fell apart, he pushed all that from his mind. Not just having kids but ever getting married. It was easier to deal with the pain and the betrayal if he convinced himself that it had never been real in the first place. That there was no such thing as true love and that marriage was nothing more than a contract negotiation, one that could easily be deemed null and void.

But when Spencer married Traci he saw the love they shared. It was undeniable. And then it was Nate and Chrissie. Again, love that couldn't be explained away. And when he met Sarah, all those old wounds were exposed, open. And rather than trying to hide them, avoid them, deny them, he had embraced them. She made him want to be better, to be more.

Mending his relationship with his mom had been possibly the most critical step. So when Ruzzoli asked if he wanted a family, a future with Sarah, he had been flooded with emotion. The answer was a resounding yes.

As he pulls his sweater over his dress shirt and studies his reflection in the mirror, he takes in a slow and steady breath.

A baby. Right now? At this point in his career? This early in their relationship?

It isn't ideal, that goes without saying. It isn't the way he'd have planned it, and if you'd asked about it a year ago, shit, a couple months ago, it would have scared him to death. But right now, today, he knows he can handle anything with Sarah by his side. And if he really digs deep into his heart, there is a small part of him that wants that test to be positive.

When they arrive at the doctor's office, Sarah's stomach is in knots. She couldn't be more grateful for all of Tytus's love and support. It's more than she ever expected and far more than she's ever had before. But despite that, and despite his firm grasp of her hand, she's terrified.

She believes with her whole heart that Tytus is ready for the results one way or the other, and maybe that's why she feels so panicky. She doesn't feel ready. Not at all.

Over the past few days, she had run the entire gamut of emotions multiple times. And she is exhausted. Drained emotionally and physically. Even though she had dipped her toe in the waters of potential motherhood, she just can't seem to let the idea take hold.

They are checked in and brought into a room almost immediately. The whispers and stares of the office staff don't go unnoticed by Sarah. It is clear that the girls recognize Tytus. If he notices their reactions, he doesn't let on.

It only makes Sarah feel less secure.

They are in the room for only a few minutes before the door opens.

"Ms. Dalton." The doctor enters the room with her head in a file. When she looks up to find two of them in the room the surprise that flashes across her face is undeniable.

"This is Tytus Hayes, Doctor Elam, my boyfriend."

A look of recognition passes over the doctor's face when her eyes focus on Tytus, but she plays it off.

"It's nice to meet you, Mr. Hayes." She smiles softly at him before taking her seat.

Sarah feels a sense of awkwardness in the air. As though the doctor wasn't expecting her to have company and it's thrown her off her game. The idea of what that implies fills Sarah with dread.

"I'm assuming that since you brought him with you, you are comfortable with me sharing the results of your exam with both of you?"

"I am," Sarah replies, squeezing Tytus's hand.

"Okay, then I will get right to it." Doctor Elam looks from Sarah to Tytus, and back to Sarah. "The reason you have been suffering from fatigue and headaches is a deficiency of iron in your blood." The doctor takes a report from the file and hands it to Sarah. "You're anemic, Ms. Dalton."

Sarah takes the paper from the doctor and stares blankly at it while the doctor continues talking. She hears something about red blood cells and iron supplements but none of it is really registering.

"Ms. Dalton? Do you understand? Your case is fairly mild, and controllable, but it shouldn't be taken lightly."

"You're saying she needs more rest? And a change in her diet?" Tytus speaks up while Sarah just blinks at the report in her hand.

"Yes, exactly. And iron supplements." The doctor lays her hand on Sarah's knee. "Anemia is very common in women and as long as you make the needed adjustments, you should be able to avoid more invasive treatments."

"Invasive?" Tytus responds with a touch of alarm in his tone.

"In more severe cases, iron infusions and even blood transfusions may be required."

"So, I'm not pregnant?" Sarah blurts it out. She hadn't intended to say it but it happened anyway.

Both Tytus and the doctor turn their attention to her. Concern and surprise on their faces.

"No, Ms. Dalton. You are not pregnant."

Sensing the couple might need a moment of privacy, the doctor gets up and makes an excuse about getting Sarah some additional information. Information Sarah is certain is already in the file she's holding.

The doctor walks out and leaves the two of them alone.

Tytus turns to Sarah but doesn't say anything. He just takes her in. Her shoulders are slumped, her eyes cast at the floor, her usual aura replaced with something darker.

"Hey?" He uses their coined greeting since he's at a loss for anything better. When she doesn't respond he gets down on his knee in front of her. "Sarah?"

She looks at him as if she's only just realized he's there.

"Sorry." She snaps a smile on her face. "What a relief, right?"

"A relief?" Tytus may not be the best at reading people but the emotion he had read all over her was not relief. He tilts his head and raises his right brow. "You're relieved?"

Sarah smiles softly but it doesn't reach her eyes.

"Of course. Aren't you? I'm not surprised about the anemia, actually. My mom has struggled with it all her life. I should have known that's what it was."

Tytus hears the words coming from her mouth but they are in stark contrast to what he sees in her eyes and what he had perceived from her initial reaction to the doctor's news.

"Sarah." He takes her hands in his and looks up at her, trying to break through the barrier he knows she put up between them. "It's understandable if you feel a little, I don't know...disappointed."

Sarah pulls her hands away and scoffs. A little overdramatically if you ask him.

"Disappointed? That I'm not pregnant?" She looks over his shoulder and around the room. Anywhere but in his eyes. "That I don't have to put my career on hold for a baby I hadn't planned on? Tytus, we've only been dating a few months. This is a blessing. Not something to be disappointed about."

He knows, of course, that what she is saying makes perfect sense. So why does it cut deep? He gets up from his knee and sits back down in the chair next to her. His stomach is in knots, but he can't tell if it's because he thinks Sarah isn't being honest with him, or because he's the one that's disappointed.

There is a knock on the door and Doctor Elam re-enters the room.

"Here is some information for you to review about diet, rest, and the supplements I'd like you to start on right away." She hands the paperwork to Sarah who now has a smile plastered on her face that isn't fooling anyone. "I'd like to see you back in four weeks."

Sarah nods and gets up from her chair.

"Thank you, Doctor."

Tytus shares an awkward glance with the doctor when Sarah walks out. They both seem to know exactly what the other is thinking. He nods and follows Sarah.

Miles is waiting for them at the curb and Sarah climbs in before Tytus has a chance to open her door. He knows she is hurting but he's at a loss for how to help. They are headed straight to the airport and he doesn't have much time to figure it out.

They ride in silence for a few minutes before he glances at her from the corner of his eye. She appears to be looking over the paperwork from the doctor.

"What's it say?"

"Huh?" she mumbles without looking up.

"The paperwork. What does it say?"

"Oh." She drops the papers into her lap and looks out the window of the Lexus. "Just what the doctor said. Low iron counts."

"And the treatment?"

"Tytus, you were in the room. You heard what she said." Her voice isn't harsh exactly but there is a hint of irritation. It reminds him of the way he used to speak to his mother.

He takes a chance and reaches over to stroke her cheek lightly with the back of his hand. The last thing he wants is a fight.

She stiffens at first but when she turns to him, her eyes are soft.

"I'm sorry, Tytus. You didn't deserve that." A tear leaks from her eye and she lets it fall.

"Sarah—"

"I'm just concerned about work." She turns back to the window.

Deflecting. Again. He's no expert, but he's pretty sure that's what they call it. He used to be a pro at it.

"My schedule is hectic," she continues before he refutes her. "Long hours and demanding work. It's what I do. Who I am." She shakes her head and looks back at him. "I don't know how to get more rest."

"Sarah," he says quietly. His hand on her shoulder and toying with her earlobe. "You can talk to me, you know? That wasn't the only thing the doctor said in there."

She takes his hand from her ear and squeezes it tightly in hers. "Tytus, I already told you, I'm relieved that I'm not pregnant, and you can stop pretending that wasn't exactly the news you were hoping for."

She lets go of his hand and turns away from him.

Her words sting. He clenches his jaw and looks out his own window. His eyes burn at her implication. He's the one pretending? *Bullshit*. He balls his fists. Old habits die hard and Tytus has always been one to lash out when he's put on the defensive. *The best defense is a good offense*, his high school basketball coach always said. And that advice applies to more than just sports.

A part of him had been hoping Sarah was pregnant. That they were pregnant. And hearing the news they weren't had made him flinch. He knows she felt the same way. What he doesn't get is why she is so afraid to just admit it. And then to accuse him of hoping for it?

He doesn't lash out. The therapy and breathing exercises he had learned after his panic attack are put to good use. He closes his eyes instead and calms himself down.

They arrive at the airport a short time later and they both get out of the car. She can't go in with him, so they will have to say their goodbyes on the crowded sidewalk. He decides the best thing to do for now is to let it go.

He grabs his bag from the trunk and walks over to her. Setting it on the ground, he wraps her in a hug. Not sure he can look her in the eye without giving too much away, he kisses the top of her head and speaks quietly just above her ear.

"I love you. I wish I didn't have to go."

She pulls him a little tighter and he hears a quiet sob escape her throat.

"I love you too, Tytus," she mumbles into his chest and climbs back into the Lexus without another word or a kiss goodbye.

15

Roots

Sarah is snuggled in bed under her down comforter with a hot cup of coffee. It's Wednesday, her day off, and she has never needed one more. It's been about forty-eight hours since she and Tytus left the doctor's office and he boarded a flight to California. She's been in a funk ever since.

She's pushing him away. She knows it. He knows it. She is doing the exact thing to him that she had cursed him for just weeks ago. Well, not the exact same, she rationalizes. Tytus knew what his issue was and he chose to keep it from her. Sarah has no idea what's wrong with her. Not really. So how can she share it with him?

She's started her supplements and is working on including foods high in iron—white beans, green vegetables, and dark chocolate, which she was happy to see on the list from the doctor. Physically, she feels a little better, but she just can't clear this fog surrounding her. She feels like the lady in the depression commercials who has a dark cloud following her around everywhere she goes. She can't make sense of it.

She hadn't wanted to be pregnant. The idea had scared the shit out of her. Her career is starting to take off, and despite her and Tytus being in a good place, the relationship is still brand new. A baby right now would have been really difficult. So why is she so damn sad?

When her phone buzzes on her lap she almost spills her coffee on the white duvet. It's a text from a number she doesn't recognize.

Hi Sarah, this is Tytus Hayes Sr. I got your number from TJ. I hope that's okay.
I know he's on the road but I'm filling in with that band in the city tonight,
and I thought you might like to come. Bring a friend?
Your show is dark on Wednesdays, right? I'd love to see you.

Sarah sets the phone down on her lap. Her mouth open and her hand on her chest. Her eyes fill with tears she can't explain. Par for the course these days. She's touched, she is. She wonders whose idea this had been, her Tytus or Tytus Sr.'s, but it really doesn't matter. Either way, it's sweet and thoughtful, and she appreciates it.

Of course, it's okay. What a nice surprise to hear from you.
I'd love to come. What time?

Excellent! We go on at 8:00, but if you can come early, I'd love to buy you a drink.

Sarah sighs deeply. Suddenly, she is reminded of the fact that she can drink again without concern. And she wonders if Tytus Sr. is aware of what happened.

It's a date. I'll see you at 7:00.

She hits send before she changes her mind.

Sarah sighs as she sips on her coffee. Hearing from his dad makes her miss Tytus even more. It's 11:00 a.m. in New York, which makes it 8:00 a.m. in Los Angeles. She thinks about calling Tytus but opts for a text instead.

Morning. Are you up?

She stares at the screen, waiting to see the dots pop up to indicate he's responding, when for the second time this morning she's startled as her phone starts ringing instead.

"Hey," she says softly into the phone.

"Hey." His voice has a gravel to it like he's not fully awake.

"I woke you."

"No. No, I was up."

"I just heard from your dad. You know anything about that?" There is a hint of playfulness in her tone as she smirks into the phone. It feels good to smile.

"Well, I know he texted me last night and asked for your number. And like an idiot, I sent it before asking why he needed it. Then when I did ask, he told me it was none of my damn business. Nate would be so disappointed in my tactics."

He chuckles softly and Sarah gets a vivid image of his smile. It's like a knife in the gut. She misses him so much but instead of saying so, she responds with wit.

"Good thing you chose baseball over the law, Hayes. You'd make a shitty lawyer."

"You know what, you did wake me. I'm going back to sleep."

She knows he's just teasing her back and it relaxes her a bit.

"He invited me to see him play tonight." She chews on the inside of her cheek. "I said I'd come."

Tytus is quiet on the other end of the line and it makes her nervous.

"Good," he finally says. There is a thickness in his voice that makes her breath hitch.

Sarah hears a knock on her door and remembers her plans with Chrissie.

"Chrissie's at the door. I promised her some girl time today. A chick flick and lunch in our PJ's."

"I never thought these words would leave my mouth but right this minute, I wish I was Chrissie."

She feels her stomach clench. She knows what he means, but rather than say something comforting, she makes a crack about what that would mean for Nate and Tytus, and she agrees to call him after his dad's gig.

When the team bus pulls into Chavez Ravine a few hours later, Tytus actually has butterflies in his stomach. There aren't many things at this point in his career that can make him feel like a young starry-eyed boy, but he is hit with that exact notion as he walks out of the tunnel and onto the pristine grass of Dodger Stadium. Tytus hadn't been in this historic place in nearly 20 years, but he had never forgotten the one time his father had brought him here.

Tytus Sr. was born in 1959 in Brooklyn, and his father was a die-hard Dodgers fan. When the team had decided to move to Los Angeles in 1957 it had broken Tytus's grandfather's heart. But he stayed true to his favorite team and he saved up for years to take Tytus Sr. to Los Angeles as a young boy to see the team play. And Tytus Sr. had done the same for Tytus and his siblings. They weren't Dodgers fans now, not really, his dad and sister loved the Sox, and Travis and Tytus favored the Yankees. Probably because they had dominated through much of their childhood. But there is something special about this place, and Tytus feels it in his bones.

A heaviness settles over him as he takes in the field and comes to terms with the fact that he won't be pitching here tonight. The chance that another opportunity to do so will come in his career is slim. With a heavy sigh, he walks back through the underground tunnel to the clubhouse.

Tytus spends the next few hours doing all his physical therapy and treatment when Spencer walks up to where he is stretching out.

"Doc wants to see you."

"Doc? Why, what's up?"

"He didn't say." There is a glint of something in Spencer's eye but he walks away before Tytus can get a good read.

He gets up from the training table and walks into the small office in the hall.

"Doc?" He knocks on the open door. "Kline said you wanted to see me."

"Tytus, yes. Come in, please. Have a seat."

Tytus flashes back to the scolding he received from this man a couple of weeks ago and he feels like a kid for the second time today.

"Something wrong? My new MRI results?" Tytus wipes his suddenly sweating hands on his knees.

Dr. Workman doesn't respond right away. He just looks back and forth between the files in his hand and his computer screen while he moves his mouse around.

"It is about your MRI, yes." Workman takes off his glasses and sits back in his chair, his eyes moving from the computer monitor to Tytus. "Have you been doing all the treatment I prescribed?" he continues. The expression on his face is the same stoic one that seems to be permanently affixed there.

"Of course." Tytus shifts in his seat. He had been, of course. That and then some.

"Well, it's paid off. Your shoulder is improving faster than I expected." The news is good, great even, but you'd never know it from the doctor's face. "I hadn't expected to clear you from throwing until we returned home, but if you'd like to get out there today for some light catch, I think you're ready."

And there it is. Almost undetectable, a slight twitch to the corner of his mouth, and what Tytus could swear is a wink. Or maybe the man just blinks with one eye at a time.

"You serious, Doc? Here? Today?" Tytus sits up and scoots to the edge of his seat. It's not pitching off the mound but it's enough. So much more than he expected.

Dr. Workman responds with a nod and Tytus is out of there in a flash.

A half-hour later he's back on the perfectly trimmed grass with Spencer. They start by tossing the ball from about 15-20 feet. Tytus sees that same smirk on his catcher's face that he saw earlier.

"You knew," Tytus states. He doesn't phrase it as a question.

"Knew?" Spencer shakes his head. "I orchestrated it."

"You what now?" Tytus holds the ball and tilts his head. His eyebrow raised in suspicion.

"Look. I asked Doc when you'd be cleared to throw. He said probably in a couple days when we get up to San Fran. I simply suggested maybe he clear you today. Here." Spencer gestures to their surroundings.

Tytus's lips pull together tightly as he realizes what Spencer is saying. He feels a lump form in his throat as he nods to him with his jaw clenched tightly. He throws the ball back to his friend, more grateful for this gift than he knows how to express.

The two men throw for about another twenty minutes. Carefully stretching the distance as they go. Tytus's shoulder feels great, and so does he.

Things with Sarah may be a little tough right now, but he's not afraid of a little hard work. He knows what they have is real and just like he's committed to doing what it takes to get back on that mound, he's committed to Sarah and the future with her he knows he wants.

⚾

Sarah walks into Arthur's Tavern and scans the place for Tytus Sr. She had considered asking Chrissie to join her, but for some reason, she'd decided to come alone.

"What's a gorgeous lady like you doing in a shit hole like this?"

She knows it's Tytus Sr. before she even turns around.

"I happen to know a musician who plays here." She faces him with a grin. "And this shit-hole has character, in spades."

"Gorgeous and great taste." Tytus Sr. kisses Sarah on the cheek and pulls her into a warm hug.

She follows him to the same booth she had sat with Tytus and wonders if it's reserved just for Hayes.

"Hungry?" Tytus Sr. asks. "The food's not great, but I know a thing or two on the menu that won't kill you."

"Well, as tempting as that sounds, I ate before I came." Sarah laughs. "But I could use a stiff drink."

Tytus Sr. nods his approval when Sarah orders a Johnnie Walker Blue Label, and he signals the waitress to bring him the same.

The two small-talk for a bit while they let the first few sips of liquor enter their system.

"So, why the stiff drink? My son driving you crazy?"

"What?" Sarah is thrown off by the accusation, even though she knows he's joking. "No. Quite the contrary, actually." She sips on her scotch and welcomes the burn it brings. "I think I'm the one doing the driving."

They keep the conversation going with ease, and by the time Sarah is halfway through her second scotch, she's basically told Tytus Sr. the whole story. At some point during her ramblings, when she sees the softness in his eyes and hears the tenderness in his tone, she acknowledges that this is why she had come alone. Some small part of her knew that he'd invited her because he had some clue what she and Tytus had been through, and he was offering her a safe place to talk. Maybe it isn't the same as talking directly to Tytus but it's the next closest thing.

"I just feel empty inside. Like something is missing now. Which is completely absurd, because it was never there to start with." Sarah wipes at her eye as another tear escapes. "I didn't even want to be pregnant. I mean, not now. But then once the seed was planted, so to speak," she pauses, "the idea took root and I guess I started to warm up to it." She inhales and then lets the shaky breath out slowly. "Tytus must think I'm bat shit crazy."

"Can I tell you a secret?" Tytus Sr. is still nursing his first scotch. Probably because he has to perform in a few minutes. "It's not a secret from Tytus, he knows, but it's a family secret of sorts. And one he rarely talks about."

"I wouldn't want to betray his trust," Sarah says honestly, even though he's piqued her interest.

"Oh, you wouldn't be. It's not his secret to tell. It's mine. Well, mine and Judy's."

Sarah looks into Tytus Sr.'s eyes and nods before taking another drink and then watching the liquid swirl in her glass.

"After we had Tytus and Travis, Judy miscarried."

Sarah looks up from her drink to meet Tytus Sr.'s eyes.

"Judy was devastated. We all were. But it took a piece of her, you know?"

Sarah nods as her eyes fill again.

"Travis was too young to understand, but Tytus was six, and even though he hadn't been very attached to the idea of another baby in the house, he hated to see his mother cry. He didn't really understand what had happened, but he knew his mommy was sad all the time." Tytus Sr. sips on his scotch and doesn't speak for a minute or two. "The thing is, Sarah. Everyone understood Judy's pain and all of our friends and family supported her and helped her to heal. First and foremost, me."

Tytus Sr. sets his glass on the table and takes Sarah's hand in his.

"But she wasn't the only one who'd lost a child." His eyes well up and Sarah can see that even after all these years there is still pain.

"Of course not." Sarah lays her other hand on top of the one she's holding. "So did you."

A soft smile spreads across his face as he nods at her in acknowledgment.

"And you aren't the only one whose seed planted roots." He tilts his head and looks at her knowingly. Then he brings her hand to his lips, kisses it softly, and heads to the stage, leaving Sarah wide-eyed and speechless.

When Sarah hears her phone ringing at 2:00 a.m., she reaches her hand through the dark to pull it from her nightstand. She knows it's Tytus. She had texted him to call when he got to the hotel, regardless of the time.

"Tytus?" Her groggy voice did not hide the fact that he'd woken her.

"Sorry, Sarah. You said to call, right?" he says softly and apologetically.

"Yes, Tytus. Yes." She drags her hand over her face and contemplates turning on a light but decides against it.

"How was the game?" she asks, sounding only slightly more awake.

"Ugh. Don't ask."

She hears him rustling around, most likely getting comfortable.

"How was my dad's gig?"

She can hear the smile in his voice through the phone and it makes her break out into one as well.

"Mind-blowing. I just can't get over how talented those men are. They just completely transport me to another place and time." She sips on the water on her nightstand. "The three glasses of Scotch might have helped with that, too." She giggles, sounding more like herself.

Tytus laughs out loud. "What a lush," he teases. "Was that my dad's fault or your own?"

"Maybe a little of both. But he made sure I got home okay. Those Hayes men are real gentlemen, you know?"

"I do." He pauses. "Did you bring Chrissie along?"

Sarah scoots back to a more upright position. She promised herself she wouldn't chicken out. This conversation isn't going to be a walk in the park but he deserves honesty. They both do.

"I went alone, actually. I felt like I wanted to just enjoy the jazz without conversation. A little, me time, I guess."

"I get it, trust me. I have always enjoyed watching my dad play on my own. In fact, I used to hang out in his recording studio when I was a kid. Sometimes I just closed my eyes and listened."

He clears his throat and she wonders if he's closing his eyes now. Picturing it.

"Did the two of you get to talk much, before or after the set?" he continues.

Tytus's question is the perfect segue to what she needs to say. If she doesn't do it right this minute, she may never get it out. She lets the words start to roll off her tongue. Like a snowball picking up downhill momentum.

"We did talk, quite a bit actually." She takes a deep breath. "Your father is a very wise man, Tytus."

"Oh, God. I don't think I like the sound of that," he scoffs.

"Tytus..." Her voice soft but confident. "I'm so sorry."

She hears his breath hitch on the other end of the line. She'd caught him off guard. She feels the tension from the past few days settle over them like a fog rolling in over the coastline.

"Sarah—"

"I'm sorry that I shut you out," she blurts out. Roll, snowball, roll. "At the doctor's, at the airport, on the phone after you arrived in L.A." Her eyes well up and she lets it all just pour out of her. He doesn't interrupt this time. Her hands are shaking but she needs to finish this.

"Can I ask you something?" Her voice cracks.

"Anything." Tytus's own voice has grown thick.

"Did...did you want the test to be positive? Did you want us to be pregnant?"

The silence that follows is deafening. Sarah's heart is pounding so aggressively, she wonders if this is how Tytus felt before his panic attack. Every second that passes waiting for his answer feels like an eternity. She hears his breathing and grips her sheets, bracing herself.

"I think a part of me did." The crack in his voice gives away the truth of it.

Sarah lets her face drop into her hands as she cries softly. She is incredibly grateful that he can't see her right now. Or more accurately, that she can't see him. She's not sure she could bear it.

"I'm so sorry, Tytus." She leans her head back against the wall. "I was so caught up in trying to understand what I was feeling, I never thought about what you might be feeling. It was just less painful to believe you were relieved. Happy, even."

Tytus doesn't respond for several beats and Sarah squeezes her shut tightly. Bracing herself for the potential cost of her honesty.

"So, you wanted to be pregnant, Sarah? You did want to have my baby?"

His voice is so raw with emotion it breaks her heart into a million tiny pieces.

"Oh, Tytus." She aches at the realization that she caused him to doubt what is such an obvious truth to her now. She shakes her head at the insanity of what she's about to admit. "Nothing would make me happier than having your baby. I would be lying to both of us if I didn't acknowledge the way I've dreamt about a future with you. A family of our own."

Sarah takes a minute to regain her composure. If nothing else, Tytus deserves a clear explanation. "At first, the idea of being pregnant terrified me. Because I could only think about all the reasons that the timing was bad. My career, your career, the newness of our relationship, and all we'd already endured. But when you told me you loved me. When you said you knew and you'd be there no matter what came next...it wasn't so scary anymore. I started to let myself think about what it would be like to carry your child. To have a baby with you. And even though I denied it to myself, I started to hope it was true."

"Sarah." Tytus's voice cracks just a bit and she knows she is not the only one in pain. "I felt the exact same way."

Sarah nods as she squeezes the pillow she had pulled up to her chest.

"I love you, Tytus."

"I love you, too, Sarah."

She snuggles back down under the covers. She cries softly for the next few minutes while just listening to Tytus breathing on the other end of the line. She takes in a deep shaky breath, holds it for a count of four, and slowly lets it out.

A weight has been lifted, and in its place, a sense of peace. Her eyes grow heavy as the exhaustion consumes her. She stops fighting to keep them open and lets them drift close.

"Sarah?"

She hears his voice through the receiver.

"Mmph?" she mumbles.

"Get some rest and I'll call you tomorrow."

"Mmm-kay."

"I love you, Sarah. Goodnight."

Tytus sets his phone down on the bedside table and rubs his face with both hands. The moisture from his eyes dampens his fingertips. He sits on the edge of the bed, both feet on the floor, his elbows on his knees.

Letting his lungs fill with air, he takes in a deep breath and holds it. He lifts his hand in front of his eyes and sees it trembling. He releases the air from his chest in a slow stream, his lips barely parted as if he's blowing through a straw. This breathing exercise is something he picked up from Ruzzoli and it works miracles for slowing his heart rate.

He gets up from the bed and heads into the bathroom, grabbing a hand towel from the rack on his way to the sink. He runs the water and lets it heat up before putting the towel under the stream. Leaning against the wall he presses the hot cloth to his face and relishes the burn it brings.

After a few moments, he tosses the wet towel over the shower and gets undressed. Within minutes, he's under the covers in the dark staring up at the hotel room ceiling.

A smile slowly spreads across his lips as he's finally able to process everything Sarah had told him. And what he had told her. She wants a baby with him. That's the bottom line. She loves him, maybe even as much as he loves her. She wants a future with him. A family. And as far as he sees it, that future begins right now.

He turns on his side and falls into a deep sleep. Dreaming of a house with a yard, a dog, a couple of kids, and a beautiful redhead sitting on the porch.

Tytus stands in the open bullpen at Oracle Park, just taking in the view. The San Francisco stadium is even more fantastic than it looks on TV. Watching his team take the Giants deep into McCovey Cove three times in the past two nights was a thrill he won't soon forget. It's an unusually crisp morning for June, but the sun is shining and there is not a single cloud in the sky. After they wrap up the series this afternoon, they head to Colorado for a three-game stint with the Rockies. And then, finally, home.

The way he misses her is palpable. After their talk the other night, he feels more connected to her than ever and he needs to see her. To hold her.

Spencer walks out to meet him on the field and tosses him a ball.

"Mound today?"

"That's what Doc said," Tytus responds with a wide-eyed grin.

His arm feels great and Workman cleared him to start throwing off the mound. Lightly, of course. But progress, nonetheless. He is officially off the injured list and could even be assigned a rehab outing for the Triple-A RailRiders later this week. The positive of that being, he could be closing for the Yankees in the next homestand. The negative, it could delay his arrival back to New York by a day or two considering the Triple-A Club is based in Scranton, Pennsylvania.

The team is still ahead in the division by two games as they near the midway point of the season. Tytus's name continues to be in the All-Star discussions, despite his injury, and if he can get back on the mound soon, and pitch well, he should have his first-ever appearance in the Midsummer Classic.

"You seem...happy?" Spencer comments with a suspicious look in his eye as he throws him the ball.

"And?" Tytus chuckles returning the ball.

"And it's weird." He throws the ball back. "It's throwing me off."

Tytus just shakes his head and steps up onto the mound for the first time in weeks. He taps his toe into the ground a few times to knock off any wet brick dust trapped between his spikes. As is his normal routine, he places the ball of his right foot against the edge of the far end of the rubber and slowly slides it backward toward him. Feeling the familiar pressure of the firm rectangle beneath his foot is like returning home after a long trip.

"So is it personal or professional?"

Spencer's question draws him out of his reverie.

"What?" Tytus calls back as he gets set to throw his first pitch.

"Your mood? I've noticed the past few days you seem, I don't know, different." Spencer raises his catcher's mitt in the air. "Just curious if it's getting back in the game that's got you smiling, or—"

"It's both."

Tytus positions his left leg in front of his right and turns to look at his catcher over his shoulder. He bends his knees and drops into a deep squat before standing tall again. Lifting and coiling his front leg, he rotates backward at the waist and pauses briefly before swinging the leg back and extending it out in front of him while pushing off the mound with the incredible power of his back thigh. The ball zips through the air and causes a loud "pop" in Spencer's glove.

Spencer immediately stands up and pulls off his mask. He looks at the ball planted squarely in the web of his mitt and then looks back to Tytus. His eyes sparkle as he grins like a kid in a candy shop.

"It's nice to have you back, Hayes. But remember," he puts both hands up in front of him, "easy, boy. Easy."

As Sarah finishes up her Sunday evening show, she notices that she feels a million times better than she had last Sunday night. Physically and psychologically. Her energy level is improving and after her heart-to-heart with Tytus the other night, she has been in a much better headspace. She is working on getting back to the *real* her. The confident, sassy, kick-ass redhead everyone knows and loves. And it feels great.

She stands in her dressing room and takes a good look around. Her closing night is just over two weeks away and she still isn't sure what will be next. Oh, she has offers, and there are plenty of opportunities out there, especially after the raving review from Cam Stewart. She just isn't sure what she wants. She has already committed to a break. She and Tytus had talked about a get-away of some kind during his mid-season break and she had refused to commit to anything that didn't give her at least a month off. Lord knows she's earned it.

Checking the time and seeing it's just before 10:00 p.m., she knows that Tytus will already be on board his flight to Colorado. He's moving one time zone closer at least which will put them at a two-hour difference. If she gets moving now, she can be home and in bed by the time he calls.

His timing couldn't have been better. The phone rings just moments after she sits down on the balcony with her wine. It's a warm night and she's opted for the fresh air.

"Took a broom to those Giants, eh?" She smiles into her wine glass, proud of her sports quip.

"That we did." She can hear the smile in his response.

"How was your flight?"

"Fine. Your show?"

"Great, actually." Sarah sighs and bites on her lip. "I'm going to miss being Roxie." She surprises herself with both the comment and the unexpected emotion it stirs.

"You still have a couple weeks, right?" His voice softens.

"Yes. We close on the twenty-sixth." She sips her wine and looks out at the city she calls home. "I was just musing about what's coming next, actually."

"Is that so? Well, what did you come up with? Leaving the theater and following me around on the road?"

She knows he's teasing, but she doesn't offer a response. Instead, she asks a question of her own.

"Speaking of what's next, how's the arm? Any news?"

"As a matter of fact…I'm throwing on Wednesday night."

"In Colorado? Tytus, that's great."

She hears a soft laugh on the other end of the line.

"Not in Colorado, unfortunately. In Pennsylvania. Scranton to be exact."

"Scranton? What the heck is in Scranton?" Sarah sits up and crinkles her nose.

"The RailRiders."

"The what?" Sarah laughs out loud.

"You know what, if I wanted this kind of abuse, I'd call Travis." He chuckles. "Aren't girlfriends supposed to be supportive?"

The sound of the word girlfriend coming from his mouth does things to her insides. They've said they love each other and even talked about a family. So it's childish, really. But she can't help it. Sometimes he just makes her feel like a schoolgirl.

"I'm sorry, we both know how fragile your giant ego is." She leans back in the chair. "Is this typical? To have you pitch for a different team?"

"Yeah, it's standard. Usually, any time a player is coming off the injured list, they have what's called a rehab assignment. We have three levels of Minor League clubs and that's generally where we take a test drive, of sorts. You know, to make sure you won't embarrass yourself, or the Yankees, on national TV."

"How thoughtful."

"Yeah. Exactly."

"So does that mean you won't be home on Thursday morning?" The thought just occurs to her and her heart sinks.

"It might." He pauses. "If I throw well, and feel good, I'll probably just pitch that one game and then return to NY for the home series. If not, I'll stay in Triple-A until they deem I'm ready."

She notices a hint of uncertainty in his tone and she regrets teasing him before.

"Did you throw today?" She winces a bit waiting for his response.

"Yeah." She hears a quiet laugh. "I threw off the mound for the first time since…you know. And it felt amazing."

"That's great, Tytus." She stands up and leans on her railing. "I have complete faith I'll be seeing you on Thursday then."

"I hope so. I miss you."

239

"I miss you, too."

They talk for a few more minutes about this and that. Sarah makes her way to the bedroom after finishing her wine because she loves listening to his voice on the phone just before falling asleep. It's 11:30 before they finally say their goodnights.

The minute she hangs up with Tytus she texts Nate. She would have called, but it's late.

I'm assuming you will be going to see Tytus pitch in Scranton on Wednesday.
I'm coming with! No discussion. Road Trip! How fun. XOXOXO

16

Road Trip

*I*t's been over five years since Tytus played in the minors. The atmosphere is completely different than Yankee Stadium but not in a bad way. It's actually pretty nostalgic. Most of the guys are new to him. His old teammates had either made it to the *Bigs* or hung it up by now, but the manager is the same, and so is this town.

Playing in the minor leagues reminds him of the State Championships in high school. A small stadium but packed with the most loyal and die-hard fans. The love and support of a crowd like this is unconditional. Win or lose, strikeout or homerun, they love their team and its players. Sometimes he misses that.

The stadium is bursting at the seams of its nearly 11,000-seat capacity and Tytus is well aware that it is mostly due to his presence. When word gets out in a town like this that a major leaguer is making an appearance, people come from all over to take a gander. It may very well be the only time they see a player of his caliber pitch.

It's when he and his team line up along the baseline and remove their caps for the National Anthem that he spots them. Sitting just behind home plate, in the third row, a bag of fresh peanuts and a cold beer in hand, are Sarah and Nate. He clenches his jaw at the sight of them, a swelling feeling of gratitude and love flowing through his veins as the first notes of *The Star-Spangled Banner* echo through the stadium speakers. He silently blames the glistening in his eyes to the emotion of this song and his return to the game he loves, but under the surface, he knows it's much more than that.

In Sarah's opinion, this game is even more fun than the ones at Yankee Stadium. The fans aren't on their cell phones or coming late and leaving early. People are actually watching the game and hanging on every pitch. She loves it. And it doesn't hurt that her boyfriend is the main attraction. As much as she had feared his fame early on, she has to admit there is a certain element of excitement to it. And now that she knows he loves her, and what they have is real, she actually enjoys it quite a bit.

Their seats are next to a father and son who explain they had driven over four hours from Pittsburgh just to see Tytus Hayes Jr.

"Sean, Sean Cooper. And this is my boy, AJ," the father introduces himself.

"Nice to meet you both." Sarah smiles as she shakes their hands. "I'm Sarah Dalton and this is Nate Richards."

The four talk throughout the game and Nate is tickled by the fact that AJ knows every single statistic of Tytus's entire career. The boy proudly shares his rookie Tytus Hayes Jr. baseball card, encased in protective plastic, that he has been clutching in his hand the entire game. And when Tytus comes in to pitch, and strikes out the side on 12 pitches, the entire place goes ballistic but none louder than little AJ and his dad.

The father and son have no idea who either Sarah or Nate are, or that the two of them are about to make this little boy's dreams come true.

After the game, she and Nate stand back at a distance and watch as Tytus is mauled by the thousands of fans who had come just to see him. AJ is on pins and needles and he can't stand still.

"Are you sure about this?" his father asks. "He looks a little busy."

"Trust me," Nate smiles and winks at the nervous father, "he's got time for this."

When Tytus finally makes his way over to them, he drops his duffle bag and lifts Sarah up off the ground in a twirling embrace. As if they are the only two in the entire parking lot, he takes in a deep breath of her hair and plants a kiss on her lips.

"God, you're beautiful," he says just loud enough for her to hear as he places her unsteady feet back on the ground.

"And who is this?" He squats down and tugs on the bill of the worn Yankee hat on AJ's head. "A new member of the team?"

The boy just stands there blinking at his idol, speechless.

"This is AJ, Tytus. He drove all the way from Pittsburgh to see his favorite player," Nate pipes in. "And this is his father Sean."

"Nice to meet you, Sean." Tytus stands and gives the man a firm handshake.

"So you came to see your favorite player, and you got stuck just meeting me?" Tytus looks down at the starry-eyed boy. "Who is he? You want me to go find him?" he jokes.

"Oh no, Mr. Hayes. It's…it's you. You're my favorite player," AJ says excitedly, finally finding his words. "See," he juts out the hand holding Tytus's card, "it's your rookie card. I saved up my allowance for months to get it."

Sarah isn't sure when exactly it happened, but her eyes are now full of tears. She can't be certain if it's the look of admiration in this little boy's eyes or the sweet and sincere expression in Tytus's.

"Wow." Tytus raises his eyebrows. "Do you mind?" He nods at the card, and the boy hands it over without hesitation. "I see you have it in a nice case, would it be okay if I took it out? You know, so I could sign it for you?"

AJ's eyes grow like saucers as he blinks at Tytus and then looks up to his father. When Sarah sees the man swallow and nod down at his son, she can see she's not the only one on the verge of tears.

Tytus smiles and carefully removes the card. Nate holds a pen out to Tytus which he takes and kneels back down in front of AJ. He autographs the card, carefully puts it back in the case, and hands it to his grateful fan.

"How about a picture?" Sarah suggests as she wipes a tear from her beaming face.

After Sean and AJ pose for a photo with Tytus, they say their thank yous and goodbyes. Sarah, Nate, and Tytus head out for a bite to eat. No one talks much more about what had just transpired. It may have been a typical experience for Tytus and Nate, but for Sarah, it had been anything but.

"You can sit up front, Sarah," Tytus calls as she starts to climb into the back of the Navigator the following morning.

"What? No. Your legs are longer than mine." She smiles at him as he approaches the SUV.

"Yeah, and this thing is a damn boat, the back seat has plenty of legroom." He reaches for her arm to stop her. "Really, please. I'll sit in the back." The look in his eyes says he doesn't want to argue.

"Okay, Tytus. Thank you." She raises up on her toes and kisses him square on the lips.

For the first thirty minutes of the drive, the three friends talk about last night's game, the weekend series against Tampa Bay, and the upcoming closing night of Sarah's show. It's when the conversation dies down that Nates throws out a suggestion.

"Cell Phone Karaoke."

"What? No. No way." Tytus shakes his head vehemently looking at Nate in the rearview mirror. "Plus, that's a drinking game and we can't play it while driving. Pretty sure that's illegal."

"What's Cell Phone Karaoke?" Sarah asks, looking back and forth between the two men. She'd been sitting with her body turned sideways, one leg tucked under the other, the whole time so she could see Tytus.

"It's a great game we used to play in college," Nate says, his face practically glowing in excitement.

"It's a stupid game that's meant to be played when you're drunk. Not sober as a judge. And definitely not in the car where I can't run away from Nate's freakishly underdeveloped prepubescent voice."

"He's scared." Nate looks at Sarah and tilts his head. "He knows he can't beat me, and he's afraid to sing in front of you." He nods and purses his lips.

"Afraid? I'm trying to protect her. From you!" Tytus scoffs. "And I can't beat you? Please. The two of you combined don't have half my knowledge of music and you know it."

"Oh. Now it's ON." Sarah chirps with mock offense. "I have no idea what this game is, but if it involves singing, I'm pretty sure I have the advantage over you two jocks."

"Seriously, Ty," Nate pipes back up, looking at his friend through the mirror. "She doesn't stand a chance and we both know it." He raises his brows teasingly. "Sarah will be the one doing ninety percent of the singing anyway. Are you really telling me you wouldn't like to spend the rest of the ride listening to your beautiful and talented girlfriend sing?"

Sarah looks back at Tytus with a pout. "Well, Hayes?"

"Fine," Tytus agrees begrudgingly. "But I'm picking first."

Nate explains the rules to Sarah. Each of them takes a turn selecting a song on their cell phone and playing it. The other two have to shout out the title as fast as they can. Whoever loses, has to down a shot, and sing that song aloud, karaoke style. Obviously, they will skip the drinking step.

"What if you don't know the song?" Sarah asks.

"The idea is to pick popular songs. Songs everyone should know. It's more fun that way. The point isn't to stump people, just to see who can name it faster." Tytus shrugs, "And usually to see who gets the most hammered and then laughing at them all night. But I guess today, it's about watching you lose and listening to you sing." The grin he flashes is so cocky, Sarah hates that it simultaneously annoys and excites her.

"And you can read the lyrics from the screen. You know, karaoke style. So, you don't have to have it memorized or anything," Nate adds glancing over to Sarah.

"How are you going to read the lyrics? You're driving."

"Sarah." He rolls his eyes playfully. "Number one, no one will be faster than me, so I won't have to sing. And two, I have a memory like an iron trap. If, by some miracle, one of you beats me, I won't need the lyrics, trust me."

Tytus starts the game by skimming through songs on his phone. The shit-eating grin on his face is making Sarah nervous.

"Would you just pick something already." She reaches back and slaps his leg.

"This is going to be fun, actually. Nate, great idea." Tytus winks at Sarah and scoots up in the seat so he's closer to both of them. You two ready?"

Nate connects Tytus's phone to his Bluetooth so they can get the full effect of the music, but he places a paper from the glove box over the display screen so they can't cheat.

Tytus presses play and Nate shouts, "Like a Virgin," before Sarah even hears a second note.

"What? No way you could be that fast." She looks accusingly between the two of them. "You guys cheated."

"Prove it." Tytus sits back. "The rules are the rules, Sarah." He hands Sarah the phone and chuckles.

She's pretty sure she's been duped, but she actually loves this song, so she plays along and doesn't hold back.

Sarah plays into it and lets the hair she'd pulled back for the drive down, shaking it as she runs her hand through it and belts out the chorus. She is an actress after all and she can see what she's doing to Tytus, which only makes her play into it more.

As Sarah finishes the song, she wishes she had a mic to drop. She feels like a winner with the way she shut these two up, but the realization slowly creeps in that this may have been their end game all along.

"Okay, my turn to pick!=," she says excitedly.

"Uh, no." Tytus laughs. "It's Nate's turn. The winner from the last round picks next."

"Oh, that's ridiculous." Sarah hands the phone to Nate. "So, if you win this time, I sing again, and then it's your turn to pick? I'll never get to pick a song."

"That's the plan," Nate teases. "Basically Ty and I are just going to take turns picking songs for you to sing."

"Not if I beat Tytus." She huffs. "Or you."

But she doesn't. She loses to Tytus by a millisecond on Nate's choice and she sings *9 to 5* by Dolly Parton while the two men eat up every second of it.

She loses a third in a row when Tytus plays *Billie Jean* by Michael Jackson and Nate only needs three drum beats.

"I thought you'd get that one." Tytus acts as if he's disappointed. "I really wanted Nate to sing this."

"No, you didn't, Tytus. Don't be a sore winner." She scowls at him but her eyes are still playful. She's actually having fun. She's always liked karaoke.

The next song played by Nate begins with a few soft notes on the piano and Sarah knows it immediately.

"Piano Man," she yells, clapping excitedly. "I got it. I got it."

Tytus says it as well but a good second or two after Sarah.

"What?" He raises both hands up in the air. "No way, that was totally me."

"No arguing, Ty." Nate tsks from the driver's seat. "Those are the rules. My turn, I decide. And that one goes to Sarah. Hands down."

"Billy Joel, Nate? Really?"

"What? He plays piano, it's kinda jazz-ish," Nate defends his song choice.

"My dad loves Billy Joel." Sarah seems genuinely offended by Tytus's criticism. "I grew up listening to him." She smiles back at Tytus, enjoying the moment immensely.

"Here. I'm guessing you'll need the lyrics." She hands Tytus the phone and he takes it but keeps his eyes right on hers.

"Just play the song."

The music starts and Sarah turns in her seat even more to get a clear view of Tytus, which makes Nate laugh out loud.

Tytus holds the phone in front of his face and looks right at Sarah as Billy starts to tickle the ivories. The moment the harmonica starts, he turns the phone over and places it face down on the center console. Signature smirk intact. He raises his eyebrow and gives her a wink.

As the first line of the song leaves his lips, his voice is soft and a lower register than his speaking voice but good. Quite good. Sarah's eyes widen and she just might be gaping.

Tytus pretends to pull a harmonica from his pocket and plays the invisible instrument along with the music.

His voice grows louder and more confident with every line. Sarah is in complete shock. He sounds amazing as he nails every word and every note without fail. He has the slightest gravel in his tone that makes her feel warm all over. She's pretty sure Nate is laughing his ass off in the front seat, but she can't tear her eyes away from Tytus to look.

She's completely awestruck. She's also aware that Tytus is feeding off her flabbergasted expression but she doesn't mind it one bit.

The harmonica is back before he rolls right into the chorus. Literally belting it in the back seat like he's sung this song a million times.

As he plays the air harmonica again, with his eyes playfully fixed on hers, she realizes she's been played. He knew he could sing and he wanted to catch her off guard. To impress her. And he has done both in spades. Nate is now playing back-up piano on the steering wheel and she gets the feeling they've done this before.

Tytus goes on singing about John and Bill, and Paul and Davy. Sarah can literally feel herself falling deeper in love with this man with every word that comes from his beautiful lips. As if he wasn't already perfect enough.

The two men continue to play their pretend instruments and Tytus sings verse after verse. Then he scoots up in the back seat and places one hand on the backs of Sarah's and Nate's seats so that his face is only a short distance from hers.

He leans in and gives Sarah a quick, hard kiss on the lips before pulling away and leaning back to bellow out the last verse like he's on stage at a concert.

As the chorus gets ready to play for the final time, the three exchange looks between them and with a quick nod they all join in and sing the chorus together, and Sarah can't remember the last time she had this much fun.

When the music dies down, Tytus leans in close to her.

"My dad is a big fan of Billy Joel, too."

He winks, smiles, and places another kiss on her parted lips.

Saturday afternoon, Tytus sits in front of his locker holding his jersey in his hands. He had dressed out last night and warmed up with the team, but tonight is different. Tonight he knows that if the need for a closer presents itself, he will make his return.

He had just finished an interview with Alex Rodriguez from ESPN, a former Yankee legend and possible future Hall of Famer. They spoke about his injury, rehab, and pending return to the closer role. They also spoke about the Yankees' success, playoff hopes, and Tytus's bid for the All-Star closer for the American League.

As he pulls on his uniform, he listens intently to his pregame playlist and reflects on the recent changes in his life. Meeting Sarah, reconciling with his mom, his panic attack, Ruzzoli, his injury. He's grateful for all of it. The good with the bad. Everything that has transpired over the last several months has led him here, and he feels blessed.

"You ready?" Spencer stands over him with a shit-eating grin.

"You bet your ass I am." Tytus laces up his spikes, sets his headphones in his locker, and grabs his glove.

Showtime.

The Yankees continue to outperform the competition and when they lead 3-1 in the eighth inning, the bullpen phone rings.

"Hayes!" the pitching coach shouts after answering the call. "You're up."

Tytus nods to his coach and swallows. It's time.

Before he even throws his first pitch in the pen, the Jumbo Tron camera displays him taking off his jacket and the place goes apeshit. Tytus fights back the smile that threatens to split his face. He's not the type of player who gets off on the attention. He's always been the *all-business* type. But even he can't deny that it feels good to hear the fans chanting his name. It feels damn good.

Tytus channels the excitement of the crowd into pure adrenaline. The combination of that, his arm never feeling stronger, and the power in his legs from the extra rest, has his confidence through the roof. The last out of the 8th inning is made when the Yankees have a runner caught stealing, and the announcer wastes no time announcing his entry to the game.

"Ladies and gentleman," the guitar solo of *Thunderstruck* blares through every speaker, "now pitching for your New York Yankees," Tytus pushes through the gate and starts his sprint to the mound, "Ty-tus Haaaaaayes Jr.!"

⚾

Sarah hands her phone to Sebastian backstage as she awaits her next cue. It's killing her to miss Tytus's return, but she only has so many performances left and she's committed not to miss any more of them. She knows from her MLB app that they are headed to the top of the 9th with a 3-1 lead, and as long as everything is going according to plan, he should be taking the mound this minute.

She knows he's ready, and that he will do great, but it doesn't stop her from wishing she could be there cheering him on.

"Pay attention to the game. I want every detail," she says to a scowling Sebastian before running on stage.

⚾

The first pitch Tytus delivers is hit hard, a line drive right into the glove of his second baseman. It was hit hard, what the announcers call a 'frozen rope', no doubt about that, but an out is an out. And getting that first one always helps him to relax. One pitch. One out. Can't beat that.

Spencer walks out to the mound for a quick meeting while the Rays announce a pinch hitter entering the game.

"How you feelin'?"

"Listen to this place," Tytus says into his mitt so the cameras can't pick up their conversation. "How do you think I'm feeling?"

Spencer winks and gives him a quick smack on the butt. "Let's finish this."

Tytus gets a read on the pinch hitter the minute he steps into the box. He's young, nervous, and out of his league. Tytus keeps him completely off balance and sits him down on three straight-breaking balls. The batter was guessing fastball every time and never stood a chance.

The cleanup hitter gets jammed on an inside fastball on the first pitch and Tytus picks up his 13th save of the season on a five-pitch inning, a new personal best.

Sarah heads straight to Sebastian once the curtain falls.

"Well? How'd he do?" She grabs the phone from him and starts clicking wildly.

"They won," he says with a slightly irritated expression Sarah ignores.

"They won? Well, good. But how did Tytus do?"

"Good. I guess?" Sebastian shakes his head with an indifferent shrug.

"Oh my God."

"What?" Sebastian cries out as Sarah covers her mouth with her hand.

"Five pitches." She rushes toward her dressing room. "He only needed five pitches," she yells as she disappears around the corner.

As soon as she closes the door to her dressing room, she calls Tytus. She's not surprised when he doesn't pick up but she leaves him an excited message.

"Tytus. Oh my God. I saw your stats. 5 pitches." She paces around the room with nervous energy. "Save number 13. How's your shoulder? Good, I hope? Okay. Okay. I'm rambling. Call me as soon as you can. I love you."

She hangs up the phone and sets it on her makeup counter. She looks at her reflection in the mirror. This is what people mean when they say someone is glowing. She feels fabulous.

Things with Tytus have been so much better since they had that talk on the phone. She still gets a wave of sadness now and then, and getting herself *balanced* is a work in progress, but she knows that the reality of it all is that this wasn't the best time for her and Tytus to start a family. They are both enjoying success in their careers and she the incredible feeling of finding her soul mate, a revelation she has yet to share with Tytus. Someday, when the timing is right, she will carry his child. She believes that with her whole heart.

"Sarah?"

There's a soft knock on her door.

"Come in."

Sebastian walks in with a crazy look on his face that Sarah can't quite read. He may not be a man of many words but she's not sure she's ever seen him struck dumb.

"Sebastian? What is it?"

He seems to be in some sort of trance but he manages to drag his eyes to Sarah's.

"You'll never believe who is waiting outside to talk to you."

Tytus is dogpiled by his teammates as if they just clinched a playoff berth. It's a bit of an overreaction if you ask him. He's only doing what he's being paid millions of dollars to do. But he can't deny it feels good.

Before he can even make it off the field, he's got half a dozen microphones in his face and twice as many cameras flashing.

"Tytus! Tytus!"

"How's your shoulder?"

"Is it good to be back on the mound?"

"Tytus, what do you think about your All-Star chances?"

He takes each question in stride.

"The shoulder feels great."

"The mound is where I belong, of course, I'm glad to be back on it."

"I'm just trying to help my team win games. Today, I was able to do that. Now I just want to do the same tomorrow. It's as simple as that."

He politely, but deliberately, makes his way through the media and into the clubhouse. Waiting for him just inside the door is Nate. Tytus stops in his tracks and looks into the eyes of his best friend. He extends his hand with a swallow and a nod, but Nate steps past it and wraps his arms around him.

"You were amazing."

Tytus lets all the emotions of the past few weeks rise up to the surface. There had been moments he had felt so weak and helpless. He was on the verge of losing the things that mattered the most to him, his career, Sarah, but at this moment, he feels invincible.

"Thanks, Nate," he croaks out and walks away before he fucking cries in the middle of the locker room.

He sees he missed a call from Sarah, but he wants to quickly shower and change before he calls her back. He's feeling like his old self and a mischievous grin spreads across his face. Tonight, he feels cocky as hell and he can't wait to get Sarah to bed and remind her just how good a closer he is.

Sarah exhales a shaky breath as she checks herself one more time in the mirror before going to meet her guest. She tries to ignore the butterflies in her stomach but she's pretty sure one has made its way into her throat.

When she enters the backstage area, she spots him immediately. He's looking at his phone in the corner and is almost a foot taller than anyone else in the room. She had always found him incredibly handsome on the big screen, but he's even more spectacular in the flesh. She slowly walks toward him and his eyes shift upward to meet hers.

"Sarah Dalton." His smile is soft and warm as he takes her extended hand and kisses the back of it like they've been transported back in time. "I'm Pierce—"

"Evans. I know who you are." She blushes despite herself. Starstruck doesn't come close to depicting her current state. His British accent is even more delicious in person.

"I'm flattered."

Such a simple response but it leaves her without one.

"I was wondering if I could buy you a cup of coffee?"

"Oh. Um. Of course." She stumbles over her words.

Sebastian had explained when he came in that Pierce Evans, the very well-known stage and screen actor turned producer, had seen her performance and wanted to speak with her about her future career plans. And knowing what a huge fan of his Sarah is, he had offered to stall him while she pulled herself together.

The first time she had seen Pierce on stage was a few years ago when she first relocated to downtown to start her career on Broadway. He had given a breathtaking performance as the Phantom, in the world-renowned musical and Sarah had never been more inspired. His career skyrocketed from there and he was cast in several lead Broadway roles and eventually made his way to Hollywood. He earned a Golden Globe nomination last year when his first movie took the box office by storm. The word on the street is that he is delving into producing his own work now.

After agreeing to his offer for coffee, she makes her way back into the dressing room and tries desperately to calm her nerves. *Pierce Evans wants to buy me a coffee and talk about my career plans? Is this a fucking dream?*

She grabs her coat and tosses her phone into her purse, not noticing she had just missed a call from Tytus.

17

Jealousy

*T*ytus sighs when he hears Sarah's recorded voice on the other end of the line instead of her live one. Figuring she must be mingling backstage, he leaves her a message about meeting up when she's done. He decides to accept the offer for a celebratory drink with his dad and brother, who drove down for the game, and invites Nate and Chrissie to join them.

When they climb into the Lexus and Tytus suggests *Beleman's*, which is quickly becoming tradition, Tytus Sr. immediately agrees, hoping to see his old friend Earl. Tytus texts Nate to let him know where to meet them and then he texts Sarah.

Headed to Beleman's with my dad and Travis.
Nate and Chrissie are meeting us there.
I'll send Miles to pick you up.

Before they've even climbed into the booth, Tytus Sr. orders a round of Blue Label and within minutes the group is toasting to Tytus's triumphant return.

As the first sip of Scotch warms his throat, Tytus's eyes drift to the doorway. As grateful as he is to be surrounded by four people he loves, the absence of Sarah dilutes the experience. The amber liquid, not mixing well with the taste in his mouth, has him picking up his water instead. Silently cursing himself for continually checking his phone, he decides a distraction is in order.

"Dad, should we go see Earl?"

As the three men catch up between songs, Tytus feels his phone vibrate in his pocket. The anticipatory smile on his face quickly fades as he reads the message on his screen.

She's not here, Boss. Want me to come back to the bar?

Tytus reads the message twice as his brows pull together. *Not there?* The hair on the back of his neck stands on end as his mind starts racing for answers.

"Everything okay, TJ?" Tytus Sr. reads the concern on his son's face.

"What?" Tytus looks up. "Yeah. Uh…yeah." He looks back to his phone and answers Miles.

That's okay, Miles. You can head home.

What had started out as mild disappointment slowly morphs into something bordering between concern and irritation. This is not like her at all. She had left him that message and she sounded so excited to talk to him and then, poof, nothing? It just doesn't make any sense.

"Excuse me." He nods toward Earl and Tytus Sr. "I need to make a call."

Tytus heads out to the back entrance and tries Sarah again.

When Sarah and Pierce walk into the small cafe it's nearly empty. They sit across from each other at a small round table and a young waitress comes right over with a pot of coffee.

Sarah sees the way her eyes widen at the sight of Pierce, but everyone plays it off well.

"So, Sarah." He smiles as the waitress disappears behind the counter. "I know that your time is valuable, and you have two more shows tomorrow, so I will make this brief."

Sarah sips on her coffee, it's not the same without her usual splash of vanilla, and she's fairly certain caffeine is the last thing her nerves need at the moment, yet it feels like it's the logical thing to do.

"The four show weekends can definitely be challenging." Her smile is sheepish. She still isn't able to get a grip on what is happening here.

"I read the review Cam Stewart wrote about you. He and I go way back and I value his opinion greatly." Pierce sets his coffee down and intertwines his fingers on the table. "And after seeing you tonight, everything he told me about you over the phone was confirmed."

Sarah smiles nervously and takes another drink of the unwanted coffee. God forbid she try to find words to respond to that.

"You have something really special, Sarah."

He tilts his head, just slightly, as if he's asking her something more than telling. He purses his lips thoughtfully before continuing, and Sarah thinks absently that she might pass out.

"I've started producing my own work and I have a few projects coming up that I'd like you to consider. Nothing is set in stone at this point, but I know your closing night is coming up, and I wanted to reach out to you before you accept any other job offers."

He smiles then and raises his eyebrows, signaling politely that it's her turn to say something.

Before she finds the ability to speak, her purse begins to vibrate on her lap. Normally, she would ignore her phone in the middle of a conversation, but since she's speechless at the moment, she welcomes the interruption.

It's not until she sees Tytus's name on the screen that she remembers about the game. About his big night.

"I'm so sorry, Pierce. I need to take this."

She pushes her chair back and accepts the call just as she steps outside.

"Tytus. Oh my God, great game."

"Sarah, where are you?"

There is a hint of something in his voice that straightens her spine. Is he...mad?

"I'm just having a quick coffee, you'll never believe who—"

"A coffee? Now? Didn't you get my voicemail? Or my text?"

Sarah looks at her phone and indeed sees she had missed both. Quickly skimming his message she responds apologetically.

"I didn't. I'm sorry, Tytus, my phone was still on silent." She bites her bottom lip and looks through the glass window at the man waiting inside. "This is a work thing, and I'm almost done. Meet up with you guys in a few?"

"Shit, Sarah," Tytus exhales into the phone. "I was really getting worried."

He doesn't sound mad anymore, but he doesn't sound happy either. It makes her already woozy stomach turn.

"Should I send Miles?" he adds after neither speaks for a moment.

"No, no. I'm not far. I'll catch a cab." She feels bad that his big moment had slipped her mind. "And Tytus, I was following the game on the app you downloaded for me. Five pitches. You were amazing."

She hears him chuckle softly on the other end of the line and it soothes her just a bit. "Thanks, Sarah. Hurry up, okay?"

"Okay. I will."

She sighs after disconnecting the call. She had hurt his feelings, but she would make it up to him. Plus, he'll understand once he knows the whole story.

Tytus feels a shift in the air around him and he knows Sarah is there without needing to turn around. And if he hadn't sensed her presence, the grin on Tytus Sr.'s face would have given it away.

"Well, there's my favorite redhead." Tytus Sr. scoots off the edge of the booth to give her a hug. Tytus follows his father's lead and stands up behind him.

"Sorry I'm late." She smiles and kisses Tytus Sr. on the cheek.

When his father steps aside, Tytus moves in for a hug of his own. He can't quite shake the feeling in the pit of his stomach, but he tries his best to ignore it. He knows Sarah is his biggest supporter and he's a grown-ass man. Just because she had some work stuff to take care of, is no reason to get his panties in a wad.

"Tytus." Sarah lays her hands on his cheeks and plants a loud smacking kiss right on his lips. "What a comeback performance."

He can't help but smile. Her sparkling eyes, her beautiful face, he is such an idiot to let this get under his skin.

"I wish you had been there," he says softly, but there is no sign of guilt or malice in his tone, only longing.

"So do I," she whispers back.

She wraps her fingers tightly between his and squeezes into the booth, sandwiching herself between Travis and Tytus.

Sarah asks for a play-by-play recount of Tytus's save as she sips on the Scotch they had waiting for her. The group has already heard it, and watched it live, but nobody seemed to mind going through it again.

"Tytus mentioned you had a work thing holding you up?" Chrissie asks when Tytus finishes his story. "Everything go okay tonight?"

Tytus notices something flash across Sarah's face as she shifts slightly on the bench next to him.

"Actually," she smiles and sits up straighter, "you'll never believe who I met tonight."

Tytus lifts his drink to his lips with one hand while caressing Sarah's thigh under the table with the other.

"Pierce Evans."

She doesn't hide the giddy excitement in her voice and she actually brings both hands up to cover her mouth as if she can't believe those words just came out of it.

Tytus almost chokes on his Scotch and he struggles not to spit it across the table.

"As in...*the* Pierce Evans?" Chrissie gasps. "The actor? He was at your show?"

Tytus pulls his hand slowly from Sarah's knee as the wheels in his head start to spin. That *feeling* from earlier swirling again in his stomach.

"He wasn't just at the show," Sarah continues looking at all her wide-eyed friends, seemingly oblivious to Tytus's discomfort. "He stayed afterward and asked to buy me coffee!" She's practically beaming now and Tytus is not a fan of the way it makes him feel.

"No way." Travis shakes his head. "Pierce fucking Evans took you out for coffee? That guy won like an Oscar or something for that secret agent flick last year."

259

Tytus shoots daggers from his eyes at his brother, but it seems he's become invisible to everyone at the table.

He is well aware of who Pierce Evans is. He's your prototypical tall, dark, and handsome Hollywood type, and although he never disliked him before he suddenly finds him unequivocally irritating.

"It was a Golden Globe, actually," Nate chimes in.

"Golden Globe, Oscar, all I know is that man is a tall drink of…something way better than water." Chrissie's doe-eyed expression earns her an elbow from Nate.

"He wanted to talk about my future career plans," Sarah adds, stifling a laugh at Chrissie's comment.

This time Tytus does choke, and every eye at the table turns to him.

He wants to lash out. He feels his heart rate quickening as he clenches his fists below the table. He fights the urge to blurt out, *That's the work thing you had to do? Have fucking coffee with Pierce Evans?*

But as he looks around the table at the expressions of his closest friends and family, he thinks about his sessions with Ruzzoli. He takes in a deep breath instead and holds it.

He clears his throat and guzzles from his water glass.

He's fairly certain that Nate sees right through him when he takes the attention off of him by asking a question of his own.

"That's amazing, Sarah." Nate glances at Tytus from the corner of his eye but keeps his main focus on her. "Is he coming back to New York? Returning to stage acting or something?"

Sarah hesitates momentarily, most certainly picking up on the tension now emanating from Tytus.

"Possibly." She smiles tentatively. "We didn't talk long, but he explained that he's shifting his career toward producing and that he wants me to consider some of his projects before deciding on my next move." Sarah breaks eye contact and takes a drink from her glass.

"That's amazing Sarah. Holy shit," Chrissie exclaims.

If one more person fucking gushes about this guy, Tytus's going to hurl right there on the table. He wants to be happy for her. Correction, he knows he should be happy for her. But the weight on his chest doesn't feel anything like joy. And if he doesn't get some fresh air soon, he's either going to say something he will surely regret, or implode from trying to hold it in.

"Can you excuse me for one second?" He plasters on a forced smile that doesn't fool anyone and practically pushes Sarah off the end of the booth to get out.

Tytus is standing outside the hotel bar with his back and one foot propped against the brick wall. If he smoked, now would be the time for a cigarette. Or better yet, a joint.

"You okay, Son?"

He hears his father's voice and looks up from the spot on the pavement he was analyzing too closely. He's relieved, actually, that it's him and not Sarah who came to check up on him.

"Just needed some air," Tytus says without making eye contact.

"You're jealous."

That snaps Tytus's head up and he meets his father's eyes with a dangerous glare. His jaw clenched tight enough to chip teeth.

"I'm just not sure if it's of Sarah's potential success or of the man who's offering it to her?" His father adds.

Tytus feels like he could spit nails, and whatever calming effect the cool air had provided is replaced with the need to stomp his foot and pout. "I'm not jealous."

"Listen, TJ." His father steps closer and puts a hand on his shoulder. "I'm not sure you've ever had much cause to be jealous of anyone in the past, so you may not recognize it for what it is. But I'm telling you, if you plan to spend your life with a woman as beautiful and successful as the one inside that bar, this won't be the last time you battle with it."

Tytus looks back to his father with resigned understanding in his eyes and swallows. He hates that he feels this way but he's not sure how to stop it.

"I'm not threatened by her career," he says with a huff.

"I know."

"It's got nothing to do with her potential success."

"I know," Tytus Sr. says again, resulting in Tytus giving him a slanted look.

"Sarah loves you, Tytus." He squeezes his son's shoulder. "This...opportunity, doesn't change that in any way."

Tytus looks out toward the street and lets out a deep breath he hadn't realized he was holding.

"Now how about you get back in there and congratulate her? The same way she congratulated you."

Tytus Sr. raises his brows, questioning his son without actual words.

"Thanks, Dad." Tytus runs his hand through his hair and exhales one more steadying breath before taking his father's advice and heading back inside.

As Sarah stares up at her bedroom ceiling she wonders where the past few months have gone. Tonight she will take the stage as Roxie for the last time and the feeling is more bitter than sweet.

The sun starts to shine in her eyes as a beam of light creeps through the gap in her drapes. She turns on her side, away from the window, and stares thoughtfully at the empty pillow next to her.

Tytus had decided not to stay last night. He blamed it on the fact they were playing a day game today and he'd have to get in early for treatment. But she isn't so sure that is the real reason.

Ever since she'd had coffee with Pierce Evans, his name had been a sore spot with Tytus. They hadn't fought, exactly, and he said he was excited for her, but something was definitely off. She had seen it that night at *Beleman's* and every time she brought him up since.

She had only spoken on the phone with Pierce a couple times since that night and he hadn't made any formal offers. She explained to him that she plans to take some time off after the close of the show. She isn't ready to jump right into another full-time project and he'd said he understood.

She and Tytus plan to take a short vacation during the All-Star break he has coming up, and she's thinking it might be fun to follow along with him on his next road trip. She could stay in the hotels with him and go to all his games. Maybe she'd get a jersey with his name on it like one of his real fans. The thought makes her smile, but it doesn't stick.

Last night Sarah had mentioned to Tytus that Pierce was planning to attend the closing show and that she was hoping to introduce them. She had put off telling him for several days because she was nervous about how he would react. Turned out her instincts had been spot on. While he played it off fairly well, something dark flashed in his eyes and he decided to call it a night shortly afterward. Sarah knows how to read people, and she certainly knows Tytus well enough to see through his façade. She just wishes she knew if it is *Pierce* who bothers him or the opportunities he represents. Either way, it makes her stomach turn.

She eventually throws the covers off and gets up to take a shower. This is a big night for her, she thinks, looking in the mirror. And if she can deal with Tytus's fame and the thousands of girls pining after him every single night, then he should be able to handle her getting a little attention for once. In fact, maybe a small part of her wants him to be the jealous one for a change.

Tytus picks up his 23rd save of the season which puts him only 2 behind the MLB leader, the Toronto righty, Jordan Romano. Considering his injury, it is quite an accomplishment and puts him on pace for his goal of being the best closer in the game.

The minute he finishes his post-game interviews, he showers and changes as quickly as possible. He needs to pick up some flowers and meet Nate for a drink before Sarah's show. And he could really use a drink. Make that a double.

Miles anticipated Tytus's needs and picked up the bouquet Tytus had ordered before coming to the ballpark. When Tytus sees them in the back seat, he squeezes Miles's shoulder.

"You are a good man, Miles. What would I ever do without you?"

"It's really nothing, Mr. Hayes. I knew you were running behind schedule when I listened to the post-game show on the radio." He smiles at Tytus in the mirror as he pulls away from the back tunnel. "You had already ordered them, all I had to do was pick them up."

"A good man, Miles. Don't argue with your boss."

"Yes, sir." Miles chuckles. "They say you are a shoo-in for the All-Star closer. The selection show is this Sunday night, right?"

If Tytus had a dollar for every time he'd been asked about the All-Star game he could retire early. But Miles had just done him a favor, so he plays nice.

"Sunday night. Yep. I guess we'll see." Tytus looks out the window and tries to downplay how much the selection would actually mean to him. To his father. "These things don't always go the way you expect. Emmanuel Clase throws a lot harder than me, so you never know."

Miles drops Tytus at the bar and agrees to pick up Sarah and him when Tytus texts that they are ready.

"I hope she steals the show," he calls as Tytus climbs out.

"Oh, you can count on that, my friend. You can count on that."

The text from Nate indicated that he is sitting in a booth near the back and Tytus keeps his head down as he makes his way through the bar. Luckily, if anyone notices him, they don't make a thing of it.

"Double shot of Blue Label." Tytus nods at the glass already awaiting him on the table. "I really do have good friends."

Nate smiles and raises his glass to Tytus's.

"To save number 23." He nods.

Tytus clinks his glass to Nate's and returns the nod before shooting more than half of it down in one gulp.

"Woah. Easy man." Nate raises his brows and sits up in his seat. "What was that about?"

"I'll tell you what it's about," Tytus says as he downs the remaining liquid with a second swig. "Pierce fucking Evans."

Tytus raises his hand to indicate the need for another drink.

She's magnificent. Absolutely breathtaking. He had known she would be, and he'd seen the show several times, but somehow, he finds himself in awe of her anyway. Maybe it's because he's still a little buzzed from earlier, but he swears she sparkles up there like an angel. And as the noise of the crowd rings in his ears, and the lights shine brightly on the stage, a strange feeling resonates through his entire body. That's the moment when he knows for certain, she's going to be a star.

The crowd is relentless in their applause and he watches as her cast showers her in hugs and flowers from the audience. Sebastian brings her a bouquet of his own and he watches as the tears spill from her eyes. She had prepared him for this, but still, he's the slightest bit jealous that he's not up there with her. But he'd had his moment, and she had asked weeks ago if he'd be okay with it, and he is. At least it's not Evans.

It takes even longer than usual for the final bows and for the crowd to make their way from the theater. Chrissie and Nate are waiting with Tytus to head backstage, but when Chrissie runs into an old friend from Yale, they agree to catch up with him later.

He makes his way backstage, flowers in hand, and one eye scanning for Evans. He hasn't seen him yet, but he's sure the man is here somewhere. The moment his eyes find Sarah on the opposite side of the crowded room, he finds Evans as well. The two of them huddled a little too close for his liking, and Sarah seemingly laughing at whatever Evans has to say.

"It's crazy isn't it?" Sebastian appears out of nowhere at Tytus's side and follows his gaze across the room. "I mean, Pierce Evans? There isn't a bigger name right now in Hollywood than his. And the way Sarah has had a crush on him since…well, as long as I've known her." He tsks and shakes his head. "It's like a scene straight out of a romance novel."

Tytus feels the tightness in his chest first. It's become the go-to indicator of his stress level spiraling. It's generally followed with him locking his jaw and clenching his hand into a fist. He fights the urge to drop the flowers right there and ring this guy's scrawny neck, but he knows that Sebastian is just trying to get his goat so he exhales a slow breath of air instead. Tytus had spent hours in therapy the past two weeks talking through his jealousy with Ruzzoli, but at the moment, he's scrambling to remember the reason the doc had told him he had nothing to fear.

"You want me to put those in her dressing room with all the others?" Sebastian says with a disinterested wave of his hand.

And when he gets no response, he reaches for them, but Tytus pulls them away and pushes past him.

As Tytus makes his way across the room he uses the breathing exercises that have become second nature. By the time Sarah's eyes meet his, his heart rate is back to normal and his ego…maybe slightly inflated. His façade firmly in place.

"Tytus."

Sarah smiles and starts to say something else, but Tytus steps right between her and Evans and places a firm kiss on her lips. With his back purposefully to the other man, he wraps his hand around the side of her neck as his fingers slide through the back of her hair.

"You were incredible." His eyes bore holes into hers as he is filled with a rush of adrenaline. Suddenly tampering down the desire to beat his chest and claim her as *his* to everyone in the room.

Sarah looks back at him breathlessly as her cheeks flush. Feeling he'd accomplished his first task he turns to Pierce.

"Tytus Hayes Jr." He extends his hand toward Evans and flashes his million-dollar smile.

"Of course." Pierce clears his throat and shakes Tytus's hand. "Pierce Evans."

His smile seems sincere, as do his eyes, but Tytus has his mind made up. This guy is up to something shady and he won't be played for a fool.

Tytus slides his way next to Sarah and wraps his arm around her waist.

"Tell me, what were you two talking about that had my girl here in stitches?" Tytus pulls Sarah's hip tighter against his.

"Oh." Sarah raises her brow at both his gesture and his question.

"I was just telling Sarah about my closing night as the Phantom, it was—"

"Hey," Tytus cuts him off. "There's Nate and Chrissie." Tytus waves and gestures for them to join them.

"Nate, Chrissie, this is Pierce Evans." Tytus introduces them, his voice still dripping with fake friendliness.

"Nice to meet you." Nate offers a firm handshake. "Nate Richards. And this is my wife Chrissie."

Before Pierce has a chance to respond, Chrissie speaks up, making Tytus regret the fact that he's waved them over.

"I am such a huge fan," Chrissie gushes, wrapping both her hands around his. "I saw you as the Phantom and it changed my life."

Tytus coughs and actually vomits a bit in his mouth.

"Can I get you a drink?" he asks Sarah. "I need a drink." And he walks off before Sarah even has a chance to answer him. Once he chases down a beer and takes a long slow pull from it, he grabs a glass of champagne for Sarah and rejoins the group.

They talk all about how amazing Sarah had been and Pierce asks Nate about life as a sports agent. He doesn't seem interested in life as an athlete because he doesn't ask Tytus a single thing.

A while later, in the middle of Pierce answering Chrissie's question about the main differences he found between Hollywood and Broadway, Tytus interrupts with a question of his own. One that's been burning a hole in his brain for two weeks.

"Speaking of Hollywood, when will you be going back?"

Pierce opens and then shuts his mouth as the entire group falls into an awkward silence. Sarah slips her hand from Tytus's and moves a half step away from him. Indicating, most likely, that she doesn't appreciate his line of questioning.

"I only mean that a man as successful as you must be very busy," Tytus tries to recover. "I'm guessing someone is anxiously awaiting your return?"

Although harmless on the surface, Pierce's eyes flash with understanding.

"No one in particular, actually." Pierce stands up straighter, exaggerating the height difference between the two men. "In fact, I'm in no hurry to return to L.A." His eyes shift slowly and deliberately from Tytus to Sarah and back again. "I'm quite enjoying my time here."

"I'm going to change. It's been a long night." Sarah smiles but it doesn't fool any of them. "Good night. Nate, Chrissie, Pierce." She nods at her two friends but reaches for Pierce's hand, letting her fingers linger in his palm for an extra beat or two before casting her eyes toward Tytus and walking away.

Leaving Tytus with that pressure in his chest, his jaw locked, and his fists clenching at his sides.

Sarah walks into her dressing room and shuts the door with a little extra force.

That was more than a little awkward and she's pretty sure it may have ruined any shot she had for a job offer from Pierce. Tytus had acted like a spoiled child and he is going to hear about it just as soon as she calms down.

Not the mad part of her. She wants to hang on to all of that anger so she can hurl it at him the minute they are alone. What she needs is a cold glass of water, or better yet, a cold shower.

Sarah looks in the mirror at her reflection and shakes her head. Whatever she is going to say to Tytus, she needs to make damn sure he can't tell that his jealousy had downright turned her on. She is pissed at the way he had acted, and she expected far better from him than that, but something about him spreading his feathers like a peacock, and clearly staking his claim on her with that kiss and his comments, made her panties damp. And the flirty move she made at the end…letting her hand linger in Pierce's, it hadn't been one of her proudest moments. But she liked the way Tytus's body had stiffened, and she rationalizes that he had it coming.

By the time she makes her way out of the dressing room, the backstage area has completely cleared out. With her arms full of flowers, she pushes her way through the back door and finds Tytus leaning against the Lexus.

Neither of them say a word the entire ride and by the time they walk in Sarah's door, her temper is simmering dangerously close to the surface.

"You want to explain what the hell is wrong with you?" She raises her voice the minute the door to her apartment closes.

"Oh, I'm sorry." He matches her volume. "Did I interrupt your little date?" Tytus strides across the room until his face is inches from hers. "Admit it, you've been lusting after the man for years." His voice is full of disdain as he tilts his head and looks down at her.

"What the hell are you even talking about?" She is caught off guard by his comment but even more so by the dangerous look in his eyes.

"Sebastian told me," he scoffs. "You've been pining after him ever since you moved to Manhattan." Tytus raises his chin as if he's challenging her to deny it.

She can hardly believe the words coming out of his mouth. Is he serious right now? *Sebastian told him? Pining after him?* Sarah laughs out loud in exasperation.

"Sebastian's always had it out for you." She shakes her head mockingly and leans in even closer. "He'd say anything he could to get a rise out of you. Looks like it worked."

She rolls her eyes and turns to walk away from him, but Tytus grabs her wrist. Sarah's heart lurches in her chest as heat courses through her veins like electricity through a live wire. Purposefully, she keeps her back to him trying to catch her breath, but Tytus tugs on her arm and pulls her back into him.

They stand there, face to face, chest to chest, as his eyes search hers for the truth. Neither of them speak for several beats.

"Are you saying it isn't true?" His voice is hoarse. "I saw the way you ran your fingers across his palm."

The way he tightens his grip on her wrist ever so slightly, and presses his chest tighter against hers, makes her weak in the knees. They are teetering on a dangerous ledge, and it makes her breathless. She stands her ground and pushes him even further.

"Did it make you *jealous?*" She looks up at him through her long lashes, a teasing glint in her eyes.

His brows draw together and she sees the twitch in his clenched jaw which only turns her on more.

"Sarah," he rasps. There is a warning there. His control is slipping.

"You're the only one I want, Tytus." She licks her lips as she lets her eyes drift down to his. "You want me all to yourself?" Her eyes drift back up to his and his irises are black and full of need.

She takes a finger from the hand he's not gripping and runs it slowly over his bottom lip. "Show me."

The hand Tytus has clenched at his side is around the back of her neck before she takes her next breath while the one holding her wrist quickly pins it behind her back. His tongue is down her throat and he pulls her into him with an aggressive jerk, simultaneously grinding his protruding crotch into her abdomen.

Sarah's drowning in his kiss. Growing dizzy from the lack of oxygen as his tongue ravages the inside of her mouth. And just when she's ready to give in and let her legs buckle beneath her, he tears his mouth from hers and she gasps for air.

"You're mine." The gravel in his tone combined with the heat of his breath on her lips only stokes the fire in her core.

"Prove it."

She is *messing with the bull* and she knows it. She wants it. Knowing she can drive him crazy and test his control makes her feel powerful, but he is about to take the reins. And she is all for it.

Tytus spins her around and presses her firmly against the wall in the hallway. He releases her wrist and she braces herself with both palms against the cool textured surface. He ravishes her neck and thrusts into her backside repeatedly. He could make her come without removing a single layer of clothing if he wanted to.

But that's not what he wants. That becomes very clear.

She feels his hands come up and under her dress, lifting it above her hips as he continues to suck on her neck and growl words she can't quite make out. Hooking his fingers in her thong at the base of her tailbone he tears them off with a frenzied yank, causing a yelp from her she didn't see coming.

Tytus's hands wrap around the front of her thighs and his long fingers slide just to the edge of her soaking folds. She wants him so badly she nearly draws blood biting her lower lip. She pushes her exposed ass back into him, urging him to touch her, to take her, but he doesn't.

Tytus grips the front of her thighs, meeting her backward motion with his forward pressure, but he doesn't move his fingers. He doesn't touch her. Not yet.

Instead, he brings his right hand around to her firm ass cheek and caresses it. With every glide of his hand, he increases the pressure. Sarah's breathing is erratic, to put it mildly, and when she glances back at him over her shoulder she sees that his eyes are fixed downward. He's watching intently as he rubs her warm pale flesh.

"Tytus. Tytus, please." The coiling in her abdomen is nothing compared to the throbbing between her legs. The way she wants him. Needs him. It's as though she's never felt him inside of her before. Like she's been waiting for him her entire life.

"You want me to prove it?" He reaches up and takes a handful of Sarah's long, red hair. Wrapping it around his fingers he pulls down, slowly, deliberately, causing her neck to lift and exposing her throat. "I'll make you come so hard you'll never think of fucking anyone but me."

He tilts her head toward him with another tug on her hair and invades her mouth again with his tongue. It's as though he needs to devour every whimper that escapes from her wanting mouth. As though each time she moans, she feeds the fire. Sarah has never been this turned on. Not. Ever. She knows, without a doubt, she would do anything he asked.

Tytus keeps her pressed up against him. His rock-hard erection secured firmly between them as he guides her toward the bedroom. All the while, his hands are roaming her body possessively. Whatever skin he can reach, considering her dress is still on, touching her everywhere except where she wants him to the most.

When they reach the bed, she starts to climb on but he stops her. He steps between her legs and pushes them further apart with his knees.

"Bend over."

It's not a request and she complies without hesitation. Her elbows land on the mattress in front of her, her ass angling upward toward him. He doesn't touch her for a moment or two and she dares to look at him over her shoulder. His eyes are locked on her body. Just staring at her, taking her in. The desire emanating from him takes her need to another level.

His gaze shifts to meet hers and her first instinct is to look away. As if she's been caught watching something she shouldn't. But when he reaches for the hem of his sweater, she knows he wants her to watch. She wants to watch.

Tytus pulls the sweater and the t-shirt under it off with ease, quickly exposing the chest and biceps that make Sarah drool. But when he reaches for the zipper of his pants, he gives his next command.

"Close your eyes."

When she doesn't react right away, and lets her eyes drift to the protruding bulge he's about to set free, he gives her a sharp spank on the ass.

"Hey. I know you want to watch but you can't. Close your eyes."

This time she does as he says and he caresses the reddening spot with one hand as he pushes his pants down with the other. The next thing she knows, both his hands are gripping her and spreading her cheeks apart.

Just as the thrill this brings courses through her, she feels him. His length between her cheeks as he slowly glides up and down. She is so wet, that he slides between them easily and she hears his breathing start to stagger. He runs his hands across the backs of her thighs, along the small of her back. She has never wanted anything more than she wants him inside of her at this very moment.

She hears him hiss as he pulls his body from hers, and just as she's about to whimper from the loss of contact, she feels him kneel behind her and she holds her breath in anticipation. He applies the slightest outward pressure on each side of her cheeks, and wanting to grant him as much access as possible, she lifts her knees onto the bed, sliding them even further apart. Despite doing this without his instruction, he doesn't complain. Instead, he buries his tongue inside her. Gripping her possessively, he dives deeper just as he had done into her mouth when she first dared him to.

The orgasm is immediate and all-consuming, she bucks and shakes and cries out, and all the while his mouth stays on her. Lapping up and taking in everything she has to give. When the orgasm finally subsides, she collapses onto the mattress, but only for a moment. Because he's not done with her yet.

Tytus lifts her hips and brings her back onto her knees. He reaches for her hair and wraps his hand around it, the same way he had done in the hallway. He has never pulled her hair this way, before tonight, but Sarah will make sure he knows how much she likes it.

With a firm grip on her hair, and his knees braced against the side of the bed, he enters her. One long hard thrust and he's as deep inside her as her body will allow. The sound he lets out is primal and hungry, and with every thrust in and out, with every pump of his hips into hers, he takes her right back to climax in a matter of seconds. Only this time, they fall from the cliff together.

Moments later, she has her head on his naked chest as they lay side by side. Her dress, finally discarded, and a light sheet draped over them.

"Tytus?" she asks while running her fingers through his chest hair.

"Hmm?"

"That was...wow."

Tytus doesn't respond but he pulls her a little tighter against him and before she knows it, she's sleeping like a well-swaddled baby.

Tytus sits in Dr. Ruzzoli's waiting room the following morning, drumming his fingers on his knee nervously. He'd called and asked for a last-minute appointment and the doctor had agreed. He doesn't usually get nervous before their sessions. He's grown to enjoy them, actually. But today is different.

"Tytus," Levi's voice breaks through the silence. "Come on in."

His warm smile makes Tytus feel both better and worse, somehow. How the fuck is he going to talk about this?

"Levi." Tytus nods when he stands. "Thanks for seeing me, last minute."

"Of course, Tytus. I'm just glad my schedule allowed for it."

The two men sit down in their usual spots and Tytus's knee drumming picks right up where he left off. Ruzzoli waits patiently for him to begin. He's the one who asked to see him, after all.

"So, something happened last night. With Sarah and me... and I'm having trouble processing it."

Ruzzoli looks up at Tytus, thoughtfully. "Well, I'm glad you called, Tytus. It shows how much you value your relationship with Sarah."

Tytus coughs nervously, and breaks eye contact, running his hand over his face. He may as well start with the easy part.

"You know how I've been having trouble with…feeling jealous."

"I do. Is this about that? About Pierce Evans?"

"Yes. And…yes." Tytus pauses and contemplates how to continue without making it completely awkward for both of them. Finally admitting to himself that that isn't possible, he decides to just get it over with.

"He was at Sarah's closing show last night. I watched them together from across the room, and I let her pipsqueak of an assistant get in my head."

"I see," Levi responds. "And what, may I ask, did he put in your head when you let him in there?"

Tytus stares at him, momentarily dreading how stupid this is going to sound when he says it aloud.

"That Sarah has a thing for this guy. That she always has." He looks down at the rug below his feet. "That I should be worried."

Ruzzoli raises his eyebrows. "He said all that?"

"Well, not those exact words." Tytus runs a hand through his hair. "He got to me. Watching them got to me. And needless to say, I handled it poorly. I embarrassed her."

Ruzzoli just sits back and looks at him thoughtfully. Waiting for Tytus to continue.

"But this isn't even about that. Not really." Tytus shoos the topic away like a fly. "It's about what happened once we got back to Sarah's place."

"You had a fight." It's phrased as a statement.

"You'd think, right?" Tytus fixes his eyes on his therapist. "A fight would make sense. But what we had was…sex." He purses his lips thoughtfully and lets out a stream of air. "We had sex." Tytus looks away from the therapist like he's confessed to some terrible crime.

"And you see that as a problem. Not a solution?" The doctor works his usual magic. No judgment. No opinions, just another question.

"Isn't it? I mean, we didn't even talk about it. Not really. Instead of addressing the real issue, she turned it into some kind of sex game. She dared me to take control and I..." Tytus stops himself. He hadn't meant to say quite that much. His neck feels a little warm and he's guessing Ruzzoli can see he's embarrassed.

"Tytus. I heard you say you didn't address the 'real issue'." Ruzzoli steers the conversation in a different direction. "What do you see as the real issue here? Are you worried that Sarah has feelings for Pierce? Do you think she will leave you for him?"

"What? No. Well, not really." He shifts around in his seat and runs his hands down his thighs, it's his tell that he's getting uncomfortable with the waters they are treading in. He inhales, holds it, and lets it out slowly. He's become quite dependent on that strategy of self-calming.

"Maybe I was at first. The idea of Sarah being touched by another man." He pauses. "It makes me crazy. Seeing her across the room smiling at him, laughing, and then having Sebastian whispering in my ear." He clenches and relaxes his fists before looking back up. "It made me boil inside. And I acted like an ass."

Levi just nods at him before offering, "Jealousy is a dangerous emotion. But it's also natural. We want to hold onto the things and the people whom we love."

"But, Sarah wasn't even mad about the way I acted. I...I think she liked it." He shakes his head. "How am I supposed to make sense of that?"

"Do you want my opinion, Tytus?"

"That's why I'm here."

"Maybe the reason she wasn't angry is because she's confident in how she feels about you. How you feel about her. I think she knows that Pierce is not a threat to what the two of you share." Levi waits for Tytus to look back at him. "And it's natural for a woman to want to feel wanted by a man. Jealousy, when it doesn't get out of hand, can let others know how much you value them. Need them. Maybe that feeling is what Sarah needed from you."

Show me.

Prove it.

Tytus thinks back to the night before. To the things Sarah said and the hunger and need in her eyes. Maybe Ruzzoli had a point. Tytus feels some of the tension in his shoulders relax. He takes another deep breath.

"That makes sense, I guess. Honestly, I was feeling a little uneasy about the way I…" He looks away and clenches his jaw.

"Tytus, was Sarah upset at all with what happened between the two of you? Afterward, I mean. Did you cross any lines that might be hard to come back from?"

"No. No, she was fine. Better than fine, actually."

"Then I think you have no reason to regret what happened. Quite the opposite."

When Tytus looks at Ruzzoli and tilts his head, he clarifies his meaning.

"I think the two of you communicated more than you realize last night. Sometimes we share how we feel more clearly without any words at all." He smiles and adds, "Maybe now you can both move on? Put this issue with Pierce Evans behind you?"

"That's just it." Tytus hesitates, bringing his eyes back to Levi's. "I don't think it's really Pierce that's got me worried, after all."

Sarah and Tytus arrive at Nate and Chrissie's around 6:00 p.m. on Sunday, armed with two bottles of wine. Tonight at 7:00 is the MLB All-Star show where they reveal all the players who were voted on the team. Even though Tytus is a lock to make the team, she can tell he's a bit nervous. Imagine attending a party in your honor and then not getting selected.

She slides her fingers through his as Nate answers the door with a much louder than necessary greeting.

"There he is, Ladies and Gentlemen. My best friend, and my biggest client, the soon-to-be All-Star, Tyyyytussss Haaaaayes Jr.!" He waves his hands in the air and makes fake crowd cheering noises.

"Wow. Somebody knocked a few back already." Sarah laughs at Nate's introduction. "Where's your wife? Shouldn't she be babysitting you?"

"I'm right here." Chrissie walks up to greet them. "And I'm busy hosting a party, so he's on his own."

The men head to the oversized family room where the large flat-screen TV is already tuned to ESPN and the women head to the kitchen to pour Sarah some wine.

Within a few minutes, Traci and Spencer arrive and the three of them catch up and gossip about their husbands.

"Speaking of Tytus," Chrissie segues, "did you two have it out the other night after your show?"

"This sounds juicy." Traci raises her brow. "Have it out about what?"

Chrissie starts at the beginning and explains how Pierce Evans burst into Sarah's life and how Tytus hasn't exactly welcomed him with open arms.

Sarah is careful not to let the conversation get too carried away and eventually puts an end to it by saying Tytus was fine, and that she'd assured him he had nothing to worry about with Pierce or any other man for that matter.

"But, it's Pierce Evans," Chrissie teases.

"Yeah," Sarah says. "And he's Tyyyyytusssss Haaaayes," she draws out his name like Nate had earlier and the other two girls burst into laughter. Sarah smiles into her wine glass, but it's mostly for show. There is a small part of her that worries the issue isn't as cut and dry as she makes it out.

By the time the selection show starts, everyone is gathered in the room with the TV. Most everyone has a pretty good buzz going and the room is loud with chatter.

"Okay. Shut up, shut up. It's starting."

Sarah is seated next to Tytus on the couch, one of her legs draped over his casually. He's playing it off well, but he's nervous. She can tell. His hand is on her knee and she lays her palm on top of it. When he looks at her from the corner of his eye, she mouths *I love you.* He smiles and squeezes her knee before casting his gaze back at the TV. The sports broadcasters hosting the show announce that they will begin with the American League, and everyone breaks into applause.

This is it.

They begin with what they call the starting lineup of 'position players', which excludes pitchers. These players are voted on by the fans and to the delight of everyone at the party they hear the name Spencer Kline come through the surround sound speakers Nate has splashed around the room.

Sarah watches as Tytus's grin spreads from ear to ear, and Traci jumps into her husband's arms despite the now visible baby bump. Sarah slides her fingers through Tytus's as they watch their friends celebrate. While Tytus is considered a favorite for the closer role by most sports stations, Spencer had been more of a long shot.

A few minutes later, they move on to the pitchers, who instead of being selected by fans, are chosen by their fellow players, making some feel it's an even higher honor.

The hosts start by naming the starting pitchers that were selected. Moments later, the entire room goes silent with anticipation as the word "Closer," leaves the lips of one of the men on the screen.

Sarah can feel her heart beating in her chest, pounding loudly as she holds her breath.

"Tytus Hayes Jr.!"

His name comes from the TV and every speaker surrounding them and the room erupts for a second time. Since they are already seated, and she can't jump into his arms, Sarah improvises and swings herself around to straddle Tytus on the couch. She lays a kiss on him that she's sure tastes of wine and he chuckles right into her mouth.

"Congratulations, Tytus Hayes Jr."

He smiles up at her and she can see the pride swelling in his eyes. She slides off of him and helps pull him to his feet so he can shake every hand and slap every back of the friends who came here tonight to support him. None of them are more excited than Nate.

"Sarah, Sarah," Nate whispers and waves for her to follow him. "I got you something."

She follows the now very drunk Nate down the hall with a mixture of apprehension and curiosity.

"Shhhhhh." He spits a raspberry at her with his finger on his lips, even though she hadn't made a sound. "It's a thurprise."

Sarah giggles as Nate grabs a bag from his bedroom closet. But the moment she pulls out what's inside, the giggles turn to a gasp. She drops the bag and uses both hands to hold Nate's gift up in front of her eyes which are now welling in gracious tears.

"Nate." She looks back and forth between him and the jersey in front of her. "It's perfect!"

Nate's *thurprise* was a custom American League All-Star jersey, embroidered with the number 42, and Hayes Jr. written in large bold script. In the All-Star Game, he will have his name on the back of his jersey so hers will match his exactly.

She wraps her dear friend in a bear hug as he encourages her wildly to put it on.

And when the two of them walk proudly back into the crowded living room, the look on Tytus's face is priceless.

18

Foreboding

*T*ytus sips on his coffee as the plane reaches its cruising altitude. The smile plastered on his face while looking out the window is completely out of character. Generally, a departing flight for a road trip that will have him away from New York for nearly two weeks would bring a scowl, not a grin. But this trip is different.

"Can I get you anything else, Mr. Hayes?"

"No. Thank you. I'm fine." He offers a half smile to the flight attendant and turns his focus back to the clouds. The flight isn't even two hours and he's chasing a headache from the celebratory drinks and lack of sleep last night. Again, he can't help but grin.

Last night was one of the best nights of his life. Getting the All-Star nod had been a dream of his since he was 8 years old when Derek Jeter, his favorite player, was selected to the All-Star team for the first time. Now he, himself, would be a part of the Mid-Summer Classic wearing a navy pin-striped jersey of his own.

But, while it was a dream come true, that wasn't the only thing that had Tytus's head in the clouds, so to speak. He'd shared an incredible night with Sarah. And as his mind drifts to thoughts of her, his eyes fall shut and blood rushes to his crotch.

They barely made their way through Tytus's door before their hands were all over each other. They were both drunk which meant two things, sloppy kissing, and compromised balance. Sarah tripped over Tytus's clumsy feet and the harder he tried to hold her up, the less he could regain his footing. They both went down hard.

Thanks to being drunk…it didn't hurt.

Tytus removed his clothes and Sarah's jeans with surprising dexterity, but when she moved to unbutton her new jersey, he stopped her.

"Leave it on."

Sarah just giggled and buried her fingers into his hair instead.

And as he glided in and out of her on the floor of his condo, her long auburn waves spread carelessly around her face, wearing nothing but an All-Star jersey bearing his name, he realized she had never looked more beautiful. And as he emptied inside of her while she screamed his name, he wondered absently if that made him romantic or incredibly vain.

He opens his eyes and glances over his shoulder self-consciously. Worried that someone may be watching him and be onto where his mind had gone. He just isn't sure if it's his shit-eating grin or the tent in his pants that might be giving him away.

Luckily, Spencer is fast asleep across the aisle and no one else is close enough to notice. He unlocks his phone and swallows thickly at his new screensaver. Sarah, looking back at him over her shoulder while pointing both thumbs down at the name Hayes Jr. printed across her back.

He is such a fucking goner. His chest swells with an overwhelming combination of love and pride.

This morning Sarah had surprised him with a plane ticket of her own, another reason for his impenetrable good mood. She is meeting him in Cleveland, following him to Boston, and then the two will spend four days together in Toronto for the All-Star festivities. He's never been happier.

Getting to spend so much time with Sarah is going to be amazing. They both have such demanding schedules, and as much as he loves how talented and successful Sarah is, there is a small, selfish, part of him that wishes she could just spend all her time with him.

Sarah is half-naked and working her way toward the shower after her morning yoga class when her phone starts ringing on the nightstand. It seems too early for Tytus to have landed in Cleveland, so she's guessing it's Chrissie.

She's wrong.

The name Pierce Evans has her display brightly lit, and there is just no getting used to that.

"Pierce?" She doesn't hide the surprise from her tone.

"Sarah. I'm glad I caught you. Do you have a few minutes?"

Sarah looks down at her naked bottom half and then glances into her bathroom at the open shower door with the water running.

"Or, if it's a bad time—" Pierce says when Sarah doesn't respond to his question.

"No, no. It's fine. Can you just hang on one second?" She's pretty sure she's blushing as if he can hear her nakedness through the phone.

She sets her phone down and runs to shut off the water in the shower. She grabs a pair of pajama shorts from her drawer and throws them on before picking up her phone from the bed.

"Okay," she says into the phone awkwardly as she heads to her living room sofa. "Sorry about that."

The next fifteen to twenty minutes are like a scene straight from an episode of *The Twilight Zone*. And when Sarah eventually hangs up, her hand is shaking as she sets her phone on the coffee table. It's a little early for a drink, but she heads straight to the kitchen to pour one anyway. She just spent an hour doing hot yoga to rid her body of the alcohol from last night, but in spite of that, she opens the freezer and pulls the bottle of vodka from it. As her hand trembles, she pours a double into a small glass and does her best not to pour it all over the counter. She picks up the shot, tilts it back, and empties the clear liquid right down her throat. Both the burn and hiss it brings a necessary and welcomed distraction.

Pierce Evans has just offered her a job.

In California.

The range of emotions she has just experienced reminded her of *Mr. Toad's Wild Ride* at Disneyland. While it may seem a strange comparison to some, it is the first thing she thought of when the call ended. Maybe it had something to do with her visit to Disneyland on her one and only trip to California.

Steading herself by gripping the countertop with both hands, she works desperately to regain control of her breathing.

Pierce is beginning the casting for his first film as a producer. He explained that it is a suspense-filled drama about the disappearance of a young aspiring Broadway actress. He thinks she is perfect for the role. Apparently, this role was the reason he sought her out in the first place, but the film hadn't been picked up yet, and he didn't want to get her hopes up until he knew for sure it was moving forward.

Sarah is shocked and flattered of course, but it is so much to take in. California? A movie? She is a stage actress. The theater is her first love, and despite her respect and admiration for screen actors, it has never been a dream of hers. Still, a move like this could change her entire career. Her life.

His offer, and all the wonderful things he said about her talent, make her heart race. The idea that she could star in a blockbuster film in Hollywood…is beyond anything she had ever imagined for herself.

Her eyes wander around the room and then settle on the envelope on the counter in front of her. As she reaches down and slides the contents out of it, her heart skips in her chest. Her plane ticket.

She closes her eyes as she thinks of Tytus. The smile on his face when he kissed her goodbye early this morning. The sparkle in his eyes when she told him of her plan to spend this road trip by his side. The hurt and jealousy she had seen in those same eyes weeks ago when they had fought about Pierce.

She presses her eyes closed tighter as she turns and leans her back against the countertop. Both hands come to cover her face as another wave of emotion washes over her. Her mind is racing with a million questions she doesn't have the answers to.

How is Tytus going to take this news? Is this even something she wants to do? Could a long-distance relationship between an actress and an athlete actually survive?

She considers looking for the answers at the bottom of another shot of vodka but opts for the shower instead. A quick glance at the clock reminds her she has a plane to catch.

By the time the wheels hit the runway in Cleveland, Sarah has made up her mind. Made up her mind, that is, that she's not ready to make any decisions. Pierce told her she could take her time, and she is going to do just that. If she does decide to make the trip to Los Angeles, she wouldn't need to leave for a couple of weeks, and even if she does go, she doesn't have to commit to the role right away. Pierce had simply asked that she come out, read the script, run some lines, check out the studio, and then decide.

She has also made up her mind not to tell Tytus about the offer. Yet. She hadn't even called to tell Chrissie. Granted, there hasn't really been time, but when you have a friend who is married, telling her basically means telling them both. And when her husband is best friends with your boyfriend, no secret is really safe.

She wants to make this trip about him. Sure, it's about them as well, but mostly it's an opportunity for her to celebrate his success and enjoy her two new loves. Tytus and baseball.

She had missed so many of his games, with her schedule being just as demanding as his, and there is a reason she requested this break. They need some time together to just be Sarah and Tytus. The thought of that soothes her far more than the vodka had. This week will be about Tytus and supporting his career, and once they are back home, she can think about hers.

Sarah bobs and weaves her way through the sea of people on her way to the baggage claim carousel. She had tried, and failed, to pack light with a simple carry-on. She isn't sure who she was trying to fool.

Once her bag is offloaded, she heads outside to find the Uber/Lyft pick-up area while digging back into her purse for her phone.

"Miss Dalton?"

Sarah nearly runs smack into the man in front of her who is holding a small sign with her name on it.

"Oh," she practically yelps. "Yes, I'm Sarah Dalton."

"Excellent," he responds. "My name is Jonathan. Mr. Hayes sent me to bring you by the hotel and then on to the stadium." The man looks as though he takes his job very seriously, and when he sees the hesitation in Sarah's eyes he adds, "He said he sent you a message?"

Sarah looks down at the phone she finally fished out and reads a text from Tytus that must have come in when her Wi-Fi resumed.

Be nice to Jonathan. He's no Miles, but he'll take good care of you. XO

A slow smile spreads across her face at what has become his new signature. The man refuses to use emojis. Jonathan clears his throat to remind Sarah he's waiting to take her bag, and she slides it toward him with a soft smile.

The ride to the hotel is quick and Sarah tells Jonathan she'll only need a few minutes. Tytus had explained in his excitement about her coming on the road trip, that while she may not always be able to travel with the team, she can stay with him in the hotels.

A quick show of her ID and she's on her way up the elevator, key in hand. The room is massive. An oversized suite with a balcony overlooking the city and a large bathtub that catches her eye. She will definitely be taking advantage of that. She knows she told the driver she wouldn't be long, but the large bed is lifted high above the floor and the down comforter is calling out to her. As she flops backward onto the bed she can almost hear her mom scolding her. As a child in the Dalton home lying on top of the down comforter was strictly forbidden. Sarah feels like such a rebel, and it makes her laugh.

As she lies there, looking up at the crown modeling around the ceiling, she thinks about the luxuries of being a star like Tytus. She knows it comes with its pressures and drawbacks. And she has tasted some of that kind of attention in her line of work. But she can't help but wonder what it would be like on a larger scale. What if she took this job and ended up a famous Hollywood star? Is a life on the front page, with every move under a microscope, worth a personal driver and a fancy hotel room?

She pushes herself up from the bed, brushes those thoughts away, and quickly freshens up before heading back down to Jonathan.

When they pull up to the VIP area of the stadium about thirty minutes later, she gets out and thanks the driver graciously. She tries repeatedly to tip him, but he assures his fee has been more than taken care of. It's not until she turns and faces the stadium that she's hit with an influx of butterflies. She's not sure why exactly, but she finds it equally exciting and nerve-racking to head into the stadium alone.

Tytus had asked if she wanted to sit with some of the other women who would be on the trip, or if she'd like a seat next to the bullpen where he'd be spending the majority of the game. She chose the latter. Not that she wasn't interested in meeting the other women, but she knows that they are mostly *wives* and not *girlfriends* and she prefers to meet them in the company of Traci or Chrissie, neither of whom would be attending this series.

In Boston, she'd have Tytus's family. In fact, she's pretty sure they are going to be watching from a luxury box, similar to the one they have at Yankee Stadium. And in Toronto, for the All-Star Game, Nate, Chrissie, Traci, and most likely Tytus Sr., Travis, and Tess will all be joining her. In fact, it looks like even her dad might be coming to the game. Now that will be interesting.

Tytus is in the bullpen playing grab-ass with his buddies when he catches a glimpse of red hair from the corner of his eye. It actually causes a flutter in his gut.

He turns his head and takes a tossed ball to the chest, but it bounces off of him like he's made of steel.

Sarah.

He saunters over to the gray padded wall that separates the outfield seats from the pen. Considering the way the seats overlook the field level, he has to step on a folding chair to reach her.

"You're here."

He extends his hand up and through the guardrail to take hers. It never ceases to amaze him how her beauty takes his breath away.

"I'm here." Sarah smiles and shrugs both shoulders up in excitement.

Tytus matches her smile with his own and neither says anything more for a solid minute. He has been excited for her to come. To spend this whole road trip by his side, wearing his jersey, cheering for him in the stands, being his...girl. He'd always convinced himself he didn't need that. Want that. That he wasn't jealous of the guys who always had a girlfriend or a wife waiting at the end of the tunnel after a long night. But as he stands here, in this moment, looking up at Sarah's beautiful face, he knows he could never imagine living without it now. Without her.

"You wash that?" he jokes, flaring his nostrils, and eyeballing the jersey she is wearing.

"Why would I do that?" Sarah lifts the front of the jersey and takes an exaggerated whiff. "It smells like sex with Tytus Hayes. You know what I could get for this on eBay?"

Tytus chuckles out loud at the serious expression on Sarah's face. Her wit and sense of humor make her that much sexier. They chat for a few more minutes about her flight and the hotel suite before Tytus has to get back to his team.

Once the game starts, he is all business, and his game face is plastered on throughout all the action. But that doesn't mean his eyes don't wander in Sarah's direction. He can't help the way his gaze drifts over to the seat where she's perched above him. He knows it's not rational, but a part of him feels like if he doesn't keep checking, she might just disappear.

Sarah can't get enough of this fangirl stuff. Progressive Field, home of the Cleveland Guardians, is almost as impressive as Yankee Stadium, and surprisingly she thinks she likes this perspective even more than the view from the luxury box. Or maybe she just likes the view of her super sexy boyfriend. Her seat is right along the railing between the right field pavilion and the bullpen. The vantage point from the way it overlooks them is amazing. She has been watching the game, mostly, but she has a hard time keeping her eyes off Tytus. As she sips on her cold beer and cracks peanut shell after peanut shell, it reminds her of the night in Boston when she nearly creamed her panties watching Tytus stretch. It brings on a serious case of the giggles which has her choking on her mouth full of beer. The struggle to keep from spitting it all over the heads of the couple in front of her is real.

"Are you alright?" The older man sitting to her left reaches over and places his hand on her shoulder.

Sarah gulps down the beer in her mouth and smiles at her new friend Jerry.

"I'm fine. Just," she shrugs her shoulders, "wrong pipe, you know?"

The couple sitting next to her had become her new best friends. Jerry and Barbara are visiting from California for their anniversary. They had met in Ohio when they both attended Dayton University and Barbara was a die-hard fan of 'The Tribe'.

Sarah just loves meeting couples like them. Still so in love after more than 50 years of marriage. Listening to their story, combined with enjoying watching Tytus in his element, causes her mind to wander to the call from Pierce, and the looming decision that hangs over her. She had always thought her career was the most important thing in her life, but as her eyes wander down to Tytus, and he lifts his chin to meet her gaze, she wonders if all that has changed.

The Yankees lose the game 3-1 and although Tytus isn't called on to pitch, Sarah did get to watch him warm up and the view was enough to heat up her body despite the drop in temperature after sunset. The thing that really caught her eye was the power of his thighs and the way he'd balance on one leg before driving his weight forward when he pushed off the mound. Who knew how hot watching a pitcher warm up could be? She curses Mason silently for turning her off of athletes for all these years. She's beginning to realize she has really missed out.

Tytus has to ride to the hotel on the team bus, and Sarah finds Jonathan waiting for her in the same spot he'd dropped her off. Apparently, he's going to be her personal driver for the next couple days, which is actually really nice since she'll be mostly traveling without Tytus.

The two finally find their way into each other's arms as Tytus wraps her in a bear hug and spins her around. Sarah had beaten him back to the hotel and the minute he walked through the door, he'd gone straight to her.

They order room service, take a bath neither of them really needs, and climb into bed still damp under their robes.

"How about a massage?" Sarah says lifting the lotion from the bedside table.

"For you or for me?" Tytus answers her question with another. "Nevermind. Either way, it's a yes."

Sarah giggles as Tytus wriggles his eyebrows at her.

"I meant for you, but if one thing leads to another, who am I to stop natural progression?" Sarah moves herself down toward the end of the bed and lathers the lotion in her hands.

"Now, let's start with your thighs…"

The charter plane that carried the team from Cleveland to Boston landed at Logan International about thirty minutes before Sarah's commercial flight, so Tytus is waiting for Sarah by baggage claim.

The team had taken the next two games, and therefore the series, and Tytus had picked up another save. Sarah got to know a few of the other women on the trip and even chose to sit with them for the game last night. Tytus can't remember the last time his life had ever felt so perfect. Deep down he knows that's because it never has.

Since today is an off day for the team, Travis will be picking them up to head to Tytus Sr.'s for an early Fourth of July Barbeque. Independence Day has always been a big deal for the Hayes family, and despite the fact that today was just the 2nd, they'd take what they could get. You can't grow up in a town with a history as deep as Boston's and not be a Patriot. It's in your blood.

He spots Sarah coming down the escalator with her hair pulled back and her Yankee cap pulled down low. She almost looks like she's in some kind of disguise.

Not that Tytus can talk. He's wearing a hat of his own, not Yankees, but a Chicago Bulls cap he'd picked up when he was in town, and a pair of dark glasses despite being inside. Airports are one of the places you can really get mobbed.

"Hey." He leans in for a soft kiss and slides his fingers through hers as their palms press together and find their familiar place.

"Miss me?"

"Terribly."

They grab Sarah's bag the minute the carousel starts to spit them out and Travis is right on time when they step out to the curb. The strange thing is, he's not alone.

Travis jumps out and runs around the car to give both Tytus and Sarah a hug. He knows his brother all too well so he leans in close before Tytus has a chance to say anything smart.

"Her name is Katie. We've been dating for a few weeks and she's coming to Dad's with us."

Tytus smirks at his little brother's rambling and sees this as a perfect opportunity to torture him.

"A few weeks?" Tytus whispers. "And you're bringing her to the Hayes Circus? Either you're crazy about her or you're trying to get rid of her, I'm just not sure which." Tytus chuckles as he slaps Travis on the back and puts their bags into his trunk.

"Seriously, TJ. I really like this girl. Please don't embarrass me."

"Me?" Tytus puts his hand to his chest in mock offense. "Never." Tytus crosses his chest and puts his fingers in the air like they did when they were kids. "Scout's honor."

Travis shakes his head and climbs back into the driver's seat as Tytus whispers to Sarah, "Let the games begin."

Introductions are made all around as the two couples make the forty-minute drive to their father's place. They learn that Katie grew up in the suburbs of Boston and is the oldest of three. She recently graduated from UMASS and moved back to the area to look for a teaching job. She and Sarah hit it off right away, and they spend most of the drive talking about the theater.

After the divorce, Tytus Sr. had purchased a small two-bedroom fixer upper and spent most of his weekends working on it. Tytus spent quite a bit of time there during the offseason and helped his dad with much of the needed repairs. It has been a big part of the healing process for the two of them and for Travis. Honestly, he feels like this place holds a piece of him.

"Oh," Travis says nonchalantly over his shoulder as they walk toward the front door. "Dad has a surprise to share."

His younger brother raps his knuckles on the door and then opens it without waiting for a response.

"Dad. We're here."

"We're out in the back." Tytus Sr.'s voice carries through the sliding screen leading from the small living room out to the backyard. For as small as the house is, the yard is actually perfect for entertaining.

Tytus makes his way outside and sees that his mom and Danny are already seated with cold drinks in hand. He knew that Danny would be here and after some extensive role-play with Ruzzoli in his last therapy session, he is sure he can handle it. He walks over to give his mom a kiss, and Danny's hand a firm shake.

"TJ." The shriek comes from out of nowhere and precedes a flying tackle from Tess. Tytus hasn't seen his baby sister since the start of the season, and he didn't even know she'd be back from school for the holiday. Bracing himself using his core and a small step back he keeps the both of them from knocking over the grill.

"Tay. I thought you were knee deep in summer classes." He lets her go and gives way to a giant grin at the sight of her. "Isn't this Master's program basically absorbing your entire life?"

"Without a doubt," she replies, reaching for a bell pepper from the barbeque and gets a smack on the hand for her efforts. "But my big brother is a freaking MLB All-Star so I will be keeping up with my classes online for the next week or so."

Tytus's chest puffs out just a bit. For a long time he hadn't been the big brother to Tess that she deserved. Travis had to fill that role for the both of them. But in the past few years he'd really put forth an effort to make up for lost time. Looks like it may be working.

As Tytus turns to greet his father at the grill, he bumps straight into a very unexpected face. He stands there just blinking rapidly as he lifts his sunglasses to the top of his head. He's pretty sure he hears Travis snickering but everything's gone a bit hazy.

"TJ." Tytus Sr. walks up and slides his arm around the waist of the woman in front of him. "You remember Mrs. Maguire, don't you?"

Tytus swallows thickly and nods. He knows he should say something, but instead he just stares. Her red hair is much lighter than the last time he'd seen her. But he definitely remembers Mrs. Maguire.

"Tytus." She leans in and plants a kiss on his cheek. "Joey just can't stop talking about what an amazing year you're having. Tytus Sr. tells me you're an All-Star. Congratulations."

Tytus smiles bashfully and tries again to find his voice.

"Thank you, Mrs. Maguire. How is Joey?"

"Oh, he's just fine. Still coaching football at the high school. And please, call me Charlotte."

Now he's certain he hears Travis snickering.

Tytus makes his way to the cooler and downs half a beer before Sarah finds her way to him.

"What was that all about?" There is humor in her eyes as she gives him a knowing look.

"What was *what* all about?

She shakes her and laughs at his weak denial. "So you've always had a thing for redheads, I take it?"

"I...what...no..." Tytus shakes his head as his eyebrows pull together.

"It's okay, Tytus." She kisses him softly on the lips. "We all have a Mrs. Maguire in our past. Yours just happens to be sleeping with your father." She taps him on the nose and lets him finish his beer in private.

Sarah is having an amazing time with Tytus's family. Tytus Sr. made some delicious steaks and corn on the cob on the grill and Judy had brought a fruit salad that Sarah can't get enough of. They all talk and laugh and drink until, before she knows it, the sun begins to set.

The rest of the group looks on as the Hayes family plays cornhole. Tytus has been partnered with Tess and they are just about to beat Travis and Tytus Sr. in best two out of three. She is so proud of him. Not for the cornhole, but for the way he is handling everything. She wonders if Tytus Sr. put the two of them together so they could work as a team. She knows Tytus is still working through a lot of regrets in therapy, and his relationship with his sister is one of them. Watching them together now makes her heart swell.

She and Judy share stories about everything from where they grew up, to Tytus's childhood, to Nate and Chrissie's wedding. Sarah is on her third glasses of wine, and her lips are getting looser by the minute. But when Judy asks her what's coming up next with work, Sarah almost swallows her tongue.

"Oh. Um." Sarah's mouth goes dry and she stumbles to answer the seemingly harmless question. "I'm not really sure. Still weighing my options." Her smile is forced. It's the first time since Pierce had offered her the job that she feels like she's hiding it. And she doesn't like that feeling one bit. She can see the confusion on Judy's face, and to make matters worse, enter Tytus.

He plops down in the chair between Sarah and his mom with a cold bottle of water. "Okay," he looks back and forth suspiciously between the two women. "You two have been gabbing nonstop all evening, and now that I'm here, you've run out of things to say?"

Sarah swallows another gulp of her wine and prays that Judy doesn't repeat her previous question.

"Sarah was just telling me about you singing Billy Joel for her. She says you and Nate set her up."

Tytus lets out a booming laugh and Sarah exhales the breath she's holding. Judy must have picked up on Sarah's discomfort and she couldn't be more grateful.

"Well this has been the best day I can remember having in years," his mom continues. "But Danny has to work in the morning and we should be on our way." Judy stands up and so does Tytus. "I can't tell you how excited I am to see you play this weekend, TJ." Her eyes fill with tears and Sarah decides to give them a moment alone.

She heads into the house to use the restroom and stops to take in the photos adorning the walls. There are photos of Tytus, Travis, and Tess everywhere. From black and white baby photos, to color action shots of them from football and baseball games. There is even one of Tytus on the pitcher's mound on the cover of a mock *Sports Illustrated Magazine*.

"I knew it back then, you know?" Tytus Sr.'s voice startles her and she looks back at him. "He was always special. Just a little better than everyone else."

Sarah smiles softly and nods. She doesn't doubt it one bit.

"Can I ask you something?" Tytus Sr. says softly.

"Anything."

"Has Evans made you an offer?"

Sarah is so caught off guard by the question she just opens and shuts her mouth.

"I know it's not my place to ask." Tytus Sr. looks away and wipes his mouth with his hand. The stalling gesture is a spitting image of Tytus. "I'm sorry. I overstepped."

"No," she croaks. "The answer is yes." She has no idea why she's always so quick to open up to this man.

"Does Tytus know?"

Sarah's bottom lip trembles as her eyes grow misty. She shakes her head from side to side.

"He's not going to like it?"

Sarah just looks up into his concerned eyes and swallows.

Tytus Sr. pulls his lips tight as he gives her a curt nod. "He's never been in love before, Sarah. He's kept his heart guarded for so long now." Tytus Sr. takes her hand and gives it a gentle squeeze. "Just, be careful with him, okay?"

She reaches for his arm as he turns away and quickly swipes at the tear that escapes from her eye.

"It's not that I don't want to tell him." She bites the inside of her cheek hoping to keep the tears at bay. "It's just a lot to take in, and I don't even know how I feel about it yet." She looks away from him and drops her hold on his arm. "I don't know. Maybe that's just an excuse."

"Sarah." He looks over his shoulder to make sure they are still alone. "There is nothing wrong with needing time to process it before you talk to Tytus. It's probably smart that you know what you want before you hear what he wants." He takes her hand in his again. "This is your career and your future." He pauses briefly before adding, "I'm always here if you need to talk."

She forces a soft smile and nods in agreement before finding the bathroom she'd come in for in the first place.

The Friday night game had been a blowout. The Yankees beat the Sox 5-0 and Sarah enjoyed every minute of it from the luxury box Tytus had set up for his family. The whole gang had been there and even though they were all disappointed Tytus didn't get to pitch, Sarah was secretly relieved. She knew that despite his vehement denial, he was nervous to pitch with his mom there. She hadn't seen him play since high school and he had really wanted to do well.

Tonight, however, is the Fourth of July and the energy in the stadium is downright electric. Fans decked out in patriotic garb, USA mini-flags passed out to every fan in attendance, and Lee Greenwood blaring through the speakers before the National Anthem. Sarah gets a flurry of goosebumps when the Air Force jets fly over the stadium and the sky lights up with an explosion of color. The long tradition of fireworks has always been one of Sarah's favorites.

For a few brief moments, the team colors are forgotten. There are no Yankees or Red Sox, just Americans and the feeling of unity and pride is palpable.

But the minute the first pitch is thrown for strike one, the Boston fans roar with excitement and the rivalry is back on. Just like that.

"What do you think of all this?" Sarah asks Katie, gesturing to the suite, the food, the stadium. It wasn't long ago when she was quite overwhelmed by it all herself.

"It feels like a dream." Katie smiles with a sparkle in her eye. "My dad and brother are huge Sox fans. I mean my whole family, really. They would die to be here."

"Well, they should come. There's plenty of room. Have them come to the day game tomorrow."

"Oh, I don't know. I'm not sure how Travis would feel about it." Katie looks away like she regrets bringing up the topic.

That comment sparks Sarah's curiosity, so she pushes a little deeper. "What? Why? I'm sure he wants to get to know your family better." Sarah gives Katie a little elbow jab. "Anyone can see he's crazy about you."

Katie blushes at Sarah's comment before answering her question awkwardly.

"It's my brother. He's got such a big mouth." She looks at Sarah with trepidation, seemingly unsure whether or not to go on. "He told Travis that I've always had a crush on Tytus. I used to have his posters up in my room."

Sarah disguises a burst of laughter as a cough but Katie isn't fooled.

"I shouldn't have said anything," she says looking down. "It's just, I really like Travis. But I'm not sure he can get past this. It was just a stupid crush. I mean, every girl in my town was in love with Tytus Hayes Jr. at some point."

Now, it's Sarah's turn to force a smile. She doesn't doubt the truth in that comment one bit, and it brings back the weight of old baggage that she quickly pushes past.

"I'm sure it hasn't been the easiest thing for Travis to grow up with Tytus as a big brother, but I can see what the two of you have is special." Sarah means it completely. "Let me talk to Travis. I think this would be a great opportunity for your families to meet." Sarah offers Katie a cold beer from the ice chest. "You know Tytus Sr. is a Red Sox fan, right?" Sarah laughs and Katie smiles back at her, the worry mostly gone from her eyes.

"I'd love that, Sarah. Thanks."

Tytus absently spins the baseball in his hands as he sits in the bullpen staring up at the scoreboard. The game is still scoreless in the bottom of the seventh inning and he knows his manager will have him start warming up soon. If the game remains tied or his team scores a run or two, he'll be out there for the ninth.

He stands up and walks to the fence, leaning over it and taking in the stadium. He'd grown up attending games at Fenway. His dad had brought him and Travis countless times over the years, never giving up hope that he could turn them away from being Yankee fans.

But when it came to Tytus's own games growing up, it had always been his mom who was there. Driving him to every practice, cheering for him in the stands. She was his biggest fan and everyone knew it.

When they finally had it out, nearly 10 years ago, he had told her she wasn't welcome at his games. He didn't want her there. And it had taken a piece of them both.

He glances up behind home plate where he knows his entire family is watching. Other than Nate and Chrissie, every single person that matters to him is up in that box. His chest swells with a mixture of pride and gratitude. A sudden crack of the bat, and a roar from the many Yankee fans in attendance, wakes Tytus from his trance. Spencer had just slugged a solo home run to lead off the eighth inning.

Yankees - 1. Red Sox - 0.

Time to get to work.

"Here he comes, here he comes!" Travis shouts like a proud kid brother as Tytus makes his signature sprint from the bullpen to the mound.

Sarah is struck immediately by the difference in atmosphere here than in New York. Granted, she had just seen Tytus pitch on the road in Cleveland, but this. This was not Cleveland.

Instead of the iconic ACDC's *Thunderstruck,* it's the riff and bagpipes of *I'm Shipping up to Boston* by the Dropkick Murphys. The Red Sox fans scream, boo, and heckle Tytus mercilessly, while the Yankee faithful do their best to cheer over them.

It's one of the most amazing things Sarah has ever seen.

Judy comes up from behind her and wraps her arm around Sarah's as if she needs her help to balance. Judy's eyes are already spilling over as she looks down at her son with a sense of pride that only a mother can feel.

Boston will send the heart of their lineup to the plate including two players who will be joining Tytus and Spencer in Toronto in a couple of days. With a measly one-run lead, Tytus has his work cut out for him.

Devers leads off and drives a fly ball to center field that the Boston fans think will tie the game, but it is well short of the fence and caught, for out number one.

Judy bounces up and down next to Sarah and she squeezes even tighter onto her arm.

Bogaerts, the Red Sox shortstop, steps into the box. An All-Star himself, he digs in his back foot and waggles his rear end confidently.

"Better be careful with Bogaerts, TJ," Tytus Sr. pipes up and earns a smack on the arm from Judy. "What?" Tytus Sr. objects. "He's a dangerous hitter."

Before the words are out of his mouth, the shortstop hits a bullet down the left field line for a stand-up double and the home crowd erupts.

"Oh my God, Tytus," Judy squeals. "See what you did."

Tytus Sr. mumbles something about not being the one with a bat in his hand and walks to the far side of the suite.

You could slice through the sudden tension in the room with a knife as the potential winning run steps to the plate. A base hit here would tie the game.

Tytus starts him out with a changeup and the hitter is fooled by the off-speed pitch, swinging and missing badly. But the ball bounces in the dirt causing Spencer to drop to his knees to block it, keeping the runner from moving to third base.

"Atta boy, Kline. Way to work back there." Travis Sr. screams as if Spencer can hear him over the hundreds of feet and thousands of screaming fans. Sarah can't ever remember feeling this nervous in her entire life.

The next pitch is a high fastball that Verdugo can't catch up to and Tytus is quickly ahead of the batter with no balls and two strikes.

"Come on, baby. Sit him down," Judy yells with fire in her eyes and Sarah's eyes widen in shock. This is a whole new side to the Hayes clan, and she loves them even more for it.

"Yeah, sit him down," Sarah repeats, not sure exactly what the expression means, but guessing it's a good thing for Tytus.

And sit him down he does, as Tytus paints the outside corner of the plate with a perfectly placed fastball and the umpire wrings out the batter with a violent pump of his hands.

That quiets down the Sox faithful and ramps up the Yankee fans and Sarah is flooded with confidence that Tytus has this completely under control. There is a reason he's an All-Star.

She leans over to his mom and says with conviction, "He's the best damn closer in the game, Judy. He's got this."

And moments later, the batter grounds out to end the game and it's nothing but hoots and hollers and clapping and back slaps for the Hayes family and their guests. Tonight, in this room, there are no Yankee fans or Boston fans, there are only Tytus fans.

The adrenaline pumping through Tytus's veins makes him feel like Superman. As Spencer comes jogging toward him on the mound he feels like he's literally invincible. Man of Steel. The majority of the fans at Fenway Park are pouring out of the exits as fast as they can, but those who came to see the first-place Yankees are loud and proud and on their feet.

"Nice work, Hayes," Spencer slaps him on the back.

"Nice work to you, Kline. You hit the game-winning dinger." He slaps his friend's glove with his own and the two men line up to fist bump with all their teammates.

Tytus showers and changes as quickly as possible and meets his family by the player's exit.

"Oh, TJ," his mom exclaims as soon as she gets her arms around him. "My God, you were amazing out there. It's so much better in person."

Tytus squeezes Judy tightly in both arms as her words fill him with a warmth he has dearly missed. He pulls back so he can see her face. "In person? You mean you watched me on TV?"

Judy places her hand on her son's cheek and looks into his deep brown eyes. "I never missed a game, son. Not a single game."

Tytus pulls his mom into his arms again and fights the urge to cry.

Sarah fumbles with her phone on the nightstand for the third time in five minutes. She thought she shut it off the last time it started buzzing but apparently not.

The beautiful hotel room that Major League Baseball had provided them in Toronto is still dark. They had pulled the thick drapes shut tight when they arrived from Boston late last night. She finally gives up, fearing that her constant rustling will wake Tytus.

She stumbles out of the bedroom and into the small living room of their suite. When she finds her way to a chair she sits down and unlocks her phone. While the three missed calls from Chrissie are just coming into focus, her phone starts to buzz in her hand. Chrissie. Again.

"Chrissie?" Sarah answers, her tone somewhere between worried and annoyed.

"Sarah. Finally," Chrissie responds with exasperation. "I've been trying to reach you since last night."

"I'm sorry, Wis. What is it? Is everything okay?"

"Sarah. There is something I need to ask you before Nate and I join you guys in Toronto this afternoon."

"Okaayyy," Sarah exaggerates the last syllable, having no clue where this is going.

"I had drinks last night with my friend Stacie. The one from college?"

She phrases it like a question so Sarah confirms. "The one who works in Hollywood now?"

"Yes. Exactly."

Sarah doesn't want to be rude to her best friend, but she hasn't had any coffee and this conversation seems to be going nowhere.

"Sarah, she heard Pierce cast you in a role for his new movie?" She hears Chrissie gulp through the phone line. "Are you...moving to L.A.?"

19

Inevitable

*T*ytus and Sarah pull up to the yellow Loading/Unloading zone at Pearson International, but they don't see Nate or Chrissie. Tytus has always had a preference for fast cars. He's never driven a truck in his life, but there are some occasions where an SUV just makes sense. So when he and Sarah agreed they should rent a car for their stay in Toronto, he decided on a Range Rover. It was more than enough space for the four of them.

Airport security gives Tytus a wave and an irritated look, signaling that he needs to circle back around. Sarah is busy looking through her *What to do in Toronto* book and humming along to the radio when he pulls out from the curb.

"Where are you going? Isn't that their terminal?" She looks back over her shoulder in confusion.

"Yes. But security was giving me the stink eye. Loading and Unloading is apparently not the same thing as Sitting and Waiting." Tytus shakes his head as he tries to change lanes in the crowded airport. "It's Monday afternoon, for Christ's sake. Why aren't you people at work?"

Sarah laughs out loud.

"You know, I think there is some kind of big event here this week." She smirks playfully when Tytus lifts an eyebrow in her direction. "Some kind of stupid sports thing," she adds.

"Very funny." He tries his best to sound irritated but the way his eyes crinkle gives him away. "This is just a reminder why I don't own a car. I'd much rather sit in the back and let someone else deal with the traffic."

By the time the couple makes their way back, Nate and Chrissie are on the curb with smiles that may not fit in the Range Rover after all.

Tytus puts the car in park but keeps it idling when he hops out to greet his friends.

"It just occurred to me," Tytus says as he approaches Nate, "you're the one who works for me, what am I doing picking you up at the airport?"

"Oh Ty," Nate says as their handshake morphs into a one-armed hug, "it's so cute that you still don't see you're the one working for me."

The girls squeal and squeeze, and squeeze and squeal until Nate finally peels Chrissie off of Sarah so he can get a hug of his own.

"You two act like it's been seven years instead of seven days since you've seen each other." Tytus laughs as he throws their bags into the back. And after a quick kiss on the cheek, the four friends hop in the car and get the hell out of the airport.

"Hey, I've never seen you drive a car with four doors, much less a beast like this, you sure you're man enough for this machine?" Nate ribs Tytus from the passenger seat while Sarah and Chrissie ramble excitedly about all the places they hope to visit this week.

"I outweigh you by fifty pounds. You want me to show you just how much man I am?"

When Nate's eyes go wide and he bursts into laughter, Tytus can't help but join him.

"Okay." He gasps for air between chuckles. "That came out wrong."

Tytus laughs so hard he can barely concentrate on the road. As he catches his breath and listens to the other three start talking about their plans for tonight, he is struck with an unexpected wave of gratitude for the group of people in this car.

In just a matter of months, he'd gone from spending nearly every night alone, closed off from so many people in his life, and pretending he wanted it that way, to watching his best friend get married, reconciling with his mom, and falling madly in love. He glances briefly in the rearview mirror as Sarah smiles and laughs with Chrissie. He's never seen anything more beautiful. He's never been so grateful. And he could never imagine his life without her.

A couple of hours later, the group is back in the car after stopping by the hotel to get Nate and Chrissie checked in and changed. They are on their way to the Rogers Centre for the Home Run Derby. Tytus doesn't have to do anything but watch and cheer on his American League teammates, but all the players are expected to attend.

Once they arrive, Nate and Tytus head to the clubhouse so Tytus can change and Sarah and Chrissie find their seats. Sarah knows that Chrissie had been chomping at the bit to continue their earlier conversation, and the minute they are alone, she does just that.

"So?" Chrissie turns and stands in front of Sarah. "You said we'd talk when I got here. I'm here."

"Let's at least get a beer first?"

"Oh my God, you are stalling," Chrissie calls, trying to catch up to Sarah who had moved around her and kept walking.

"I'm not stalling, I'm thirsty."

If the beers are in fact a stall tactic, they are a good one. The stadium is packed and the lines are long. Sarah manages to keep Chrissie talking about the new design project she is knee-deep in at work, and she updates her on the time she spent with the Hayes family.

"It's almost like I've known them all my life, Wis. It's so...different than with my family."

Clearly, the wistful look in Sarah's eye doesn't go unnoticed by Chrissie because she steers the conversation back to Pierce's offer.

"Okay, I know you said you wanted a beer first, but at this rate, Nate will be back before we take our first sip." Chrissie takes Sarah's hand and waits for her to return her gaze. "What are you going to do, Sarah?"

Sarah looks at her best friend and exhales slowly. There is a part of her that is dying to talk this through with the one person she had always been able to go to when life got rough. And there had been plenty of those times over the decade they had been friends. But talking about it makes it feel so real, and she isn't sure she is ready for that.

Finally, Sarah nods in agreement. "I don't even know where to start, Chrissie. This whole thing is so overwhelming, I just keep pushing it to the back of my mind. I—" She swallows and squeezes the hand that is still holding hers. "I can't even wrap my mind around what this would mean."

The line moves and the two scoot forward as Sarah's statement hovers over them.

"Let's just break it down, piece by piece," Chrissie offers. "When I have a big project at work and I feel like I can't see through all the details, I just try to tackle it one step at a time." She laughs and adds, "You know, my dad used to say, *You can't eat a whole ribeye in one big bite, you gotta cut it up, eat one piece atta time.*"

That gets Sarah laughing. "Why does every life lesson you get from your dad have to do with food?"

They finally get to the front of the line and order their draft beers. Chrissie gets one for Nate too, because nobody wants to stand in this line again. They can get beer from the hawkers once they find their seats, but not the good stuff.

Sarah takes a few big gulps and wipes her mouth with the back of her hand. "Okay. Baby steps. Got it."

They hold the conversation while they fight the crowds again and carefully make their way down the concrete steps to the amazing seats Tytus secured for them. Right behind the Blue Jay dugout, which is currently occupied by the American League All-Star team. It only takes Sarah a quick survey of the field to spot Tytus. He's standing in a group of other All-Stars, talking with Spencer and another player. He looks so natural out there, in front of thousands upon thousands of fans, so in his element, and she couldn't be happier for him. It's the first time she's seen him in this uniform and it pushes her to take another long pull from her plastic cup to cool the heat building in her core.

Damn, he sure is something to look at.

306

"Okay, for starters," Chrissie brings her focus back, "can I just say, congratulations. I get this is a big decision and it's scary and there's a lot to consider, but…holy shit, Sarah, a role in a movie. Like a real movie. Filmed in Hollywood. Opposite Pierce Evans."

"Wait, what?" Sarah's eyes shoot from admiring the view and lock on Chrissie. "What do you mean opposite Pierce Evans? He's producing it, not starring in it."

"That's not what Stacie said. She's working on mockups for the film already and she said Pierce was starring in it. The role you'd be playing is his mistress."

Sarah just stares blankly at her friend and lifts her beer back to her mouth. Pierce had gone over the role with her in detail, a small-time stage actress, who is the mistress of a senator, goes missing. He just failed to mention that he was playing that politician. Not that it mattered. Well, maybe it mattered a little.

"Anyway, my whole point is to say, congratulations," Chrissie squeals and spills her beer.

Sarah smiles over her cup as she takes another drink. She can almost feel the alcohol trying to settle her flaring nerves like an internal war she has no control over. Baby steps…

"The opportunity is exciting." She tries to focus on that single aspect. "If you had told me a year ago that I'd be offered a role in a film from Universal starring Pierce Evans, I'd have laughed you out of the room." Sarah lets the reality of that sink in, maybe for the first time since Pierce had called. She lifts her head to search for Tytus on the field, but quickly closes her eyes and then turns back to Chrissie.

"Can you imagine? Sarah Dalton, me," she puts her hand on her chest and shakes her head, "on the big screen in theaters across the world?" She moves her hand from her chest to her mouth, covering it.

"It's incredible, Sarah." Chrissie smiles as she sets the beers down and places a hand on her friend's knee. "And, yes. I can imagine it. You've earned this, Sarah. You know that right?"

As if putting on a pair of glasses after staring at a blurry screen for days, everything suddenly becomes clear. She has earned this. Maybe it will work out and her future will be in the movie business. Maybe she will hate it, and return to the stage for good. She honestly has no clue how it will turn out for her. But one thing she does know for certain is that she'll never find out if she doesn't take the chance. She had worked her ass off to get her career moving in the right direction. This is the opportunity of a lifetime, and she can't, won't, let it slip by.

"I do know that." This time the smile that spreads across her face is genuine. "I guess I just needed a reminder."

As Chrissie smiles back at her, Nate appears behind them with a tray holding three more beers. He looks down at them and chuckles.

"Guess we're getting wasted." He shrugs and sits beside Chrissie. "Good thing we have Ty as our DD."

Yesterday had been all about fun and hanging out with guys he was honored to share the field with. Some of them, players he'd admired for years, some far younger than him. Being out on the field wearing that star on his chest has been everything he dreamed it would be.

But that was yesterday. And this is today. Today, he has a job to do.

As he buttons the last button of his jersey, Spencer walks up with a wide grin and a fire in his eyes.

"Here we go. You ready?" Spencer smacks his back and starts to walk toward the tunnel.

"Spencer?"

Tytus rarely calls him by his first name. He could probably count on one hand the number of times he'd done so and at least two of those times he'd been mocking him. It stops Spencer immediately and he turns.

"I never would have made it here…" Tytus pauses and clears his throat. This kind of shit had never come easy to him. He and Spencer spent years as enemies, but no one could deny the great team they are now. "I wouldn't be here if it wasn't for you. I just want you to know that I know that."

Spencer tilts his head, his expression serious, as he steps back toward him. He puts his hand on Tytus's shoulder and looks him straight in the eye.

"You gonna be alright, man? Can I get you anything? Glass of water? A hankie?"

Tytus shoves Spencer back with two hands to the chest and both friends laugh loud enough to get the attention of the few players still in the clubhouse.

Neither says another word but they share a knowing look before heading out onto the field together. Tytus knows what his catcher really meant was, *me too, Tytus…me too.*

The Hayes/Richards/Dalton party takes over a large portion of seats near the home bullpen, and every single one of them is wearing some kind of Hayes shirt. Well, everyone but Sarah's father Dave, who is proudly sporting an old Blue Jays T-shirt that looks like it's been through the wringer.

Sarah introduces her dad to everyone, Tytus Sr., Travis, Tess, Nate, Chrissie, and even the surprise addition of Judy and Danny who made last-minute arrangements to come. She had been a little nervous about it because, ever since she was a child, her father could be a little…unpredictable. When she had first told him about dating Tytus Hayes Jr., he had laughed and made some snide comment about her being Tytus's flavor of the month. It had stung, but she is used to his lack of faith in her. He loves her, he always has, but he seems to disapprove of every decision she's ever made: moving to New York, pursuing acting, and now, dating Tytus. It doesn't really bother her though. Not anymore. She disapproves of most of his decisions, too, so it seems fitting. Sarah had heard people use the phrase, 'daddy's little girl', but it had never meant much to her. Dave had never been the person she would run to with a problem, or for advice. In fact, she probably had more of that from Tytus Sr. in just a few months than she ever had from him. He hadn't complained about the free ticket to the All-Star Game, though, and so far, he's been quite pleasant. Granted, he hasn't met Tytus yet.

The group has a fabulous time and the game is an exciting one. Normally the All-Star game is dominated by strong pitching which equates to a low-scoring, sometimes boring, game. Not this year. The batting line-ups for both sides have recorded multiple hits and two home runs. Spencer has an RBI double to put the American League up 5-4 in the seventh inning and Sarah knows exactly what that means. Tytus could be set up for a save.

Nate had assured everyone that Tytus would pitch in the game regardless of the score because it was only an exhibition and his typical closer protocol would not apply. He had been voted on the team because the people want to see him pitch, regardless of the score.

But Sarah knows that this scenario is exactly what Tytus had hoped for. He wants that save tonight, and it looks like he just might get that chance.

⚾

Tytus knows the minute the bullpen phone rings that it's time. He pulls the lightweight jacket over his head as he exhales a shaky breath. He's not nervous, per se, but anxious…excited. He had dreamt about this moment and now that it is here he wants to be sure to savor it. He brings his right arm behind his head and pushes his elbow back with his opposite hand, arching his back and taking in a deep breath of air as he looks out at the packed stadium and the section of seats beside him where everyone who matters to him is watching.

It's a bit foreign to him. This stadium, this bullpen, this uniform, even the players surrounding him are different. But the feeling brewing in his core, that's not foreign at all. He was born to play this game. Every pitching lesson as a kid, every mile he ran, every weight he lifted had led him here. To this moment. It isn't the World Series, and God willing he'll experience that soon enough, but it is the biggest moment of his career so far and he is ready.

⚾

"Ladies and Gentleman, now pitching for the American League, representing the New York Yankees, Tyyyytusss Haaaayess Jr.!"

Tytus's heart pounds wildly in his chest as he pushes through the bullpen gate. The peeling guitar solo from ACDC ignites the roaring crowd and Tytus has to bite his tongue to keep from breaking out into a shit-eating grin.

They're playing my song.

He's got his work cut out for him. Facing the middle of the most dangerous lineup in Major League Baseball. He'll face Betts, Martinez, and then Arenado, any of whom could tie the game with one swing.

Tytus digs his toe into the dirt at the far end of the rubber and slides it back, along the pristine white rectangle as he blows a slow steady stream of air through his lips. It's his signature move and it means he's ready to close the shit out of these guys.

The baseball gripped tightly between his fingers, he places his right hand behind his back as he leans out and over his front knee, the glove on his left hand tucked up under his chin. He looks to Spencer for a sign and knowing his trusted friend is the one behind the plate sends an influx of additional confidence flowing through his veins.

He'd done his homework on these guys and so had his catcher. He knows every strength and every weakness. Which pitches to throw and where to throw them. But despite all that, he misses his spot by an inch and gives Betts an inside fastball that catches too much of the plate. Luckily, the long fly ball hooks foul before reaching the bleachers in left field. And when the next pitch hits the intended spot, Betts misses hard with a powerful swing that comes up empty. After back-to-back fastballs, Tytus pulls the string on a perfectly placed curveball and gets Betts leaning out over his front foot. One down.

When J.D. Martinez steps into the batter's box he points his bat out at Tytus and looks down the barrel of it with his chin held high. Tytus knows this is a crucial moment. If Martinez gets on base, he will face Nolan Arenado as the potential go-ahead run. For a brief moment, he flashes back to his first blown save earlier this season when he gave up the walk-off home run in Houston. The dread he felt walking off the field with his head hung low while the Astros celebrated around him.

A deep breath in…and out. He crouches down for the sign from Spencer. Today is not that day.

Two pitches later, he pops Martinez up in deep foul territory behind home plate and Spencer chases it down with a sliding catch. Tytus is down to his final out.

He gets ahead of Arenado quickly with a called first strike and then a foul line drive into the net protecting the fans down the left field line. When Spencer gives the sign for the high fastball, Tytus knows he needs to dig deep into the tank and give this pitch everything he's got.

The feeling is surreal. Like it's all happening in slow motion in some baseball movie he watched as a kid. Deep breath in, and out. He finds his grip on the tight seams of the ball, crouches down on his back leg, and strides out as far as his front leg can take him, using all the power his body has to offer and transferring it into that small white ball as it whizzes from his fingertips, seemingly picking up speed as it travels, finding its way past the bat of Nolan Arenado and right into the mitt of Spencer Kline.

Before Tytus has a chance to really grasp what he's accomplished, he's being dogpiled by the best players the American League has to offer. And he, undoubtedly, is one of them.

The next two days go by way too fast, but as the saying goes, time flies when you're having fun. The two couples spend all day Wednesday together exploring the Distillery District, taking touristy pictures, and watching Tytus sign autograph after autograph. They meet up with Spencer and Traci for dinner, stay up too late, and drink too much. Sarah loves every minute of it.

On Thursday morning, they take Chrissie and Nate to the airport, and then meet up with Sarah's father, Dan, for lunch. It is about as awkward as Sarah had expected, but having been warned, Tytus handles Dave Dalton's interrogation with grace. He even tells Dave flat out, "Your daughter is the most important person in my life." And Sarah almost passes out into her salad.

By the time Thursday evening rolls around, they finally have a night to themselves. They decide on dinner at a popular Italian restaurant called Buca Bar, which was recommended to them by several locals.

As the night progresses and Tytus brings up the reality of heading home in the morning, Sarah can't ignore the churning feeling in her gut. She even considers telling him right there at dinner. Just laying it all on the table and getting it out in the open. But as she searches for the words to start the conversation, the decision to keep it to herself for this long suddenly feels like a mistake. And that tiny twinge of doubt creeps slowly up her spine like a shadow. She lifts the glass in front of her to her lips and downs the last of the wine in her glass.

Tomorrow. She will tell him tomorrow.

Even when you have a great vacation, there is still a feeling of comfort and relief to coming home. And for someone who travels as much as Tytus, there is no sound quite like the 'click' of unlocking his front door.

The couple had gone round and round on whose place to spend their first night back at, but in the end, Tytus had won out since he is the one who has to work in the morning, and his place is much closer to the stadium.

"I'm going to hop in the shower real quick if that's okay?" Sarah says as they set their bags down on the bed.

"Perfect, I'll open a bottle of wine and wait for you on the balcony."

After unpacking a few of his things, Tytus heads to the kitchen to grab a bottle of wine and two glasses. It's a beautiful summer night and he's glad they can have a little more quiet time together before life returns to normal tomorrow. As he rounds the island to head outside, he hears Sarah's phone buzz as the screen lights up. He hardly casts a glance in its direction but the name on the screen is bold and it stops him in his tracks.

Sarah throws on some black yoga pants and a loose-fitting sweater. Her hair is still damp but it's a warm July night, so she just shakes it out and heads out to meet Tytus.

"Much better," she says, referring to the refreshing feeling of a cool shower. Tytus doesn't respond but just sips on his wine, looking out at the cityscape.

Sarah picks up her glass and takes in the view as well. "What a beautiful ni—"

"You got a message."

Something about his tone and the way he cuts her off stops her in mid-sip. She turns her head to face him, but his eyes are still cast forward.

"While you were in the shower."

313

And instantly, she knows. She swallows the lump in her throat and sets her glass on the small table between them. Her phone is lying there face up. When she reaches for it, the black screen vanishes and the banner message on her lock screen appears.

Just checking in to see if you've had enough time to consider my offer. — Pierce

Sarah swallows again and sits down for fear her now shaky legs won't hold her weight.

"I was going to tell you. Tonight."

Tytus simply turns his head. His jaw clenched so tightly that the dent in his cheeks is clearly visible. His eyes dark with something, not anger exactly, but…pain.

"Were you?"

He's hurt. She can hear, see it, feel it.

"Yes. I was, Tytus." She scoots forward on the chair so she can reach the hand he has balled on his lap. She wraps her slender fingers around his fist. *No excuses, just the truth.*

"He called the morning you left for Toronto."

Tytus's eyebrows shoot up in surprise and he takes his hand from under hers and rubs his forehead with it. He lets out an exasperated puff of air and sets his glass on the table next to hers. Interlacing his fingers, he brings his joined hands up to his mouth and leans his elbows on his knees. The fact that he doesn't say anything may speak louder than any words he could have chosen.

Sarah can feel her eyes fill as she once again questions her decision to wait this long to tell him. But she had done so with the best of intentions. And this offer is a dream come true for her and she shouldn't have to feel guilty about it. If he loves her, he should be happy for her.

"He called just before I left for the airport. I made the decision to wait until after our trip to tell you about it because this week was about you, Tytus. It was your moment, and I didn't want anything to get in the way of that." Sarah can hear the shakiness of her own voice and she curses herself for it.

Once again, she is met with silence as Tytus simply stares out at the buildings in front of him.

"And to be completely honest, I couldn't even process the information myself. I had no idea how I even felt about the offer he made, so…how could I really talk with you about it?"

"And now?"

He has been silent for so long, his words actually surprise her.

"What?"

Tytus turns his head and meets Sarah's eyes. "And now?" he repeats. "Now, do you know how you feel?" He looks away for a moment and then locks his eyes back on hers. "About his...offer?

The bitterness dripping from the word 'offer' makes her cringe internally, but remembering her conversation with Chrissie, she stands firm and nods.

"I do."

Tytus's lips pull tight into a grimace as he pushes up from the chair, placing both his hands on the railing.

Sarah stands as well and makes her way over to him.

"Can I tell you about it?"

He nods and she can see, just in his body language, that any initial anger he had been harboring is subsiding. He is hurt that she hadn't told him sooner, but he is ready to listen now.

She takes a chance and reaches for his hand. A sense of relief washes over her when he slides his fingers through hers and opens his shoulders to face her.

"Tell me."

He's tense. Nervous. But God, she can see he is trying and she can sense how difficult this is for him. It's not easy for her either.

"A role in a movie, Tytus. A film he's producing, and apparently starring in. It's a drama." She shakes her head. "A thriller of sorts." She can't hide the excitement in her voice and the more she lets out, the happier she feels. "Can you believe it? A movie? This could change my whole life."

The moment those words leave her lips she wants to grab them from the air and shove them back down her throat. *Career*. She'd meant it could change her whole *career*.

There is no mistaking the look that flashes on Tytus's face. He's smiling at her. Doing his damnedest to mirror the happiness emanating from her. But it's a façade. She knows it as well as he does.

"That's amazing, Sarah." He pulls her into a tight embrace, but something is off. She has the bad feeling he's only holding her this tightly so she can't see his face.

"Where?"

It's just one simple word but the weight of it crashes into her like a semi-truck. She's still wrapped in his arms and maybe it's better for the both of them. That way neither has to look at the other as her answer reverberates off the concrete walls.

"California."

As the word leaves her lips and makes its way to his ears, his heart shatters into a million tiny pieces. Like a vase falling from a table and crashing on the floor, shards of glass shooting in every direction. All of the air fleeing from his lungs in an instant, he's not sure if the gasp is audible or not, because the ringing in his ears makes it impossible to tell.

He had seen this coming. All those weeks ago, he had seen it…

"That's just it, Doc." Tytus hesitated, bringing his eyes back to Levi's. "I don't think it's really Pierce that's got me worried, after all."

"What is it then, Tytus?"

"Ever since my mother…ever since she made me keep her secret, I haven't been able to…trust people."

Ruzzoli didn't respond, he just waited for Tytus to continue.

"I felt like my mother cared more about her lover than she did about me." Tytus wiped his mouth with his hand. Talking about this was even harder than he thought it'd be. "And when I told my dad what had happened, the way I told him." He shook his head as tears filled his eyes. "And then I just…left. I just left Travis and Tess there to deal with the mess I made."

"You didn't make that mess, Tytus. What happened to your family wasn't your fault."

"The thing is, Doc. deep down, I'm not sure I'm worthy." His voice cracked as he draped a hand through his hair. "I mean if my own mom didn't love me enough to…" He stopped mid-sentence. "How can I deserve the love of someone like Sarah? The deeper I fall in love with her, the more I fear that losing her is inevitable."

He looked up at Levi and said what he really came in here to say.

"I'm not jealous of Pierce, not really. I'm terrified of what he represents."

Tytus paused and swallowed. Afraid once he spoke the words out loud, they would become a reality.

"A future for Sarah, that doesn't include me."

He feels the panic attack coming and searches his mind frantically for the strategies he's worked so hard on in therapy. But he can't find them. He can't remember if they ever existed at all. He had seen this coming and had asked Ruzzoli for help. If only he could remember a single word his therapist had said.

All he can feel now, besides the bubbling panic in his chest, is fear. Gripping him like a vice, it's as though a switch inside of him has been flipped, and he responds to the fear the way he has all of his life.

"I'm happy for you." He grips her shoulders as he pulls back from the embrace. His tone and expression are in complete contrast to his words.

Dropping his hands to his sides, he picks up his glass and empties the contents of it into his mouth. When he grabs the bottle to refill it, his hand is visibly shaking. He had known all along that this day would come.

"Tytus?" Sarah exhales a shaky breath.

The way her voice breaks pains him like a knife in his side.

She's leaving me.

He grapples for control, but keeping his voice even is the best he can manage.

"Tell me about the role."

"I don't know what that has—"

"Just tell me, Sarah. I think I deserve that much." He doesn't raise his voice. To raise his voice, he'd have to feel something. But he's gone completely numb.

She's leaving me.

"A dancer. A rising stage actress who goes missing."

"And Pierce? You said he was acting in the movie as well?" He doesn't know why he's asking these fucking questions. Nothing good will come out of her answers. But he can't stop himself. He's spiraling now.

She's leaving me.

"Yes. A Senator caught in a scandal."

"A scandal?" He doesn't even try to hide the mocking sound in his voice.

317

He drags his eyes to hers for the first time in minutes and notices a fire building there that hadn't been present earlier. She straightens her spine and lifts her chin just slightly. He's put her on the defensive.

"Yes, Tytus. A scandal. The actress who disappears is his mistress."

He knew it. Evans wanted her, and not just for her acting ability. He had seen it in the man's eyes the night they met. In the way he looked at her. Any semblance of control Tytus had left dissipates.

"I knew it." Tytus shakes his head with a mirthless laugh.

"You knew...what?" Sarah challenges him, her voice escalating.

"Come on, Sarah. Why do you think he offered you this role?" It's a shitty thing to say. He knows it and he loathes himself for it. But maybe if he pushes her away, then he can use that as an excuse when she's gone.

"I'll tell you why," she's yelling now, "because I fucking earned it!"

He watches her walk into the apartment and grab her purse. He wishes he could follow her. Stop her and say he's sorry. That he loves her more than he has ever loved anyone in his entire life. He hadn't meant any of it. The way he's acted, the things he's said. But he can't move. In fact, he can't breathe.

And as Sarah walks out and slams the door behind her, Tytus drops to his chair and lets the panic attack wash over him. His heart pounds uncontrollably as his throat begins to close off his airway.

Breathe. He scolds himself. Gasping deeply, he's able to draw in just a small amount of oxygen. Pressing his eyes shut, he's flooded with a vivid image of the look on Sarah's face before she walked away. The pain it stirs inside him far surpasses anything this fucking panic attack can bring. He lifts himself from the chair and stumbles into the living room.

His vision blurs significantly, and he gasps for air again, fumbling for the decanter on the side table. He gulps the water down with a shaking hand and coughs out more than he swallows.

After a second drink, he's able to get some down, and as his throat clears, so does his mind. The doc's words finally resurface. Clear as day.

Sarah loves you, Tytus. And if she ever leaves you, I'm afraid it will be because you left her no other choice.

The gravity of what's happened sinks in and takes hold. Slamming the glass back on the table, he pushes off the wall and staggers to his door.

Fuck this. There is no way he is losing her. Not today. Not like this.

Tytus nearly rips the door from the hinges and stares down the empty hallway. His heart rate is back to a dangerous level, and his breathing is wheezy and shallow but it's going to take more than that to slow him down now.

The hallway is empty but he sees the doors to the elevator close. If he's going to catch her, he's got to hurry.

He breaks into a sprint and pounds the elevator button incessantly.

"Come on, come on. Fuck!" He drags a quivering hand through his hair while using the other to brace himself on the wall. It only takes a few seconds but they drag on mercilessly before the double doors finally begin to separate.

With his eyes cast at the floor, he taps impatiently on the wall as the doors open. Before stepping on, he lifts his eyes and his whole world stands still as they lock right on Sarah's.

20

Distance

*B*efore Sarah even makes it to the elevator, she stops to catch her breath. She's so furious about Tytus's accusation that she has forgotten how to breathe properly. She steadies herself with a hand on the wall outside his apartment as tears stream down her face. His comment had cut deep, and while a third-party observer may see a woman scorned, it was the pain his words had caused that really had her spiraling.

Once she catches her breath she continues down the hallway and pushes the button frantically in hopes of it quickening the car's arrival. She doesn't look over her shoulder. She's afraid he will be there watching her go, or coming after her, or worst of all, that he won't be there at all.

When the doors finally open, she climbs in without a single look back and rides the elevator down while wiping away the constant tears. *God damnit. What had happened up there?*

Before she reaches the lobby, Sarah leans against the elevator wall and closes her eyes, but what she finds in the darkness only unsettles her more. Tytus's eyes. There was so much pain.

He had tried, she had seen it. He was fighting the anger and pain brewing inside him from the moment she stepped out onto that balcony. But instead of accusing her, he simply asked for an explanation. She had kept something from him. She hurt him and he lashed out. Had she just done the same?

"He's never been in love before, Sarah. He's kept his heart guarded for so long now."

"Just, be careful with him, okay?"

When the elevator dings to signal its arrival at the lobby, the doors open, but Sarah doesn't step out. She stands there blinking repeatedly as Tytus Sr.'s words replay in her mind. And as the doors slowly begin to close, she reaches for the button and composes herself before she begins the climb back up to Tytus's floor.

In her heart, she knows that he didn't mean what he said. He had been her biggest fan since the moment he first saw her on stage, and he had told her again and again that she was destined for greatness. He was just scared. Scared of giving too much and then losing it all. Just the way she had been terrified of falling in love with him. Of his success, his fame, his career.

Maybe if she had trusted him to understand, maybe if she had shown a little more faith in him, maybe if—

The elevator dings again and this time when the doors slide apart, Sarah finds herself looking straight into the eyes of a panic-stricken Tytus.

The two stand there blinking until the doors start to shut again. Tytus's hand darts up from his side to stop the closing doors, and they reverse direction at the contact.

"You came back." His voice is hoarse and barely louder than a whisper.

Sarah can see that his pupils are dilated, and his chest is heaving noticeably.

"Tytus? Tytus, are you okay?" She steps out of the elevator and takes both his hands in hers. Although she hadn't experienced his last panic attack first hand, she has a feeling she's witnessing one now.

"Let's get you back inside." She places her hand on his back and guides him back toward his apartment.

"I'm...so...sorry." He tries to stop and face her but Sarah isn't having it. His eyes are still bulging and his breathing is erratic. She can't begin to guess what his heart rate must be.

"If you're really sorry, you'll shut up and get back inside. You are scaring me half to death."

"I ...I was coming..."

"I can see that, Tytus." Sarah's own voice is weak. Seeing him this way is tearing her apart. Her strong, confident, powerful Tytus, reduced to stuttering, stumbling, and shaking.

She came back.

The phrase keeps repeating in his mind, over and over.

The cool hand she lays on the back of his neck feels like lowering himself into an ice bath after a tough workout. It soothes him even more than the gentle tone of her voice.

By the time he sits down on the sofa, his breathing has slowed significantly and he's able to draw in his first deep breath of air after drinking from the water glass Sarah hands him.

She came back.

Tytus closes his eyes and begins counting down from ten. Concentrating on slowing his heart in an effort to sync the beats with his cadence. He places his hand on Sarah's, which is lightly squeezing his knee, and he laces his fingers through hers as he opens his eyes and his vision clears. The pounding in his ears steadies. His breathing, gradually, returns to normal.

"You came back," he repeats the words, this time his voice is steadier than before.

"Just drink." Sarah gently pushes the glass in his hand back toward his mouth.

Not wanting to start another argument, he does as he's told and empties the glass in a few large gulps. As he places the glass on the table in front of them, he closes his eyes, takes in one last deep breath, blows it out slowly through his barely parted lips, and counts up this time from one to ten.

"Sarah—" He turns his body toward her on the couch.

"Tytus—" She tries once again to stop him from talking but this time he's not having it.

"Sarah. Just...let me talk, please." He takes both her hands and squeezes them lightly. Not only had he been a complete asshole, but he'd scared her half to death with his fucking hyperventilating. "I'm fine. I promise." He waits for her to look back up to his eyes. "See, I'm fine."

She nods and he can feel the tension in her body give way. Like she'd been holding her breath for hours and can finally exhale, her breath hitching as she tries to match his calm tone.

"Okay." Her eyes are still glistening with unshed tears and it breaks him even more.

"I'm so sorry, Sarah." His voice is sincere, that deep rich tone he only uses from time to time, and she opens her mouth to speak, but he tilts his head with a warning and she closes it. A single tear rolls down her face and he lifts his hand to touch her. His strong fingers slide to the back of her neck and rest in her hair as he strokes her flushed cheek with his thumb.

"You are incredibly talented." It comes out like a whisper, like a secret he doesn't want to be overheard. "You could do anything, be anything, and I hate myself for belittling that."

His eyes fill again as the horrible insinuation he'd made resurfaces in his consciousness.

"I know you earned this, Sarah. No one believes in you and your talent more than I do." Tytus scoots a little closer to her as he continues to run his thumb across her face. "Seeing you on that stage takes my breath away every single time. It's who you are, where you belong."

"I belong with you, Tytus."

His breath lodges in his throat. There is nothing she possibly could have said at this moment that would have meant more to him than that. He just blinks, unable to find words worthy of the love he feels for her. So instead of responding, he pulls her close. Wraps her in his arms and holds her, pinching his eyes closed and fighting the need to let out all of his fears, all his insecurities, and just sob in her arms like a child.

The couple sits quietly for several minutes. Both lost in their own thoughts trying to process everything that had transpired between them tonight. She's going to take this job. He knows it. He wouldn't let her turn it down if she tried. But she loves him, and he loves her. And they are going to be okay.

Tytus scoots himself back against the arm of the couch and pulls Sarah up next to him. She lays her head on his chest as the two make themselves comfortable. Deciding enough words had been said tonight, they just lay in silence. Sarah caresses his chest, and Tytus runs his hands through her hair. It had been a long week and a very emotional evening, and before the clock reached 9:00 p.m., they were both fast asleep.

Sarah wakes in the morning to the sound of Tytus working in the kitchen. The curtains are drawn but the July sun is already shining brightly and casting a glow on the bedroom. She has a vague memory of Tytus waking her in the middle of the night and relocating them from the living room to the bedroom, but it's all a bit hazy now.

Before she's fully awake, Tytus walks back into the room wearing only a pair of baggy sweatpants and carrying a steaming cup of coffee. No woman has ever laid eyes on a sight more glorious than this.

"Good morning." His sexy smirk and dark eyes stir something primal in her core, and she's pretty sure he must be flexing his pecs on purpose.

"Good morning." She tries for seductive but it comes out more like groggy.

"I have to head to the stadium in a little over an hour. I thought we could have some breakfast and...talk." He hands her the mug and casts his eyes on the floor.

She hasn't forgotten about last night, and she knows they need to talk. But honestly, there is a small part of her that just wants to pretend it didn't happen.

"Okay," she responds after a brief hesitation. "I'll be out in a few minutes."

When Sarah takes a seat at the small table, she's impressed with what Tytus pulled together after being away for several days.

"This looks delicious." She smiles up at him as he pours her a glass of juice.

"Thanks." He winks down at her. "Omelets were a necessity in college. Eggs are all protein and they are cheap." He chuckles as he returns the juice to the refrigerator and then takes a seat across from her.

Something about the domesticity of the moment coupled with the sound of his laugh fills Sarah with a warmth that starts in her chest and spreads out through her entire body.

Neither of them seems to want to start the talk. Either that, or they are both just starving. They hadn't had a real meal last night and eating is a great excuse for not talking.

Finally, Sarah breaks the silence and catches Tytus completely off guard.

"I'm sorry, Tytus."

"Sarah—"

"No, Tytus. Don't 'Sarah' me." She wags her finger at him. "Last night I let you talk. Now it's my turn."

Tytus puts his hands up jokingly and sits back in his chair.

"I'm sorry I didn't tell you about the job offer sooner." Sarah looks through the glass door to the balcony, trying to remember all the good reasons she had. "I meant everything I said last night, but I know there was more to it than that. I was afraid. At least a part of me was." She turns her head back to face him and she can see the sadness in his eyes.

"Afraid? Of me?"

"Not of you, Tytus. But of the way you might react." She hates saying it out loud because she knows he loves her and he would never intentionally hurt her.

"You mean because I acted like such an ass before?" There is no bite to his statement. No bitterness, just honesty. "And then I went and proved you right? Shit, Sarah. I'm so sorry." He props his elbow on the table and rubs his hand over his face.

"Tytus." She reaches across the table and lays her hand on his. "I know you didn't mean the things you said last night. And I also know that it was a terrible way for you to find out. And that's on me." She squeezes his hand and he looks back up at her. "How about from now on, we don't hold back? We tell each other the truth, the whole truth, no matter how scary it might be."

Tytus clenches his jaw and nods. Running his other hand through his hair, he exhales loudly.

"I don't ever want you to be afraid to tell me something." He scoots his chair around to the side of the table so he can take both her hands. "You need to understand that you are the most important thing in the world to me. Anyone else ever doubts me, it doesn't matter." Tytus looks down at their joined hands and then back up into her eyes. "But I need to know that you'll always believe in me."

The lump in Sarah's throat is accompanied by a skip in her chest.

"If there's anyone I believe in, Tytus, it's you."

The love she sees in his eyes at this moment speaks louder than a thousand *I love yous*. They are like windows into his soul and the love he feels for her shines through them like the bright morning sun. And she knows. She knows that they will be okay.

Sarah stands and pulls him up to his feet. Burying her face into his firm chest, she relishes the comfort of his strong arms enveloping her.

"I love you, Tytus."

"I love you, too."

When Sarah was a little girl she was very close to her maternal grandfather. He used to tell her over and over, *"What comes easy won't last, and what lasts won't come easy."* She didn't really understand it as a child, and as she grew up, she always thought it applied to her career. About working hard for what she wanted and not seeking the quick buck like her father always had.

But as the relief of Tytus's embrace calms her nerves, and the sincerity of his words fills her heart, she realizes her grandpa's advice had nothing to do with money or jobs. He was talking about love. Real, unconditional love.

They eventually move to the couch to continue their conversation and Sarah fills Tytus in on all the details. At least the ones she knows. She will head out to L.A. in a week to read the script and meet the director. If she is happy with how all of that goes, she will accept the role. Filming would begin in August and she would most likely be in California for about two months.

Sarah can see the flash in his eyes when she mentions being gone for that long. She can see the way his lips pull tight when he tries to smile, making it look like more of a wince than anything else. She loves him so much that a small voice in the back of her mind almost convinces her this is a mistake. That she should stay here with him. That she can't just leave and miss the rest of his season. But deep down she knows this is something she needs to do.

She reaches for his hand when he seems to drift off, staring blankly at the empty fireplace.

"Are you okay?"

"Yes," Tytus responds with a sigh as he turns back to face her. "I am so happy for you. I really am…but we said, 'whole truths', right?"

Sarah swallows and nods and her stomach flops like a fish out of water.

"This isn't going to be easy," he continues, clenching and relaxing his jaw. "Being thousands of miles apart. For weeks. Months. It isn't going to be easy."

"What comes easy won't last, and what lasts won't come easy." The words just roll off her tongue.

"What was that?" Tytus tilts his head.

"It's something my grandfather used to say." Sarah reaches up and places her soft palm on Tytus's cheek. Still rough from the day of travel yesterday. "Nothing about being in love is easy, Tytus. But what we have is strong enough to get through this, and anything else life might throw at us."

She leans in and kisses him softly, just at the corner of his mouth where his upper lip meets his lower one. And then again on the lips. Letting her tongue slip through his, just barely, before pulling away.

"We got this," she whispers.

Tytus leans in and lays his forehead against hers, smiling.

"We got this."

The next few weeks pass in a blur. Sarah makes the trip to Los Angeles and is completely swept off her feet by the entire experience. The studio, the cast, the palm trees. She loves everything about it. Well, except for the absence of Tytus. She accepts the role and is blown away by the compensation. She will make more in two months on set than she had in two years on stage.

Tytus, on the other hand, has struggled a bit with their new normal. Sarah did return to New York for a couple of weeks after her initial trip, but it went by in a flash and then she was gone again. Some nights, like tonight, he sips on a glass of scotch on the balcony and wonders how he ever thought his life was perfect before. The way he used to scoff at Spencer and even Nate for being whipped or tied down. And now the loneliness aches like a tooth that needs to be pulled, and he just counts the days until his upcoming trip to L.A. She was supposed to call tonight, once she got home, but it is getting late.

"Hey." He picks up the phone with a smile when her call finally comes in.

"Hey. Sorry, it's late."

Just the sound of her voice melts his insides. He plays it cool whenever they talk because he knows she's loving it out there and the last thing he wants is her worrying about him.

"I haven't been home long." He sips on the amber liquid in his glass. "How was your day?"

"Incredible. I mean, overwhelming, but incredible. I'm still adjusting to all the people, and the cameras, the lights. It's a completely different world." He hears her moving things around before she continues. "I saw you guys won tonight?"

"Yeah. Five games up now. We'd have to really go in the shitter to lose it at this point."

"Well, you better keep that from happening because I plan to be home for the playoffs."

Hearing her talk about coming home makes him smile into his glass.

"I'll do my best." He chuckles softly.

"I can't wait for you to come out here," Sarah says excitedly. "Thirteen more days."

The way his heart flutters at the idea that she's counting down makes him feel like he's in Junior High. He's also been ticking the days off on his calendar, but knowing she's doing the same is comforting.

"Twelve and a half, actually, but who's counting?"

"I miss you, too, babe." She giggles.

When the team checks into the hotel in Anaheim, Tytus can't get out of there quickly enough. He has been given permission to miss the team meeting this evening so he can go and surprise Sarah on set. It's a forty-five-minute drive to Santa Monica, and the Uber will cost him an arm and a leg, but he'd gladly give a kidney to see her right now.

The current plan, as far as she knows, is for them to meet at her condo tonight once she wraps for the day. It will be the first night they get to spend together in weeks and he plans to make the most of it. He had made a call to an old Harvard teammate who is now an Amazon Executive, and he agreed to meet up with Tytus and bring him on set.

The entire ride to L.A., his fingers drum nervously on his knee. He can't remember being this excited since he and Travis bolted down the stairs as kids to see what Santa had brought for them. He can't wait to see the look on Sarah's face when she sees him there.

It's not until his buddy Flynn parks the golf cart just outside the studio that the first flash of doubt strikes like a bolt of lightning.

"Something wrong?" his friend asks with a puzzled expression when Tytus stops following him.

What if this was a bad idea?

"No." Tytus shakes his head. "It's nothing."

As they walk through the back entrance onto the set, Tytus sees exactly what Sarah had meant. There are people moving in every direction, and lights, cameras, and sound equipment everywhere. There are more people just working behind the scenes here than could fit in the Ambassador Theatre.

As they walk around, Flynn introduces Tytus to half a dozen people, but he's hardly aware of any of it. He can't seem to shake this ominous feeling that maybe showing up here unannounced wasn't the best idea he'd ever had.

Considering Sarah's role in the film, watching her work might not be fun for him after all. He had been so excited just to see her, to surprise her, that the image of what he might actually witness hadn't occurred to him until this very moment. And the fact that he has yet to spot Pierce or Sarah only tightens the knot forming in his gut.

"Looks like our timing is perfect." Flynn turns and offers Tytus a grin. "She's filming right now."

He gestures out beyond the plethora of cameras and lights to a scene that looks like an almost exact replica of Sarah's dressing room in New York.

The first thing he notices is how beautiful she looks. Her hair and makeup are like that of a Hollywood star. Her skin sparkles under the overhead lighting. It's not the first time the sight of her leaves him breathless. Then just like the way a fantasy can turn into a nightmare with the snap of your fingers, enter Evans. They are too far away to hear the dialogue, and it appears that whatever Pierce is saying is meant to be whispered anyway, but what happens next has Tytus's breakfast lurching up into his throat.

Sarah swings her palm at Pierce's face but he catches her wrist before she makes contact. They stare each other down and even from this distance, the heat between them is palpable.

He knows what's coming but it doesn't mean he's prepared for it. Pierce's lips come crashing down on hers as he backs her into the dressing table. Tytus just watches and strangely the main focus of his mind is the sheer size of Evans and the way he dwarfs Sarah. She nearly vanishes into him.

"Cut!" A voice yells out and the scene stops. Just like that.

The two actors pull apart and several people start bustling around the set. The director walks out and speaks to the two of them while Tytus leans on the wall for support.

"Damn. That was hot." Flynn chuckles. "She's amazing."

"Yeah." Tytus offers a weak smile. "She sure is."

"You look a little pale there, Hayes." His friend slaps his shoulder and laughs. "Could be worse, at least it's not a sex scene."

Giving his friend the middle finger as a response to that, he grabs a bottle of water from the table beside them and drinks the entire thing without taking a breath.

Tytus doesn't understand what the fuck this director wants, but they continue to shoot the same damn scene over and over. He's beginning to feel like he's a prisoner of war sentenced to psychological warfare as a form of torture.

It's after the fourth merciless take that he finally tells everyone to take five.

And that is when she spots him. The second her eyes meet his, he watches her entire face light up. Like a brand-new bulb being screwed into the socket, and in that very moment, all the angst built up inside him vanishes. Poof. Just like that.

Sarah races through the crowd of people, dodging cameras and booms along the way, and leaps into his embrace. The kiss she plants on his lips isn't on camera, no one is watching or evaluating, there are no lights or microphones. There is just her and him. And he pours himself into it with everything he has. God, he's missed her.

"What are you doing here? Oh my God. Look at you. Feel my heart." She rambles excitedly as she lays his palm on her chest and he can feel the way it's pounding wildly. Beating out of her chest. For him.

He smiles back at her, completely and utterly dumbfounded by her love for him. But his smile fades as the excitement he feels gives way to guilt for the jealousy he had once again succumbed to just moments before.

And Sarah being Sarah, she sees it. And her smile fades as well.

"It's just acting, Tytus." She's hurt. Offended. And it breaks him.

"I know, Sarah." He reaches for her, but she pulls back.

"Places, everyone," the director bellows. "Let's get it right this time, people."

"I have to go."

She walks away without even looking back at him and he pinches the bridge of his nose and wishes for a drink. Somehow, he's so talented at being an asshole, he doesn't even need to open his mouth to put his foot in it.

The next take is over before it begins. Sarah is clearly shaken and she walks off the set announcing she needs a few minutes.

Flynn had disappeared a while ago and Tytus had been watching on his own. So when he sees Sarah leave the building, he chases after her.

"Sarah," he calls when he gets outside. "Sarah, wait."

At first, he thinks he's going to have run after her, but she turns on a dime and starts stalking back in his direction.

"Why did you come here, Tytus?" She lifts her hands in the air and drops them dramatically, clearly exasperated. "If it's so hard for you, why did you come?"

"I came because I couldn't go another minute without seeing you. Without holding you. Without looking into those beautiful eyes." He steps forward. Tentatively closing the short distance left between them. Testing the waters.

"I'm here because I love you." He takes the last step needed to reach her and takes her hand. She doesn't respond and just blinks rapidly at him. But her eyes soften and he sees her frustration dissipate.

"I know it's acting, Sarah. And you're brilliant. Your talent takes my breath away. And just because I act like an overgrown child from time to time, doesn't mean I don't get that." He reaches up to caress her cheek with his thumb the way he often does. "Plus," he adds with a coy smirk, "I remember a time you thought my jealousy was pretty hot."

Sarah scoffs and slaps his chest playfully.

"Now get back on that set, and show them just what Sarah Dalton is made of."

She accepts his apology by wrapping her arms around him and kissing him softly on the lips.

"When we get to the hotel later, I'm going to remind you about the difference between fiction and reality. Over and over and over." She bites his lip before pulling away.

"God, I hope so," Tytus says to her back as she saunters back onto the set, leaving him with a burning sensation in his groin.

Sarah has Sunday off and she is ecstatic that she will be able to make Tytus's afternoon game in Anaheim. They would even get to have dinner together and spend the night in his hotel. While she is beyond excited, there is also a feeling of sadness just below the surface. Tomorrow he will be on a plane to Seattle and then home to New York. She won't see him for another three weeks.

As she walks into the stadium, she is overwhelmed with a sense of comfort. She's never been to an Angels game, so it's not that. It's the smell of the fresh grass, the beer, and the peanuts. It just smells like baseball, and that means Tytus.

She walks up to the side of the bullpen where she sees him stretching with the rubber bands he uses before the games.

"Oh my God. Is it really you? Tytus Hayes. Can I have your autograph? On my chest?" she calls out to him, giving her best fangirl impression and making him laugh out loud.

"Sure, Red." He raises an eyebrow at her. "Just meet me in the parking lot after the game, and I'll give you more than just an autograph to remember me by." He winks and makes Sarah giggle.

They had spent the most amazing night together on Thursday and she hadn't stopped thinking about it since. They had made love over and over. They talked, laughed, and kissed. It had been the perfect night in every way.

He'd apologized again for his reaction to the filming, and promised her that even though it may be hard for him to watch, it has nothing to do with a lack of trust or faith in what they have. And that was all she had needed to hear. She wouldn't want to watch him put his mouth on another woman, no matter what the circumstances, so she figured she should cut him a little slack.

She is bubbling with excitement the entire game, knowing that she had great news to share with him at dinner tonight. Selfishly, she's a little happy that the game was low scoring and quick. And even though it was too bad they lost, it meant the game was half an inning shorter and Tytus wouldn't be exhausted from pitching. A *win-win*-loss in her mind, even though she'd never admit that to Tytus.

They sit down for dinner at The Ranch, which is a favorite of Tytus's. He made a point of eating here every time the team came to Anaheim. He orders a bottle of wine and tries not to give in to the aching in his gut knowing their time together is coming to an end.

"I have some great news." Sarah sips on her wine and looks up at her through her lashes. "I almost brought it up the other night, but it wasn't a sure thing yet."

"You're running away and becoming a full-time groupie of mine?" He gives her his best sexy smile and she almost spits out her wine on the table. "Hey, I was being serious." Tytus furrows his brow and pouts playfully.

"I've accepted another role," Sarah blurts it out like she just can't keep it in a second longer.

Her eyes sparkle with such joy and anticipation that he forces the bile down and smiles back. He will not let his fears or insecurities fuck things up again.

"That's amazing, Sarah." He's pretty sure he means it.

"It's a dream role for me, Tytus."

He swallows the lump in his throat and clenches his fist below the table.

"Well, tell me. What is it?"

"Elphaba." She beams as she waits for his response.

"Elfa—what now?" His face contorts with complete confusion.

Sarah laughs out loud. "Elphaba. The green witch," she adds when he still looks lost. "*Wicked.*"

"*Wicked?*" he whispers like he's afraid he misheard and will look like a fool. "As in… Broadway?"

She just claps her hands in front of her and nods repeatedly. "A two-year contract."

"You're coming home?" He can hardly get the words out. "For good?"

"I'm coming home, babe. For good."

Tytus feels like he is floating a few inches above his seat through the rest of the meal. The colors look brighter, the food tastes richer, shit, even the country music sounds better. Sarah takes her great news and makes it even greater by explaining to Tytus that she doesn't think Hollywood is for her. She misses the live audience and the intimacy of performing with a smaller cast and crew. As wonderful as this experience has been, she belongs on the stage. And selfish as it may be, he couldn't agree more.

The moment Sarah sees Tytus off in the morning, she calls Nate. An idea came to her yesterday at the Angels game and she's hoping Nate might be able to help her make it a reality.

"Hey, Nate."

"Sarah. This is a nice surprise. I heard you're coming back to New York. Told you the sunny weather every day is overrated."

"You heard already? I haven't even had a chance to call Chrissie."

"Tytus texted me. Pretty sure he did it at dinner when you went to the bathroom." Nate chuckles. "Such a pussy."

"Hey." She was going to say 'He's my pussy'. But luckily, she caught herself. "He could whip your scrawny ass, and you know it."

"Fair enough," he concedes. "So, what's up? Everything okay?"

"Actually, I have a favor to ask." She bites her lip suddenly second-guessing herself. "A big one."

"Anything for you, Sarah."

"Do you know anyone in Public Relations for the Yankees?"

"Suuure…" She can hear the curiosity in his voice and it makes her grin.

"Okay, I need you to set up something for me for the first home playoff game. But, Nate, you have to swear to keep it a secret."

21

Surprise

*S*eptember may only have thirty days, but it feels like three hundred to Tytus. The month has been crawling by, painfully slow, and he still has over a week until Sarah comes home. The weather may have cooled considerably, after a hotter than usual August, but with the colder weather comes rain, and with rain, comes rain delays and rainouts. Bottom line, it sucks.

The only saving grace is that the Yankees have clinched not only the American League East, but they are guaranteed home field advantage throughout the playoffs since they have the best overall record in baseball. This means that most of the starters are getting plenty of rest and they use Tytus sparingly with the expectation of needing his arm to last deep into October.

"My God, Hayes. Are you really looking through the photos on your phone again?" Spencer stands over his shoulder in the locker room scoffing. "Christ, you're pitiful."

"Fuck off, Kline." Tytus puts his phone back into his locker. "You seem to have forgotten I was your roommate in Triple-A when you and Traci broke up every other weekend and you used to cry yourself to sleep at night."

"Hey. It was more like every couple months," Spencer fires back. "And I only cried that one time."

The two friends exchange playful punches before continuing to get dressed for their game.

"When's she coming home? Soon, right?" Spencer asks while lacing up his spikes.

"Yeah, on the 2nd." Tytus tugs on the bill of his hat and can't help but smile at his reflection in the small mirror. "She'll be back just in time for our first playoff game."

"Thank God for that." Spencer laughs. "You need to get laid."

As Sarah sits on the 405 freeway in bumper-to-bumper traffic, she thinks about how much she misses New York. Sure, she loves Southern California, but the longer she stays the more she's ready to go home. She knows, of course, that it's really Tytus she longs for, and if he were here with her, she might even consider living in LA long term. But he's not, and thinking about him being in New York, makes her miss everything about the city. And with her return being only a few days away, the feeling is only that much more intense.

The production of the movie has been amazing in every way. Not just the experience she's gained as an actress, but the knowledge of the entire process, the networking, the feedback from so many talented people in the industry; some uplifting, some constructive, but all of it incredibly invaluable. She doesn't regret the decision to accept this role in any way. And she may even decide to return to the silver screen in the future if the right opportunity should arise, but her home is in New York, on the stage, and she can't wait to get back to it.

Everything is going according to plan for her big surprise, but the trickiest step is still in front of her. Nate has been instrumental in helping to orchestrate everything in New York and she is going to owe him big time for keeping her secret. Chrissie is in on it too, of course. Her best friend has a crucial role to play as well. It will take all three of them working in sync to pull this off.

When Tytus wakes up on October 2nd, his stomach is in knots. This is the biggest day of his life and regardless of the fact that he is confident it will go as expected, he's nervous as hell. Sarah's flight won't get in until he's already at the field so Chrissie will be picking her up and bringing her to the game. He is beyond excited to see her, to hold her, to share this incredible night with her.

The nervous energy coursing through his veins is making him antsy, so he decides on an early run. It's barely 6:30 when he hits the streets in his usual black sweats and hoodie. It's still dark as he starts to pick up his pace, and he knows he's going to have the added benefit of catching the sunrise.

As the music pumps loudly in his ears, he takes in the city that has become his new home. He thinks about all the hours of working out, the rehabilitation to come back from his injury, all the exciting wins and tough losses, the strikeouts, and the blown saves. All of those experiences have led him to this day. He knows it's only game one of the series, but it's his first playoff game as a closer, and it's the most crucial step to bringing home that World Series title.

With his body warm, and sweat dripping down his face, he watches as the sun makes its way over the horizon, casting a stunning red haze over the downtown skyline. His mind drifts to Sarah. He had heard the phrase *'absence makes the heart grow fonder'*, but he'd never realized how accurate it had been until now. The way he had missed Sarah over these past couple months had opened his eyes to a number of things, and he plans to make sure she knows just how much he loves her. The thought of seeing her tonight, of tasting her lips on his, causes him to quicken his pace even further as he pushes his body to its limits, sprinting the last couple hundred yards to his condo.

Sarah scans the crowded baggage claim area at JFK while she's riding down the escalator. Chrissie had texted that she was there waiting, and Sarah is hoping to catch sight of her before getting to the ground level. They had figured that the airport would be a madhouse due to the game tonight, but it's even worse than they'd imagined.

"Sarah," Chrissie calls out. "Sarah."

She spots her best friend off to her right and runs to greet her.

"Oh my God," Chrissie squeals, pulling back from Sarah and taking her in. "You even glow like a Hollywood actress now."

"Oh, Wis." Sarah shakes her head. "Don't be silly. I always glow."

"Right." Chrissie chuckles. "Of course, you do." She grabs her friend's hand and pulls her toward the luggage carousel.

"Did Nate get it? Is everything ready?"

"Yes, Sarah. I've told you a hundred times, everything is ready. It's going to be perfect."

Sarah doesn't usually get anxious like she is about tonight. She's always been a planner and when she decides to put something in motion, you can count on it getting done and getting done right. But this is such an important night for Tytus and she had wanted to do something really special. Something completely unexpected to celebrate his amazing success, and also her homecoming. This night has to be perfect.

When the girls get to Sarah's place they take her bags upstairs and rush to get ready. Sarah showers just to rinse off. She'd done her hair before the flight because she knew time would be limited once her flight got in.

Standing in front of her full-length mirror she takes a deep breath. Pumps, jeans, and the brand-new Yankee home jersey with Tytus's number on the back Nate had gotten her. It's perfect. An exact replica of the one Tytus would be wearing.

"Sarah, come on," Chrissie yells from Sarah's entryway. "The car's waiting out front. We have to meet Nate at the back gate in less than thirty minutes."

Sarah inhales slowly and takes in all the oxygen her lungs can hold. Then she lets the air out with an excited squeal and grabs her purse. Here we go.

The energy in the stadium even an hour before the game time is incredible. The ballpark is already packed and there is a buzz running through the place that makes your fingers and toes tingle. The field looks even more pristine than usual and is adorned with brand new paint and logos for Major League Baseball and the American League Divisional Series.

The Yankee clubhouse has an energy of its own. Every member of the organization has his or her game face on. From the trainers to the vendors, to the coaches and players. There is no mistaking it. This is no ordinary game. This is playoff baseball.

Tytus's hands tremble as he fastens the last few buttons of his shirt. He has prepared for this night and he knows he's ready. In fact, he's never been more certain of anything in his entire life.

When he walks out of the tunnel and onto the grass of Yankee Stadium he is overcome with emotion. All these fans are here to see his team take down the Minnesota Twins. He knows his family is in the stands tonight and he casts his eyes toward the section their seats are in. Most importantly, he knows that Sarah is here, somewhere, and that thought makes him smile and tear up at the same time. His chest puffs out with pride and gratitude as he jogs onto the grass to start his warm-ups.

Sarah, Nate, and Chrissie make their way through the underground hallways that lead from the back entrance to the elevators that will take them up to the Public Relations office. Nate has been talking non-stop since she and Chrissie had arrived and Sarah's beginning to think he's more nervous than she is.

On the ride up, he tells Sarah the ins and outs of how this will all go down and also repeats at least a hundred times how much she owes him for keeping this from Tytus.

"God, I cannot wait to see his face," Nate says excitedly as the elevator doors open and the three of them step off.

As soon as Nate pushes open the PR door, they are greeted by a beautiful brunette.

"Amanda," Nate says, the excitement still emanating from his body. "You're here."

"Yes, Nate." She laughs. "I work here." Amanda smiles and it lights up her entire face. "You must be Sarah." She extends her hand.

"Yes," Sarah replies, taking the offered hand with a smile. "I can't thank you enough for helping to organize all this."

"Are you kidding? This is a PR dream come true. I'm the one who should be thanking you."

Amanda takes the three of them into her office and walks them through the pre-game agenda.

"Because it's a playoff game, both teams will line up on the baselines and the coaches and lineups will be announced." She shows Sarah a diagram of the field and explains where they will be standing in order to keep Tytus from seeing her until they announce her.

"Once the lineups are done, it will be time for the National Anthem, and that's when they will announce you."

Nate is bouncing in his seat like a middle schooler with ADHD while Chrissie squeals and covers her mouth with both hands.

Sarah just nods. Deep breath in and out. She's ready.

"Okay. Sounds great. How much time do we have?" she says after a moment or two of silence.

Amanda checks her watch. "None. Time to go."

The four of them push up from their chairs and head to the field.

Sarah isn't nervous about singing. She'd sung the National Anthem at many events throughout her life and she had practiced multiple times this week. But she is nervous. She's nervous that something will go wrong, nervous that Tytus will spot her before it's time, nervous and excited, just to see him afterward, and to know the attention and media that will come with this whole experience. Shoot, she's even nervous about the game itself.

Tytus makes his way out to the first baseline with the other relief pitchers and reserves as the announcer prepares to announce the starting lineups. The entire stadium erupts as the words, "Your New York Yankees", resound throughout the stadium, and Tytus feels his heart pound even harder in his chest. One by one, the players' and coaches' names are called and they jog down the line of men and bump fists with each teammate. The anticipation builds with every minute that ticks by.

"Ladies and gentlemen, please rise and remove your hats for the singing of our national anthem by the renowned Broadway and film actress, Miss Sarah Dalton."

Tytus's breath lodges in his throat as Sarah's name echoes through the speakers and the fans scream and cheer in her honor. With unsteady legs and quivering hands, he steps out from the line of his teammates and lays his eyes on her. The sight of her nearly knocks him off balance. Maybe it's because he hasn't seen her in weeks, maybe it's the way her hair sparkles under all the overhead lighting, or maybe it's just the way she pulls off those navy pinstripes, but she has never, ever, looked more beautiful.

Her eyes meet his and a mischievous grin slowly spreads across her face. As the music starts, he has to force himself to turn away from her and face the flag. Her voice is rich and smooth as it permeates throughout Yankee Stadium. Nearly 55,000 fans look on in complete silence, hanging on every note.

And when the Blue Angels fly overhead in perfect formation, the entire stadium erupts into thunderous applause.

Tytus puts his cap back on his head and tugs firmly on the bill and he draws in a steadying breath and turns to face Sarah once again. As the crowd continues to whistle and clap, he waits for her eyes to lock on his. And when they do, he begins to take slow, purposeful strides toward her. His finger twitching at his side, and his heart lodged firmly in his throat.

A wave of relief floods Sarah's senses as the last notes of *The Star-Spangled Banner* fade from the speakers. All that is left in its wake is resounding approval of the thousands of fans in attendance. But when her eyes find Tytus's, standing nearly 30 yards down the baseline, it's a wave of something else that washes over her.

Love.

She watches as he returns his hat to his head and begins walking in her direction. With each step he takes toward her, the noise and excitement surrounding them seem to wane.

And then…as Tytus closes the distance between them, a new set of notes begins to flow from the hundreds of speakers encompassing them. Notes that immediately transport her to a moment in Los Angeles weeks earlier.

"Pull over there, by the park," Tytus said pointing to Sarah's left as they were driving to her place after dinner at The Ranch. "Let's just sit and talk awhile."

Sarah did as he asked even though she was a little perplexed by the suggestion.

"You want to just sit here? In the car?"

"Yeah. Exactly." Tytus reached for Sarah's hand after she shut off the ignition of the rental car the studio had provided.

The two sat and talked while Sarah's 'Billy Joel Essentials' playlist hummed quietly through the car speakers. It had become her 'most played' list ever since their road trip back in June.

Their conversation was relaxed and easy. Spanning from childhood friends to most embarrassing moments, to the pregnancy scare, and panic attacks. They laughed a little and teared up a little, but more than anything they just enjoyed being together. If this distance had taught them anything, it was to take advantage of every moment they had with each other.

"Hey," Tytus said suddenly, "turn that up, and get out of the car."

"What?" Sarah asked, confused by the request, but Tytus was already out of the car and standing under the glow of the lamppost on the sidewalk.

Sarah shook her head, laughed, and turned the dial on her car stereo so She's Got a Way *could be heard clearly. And when she met Tytus in front of the car, his hand was extended toward her. He pulled her into a tight embrace and began to sway to the music.*

Tytus began to sing the Billy Joel favorite just above her ear.

Sarah laid her head in the crook of his neck as he ran his fingers through her hair and gently caressed the back of her neck. As the two held each other closely and swayed to the familiar notes, Tytus continued to sing every word and made her feel like the most loved woman on the planet.

As Sarah's mind slowly returns to the present, the Billy Joel ballad bellows throughout the jam-packed stadium, Tytus is just steps away from her now and she can hardly breathe. Everything about the moment is surreal and her mind is racing for an explanation that makes sense. Even though deep in her heart, she knows exactly what is happening.

Tytus stands now, just inches from her, his eyes locked on her and filled with more emotion and tenderness than she ever thought possible. He removes his hat and puts it in his back pocket. And when his hand resurfaces, he's holding a small black box.

A steady stream of tears flows from Sarah's eyes as she watches the love of her life get down on one knee in front of her and a million others looking on. Softly, just loud enough for her to hear, he begins to sing along.

"Oh my God," is all she can manage when the music fades. Covering her mouth with both hands, she looks down at Tytus and tries to swallow back the sobs racking her body. She looks up for a moment and finds Nate and Chrissie looking on. Nate is grinning like a fool and Chrissie is crying right along with her. When she looks back at Tytus, he's holding the box open with the most glorious diamond ring she has ever seen. Despite the tens of thousands of eager fans, at that exact moment, you could hear a pin drop in Yankee Stadium.

"Sarah Jeanne Dalton," his eyes glimmer with joy, "I love you." She sees the large lump in his throat dip before he reaches for her hand and continues. "I knew I wanted to marry you from the moment I met you." His deep, thick voice booms throughout the packed stadium. "And if there's one thing I've learned over the past few months, it's not to waste any more time." Tytus blinks rapidly. "What do you say?" He smiles as his voice cracks. "Will you marry me?"

The crowd of people filling the stadium, and all those watching at home, seem to gasp in unison, collectively holding their breaths, awaiting Sarah's reply.

"I say yes, Tytus Hayes, Jr." She laughs through her tears, and nods. "Yes!"

Tytus nods back at her with his signature smile and slides the ring onto her slender finger while every spectator, Yankee and Twin fans alike, rise into a standing ovation. The applause and cheering are deafening as Sarah's hands slide around Tytus's neck. When he lifts her in the air and spins her around, she can't be sure if her feet ever reach the ground, because the kiss Tytus plants on her lips, has her floating on air for the rest of the night.

"Congratulations," Nate says, taking Sarah into his arms the minute Tytus lets her go.

"You knew." Sarah slaps his chest in mock annoyance.

"I did." Nate nods with a chuckle.

"You told him my secret." She pouts playfully.

"Guilty as charged." Nate places a soft kiss on her cheek. "But only because he told me his."

Next, it's Chrissie who is wrapped around her and sobbing like a best friend should in a moment like this.

"I'm so happy for you Sarah. No one deserves a proposal like this more than you do."

By the time the girls let each other go, Amanda is there quietly reminding them there is, in fact, a baseball game tonight, as she ushers them toward the tunnel.

Sarah breaks away to give Tytus one more lingering kiss. "I love you, Tytus Hayes. Now close the shit out of these guys."

He chuckles softly as their extended hands slip apart and Sarah leaves the field with the other two women.

Tytus is still standing behind home plate staring in the direction Sarah had gone when Spencer comes up from behind him.

"Congratulations, Romeo." He pats Tytus on the back. "That was one hell of a proposal, man. Traci's going to be talking my ear off about it for weeks."

Tytus just laughs as he turns to shake his catcher's hand. "Thanks, Spencer." He uses his catcher's given name. "For everything."

They exchange a firm shake and a nod and Tytus jogs off to take up his spot in the bullpen and Spencer crouches down behind home plate.

Throughout the game, Tytus can't shake the feeling that his entire life has changed tonight. Every twist and turn on his path to get here, every heartache, every victory, every choice, both good and bad, had brought him to this particular moment in time. And as the Yankees take a one-run lead in the fourth inning, and then increase the score to 2-0 in the seventh, he knows in his heart that they are going to win. Not just tonight, and not just this series, but the World Series. And even more important than that, he knows that the love of his life has just agreed to marry him. Sarah Dalton will be his wife and there is no trophy, no championship, that will ever mean more to him than that.

The storybook night has just the fairy tale ending it deserves. They win the game. Tytus closes and earns the save. And even the fans who leave disappointed with the outcome of the game had experienced a night they won't soon forget.

Tytus is bombarded with handshakes, back slaps, and one-armed man hugs as he leaves the field at the end of the night. He knows his buddies are stoked about the win, but they are also happy for the once wildly eligible bachelor who finally found a mate who could tame him.

The night has been so emotional for a guy who tries to keep his personal life out of the spotlight. And when he exits the clubhouse, there are hundreds of lights, cameras, and microphones to remind him that the entire world is watching.

He shields his eyes and squints to try and see beyond them.

"Sarah?" he calls out. Nate had assured him that he'd find her and that she would be there to stand by his side.

"Tytus."

He hears her voice through the crowd and he pushes through them to get to her. Reaching her, at last, he buries his face in her hair and squeezes her tight enough to cut off her air supply.

"You did it." She smiles from ear to ear and her face glows with pride.

Tytus takes her hand and lifts it in between them, running his fingers over the engagement ring and kissing her palm lightly.

"We did it."

Tytus spends the next half hour or so answering questions and smiling for the flashing cameras. He may not be one for the limelight, but if ever there was a night that called for it, this is it.

They turn down several offers from their friends about going out to celebrate. They had been apart for weeks and just got engaged. All they want tonight is to be alone.

They head to Sarah's because she's the one who hasn't slept in her bed in two months. The moment they are in the back of Miles's Lexus, Tytus covers her mouth with his. There is nothing that feels more like home than sliding his tongue slowly through her parted lips. The taste of her, the scent of her, the feel of her will never stop taking his breath away.

"We're getting married," he mumbles against her lips.

"We are." Sarah half laughs into his mouth.

Tytus slides his hand under the Yankee jersey she's wearing and groans at the feeling of her porcelain skin under his rough fingers.

"You're going to be my wife." He moans as she sucks on the skin just behind his ear lobe.

"I am," she says hoarsely, as her head falls back against the seat.

"Your voice tonight…incredible." Again, his words are muffled, coming between labored breaths as his lips and teeth scrape against her neck.

"It was supposed to be a surprise." She pushes against his chest but to no avail. He's far too strong, and focused, to be denied.

"Sorry," he says before biting her lower lip and then slipping his tongue back into her mouth when she yelps.

They barely make it through her door before every article of clothing that separates them is shed and strewn across her apartment. They make love for hours upon hours. A whole new layer of intimacy and passion seems to be uncovered by the reality of spending the rest of their lives together. And when they finally give themselves over to exhaustion, they fall into the deepest sleep either have had since Sarah left for California. And tangled in sweaty sheets, they hold onto one another, and dream of their future.

Tytus was right. About all of it. The Yankees swept the Twins in three games, then took down the Houston Astros in the American League Championship Series. And finally, won the World Series Title in game seven at home over the Milwaukee Brewers, where Tytus threw the final pitch and was dogpiled on national television. He and his teammates were on the cover of every newspaper and every sports magazine. There were parades, and talk show appearances, and even a visit to the White House. It had been everything Tytus had dreamed of since he first put on a glove at the age of four.

Yet, none of that held a candle to the day Sarah became his wife and took his name in addition to her own. They were married in front of everyone they cared about and it was the best day of both of their lives. Well, the best day so far.

The End

Acknowledgments

Writing my first novel has simultaneously been one of the most challenging and rewarding experiences of my life. This story holds such a special place in my heart and it never would have made it to print without my dear friend Stefanie. She was my editor, promoter, publisher, and most importantly, my biggest cheerleader. Her continued support and guidance throughout this multi-year project meant more to me than words could ever express. Thank you, Stefanie, for helping me make this dream a reality.

To all the friends who offered advice, read through the many, many drafts, or just lent a listening ear when I needed it the most, thank you from the bottom of my heart. Jo, your honest and valuable feedback helped this story find its truest path. Sharing this journey with you made it that much more special. Blue, thank you from the bottom of my heart for always making time to talk and answer my rookie questions. You've helped me grow so much as a writer.

Years ago, a very special group of women from all over the globe came together online and formed a family of sorts. These incredible ladies became some of my dearest friends and it was their constant enthusiasm and encouragement for my writing in its earliest stages that helped stoke a fire inside of me I didn't even know was there. Thank you to every single one of you. You know who you are.

I would not be the person I am today if not for the blessing of my three amazing children. Amanda, AJ, and Adam you are the light in my smile and the sparkle in my eye. Thank you for teaching me the meaning of unconditional love and filling me with pride that makes my heart swell day after day.

Thank you, also, to my husband Alex for believing in me and for sharing me with the characters from this book. Thank you for 25 years of marriage. For all the laughs, struggles, tears, and pain we have endured together. Rare love like ours is the inspiration for every word I write.

Lastly, thank you to my parents. Mom, you instilled in me the courage to chase the things that bring me joy and the confidence to believe that I am worthy of them. Dad, you fostered my love of reading and you inspire me every day to be the best version of myself. Thanks for giving me my first Nora Roberts novel because that is where this journey really began.

About the Author

Part time writer, full time school teacher, and mother of three, Aimee Hyde loves to tug at your heartstrings while keeping things witty and fun. The Closer is her first novel and she hopes to write more sports romance books in the future. As a college athlete herself she has a passion for sports and enjoys embedding them into her story lines. Aimee draws on her life experiences to combine light hearted humor with the angst and passion that leaves her readers wanting more.

Made in the USA
Columbia, SC
02 November 2023

25396776R00214